The charm bracelet I had put on my wrist jingled faintly. The only other possessions that remained from my three years as a sea gypsy were now packed in the well-worn suitcase I had been given.

Sam Redwing looked up from the bracelet and said, "From Daniel?"

I nodded, my throat closing suddenly so that I could not speak. He seemed to decide against another question, and held my hand firmly for a few moments, looking into my eyes. Then he said, "Goodbye. And thanks again, Casey girl."

Twenty minutes later I boarded the boat on which I was to begin my journey to a far country and strange new life. I did not know that Mr. Sam Redwing had his own plans for me, or that fate was already weaving a startling pattern with threads from my past.

Another Fawcett Crest Book
by Madeleine Brent

MOONRAKER'S BRIDE

THE LONG MASQUERADE

Madeleine Brent

FAWCETT CREST • NEW YORK

A Fawcett Crest Book
Published by Ballantine Books

Library of Congress Catalog Card Number: 81-43048

ISBN 0-449-20484-7

This edition published by arrangement with Doubleday & Company, Inc.

Printed in Canada

First Ballantine Books Edition: March 1984

1

I WAS SIX MONTHS FROM MY EIGHTEENTH BIRTHDAY WHEN I learned that I was to be married to Oliver Foy. I might have thought this announcement some strange joke except that Aunt Maude and Uncle Henry never made jokes. At the time, my main feeling was one of surprise. If I could have been granted even a glimpse of what lay in store for me as Oliver's wife I would have felt something very different.

We were at breakfast, with the french windows open wide to gather the cooling breeze, for by nine in the morning the sun was hot, even though our Jamaica plantation lay well back from the coast, in the uplands behind the port of Ocho Rios, with the house standing a thousand feet above the sea.

Aunt Maude was at one end of the big mahogany table, her girth squeezed between the curved arms of the chair in which she sat. Uncle Henry was at the other end, long brown face above a long thin neck, black hair gleaming with macassar oil. On the table near his right hand lay a folded copy of the morning newspaper, *The Jamaica Gleaner*.

The main report on the front page was something to do with celebrations in London of the Diamond Jubilee, for this was the sixtieth year of Queen Victoria's reign. I could see only

1

half the headline, and had been trying to guess the rest of it when Aunt Maude's announcement that I was to marry Oliver Foy in six weeks' time drove every other thought from my mind.

I looked wonderingly at my aunt and uncle in turn. Neither of them returned my look. Both continued to munch stolidly, gazing into space. In the silence I could hear the regular creak of the springs in Uncle Henry's false teeth, and when I looked at Aunt Maude it seemed that her heavy second chin was shaking to the same rhythm.

"Six weeks?" I said at last.

"Yes, Emma dear. That is what your uncle and Mr. Foy have arranged. It leaves ample time for the banns."

I said, "But Mr. Foy hasn't asked me, Aunt Maude. He hasn't called on me, or courted me, or anything."

"No, dear. He asked your uncle Henry, and will call on you this afternoon to make a formal proposal."

"But I scarcely know him." I looked at Uncle Henry, but while still eating he had closed his eyes, which meant that he would take no part in any discussion of the present subject.

Aunt Maude said, "Really, Emma, you are always making difficulties. Mr. Foy is one of the most eligible bachelors on the island. His coffee plantations show a bigger harvest every year, and Diabolo Hall is certainly the finest house in the parish of St. Ann."

All that Aunt Maude said was true. The Foy property and estates were huge. The house stood on the northern approach to Mount Diabolo and had a staff of twenty servants. I had visited it once, some months ago, when old Sir Anthony Foy was alive, on the occasion of his last annual garden party. Diabolo Hall had struck me then as being full of perfection but empty of heart, perhaps because it lacked a mistress. There had been no woman in the family since Lady Foy had died ten years before.

I remembered liking Sir Anthony, but found it hard to decide what I felt about his son Oliver. We had talked for a while at the garden party, and had often met briefly on other occasions, at church, at the races in Kingston, and at several cricket matches and tennis competitions, but now that I came to think about it I realized that Oliver Foy had made scarcely any impression upon me at all.

This was puzzling, for he was quite a handsome man, fair of hair, with clear blue eyes and strong regular features. I knew he was thirty-six, for his birthday had fallen on the day of the garden party. This meant he was twice my age.

"Don't wrinkle your nose, dear," said Aunt Maude. I apologized, wondering briefly how it was that my aunt and uncle could detect such a thing as a wrinkling of my nose when they never seemed to look directly at me.

"Eighteen years seems a large difference," I said.

"Not at all, Emma. Most girls are married by the time they're twenty, and a husband must naturally be of more mature years. Your uncle Henry was almost twenty years older than I, when we were married."

Her last words seemed to imply that this difference had changed since then, and on another occasion I might have smiled to myself, but not today, and especially not when Aunt Maude said, "The fact that certain persons have behaved irresponsibly and foolishly in the past should be a lesson to us in this respect, not an example to be followed."

I knew she was speaking of my mother and father, but I no longer felt angry when this happened, as I had done when I was younger. I simply said, "Yes, Aunt Maude," and went on thinking about Oliver Foy, trying to decide what I felt about him. Through the window I could see the stooped figure of Joshua working on one of the flower beds. His hair was white, his skin black, and he wore a green apron. Beyond him the lawn ran down to a curving line of trees bearing an explosion of bright blue blossoms against a paler blue and white sky. These jacarandas edged the road that wound down to Ocho Rios, and between them I could see the deeper blue of the distant Caribbean.

For the moment my mind seemed to have stopped working, and no coherent thoughts were coming into it. When I turned my head a little I could see the portrait of my grandmother as a young woman, which hung on the wall behind Uncle Henry. It was not a particularly good painting, but it showed a great likeness between us. We both had mouths that were too big, brows that were too heavy, and noses that tilted up at the tip. Over the years I had often talked to Grannie Elliot in my mind when I needed counsel, for she always seemed more understanding than my aunt or uncle.

It never ceased to amaze me that Aunt Maude was her daughter, for they were so different in looks, and I felt certain this difference extended to their characters. I barely remembered my mother, but from vague recollections and from a number of photographs I had seen I felt sure that the likeness had come down through her. Sometimes I wished I had known Grannie Elliot when she was alive, but at other times I felt glad not to have done so, for then I would have known her as an old lady, whereas I now regarded her more as a trusted older sister or friend.

I could not talk to her properly with others in the room, so I just said in my mind, "Oh dear, Grannie, I don't know what to think." Then I looked toward the sideboard, where Amanda and Cissie, the young housemaid twins, stood waiting in their frilly caps and aprons, and I beckoned Amanda to come and pour more coffee for me. They both looked very demure and straight-faced, but their eyes were even bigger and rounder than usual, and I realized the news of Miss Emma's imminent betrothal to Mr. Foy would soon be known to all the servants of the Shepherd household, if they had not already heard it even before I was told. They were usually the first to know anything.

I said, "I wonder why Mr. Foy wants to marry *me*? After all, he could have his pick of any girl on the island."

"Try not to express yourself in that rather vulgar manner, dear," said Aunt Maude. "Quite evidently Mr. Foy is somewhat smitten with you, and I think you should feel flattered."

"Well, yes, I do, Aunt Maude." It was true. Until now I had never thought of Oliver Foy as a possible suitor, never wondered whom he might marry, never thought very much about him at all. Neither had I given much thought to my own marriage prospects. But the social position of the Foy family was very much higher than that of the Shepherd family. The plantations owned by my uncle, Henry Shepherd, provided a good living, and he was well respected in the community, but the Foys had always moved in somewhat higher circles. So it was indeed flattering that Oliver Foy, now the last remaining member of the family on the island, should have decided that he wanted Emma Delaney for his wife. But I was not particularly pleased at the idea of a proposal without courtship, made through my uncle and presumably accepted by him on my behalf.

I said thoughtfully, "I'm not sure that I want to marry Oliver Foy, though."

Aunt Maude gave a gasp of horror. Uncle Henry opened his eyes, swallowed what he had been patiently chewing, and said in a shocked voice, "Don't be absurd, Emma, dear child. A refusal is out of the question."

That was not quite true, but very nearly so. Many of the girls who had been at school with me nourished a dread of being left on the shelf. I did not share this feeling, but could not have explained why. What I did know for certain was that any girl who turned down Oliver Foy would be thought quite mad; and that Aunt Maude and Uncle Henry would be enormously relieved to get me off their hands. I found it hard to believe that I would not be equally thankful to leave our home, The Jacarandas, and begin a new life at Diabolo Hall.

At once I was swept by a wave of guilt. For over twelve years now, ever since I had been brought from England to live here on the death of my mother, I had been trying to feel the gratitude and affection that Aunt Maude and Uncle Henry deserved for the kindness they had shown me. I knew that they in turn, childless as they were, had made great efforts to feel toward me the same love and affection they would have felt toward a daughter of their own. But we had all failed. For some sad reason there were barriers between us we could not penetrate.

They were not overstrict or unloving toward me. For my part I do not think I had ever been difficult or rebellious toward them. But these were negative virtues, and not enough. We simply did not understand one another. In the normal course of everyday life I found their ideas and conversation so dull and repetitious that there were times when I had to clench my teeth and mentally recite poetry to myself, otherwise I would have fled from the room. On occasions when I had something of interest to tell, or an opinion to express, they would listen with blank incomprehension and offer no real response.

I did not make the silly mistake of thinking that the uneasiness of our life together was all their fault. In a way it was nobody's fault. We simply did not fit. They were never unkind to me, apart from occasional references to my mother or father, which they perhaps did not realize were hurtful to me. For my part I tried never to upset them, but I knew that I often failed from thoughtlessness or impatience. Even in my first few years at The Jacarandas, when I was too young to think very clearly about our situation, I had felt guilty at the knowledge that I loved May Choong, my nannie, and her husband, Daniel, almost as if they had been my mother and father, while I had so little affection for my aunt and uncle. Now, twelve years later, I was ashamed to feel relieved at the thought of leaving them.

There had been a silence at the breakfast table since Uncle Henry roused himself to enter the conversation. My mind was busy with all kinds of thoughts and questions. Although I was almost eighteen I had given no serious thought to marriage, but I would certainly have to do so now, and I was beginning to realize how very ignorant I was about the whole subject. I became aware that Aunt Maude had stopped munching and was looking at me with dawning alarm. "You are not going to be awkward, Emma dear, are you?" she said anxiously.

With some effort I smiled. "No, of course not, Aunt Maude. I'm a very lucky girl."

Uncle Henry signaled for more coffee and took out his cigar case. "I'm sure you will be very happy with young Foy," he said slowly, "but pray accept a word of advice, Emma. During your brief engagement, please curb some of your—ah—youthful opinions and attitudes. I cannot imagine that Mr. Foy would wish his future wife to be of unconventional views or behavior."

I wanted to say that Mr. Foy seemed to like me as I was, but instead I smiled again and said, "I'll remember your advice, Uncle Henry, and thank you."

After breakfast, when Uncle Henry was settled on the terrace with his coffee, cigar, and newspaper, I waited until Aunt Maude had finished her morning discussion with Mabel, the cook, then followed her to the sewing room, where I knew she would spend the next hour at her embroidery. She was making new kneelers for our pew in the church, and each one was taking her between twelve and sixteen weeks, but the finished work was exquisite, and I was full of admiration for her skill and patience.

She looked surprised when I closed the door and drew up a chair to face her across her embroidery frame. "What is it, Emma? You're usually out for your morning ride by this time."

"Yes, Aunt Maude, but I wanted to talk to you about being married."

"The wedding? Oh, of course, dear. We shall have heaps of things to discuss and all kinds of arrangements to make, but I do feel it would be more correct if we waited until Mr. Foy has actually proposed to you this afternoon."

I shook my head. "No, I don't mean about the wedding, I mean about being married. I really don't know much about it, and I think it's time I did."

Aunt Maude gave me a wary look. "Well... being married to Mr. Foy means that you will be mistress of Diabolo Hall, responsible for the running of the home, seeing that the servants do their work properly, and of course playing hostess to his guests when he entertains. One cannot tell how much of that sort of thing there will be, because he has always been a very quiet and reticent young man, but in my opinion that is much to his credit."

I drew breath to interrupt, but Aunt Maude hurried on, picking over her box of embroidery silks in a rather agitated manner. "I think you will manage quite well in running the home, Emma. You have been well educated, and well instructed in the domestic arts. Your uncle and I have perhaps been lax in allowing you to be rather too friendly with servants, and you will need to adopt a more authoritative manner with them at Diabolo Hall. Also, I think you will have to cease visiting Daniel Choong. I realize that when you came here as a small girl and I employed May Choong as your nannie, you became greatly attached to her, and also to Daniel. But your uncle and I have been really most indulgent in allowing you to visit him, and go fishing and sea bathing with him, and in general to treat him as a friend rather than the immigrant Chinese laborer that he is. I know he is a good Christian, and so was poor May, but..."

I closed my ears at this point. Daniel Choong was very much more than a Chinese laborer in my eyes, and if I listened to Aunt Maude's "buts" concerning him I knew I would become angry and start an argument. After a little while, when I saw she had finished speaking, I said, "I realize that I shall have to run the house and take charge of the servants, Aunt Maude, but I want to know about the other things involved in being married."

"Other things?" Aunt Maude echoed. There was alarm in her voice now, and she was jabbing at the needle-eye with the end of her thread in a highly nervous manner. My heart sank, but I had to go on.

"Yes," I said. "Things like having babies." She gave a squeak of indrawn breath, but I ignored it. "I did ask you about it last year, and you said there was plenty of time to think about that later, but there isn't plenty of time now, not if I'm to be married in six weeks."

Aunt Maude closed her eyes tightly. "The question of babies," she said in a harassed voice, "is one that... well, that you will come to understand in—er—in the natural course of events." She finished in a rush and began trying to thread the needle again.

"Please, Aunt Maude," I said. "I hate to feel so ignorant. I know that at certain times you can put a mare and a stallion together, and the mare becomes pregnant"—another squeak of horror, but I went on—"and later she has a foal. But I don't know what happens between them. When I was at school, and again after I'd left, I've sometimes been with girls who were giggling about things to do with getting married, but I don't think they knew any more than I do—"

"Emma, *please!*" Aunt Maude's plump round face was deep pink now, and she was avoiding my eyes even more positively than usual. "These are not matters for crude questioning, child. Ladies have certain—er—*duties* in marriage, and these are . . . are made known to them by their husbands at the . . . the appropriate time."

I was becoming a little angry, and perhaps a little nervous, so I folded my hands in my lap and tried to feel meek. "I didn't intend to be crude," I said, "but why is it all such a mystery? Aunt Maude, I'm nearly eighteen and I don't know how a baby is born. I suppose it's the same way as with animals, but I don't even know that, because I've never seen a foal or even puppies being born."

Aunt Maude abandoned her embroidery, leaned back in her chair, and covered her eyes with a hand as if smitten by a severe headache. Without much hope I waited a few seconds to see if she might begin to offer some small enlightenment, but when she remained silent I went on. "I really don't want to distress you, Aunt Maude, that's why I haven't pressed you before about these things, but now that Uncle Henry has arranged for me to be married I feel . . . well, entitled to ask all about it."

Another pause, but no word came from Aunt Maude, only a quavering sigh.

"Perhaps it would help," I said, "if I told you that I do know men and women have different bodies, quite apart from the chest difference, because I've sometimes seen the little black baby boys running about with no clothes on."

My aunt made a faint whinnying sound, but that was all.

My hopes faded. The flush had gone from her face and she was pale now. After several seconds she dropped her hand from her eyes, put aside her embroidery, and stood up, all without looking at me. Pushing back the frilled cuff of her sleeve she looked at her small gold wristwatch and gave an exaggerated start of surprise. "Good heavens!" she exclaimed brightly. "I completely forgot to remind Mabel that on Tuesday it will be my turn as hostess for the weekly meeting of the Dorcas Society. I must go and discuss refreshments with her."

Because Aunt Maude was large, she rarely moved quickly, but the way she bustled to the door now was very brisk. As she opened it she said without looking round and in the same bright voice, "I do hope you enjoy your ride, Emma dear, it's such a lovely day. And perhaps later you would like to go sea bathing."

I said, "Yes, Aunt Maude," to the closed door, and sat looking down at my hands, feeling empty. My uncle and aunt had never approved of my frequent sea bathing, particularly now that I no longer had May Choong to drive down to the beach with me and stand guard over the little tent Daniel would put up for me to use while changing into my bathing dress. Aunt Maude's suggestion simply meant that she wanted me out of the way as much as possible today at whatever cost, no doubt for fear I might reopen the subject which had so dismayed her.

After a few minutes I went up to my bedroom and stood in front of the pier glass, considering myself. Emma Delaney... at present wearing a dress of fine white cotton with wide collar and sleeves, both with lace edging, the dress fastening in front with large pearl buttons. I unfastened them and slipped the dress off. Emma Delaney... not pretty, not plain. Not tall, not short. Neither fat nor thin, clever nor simple. A small waist, thick auburn hair, of which she was secretly rather proud. Legs she regarded as skinny but which May Choong had always laughingly described as "sweet-handsome honey-legs."

Emma Delaney... generally considered a rather odd sort of girl with rather odd ways. Lacking in family affection, and ashamed of it. Lacking in gratitude, and ashamed of it. Of good education, but ignorant of what might be a very important part of marriage.

I paused in pulling on my riding boots. Only a few moments ago I had mentally described myself as neither clever nor simple, but that might be untrue. Perhaps I *was* simple. Perhaps that was why people found me odd, because correct behavior was far from simple and was based on complex conventions, which I seemed always to be inadvertently breaking. Only ten minutes ago I had kept asking Aunt Maude simple and direct questions, with the result that she had been thrown into dreadful confusion while I had ended up baffled, irritated, and none the wiser.

I tried to think of any woman who might have given me simple answers, but there was only my beloved May Choong, and she had been dead these two years past. After pondering for a minute or two I gave up and went down to the stables. The youngest of Joshua's four sons, Adam, had saddled Jennie in readiness. He gave me a huge grin and rolled his eyes expressively as he greeted me. "Mo'ning, Miss Emma. Nice day fo' any gennelman fancies to ride over from Diabolo Hall."

I called him a rascal and waggled my crop at him, which made him shake with chuckling as he linked his hands to help me mount.

I rode south that day, up through Fern Gully with the cliffs rising hundreds of feet on each side of the broad winding road. The steep rocks were covered with a profusion of ferns, from the miniature varieties to the great tree ferns, and wild orchids bloomed everywhere among the trees and the long swaying creepers. Beyond the four-mile gorge lay the gentle hills and green parklands that had so justly caused the parish of St. Ann to be called the Garden of Jamaica.

I would not ride so far today, but I knew those rich pastures and pimento groves well. It was here that Uncle Henry and Aunt Maude would have lived if they had been richer, for here were some of the great estates of the island, where the more successful planters and penkeepers had built their fine houses in days gone by. Shorthorn cattle, Herefords, Ayrshires grazed on the slopes of these pens, but East Indian or Hindu cattle were the most favored, for they were by far the best working beasts when broken to the yoke.

There were sugar plantations which had survived the collapse of the industry after the abolition of slavery some sixty years before, but many plantation owners had turned to coffee, and of recent years some orange groves had been planted. In the winter I had suggested a small experiment in growing oranges to Uncle Henry, who had simply looked astounded and said, "But they are *perishable*, child!"

For thirty years he had grown coffee on his sixty-acre plantation half a mile from The Jacarandas. I greatly admired his skill and wisdom as a planter, for our Arabian coffee was of such excellent quality that it almost matched the famous Blue Mountain coffee, and he usually achieved a yield of at least ten hundred-weight from each acre. We grew a few bananas, but these were planted simply to give shade to the coffee shrubs, so the crop was small. It was also of poor quality, since bananas did not thrive in the cooler conditions required for coffee, but Uncle Henry always fretted about the perishability of his bananas until they had been cut and marketed. I really should have known better than to suggest that he might grow oranges.

As I rode on up Fern Gully I reflected that soon I should be living on the finest of all the estates that were spread across the hills below Mount Diabolo. I should be mistress of the splendid house a short two miles from Moneague, with its lofty rooms, its grand mahogany staircase and paneled hall, its satin-wood floors of pale gold, its majestic grounds where the tall silk-cotton trees and guangos marched across green lawns, where great flower beds and shrubberies blazed with poinsettias, with hibiscus, with June roses in purple and pink and lilac, and where old stone walls were smothered by the bold reds and mauves of massed bougainvillea.

The thought left me unmoved, as if it had no reality for me. I tried to conjure up a mental picture of Oliver Foy as I rode, but the canvas remained blank. I supposed that when he called that afternoon I would have to address him as Oliver. Then, when I had accepted his proposal, I would have to kiss him. After that our engagement would be announced, and he would call on me regularly, and escort me to various places, properly chaperoned. When he paid me visits we would probably be left alone together from time to time, in the drawing room or walking in the garden, so that he could court me. I supposed that meant telling me he loved me, holding my hand, and sometimes kissing it. Or perhaps kissing my cheek or even my lips. I wondered whether or not I should like it, but could not make up my mind.

As I came round a dogleg bend of the road at an easy trot I saw something that took my mind from speculation about the coming days. A hundred yards ahead a donkey cart lay almost on its side with its load of bananas spilling out into the road. The driver was a black man wearing blue cotton trousers and a gray shirt. He sat slumped on a rock beside the road, elbows on knees, chin resting in hands, gazing disconsolately at the cart.

As I drew nearer I saw that one of the two wheels had come

off. The accident had probably thrown both donkey and driver, but neither seemed to have suffered injury. The donkey had been freed from its traces and now stood gazing at the cart with that sad patience which in donkeys often made me feel close to tears. I knew the man. His name was Joseph, he lived on the outskirts of Ocho Rios and grew bananas on a small patch of poor land on a hillside above the town. He was a sour, unfriendly man with a wife and three sons who were just the opposite. I admired Joseph because I knew from Daniel Choong that he worked very hard, but I wished it had been one of his sons with the cart this morning.

He looked up as I drew rein, got to his feet, and said grudgingly, "Mo'ning, Miss Delaney."

I dismounted and said, "Hallo, Joseph, what are you going to do about it?"

He shrugged, "Cain't git that ol' wheel back on maself."

"Oh, come on, cheer up. Look, the axle isn't broken, and the wheel's sound. It's just that the linchpin worked loose and fell out, isn't it?"

He nodded and indicated the wedge-shaped pin that now lay on the ground near his foot. "Still cain't fix it," he said dourly. "Cain't lift the cart and git that wheel on all my own self."

"Well, you're not on your own now, are you? Clear those bananas off to make the cart as light as possible, then let's see what we can do."

He gave me an uneasy look, then knuckled his brow and began to lift the bunches of bananas clear of the cart. Joseph's father had been a slave, and no doubt he found it difficult to imagine that I might be ready to help him with physical labor. To my discredit I had to admit to myself that I was not doing it from kindness of heart but simply because I could not bear to ride away and leave the overturned cart with its spilled load. It would have been an offense against something—I was not quite sure what. Common sense, perhaps.

While Joseph cleared the cart I examined his donkey, led it to and fro to see how it walked, and decided that the little creature was unhurt. My riding gloves were new, and I took them off rather than risk having them ruined by grease. Two minutes later I stood holding the wheel upright while Joseph struggled to lift the cart. He managed to get it as high as his knees, but that was all. When I left the wheel and went to his aid we were able to lift the axle high enough, but still Joseph could not hold the burden at that height on his own while I slid the wheel on.

"All right, we'll put the cart down and think again," I panted. "Gently now. Mind your toes."

"I tol' you," he wheezed, wiping his brow as we straightened up. "I tol' you, Miss Delaney. Ain't no good."

"Oh, don't be such a misery," I said irritably. "We just need something to prop it up for a few seconds, taking the weight while you hold it steady. Where's your machete? You can cut a forked branch from a tree."

He ran a hand through his graying hair and shook his head. "Didn't bring no machete, miss."

I almost snapped at him again, but restrained myself as I saw the anxiety in his eyes. He was making the long journey up to Moneague and over Mount Diabolo to the rail terminus at Ewarton, because there he would get a better price for his pathetic cartload of bananas than by selling them down in Ocho Rios or St. Ann's Bay.

I smiled and said, "We don't need a branch. Look, take the tailboard off and tie it to the axle with that piece of rope. When we lift the cart, the tailboard will hang down endwise from the axle and act as a prop, as long as we lower the cart onto it carefully."

Joseph pondered for a while, then hope dawned slowly in his eyes. "Might jes' do it, Miss Delaney," he said.

Three minutes later, gasping with effort, we heaved the side of the cart up and tried to prop it in position as I had suggested, but the tailboard persisted in hanging at a slight angle beneath the cart, so it gave no support when we tried to lower our burden onto it. "No, Joseph," I panted, "lift up a little. The tailboard has to be vertical."

"Vert—? How you meanin', miss?" he grunted effortfully.

"Upright! Straight up and down. Can you nudge it over with your foot . . . ? No, *wait*! You nearly lost your balance. Oh, dear. Lower it, Joseph, right down. We'll have to try again."

Once more we let the axle-end rest on the ground. My hands and blouse were dirty now, and I suspected that I had transferred some of the grime to my brow. "Don't worry," I said, still breathless but trying to sound encouraging. "We'll do it next time. All we need is to adjust the rope to make the tailboard hang straight."

A voice behind me said, "Well spoken."

I turned in surprise. A few paces away a man sat on a red

roan, a good-looking animal and rather larger than the general run of Jamaican horses, which tended to be small. He was leaning forward, an arm resting on the pommel, gazing at us with great interest. Clearly he had been there watching us for some moments at least, and we had been too preoccupied to hear his approach.

He wore a fine check sporting jacket, white shirt, and gray corduroy trousers tucked into riding boots. A soft leather bag was strapped behind his saddle on the horse's crupper. He must have taken off his top hat just before I turned, for he was holding it in his hand. His rather fine features were clean shaven, and he had short brown hair. I judged him to be in his middle twenties. His eyes were smoky gray, and the right eye was half-closed, which gave him a rather droll appearance.

Beside me, Joseph uttered such a strangled gasp that I turned to look at him. His face was gray, and his eyes were rolled up so that little more than the whites were showing. With what seemed an enormous effort he turned slowly so that his back was to the stranger, then stood with shoulders hunched. From where I stood I could see that he was furtively pointing back over one shoulder with two fingers forked, in the age-old sign for warding off evil.

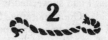

2

JOSEPH'S TERROR COULD NOT HAVE BEEN GREATER IF HE HAD found *obi* set for him—a ragged bundle left at his door, containing parrots' feathers, coffin nails, graveyard dirt, blood, and eggshells, the voodoo of the *obeah* man casting an evil spell on him.

I scarcely had time to wonder at this when the horseman smiled and said, "I must congratulate you on that penultimate effort with the cart. You came so close to success."

I forgot Joseph for the moment. Already conscious of being at a disadvantage, I was now swept with indignation and I felt my brows come together. This annoyed me further, for they were not dainty brows, and I knew that when I frowned they twisted in a rather ludicrous fashion. "I would have preferred your assistance to your congratulations, sir," I said sharply.

The stranger pursed his lips and nodded agreement. "You feel I might have helped?" he asked amicably.

"It would not be extraordinary to do so," I replied, not at all amicably.

He smiled again. "Very true. But I felt that if I helped you I would deprive you of the success you so well deserved, and I hate to spoil another's achievement." He swung down from

15

the saddle, leaving his hat on the pommel, and began to take off his jacket. "My name is Chad Lockhart from London, at your service."

My anger faded as I reflected that there was much in what the stranger had just said. It would indeed have been greatly satisfying if Joseph and I had succeeded in our task. I dropped a small curtsy and said, "Good morning, Mr. Lockhart. I am Emma Delaney, from The Jacarandas. I apologize for speaking sharply."

He shook his head and started to unfasten his cuffs. "I deserved it, Miss Delaney. I fear I often have notions that seem odd to others. Any reasonable man would have sprung to your aid without hesitation."

It occurred to me that if Mr. Lockhart was given to odd notions it was something we had in common, but I did not speak my thought aloud. I saw now that there was a thin white scar across his right temple, running from eyebrow to ear, and I wondered if the original wound might be the cause of his drooping eyelid.

He was gazing about him appreciatively as he rolled up the sleeves of his shirt, looking up at the beautiful slopes of fern and orchid, then at the donkey, the cart, at my mare, Jennie, who had moved to touch noses with his own mount, at Joseph's hunched back, and finally at me. With a glance toward Joseph he asked, "Is the man ill?"

"No, just upset." I did not want to say what I thought in Joseph's hearing, and I indicated the spilled load. "These are good stems, every one is a count bunch, and he wants to get them to Ewarton."

"A count bunch?"

"That means a stem carrying nine hands or more, so he'll get the full ruling price for it." On first impression I had thought the stranger to be slightly built, and indeed he was not a big man, but now that he had taken his jacket off I could see that he was wiry and well made, rather like our island horses.

I said, "It seems you intend to help, Mr. Lockhart, and so deny us the chance of ultimate success."

"I dare not risk your wrath again, Miss Delaney," he responded cheerfully, "but I should warn you that I am a favorite victim of an often malicious Fate."

I stared. "Whatever can you mean?"

"Well, where a more fortunate chap would simply lift the cart for the wheel to be put on, it might well be that when

Chad Lockhart lifts it, the other wheel will fall off. However, let us see if Fate is in one of her kindly moods today, rather than a malicious one. Sometimes, of course, she is merely whimsical." With the last words he moved forward, and before I could call Joseph to help him he had crouched, gripped the underside of the cart, and lifted it so that the axle was high enough to receive the wheel.

I called, "Joseph!" The graying head turned as Joseph cast a frightened glance over his shoulder, but he did not stir. I moved quickly forward, heaved the wheel onto its rim, rolled it into position, then dropped to my knees beside Mr. Lockhart so that I could align the nave with the axle. I had to lift the wheel only an inch to get it on, then I gave a twist to ease it up to the shoulder of the axle and said "You can lower it now, thank you, Mr. Lockhart."

"Well done." He lowered the cart carefully, picked up the linchpin, and drove it firmly home, using a small rock as a makeshift hammer. Together we backed the donkey between the shafts and fastened the traces.

I said, "All right, Joseph, you can load up now." He turned, keeping his head down, then began to work with great energy, picking up the stems and putting them in the cart. After a puzzled glance at him the stranger moved away and began to unfasten a water bottle strapped to his saddle. "I have towel and toiletries in my bag, Miss Delaney," he said. "Would you care to join me in simple ablutions?"

I looked at my hands, and found them even dirtier than before. "I'd be very pleased," I said.

He gave me a piece of soap, poured water over my hands, waited for me to lather them, poured more water to rinse them, then offered me the towel. Behind me I could hear a flurry of activity as Joseph loaded his cart at top speed. While I dried my hands, Mr. Lockhart tried rather awkwardly to start washing his own, but I said, "Wait," and took the bottle so that I could perform the same service for him as he had for me.

I heard Joseph climbing onto the cart, and glanced over my shoulder to see him gathering the reins. He still looked drawn, and his hands were shaking. Glancing toward us from the corners of his eyes he said hoarsely, "I wanna tell you big t'anks, Miss Delaney, allasame for gubnor man." Then he clicked his tongue and the traces creaked as the donkey began to move.

I knew it would be hard for Mr. Lockhart, out from England,

to understand Joseph's heavy accent and mispronounced words, so I said, "He was thanking us for our help."

"Yes, I understood him. He spoke in a way that's not unlike pidgin English, and I'm familiar with that."

"Oh. You must have spent some time in the Far East then?"

"Quite a few years, mainly in Hong Kong and Shanghai." He was putting away the water bottle and toilet case. "But I was surprised to hear Joseph refer to me as 'gubnor man.' That means a very high-up person in Chinese pidgin."

"Oh, it does here, too. Where the English proverb says, 'A cat may look at a king,' they say, 'Darg hab liberty watch gubnor.'"

He laughed. "You speak it beautifully. But I still don't see why the man should regard me so highly, or why he seemed upset."

"He was more than upset," I said. "He was terrified of you because of the way your eyelid droops. Oh dear, I'm sure you'll think me very ill-mannered to say that, but it's true, and I don't quite see how I could put it differently. I expect Aunt Maude would tell me that I shouldn't have said anything at all."

He rolled down his shirt sleeves, studying me all the time with friendly amusement. "I prefer your own way to Aunt Maude's, and I assure you I'm not in the least offended." He grinned suddenly. "Did the poor man think I was putting the evil eye on him?"

"I'm sure he did. He'll probably go to an obeah man and pay him money to cast a voodoo spell of protection."

"Does the law allow it?"

"Oh, no. Practicing voodoo is a flogging offense, but they do it in great secrecy and rarely get caught. Let me help you with that." He had fastened one cuff link but was wrestling with the other one-handed, without success.

"Why, thank you, Miss Delaney." He held out his wrist and I began to work the little oval plate through the buttonhole. The cuff link was not engraved, and because it was well worn I saw that it was only plated gold. This was of no importance. I discovered that I was feeling happy, and wondered why. It suddenly struck me that this was a somewhat intimate thing to be doing for a man, especially a complete stranger, and as I finished fastening the cuff I said, "I'm sorry if that seemed bold of me, but it wasn't meant to be so. It just seemed silly not to help. Oh dear, now I suppose it seems silly for me to say such a thing. I really should try to think before I speak. Aunt Maude's always telling me."

Mr. Lockhart rested his hands on his hips. "I'm sure that's excellent advice," he said pensively, "for those who don't speak from the heart. It doesn't apply to you, Miss Delaney."

I felt myself flush with pleasure, and was not in the least embarrassed by this. "You're very kind, sir. I'm glad you weren't the victim of a malicious Fate while helping us, as you feared might be the case. I mean, the other wheel didn't fall off after all."

"No . . ." he said slowly. He was gazing past me now, and with a somewhat rueful smile. "The lady is evidently in a whimsical mood at the moment."

I turned to follow his look, and put a hand to my mouth with a gasp. While we had been speaking the two horses had moved a little. Mr. Lockhart's top hat must have slipped from the pommel where he had rested it, and now it lay on its side, crushed and broken under one of Jennie's hooves.

"Oh, Mr. Lockhart, I'm so sorry!" I ran forward, lifted Jennie's foot, and picked up the hat. It was thoroughly flattened, and her shoe had cut right through it. "I'm so sorry," I repeated.

Mr. Lockhart took the hat from me, examined it, and laughed. "You really mustn't claim credit for the tricks played by a tormenting goddess," he said, and began pushing the hat into some semblance of shape. "May I ask where you were headed when I found you helping the black man with the cart?"

"I wasn't going anywhere, just out for a ride, and I was about to turn back when I came on Joseph. My home is The Jacarandas," I said, pointing down the valley, "about three miles north. I live there with my aunt and uncle, Mr. and Mrs. Henry Shepherd."

"I see." He took his jacket from the saddle and slipped it on. "I'm told this road will bring me to Ocho Rios, which is my destination. Is that right?"

"Yes, you go right on down to the coast."

"Would it be in order for us to ride together until our ways part?"

I thought for a moment, then said, "Well, I don't believe it would, really, but I can't think of anything sillier than for us to ride at a distance from each other."

"That's very well put, Miss Delaney. May I give you a leg-up?"

"Not with your newly washed hands, Mr. Lockhart. I can manage, thank you."

Two minutes later we were riding down Fern Gully at an easy walk, side by side, Mr. Lockhart wearing the broken hat on the back of his head and quite unruffled to be doing so. He told me that this was his first visit to Jamaica. He had docked at Kingston five days before, had taken the train up to Ewarton yesterday, and from the terminus there had taken a buggy for the nine-mile drive across Mount Diabolo to Moneague. There he had stayed the night, hiring a horse this morning to ride to Ocho Rios. He was quite open about having sailed from London on a steamer of the Caribbean Company because the fare was only twenty pounds, compared with thirty-five on the faster and more comfortable Royal Mail Steam Packet Company. This frankness did not surprise me, for I had concluded that he was a man without pretense.

"I greatly enjoyed the buggy ride from Ewarton," he said. "The mountain road is remarkably good, and on the descent I saw some splendid stock farms down in the valley."

"We call them pens here," I said, "and the farmers are penkeepers, I don't quite know why. But yes, we breed good cattle on the island, Mr. Lockhart. There's a lot of guinea grass, which is excellent for all kinds of stock except sheep." As I spoke I wondered what his purpose might be in crossing the island to Ocho Rios, for he seemed to be neither a businessman nor a holiday-maker.

"Is your family a penkeeping one?" he asked.

"No. Uncle Henry grows coffee. First class coffee."

"Ah, yes. You mentioned that you live with an uncle and aunt. Were you born here in Jamaica?"

I shook my head. "No, in England, but both my mother and father died when I was five, so Aunt Maude said I could have a home with her and Uncle Henry. She's my mother's sister."

"And you have never been back to England?"

"No. I'd like to see it again, but I have only vague memories of when I was small. I don't remember my mother very well, and my father not at all. He was a soldier, and abroad a great deal."

We rode in silence for a while, but it was a comfortable silence in which I did not feel I must quickly think of something to say. The day was hot, but here in Fern Gully the sun would not penetrate until noon, so we were riding in a pleasant temperature. It occurred to me that my companion must have spent a few days in the capital, so I said, "Did you enjoy seeing the sights of Kingston?"

He turned his head to look at me, one corner of his mouth twisting down ruefully. "I fear I have spent most of my time so far waiting in various offices while various clerical people pored over various tomes. My longest stay, I fancy, was in the office of the Deputy Keeper of Records. I had already discovered that there was no such person as the Keeper of Records, but nobody other than myself seemed to find it curious that there should be a deputy to somebody who did not exist. My second longest visit was probably to the office of the Protector of Immigrants, but this is all a very tedious tale. I shall, however, have some time to spare in Kingston before returning to England, so I would be grateful to have you recommend an itinerary of sight-seeing."

"Well, visitors are usually taken to see the principal buildings, but I can never think why. The theater is very pleasant, the Town Hall and public hospital serve their purpose, but it puzzles me when people are shown the Penitentiary and the Lunatic Asylum. I think you would find it much more enjoyable to ride round Kingston on the electric tramcars, and stop to look at whatever you choose. Oh, the library and museum are worth a visit, and I think you would find the market interesting because it must be so different from an English market. Then you could go out to Port Royal and see the ruins of the old town lying under the sea, from when it was destroyed in the big earthquake two hundred years ago. Were you searching for a relative when you were going round the government offices, Mr. Lockhart?"

He shook his head. "No. I was looking for a Chinaman."

I did not try to hide my surprise. "A Chinaman? A particular Chinaman?"

"Yes."

"Well, there are about five hundred on the island, and they are widely spread. I suppose there are not enough of them to live in little colonies like the East Indians. You'll find only three families in the area of Ocho Rios. Or rather two families and a man on his own. What is the name of the man you are looking for?"

Mr. Lockhart hesitated for a moment, then said, "Ma Ho."

I shook my head. "I don't think he is in Ocho Rios. Did the people who deal with immigration records say you might find him there?"

"No, they were quite unable to help, but a chance encounter with a shipping agent made me feel the trip might be worthwhile."

"The Chinese always seem to know about one another, so perhaps one of the Ocho Rios families can tell you where to find Ma Ho." I was curious as to why a not very well-off Englishman had come all the way across the Atlantic to find a Chinaman, but I had no intention of asking such an inquisitive question. I added, "Perhaps Daniel Choong will know of him."

Mr. Lockhart said, "Daniel Choong?" He tilted his battered top hat forward as if to shade his eyes.

"Yes," I said. "Daniel is my friend. Well, I'm not supposed to say that, but it's true. He came here two years before I did, as an immigrant from Hong Kong, and married a Jamaican girl called May, who was one of my aunt's servants. May Choong became my nannie, and Daniel was taken on as . . . I was going to say a handyman, but that's really quite inadequate. He's a man with great skill in his hands, who seems able to do any kind of work as if by instinct."

We were emerging from Fern Gully now, and as the sun struck down from the cloudless sky my companion tilted his hat further forward so that his face was in shadow. "I've always found the Chinese very intelligent," he said.

"Yes, I agree. Daniel can read and write as well as anyone. He's half English, in fact, and thinks his father must have been an English sailor passing through Hong Kong, but he only ever knew his mother, and he was brought up as Chinese."

"I wonder why he came to Jamaica," said Mr. Lockhart musingly.

"I don't know, but I'm glad he did, and glad he married May. They didn't have any children, and that was a great sorrow to them, but I expect it's why they treated me as if I was their daughter, except that they always had to call me Miss Emma, of course. I loved them both, and I felt quite lost when I was fourteen and Aunt Maude decided we didn't need May anymore."

"But you still see them from time to time?"

"I still see Daniel." A lump came in my throat, and I had to swallow hard before I could continue. "But my dear May died of consumption two years later. I was heartbroken, but of course it was so much worse for Daniel. When they moved out of the servants' quarters at The Jacarandas he built a small house of yellow brick and spruce for the two of them, just a little way down the hill. I often used to visit them. Aunt Maude didn't really approve, but she didn't forbid me, because May had been my nannie, and it's permissible to remain friends with an ex-nannie, up to a point."

Mr. Lockhart said, "How did they make a living when they left your aunt's service?"

"Oh, Daniel had saved some money, and he began to work for himself, building boats. He uses a big boathouse he rents down by the harbor."

"That's very skilled work," Mr. Lockhart said thoughtfully. He still rode with his face shadowed by the forward tilt of his hat.

"Yes, it is," I agreed. "But it was work he'd learned in another country years ago. He was over thirty when he came here, and he'd been employed in several different jobs before. Mostly he makes small rowing boats or sailing dinghies, but each one takes him many weeks because he works alone and uses only the simplest of tools. He's building one big boat, though. He's been working on it for almost two years, and that will bring him a lot of money when it's finished, which won't be very long now. It's a thirty-seven-foot sloop with a big cabin and an engine he salvaged from a sunken naval pinnace, to use when there's no wind or a foul wind."

"He salvaged the engine?" murmured Mr. Lockhart.

"Yes, from Kingston harbor. The boiler was no use, but Daniel made a new one. He has a metalworker friend who helped him with that, and of course he had some help in lifting the engine from the seabed after he'd disconnected it."

"I should have thought only a diver could do that," said Mr. Lockhart.

"Daniel's the best diver on the island," I said, and felt very proud. "I don't mean with a diving suit, he's never done that, but he was in Ceylon for some years, and he learned from the pearl divers there. He can quite easily work at ten fathoms for three minutes on a single breath, and from time to time he's called in by the harbor people or shipping lines for a small job. That's how he was able to save some money. If somebody wants the bottom of a boat inspected, or a propeller examined, or a cable secured under water, it's much cheaper to use Daniel than to hire a deep-sea diver. You can't see much under water with the naked eye, but you can see beautifully through glass, so Daniel uses special goggles with a wide layer of rubber round the lenses to make a watertight fit."

We had reached the point where the track to The Jacarandas branched away from the road down to Ocho Rios, and I drew rein, suddenly aware that I had been talking like a chatterbox. "This is where I must leave you," I said, "unless you would care to come to the house and take a glass of lime juice for refreshment? I'm sure my aunt and uncle would be happy to receive you."

That was not entirely true, but I could not be both truthful and polite, and I knew that Aunt Maude and Uncle Henry would receive the stranger hospitably, even though they would think my riding home with him was not quite the proper thing.

"Thank you, but I must decline," said Mr. Lockhart. He was leaning on the pommel, head bowed a little as if in thought. After a moment he went on, "So Daniel Choong is your friend?"

I stared. "Why, yes. Not socially of course, that's not possible, he's an immigrant Chinese. But he's still my friend, a very dear friend."

Mr. Lockhart sighed and lifted his head, pushing back the hat. I had thought of him as having a rather droll look, but there was nothing of that in his expression now. His face was set hard, the lips tight, the smoky gray eyes bleak and chill, the one drooping lid giving his gaze such an air of menace that I flinched, and suddenly glimpsed what Joseph must have seen in the stranger to inspire such terror.

"Then I regret to tell you," he said in a cool, soft voice, "that your friend is my enemy, and that Daniel Choong is the man I seek, his true name being Ma Ho. Your description of him leaves no doubt of that."

For several moments I could utter no word. Then I managed to say in a voice that sounded unlike my own, "But that's impossible! Daniel is a—a very good and honest man. I've never known him to harm anyone in any way!"

"Is there another half-English immigrant Chinese on the island, of the same age, with skills in boatbuilding and diving, who arrived here some fourteen years ago?"

"No . . . no, there isn't. But that doesn't mean—"

"Forgive me, but it means that Daniel Choong is Ma Ho, and my enemy."

I felt my brows come together as indignation rose in me, but I did not care about how I looked now. "You are mistaken, sir," I said very sharply. "How could Daniel be your enemy? He has lived here for many years, and you have never been here before."

The smoky gray eyes looked through me. "He ruined my family and brought my father to disgrace and death." The voice of Chad Lockhart held no emotion, but I caught a flicker of regret in his gaze, and his tight lips held a wry twist as he shrugged. "It's no pleasure to me to find that an enemy of mine is a friend of yours, Miss Delaney, but it's just the kind of trick that Lady Fate enjoys to play on me." He put up a hand to raise his broken hat. "Thank you for the pleasure of your company, and I wish you well."

He turned his horse and began to move away at a trot. I set heels to Jennie and caught up in a few yards, confused and frightened. "Mr. Lockhart, wait! Are you going to see Daniel Choong now?"

"That's my intention."

"And . . . and do you intend him harm?"

There was a long silence. Chad Lockhart was studying my face, but I could not read his expression. At last he said, "That depends, Miss Delaney. But I can't tell you what it depends on."

Again he raised his hat and turned away. After a moment I started along the track to The Jacarandas at a trot, but as soon as we were screened by a small grove of scarlet poincianas I set Jennie to a fast canter and took the smaller track, which led behind the house to the bridle path. This was steeper and less winding than the road down to Ocho Rios, and it would bring me to Daniel's house in ten minutes.

Because today was a Tuesday, I knew Daniel would be at his house till noon, for he always spent Tuesday morning cleaning, washing, and making any repairs needed. No woman had worked there since May died. It was possible that Chad Lockhart might continue down to the harbor, expecting to find his quarry at the boathouse I had spoken of, in which case I had plenty of time, but I could not be sure of this, and I bitterly regretted that I had described Daniel's house as we rode together.

The bridle path curved away from the road leaving a ridge of land between, so I knew I would not be seen by my recent companion. Jennie took the slopes well, for she was used to them, and soon I was at the little house that lay just off the road. It had been built on a small natural terrace beside a stream, and it faced away from the road so that it looked out over the narrow plain below to the creamy turquoise sea, a dainty house that May Choong had loved, and had kept shining and immaculate.

Daniel must have heard or seen me arrive, for the door opened as I was lifting my crop to hammer on it. He stood there in his faded blue working shirt and trousers, drying his hands on a towel, a smile of welcome in the dark slanted eyes. Like many Chinese he had a smooth, ageless face. Unlike any other I had seen, he had a curl in his black hair, no doubt inherited from his English father. Daniel had been to a mission school for several years as a small boy in Hong Kong, and had continued to educate himself after leaving. His spoken English was very precise, and only a slight difficulty with his r's betrayed the fact that it was not his native tongue.

"Why, Miss Emma," he said, and gave a little bow. "I did not expect you. Please come in and take some refreshment."

"No, Daniel, no," I said urgently. "There's a man looking for you, a man from England, I met him on the road from Moneague, and he said your real name was Ma Ho and that you were his enemy, and I *told* him that was ridiculous, but he wouldn't believe me, so—" I paused to catch my breath. "So I took the bridle path to reach you first and warn you."

Daniel's smile had vanished. "Did the man give a name, Miss Emma?" he asked in a low voice.

"Lockhart. He told me his name was Chad Lockhart, and that he had lived in China."

"Lockhart..." Daniel closed his eyes for a moment, and when he opened them again they held a haunted look in their depths. "After so many years..." he said in a whisper I could barely hear.

"What is it, Daniel?" I caught at his arm. "At first he seemed a very pleasant gentleman, but later he said you had ruined his family and caused his father's death. I know that can't be true, but you seem to recognize his name, and I think *he* believes what he says, so I'm very worried for you."

Daniel drew in a deep breath and gave a shake of his head as if to pull himself together. "Don't be troubled, Miss Emma," he said quietly. "I cannot explain, but I am sure everything will be all right. Perhaps it would be best if you went home now."

"Oh, no," I said quickly. "He might mean you harm. I'm going to wait, and make sure he does nothing amiss."

Daniel looked as if about to protest, but he must have seen

from my face that I was quite determined. "Very well, Miss Emma. Do you wish to come in?"

"No, I'll wait here. He might go on down to the port, but I described your house, and you can see the top of it from the road, so he may come straight here."

"I will join you in a few moments, Miss Emma. Please excuse me."

I stood with Jennie nuzzling my shoulder, my eyes on the path that led round to the back of the house and then on to the road some fifty yards away. It was not long before Daniel came and stood beside me. I saw that he had put on a clean white cotton shirt and trousers, beautifully pressed. In one hand he carried a short, thick piece of bamboo with a wooden plug in one end, sealed with red wax. I said nothing. I had no wish to pry, but simply intended to make sure that Daniel suffered no harm.

There came the sound of hooves on the brick path leading from the road, a horse moving at an easy walk. The sound drew nearer, and I felt my heart begin to pound. They came round the corner of the house, the red roan and its rider, Chad Lockhart. He still wore the broken hat, but this did not diminish his presence. He looked bigger than I remembered, and in his eyes there was none of the amiable warmth I had first seen there.

When he saw us he drew rein, and for a moment the lid of his half-closed eye twitched up as he stared. Then it fell to its normal droop, which could make him look either humorous or sinister. Slowly he took off his hat and rested it on his thigh, contemplating me somberly for long seconds before he said at last, "You are a good friend to your friends, Miss Delaney."

I gripped my crop nervously and said in a rather shaky voice, "I do not know what you intend, sir, but Daniel Choong has my support."

He looked at me a moment longer, then his gaze switched abruptly to Daniel, and he spoke in a chirruping, singsong tongue which I guessed must be Chinese. I understood no word of it, but it seemed to me that he asked a short question to which Daniel replied in the same language with equal brevity. The stranger moved his horse nearer and seemed to ask a long question. There came a longer answer. I turned my head to look at Daniel. Both his tone and his expression held no emotion, but I saw a gleam of sweat on his brow.

There was a pause. Daniel stepped forward and spoke again,

holding the bamboo tube up toward the rider. Chad Lockhart
eyed him for a second or two, then took the tube from him,
putting his hat back on his head to free both hands. He looked
at the wax-sealed stopper, took from his pocket a penknife,
opened it, and ran the blade around the seal. Putting the knife
away, he twisted the stopper to withdraw it, then inverted the
tube, giving it a little shake. A slender roll of thick white paper,
secured at each end with a small piece of tape, slid out into
his waiting hand.

Chad Lockhart pushed the tape off each end, tucked the
tube under his arm, and unrolled the stiff paper. It proved to
be a scroll almost eighteen inches in length. For a moment he
glanced at Daniel from under his brows, then he began to read.
A minute passed. Two minutes. I could not imagine what was
written on the scroll, and made no attempt to speculate. For
me the whole frightening situation was beyond all comprehension, and my only concern was for Daniel.

At long last the stranger rerolled the scroll and began to put
it back in the tube. Daniel spoke, and went on speaking quickly,
urgently. Chad Lockhart paused and stared, showing surprise
for the first time. There came a quick series of questions and
answers. The man from England replaced the stopper of the
bamboo tube, pondered for a while, then abruptly asked a short
and challenging question.

Daniel answered quietly and took a small object from his
pocket, something round in shape and gold in color. He handed
it to Chad Lockhart, who turned it between his fingers, studying
it closely. The object seemed to be a golden disk, more than
an inch in diameter. The Englishman spoke again, and this
time there was a note of wonderment in his voice. Daniel
replied, and they conversed in brief sentences for perhaps a
minute.

Then silence. Chad Lockhart slipped the coin, if such it
was, into his jacket pocket. Turning in the saddle, he slid the
bamboo tube into his bag there, and made sure the straps were
secure. His hands rested on the pommel, and now those strange
eyes were on me again in a cool survey. "The matter is unfin-
ished," he said. "I'm sure we shall meet again when the seasons
have turned. Good day to you, Miss Delaney."

He raised his hat, turned his horse, and moved away. In
moments they had vanished round the corner of the house, and
I stood listening to the fading sound of hooves. I looked at
Daniel. He took out a handkerchief and wiped his brow.

I said, "I've never seen you afraid before, Daniel."

"That one is like his father, Miss Emma. It was as if he had risen from the dead. A man greatly to be feared."

"Will he come back?"

"Not for a long time. He will return to England, and one day he will come back. Perhaps in a few months, perhaps it will be longer. But he will come back."

"Why, Daniel?"

He looked at me with troubled eyes and shook his head. "It is better that you do not know. There are some things which it is dangerous to know."

"Oh, don't be silly. How could I possibly be in danger from anybody?"

He ignored the question and said, "Thank you for coming to tell me. It was good of you, Miss Emma."

My hands were sweaty with the tension of the past few minutes, and I wiped them on my riding breeches as I said, "All right, I won't press you." I looked at my wristwatch and found it was eleven o'clock. At the same moment I was startled to realize that for the past hour or more I had completely forgotten that Oliver Foy was coming to propose to me this afternoon. I said, "Can you spare a little while to go bathing with me now?" I had long since found that there was nothing better than swimming in the sea to clear my head and wash away worries.

Daniel hesitated. "Will Mistress Shepherd approve?" That would have sounded odd to the man from England, but the old Elizabethan form was still used on the island for referring to a married woman.

I said, "Yes, it's all right. I know Aunt Maude sometimes says it's not ladylike, but she suggested it herself today."

"Then I shall be glad to, miss." Daniel felt as I did about sea bathing. "Will you go down to the boathouse with Jennie? You will find Jacob there, and he can take the tent along and put it up for you. I will follow down with Feng Po." Jacob was the small black boy who did odd jobs in the boathouse. Feng Po was Daniel's mule, who moved at a much slower pace than Jennie.

I said, "Yes, we can save time like that. Will you bring towels?"

"I have clean towels ready down in the boathouse, Miss Emma. Also your dark blue bathing dress, rinsed through and dried."

"Thank you, Daniel."

Sometimes we bathed from the beach at Dunn's River, where waterfalls tumbled down from the rocks, and sometimes below the freshwater cascades of Roaring River, but there was no time to travel beyond Ocho Rios today, so we would bathe from the western point of the bay, where little wooded islets ran out into the sea, and where there was shade to keep the sun from making my face too brown. Aunt Maude was always worrying about my face being too brown.

I moved to mount Jennie, then paused and said, "I have some surprising news, Daniel. I'm to be married to Mr. Oliver Foy very soon. In about six weeks. He's coming to propose to me this afternoon."

Daniel had started to move toward the house, but at my words he stopped, then slowly turned his head to look at me.

"Mr. Foy?" he said, and I thought his voice was unusually hoarse.

"Yes. Uncle Henry has already accepted for me, so the proposal is really just a formality. It's so strange, I ought to feel either glad or sorry, I suppose, but I don't seem to feel anything. It's as if the whole idea is unreal, and I can't quite take in the notion that I shall be Mrs. Oliver Foy, of Diabolo Hall. What do you think, Daniel?"

"Why . . . it's a big surprise, miss. Very big." He stared past me, gazing distantly out over the sea. I could read nothing in his eyes, but he folded his arms across his lean body and hugged himself as if touched by a sudden chill wind. "I hope . . . I hope you will be very happy, Miss Emma. Very happy."

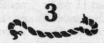

3

I AM MUCH CONCERNED," SAID AUNT MAUDE, "ABOUT THE propriety of your continuing these sea bathing trips now that you are to be affianced to Mr. Oliver Foy."

I had just put in my mouth the last piece of mango from the fruit salad with ice cream that completed our luncheon, and I swallowed hastily so I could speak. "But you suggested it this morning, Aunt Maude."

"Yes, dear. But I am thinking more of the next few weeks. What will Mr. Foy think of his fiancée going down to the shore and actually..." she lowered her voice for the word, "undressing inside that peculiar wigwam Daniel Choong made for you."

"But Daniel is on guard outside," I said, "and little Jacob is there, and Daniel always makes Jacob fetch his older sister, Lily."

Aunt Maude sighed. "I don't know of any other young lady who goes bathing with a Chinese ex-servant."

"I'm sure Oliver Foy knows about it," I said reassuringly, "and he must know I sometimes go out sailing with Daniel, too, but he's still asked to marry me, so he can't think too badly of me. Perhaps he even likes the notion of a wife who enjoys swimming and sailing."

31

I had made a point of being in the dining room ten minutes before the gong sounded so I could have a silent talk with Grannie Elliot's picture. In that time I told her how I had questioned Aunt Maude but without success, about what happened when a girl married, and then I recounted the story of my meeting with Chad Lockhart, from England. I explained that he had been seeking Daniel Choong, and had made terrible accusations against Daniel. Then I described the mystifying affair when the two men had met and spoken together in Chinese.

I never imagined that Grannie Elliot really replied to the things I told her or the questions I asked her, but usually I found I had gathered help from talking with her, probably because by putting matters into words I had clarified them in my own mind. But it was not so today. She could find nothing to say to me about my coming engagement to Oliver Foy, and offered no solution to the peculiar business of Mr. Lockhart's meeting with Daniel Choong, when the scroll and the gold coin were passed from one to the other.

While we were at table I told Aunt Maude and Uncle Henry how I had met Mr. Lockhart in Fern Gully, and ridden with him part of the way to Ocho Rios, but I did not tell them the rest of the story, for I felt this was a private matter concerning Daniel alone. Now, with luncheon ended, Uncle Henry was stirring his lemon tea and seemed to be pondering Aunt Maude's remark concerning my sea bathing. He had finished eating, but he pensively worked his jaws once or twice as if to make sure that his teeth were squeaking satisfactorily, then said, "I think, Maude, my dear, that we should not circumscribe Emma's activities during the short time that she is to remain with us."

He rose to his feet, and I thought he was about to take his tea out onto the terrace, as he usually did before retiring to the bedroom for his afternoon nap, but instead he moved to stand beside me, and a rare smile lightened his usually lugubrious features. "After all," he said gently, rather sadly, "we have always wished for her to be happy with us." He bent awkwardly to kiss me on the forehead, gave me a little pat on the shoulder, then picked up his lemon tea and walked slowly toward the open french windows.

I called, "Thank you, Uncle Henry. Thank you for everything." My eyes were suddenly moist, and once more I felt ashamed. They had taken me into their home and tried to give me a happy life for the past twelve years. No, that was unjust, they had *given* me a happy life, for I had nothing in the world to complain of. It seemed sad that I had never managed to be a daughter to them, or they to be parents to me. But some vital element of harmony had always been lacking between us.

In this moment I had no doubt that our failure had been sadder for them than for me. I wished they could have liked me more, and wished I could have liked them more. It was my hope that Oliver Foy and I would be more fortunate.

At half-past two I put on another dress and did my hair afresh. At half past three exactly, Oliver Foy drove through the gates and up the drive in his elegant black buggy with yellow wheels. I did not see this, of course, since I was seated in the drawing room with my uncle and aunt, each of us pretending to be reading a magazine or newspaper, but Amanda came scuttling in, huge-eyed, to report the arrival and to say that William, the groom, had been ready to hurry forward and take charge of the horse, as instructed.

It was little more than a minute later when Enoch, our butler, opened the door to announce Mr. Oliver Foy.

"Come in, come in, Oliver, my dear fellow," said Uncle Henry with ponderous cordiality, moving forward to greet the visitor. "No need for introductions, I fancy. All known each other a fair time, what?"

"Yes indeed, Henry."

Gentlemen usually addressed each other simply by the surname unless they were close friends, but now that my marriage had been discussed and decided it was evident that the two men had moved to Christian-name terms. I watched Oliver greet my aunt, who hid her nervousness well as he bowed over her hand. Earlier that day I had found difficulty in making a mental picture of my future husband, and now I wondered why, for he was far from nondescript. Tall, strongly built, leisurely of manner, a good-looking man by any standards, he had rather deep-set blue eyes and a short straight nose. He wore his fair hair a little longer than was fashionable, and a moustache trimmed square at the ends. His beautifully tailored clothes were worn with casual elegance, but in his manner and presence he was reserved almost to the point of reticence. This was in great contrast to his father, Sir Anthony, who had been a fiery and assertive character.

I was sitting on the long sofa, as instructed by Aunt Maude, and when Oliver turned to me I smiled and gave him my hand. "Good afternoon, Mr. Foy."

"Good afternoon, Emma. How very well and very pretty you look. Please call me Oliver."

"Thank you." I touched the sofa beside me. "Will you sit down, Oliver? We shall be having tea directly."

For the next few minutes the four of us chatted rather stiffly about the weather, last year's coffee crop, and the qualities of the Hissar breed of Indian cattle as opposed to the Nellore breed, with my uncle and our visitor doing most of the talking. Cissie and Amanda served tea under the supervision of Enoch, and when they had withdrawn there was further conversation, this time on more general subjects—a new opera called *La Bohème*; the marvel of a steam-driven flying machine invented by an American gentleman, Mr. Langley, which had actually flown three quarters of a mile; the remarkable new English newspaper, the *Daily Mail*, which was having great success; and the latest novel from Mr. Thomas Hardy, *Jude the Obscure*, which Oliver Foy had read recently. Aunt Maude did not read fiction except in ladies' magazines, and Uncle Henry did not read fiction at all, but I had always been an avid reader, and made a regular trip into Kingston every two weeks to borrow books from the library there. It held more than ten thousand books, with over a thousand in the category of prose fiction.

I had read Mr. Hardy's new story, and was thankful to be able to talk to Oliver Foy about a book known to both of us. After perhaps thirty minutes had passed, Aunt Maude rang for Amanda and Cissie to clear away the teacups and plates. As soon as this was done, Uncle Henry rose from his chair and said, "Well, come along Maude, my dear. Let us leave these two young people to their own devices for a while."

Oliver Foy stood up and waited quietly while my uncle and aunt made a somewhat awkward exit. When the door closed he smiled down at me, and I caught a glint of humor in his eye as he said, "I hope you know, Emma, that we have been left alone so that I may propose to you?"

"Yes, Oliver, my uncle told me. I must confess I'm feeling a little apprehensive. Aunt Maude was so anxious for us to be ready in good time to receive you that we found ourselves sitting here for ages before you arrived, and the longer we waited the more nervous we became, but I don't suppose I should have told you that."

He laughed and shook his head. "It's entirely typical of you, Emma, and I hope you will always be yourself. Now I must make a confession. I'm sure you feel that our acquaintance has been slight, but the fact is that we have been in the same company on more than a few occasions, and I have been guilty of watching you very carefully, increasingly so since I found myself being ever more attracted by you."

He put his hands behind his back, paced slowly away, then turned toward me again. "Emma, I have prepared and rehearsed quite a long speech explaining how I was first greatly taken by you when you were a little girl, and how that feeling has grown and changed and deepened. But the speech has quite gone out of my head, and I must simply tell you that I have long admired and respected you, and that I now realize I love you and wish you to be my wife. This is not an impulsive declaration, Emma. I am a mature man, and one of good judgment, and I now ask if you will do me the honor of marrying me."

I sat looking up at him, feeling very strange. I knew that most girls of about my age seemed to regard marriage as the end of something rather than the beginning, but somewhere in my head I kept wondering what it would be like to be married to Oliver Foy, to live in the same house, sit at the same table, and sleep in the same bed.

I said, "Oliver, has Uncle Henry told you my background?"

He nodded gravely. "I believe so. I remember your coming to Jamaica when I was in my early twenties, and I have always known that you were the daughter of Maude Shepherd's sister, who died in England. Your uncle has told me that your father was a subaltern in the British Army who was killed by the Mahdi's forces at Omdurman only a few weeks before your mother's death from pneumonia, and I understand that neither your uncle nor your aunt approved of the marriage. Is this what you meant when you asked if I had been told of your background, Emma?"

"Yes," I said. "But I wanted to tell you what I feel. You see, my mother and Aunt Maude lost their parents when Aunt Maude was eighteen and my mother was a little girl of eight. Their name was Elliot, and there's a picture of my Grannie Elliot in our dining room."

Oliver Foy nodded, giving me his full attention. "Yes, I saw it once when my father and I came to dine here some years ago. You are very much like her, Emma."

"It's kind of you to say so. She and her husband were killed with ten other people when the Fenians set off a bomb at Clerkenwell. Grannie and Grandpapa just happened to be passing through at the time. My mother and Aunt Maude went to live with a guardian, a relative of their father, I think. He was elderly, and a bachelor, and I think he was a very stern man. A year or so later Uncle Henry came from Jamaica to spend six months in England, and he met Aunt Maude. They were married, and she came back here with him, but my mother was left with the guardian, Mr. Randall. Did Uncle Henry tell you all this?"

"Not in such detail, Emma. I don't suppose he felt it was necessary."

"Perhaps not, but I want you to know. When my mother was eighteen she ran away from her guardian and married Richard Delaney, a subaltern in the Berkshire Regiment. He was my father, and he was stationed at Canterbury when I was born, living with my mother in a small rented cottage there. He was sent overseas when I was four, but I can't really remember him, and I have only vague memories of my mother. I'm told we had no private income, so on a subaltern's pay and allowances we were rather poor, but one thing I recall about my mother is that she was a happy person." I paused and put a hand to my head. "I'm sorry, but now I can't remember what I started out to tell you."

"I think it was to do with the marriage not being approved," Oliver Foy said gently.

"Oh yes, that's right. Everybody was furious with my mother. She lost her inheritance, which wasn't very much anyway. Mr. Randall, the guardian, washed his hands of her, and Aunt Maude wrote long letters of reproach before she gave up writing altogether. I've gathered this from Aunt Maude herself. She still thinks that what my mother did was unforgivably shocking, and she only ever speaks of her and of my father when she wants to hold them up as a bad example. Then she refers to them obliquely as 'certain people.' I never argue with her now, but I want you to know that I love the memory of my mother and father dearly, and I would be very distressed if you had discovered about my background later, and kept reproaching me with it. I think I've finished now, Oliver."

He stood looking down at me with the same grave expression, but I was almost sure I could see a kind of pleasure in his eyes. After a little silence he said, "Thank you for telling me, Emma. I would judge that in your character you are what your parents made you, and not the product of upbringing by your uncle and aunt. Believe me, I'm deeply grateful to your mother and father, and I shall never refer to them in other than terms of respect. Now, is there anything else you wish to tell me?"

I thought carefully. "Well . . . no. But do you mind if I ask you something?"

"I would like you to ask as many questions as you wish. I confess to having studied you, Emma, but I'm sure you have not studied me, and I'm anxious for you to know everything possible about the man who is proposing marriage to you."

I felt an unexpected wave of affection for Oliver Foy. Sympathy and understanding were gifts beyond price, and it seemed to me that in his quiet and patient way he was showing me both in full measure. I smiled and said, "I was just wondering if, as your wife, I would have to stop doing some of the things I like to do. Please don't misunderstand me. I know your wife will have household duties and social duties, and will be expected to do all the things that her position in the community calls for. That's a little frightening, because I'm not a clever person, but I would try with all my might to be a credit to you." I paused, for again I had almost lost the thread of what I was trying to say, and I wanted to collect myself, but before I could continue, Oliver spoke.

"You like to ride, and to bathe in the sea, and to sail a boat. Is that what you're asking me about, Emma?"

"Yes. You see, Aunt Maude thinks these things aren't very ladylike."

He half smiled. "I have no objection, but I think perhaps a married lady could well exercise a little more decorum than a young girl. By all means continue to ride, but I should be worried to see my wife riding at the fast gallop you're known to enjoy occasionally. I've no taste for sea bathing or sailing myself, but my wife will have two personal maids. One or both, together with a groom, could always make up a party for a sea bathing picnic or a boating trip, and I'm sure your old retainer, Daniel Choong, is the most reliable of persons to ensure your safety on such occasions. Is my answer reasonable, Emma?"

I said gratefully, "More than that, it's very kind and generous."

His smile broadened. "You may well find that sea bathing will rapidly become quite the rage among the ladies of the island, especially the younger ones. Many will be eager to follow where Mrs. Oliver Foy leads. And now may I repeat my question, Emma? Will you do me the honor of becoming my wife?"

I said, "Yes, Oliver, I will, and the honor is mine."

He reached his hands down toward me, and when I took them he drew me gently to my feet. His lips touched my cheek, then he held me lightly by the shoulders and kissed my mouth. Something stirred sharply within me, sudden and powerful. My mind was wiped clean of thought, and only sensation was left, strong and salt as the sea, burning as the sun.

I was trembling, forcing my eyes to open, struggling to emerge from whatever had taken possession of me. Oliver Foy put his fingers gently to my cheeks and looked into my eyes. "Thank you for accepting me, Emma," he said in a low voice. "You have made me very happy."

The days that followed had a strangely dreamlike quality for me. It was as if I lurked in a corner of my mind and watched Emma Delaney caught up in a whirl of new activity.

The engagement was announced in the *Colonial Standard* and the *Jamaica Gazette*, and at once I became a center of interest, not only in the parish of St. Ann but throughout the island's three counties, for with fewer than fifteen thousand white people in the population, the marriage of the only remaining member of the Foy family, leaders of society for many years, was bound to cause a great stir.

There was a complete trousseau to be made, a guest list to be decided, invitations to be sent out, a reception to be arranged, and a hundred other details to be attended to. Much to my astonishment, Aunt Maude was remarkably calm and efficient in all this, for which I was truly thankful. We had many callers now at The Jacarandas, and at church and social functions I was plied with felicitations and good wishes. Most were sincere, but I could not help sensing an undercurrent of envy among some of the young ladies and their mothers. This was hardly surprising, for I knew that many of them were greatly preoccupied with the subject of making a good marriage.

Despite all the work and responsibility, Aunt Maude was in very good humor and so was Uncle Henry, probably because they felt they would soon have discharged the duty they had accepted twelve years ago when they took me into their home. I did not blame them for this.

Two days after the announcement of our engagement Oliver

drove me up to Diabolo Hall with Aunt Maude. It was a little overwhelming to think that before long I should be in charge of such a great house with its army of servants, and I was much relieved to know that Mrs. Ferguson would be remaining as housekeeper. She was a thin Scottish woman with freckles and a pale face who was now in her early sixties, so Oliver told me, but who looked exactly the same to me now as she had looked when I first saw her at a church outing ten years before.

Sir Anthony had brought her over from Glasgow thirty years ago as a lady's maid for his wife, and she had eventually graduated to the high position of housekeeper. She had a very reserved and austere manner, but Oliver told me she controlled the staff excellently and carried out all her duties diligently and without fuss. If she seemed somewhat stiff and unsmiling when she greeted me as the future Mrs. Foy, I could well understand that she might not relish having a mistress at Diabolo Hall when she herself had been the woman in charge of the household for so long.

Oliver came to see me almost every day. Twice we went riding together, and a full afternoon during the second week of our engagement was spent at the stables where he kept half a dozen racehorses. Later that week Uncle Henry and Aunt Maude accompanied us to a race meeting at Cumberland Pen, where with great excitement we watched Oliver's horses win two of the races. It was here, between races, on a fine sunny afternoon, having left my aunt and uncle at ease in their seats with glasses of iced tea, that I was strolling on the crisp dry grass holding Oliver's arm when I came suddenly face to face with Mr. Chad Lockhart.

I had been studying the program with Oliver, and it seemed Mr. Lockhart had been similarly engaged, for we stopped short just before bumping into each other. He and Oliver were raising their hats and all three of us were starting to apologize when Mr. Lockhart and I recognized each other in the same moment. I had the feeling that he would simply have bowed and stood aside if I had not exclaimed, "Why, it's you, Mr. Lockhart!"

"How do you do, Miss Delaney." Hat in hand he gave me a courteous bow, then looked at Oliver. "How do you do, sir. My name is Lockhart and I'm a visitor from England."

Oliver looked a little surprised. "A friend of Henry Shepherd's?" he said.

I broke in. "No, Oliver, I met Mr. Lockhart in Fern Gully a week or two ago. He came riding by when I was trying to help Joseph, who had lost a wheel from his cart, and this gentleman very kindly stopped to assist. But I must introduce you. Mr. Lockhart, this is Mr. Oliver Foy, my fiancé."

"Mr. Lockhart."

"Mr. Foy."

The two men bowed to each other, and Mr. Lockhart continued. "I offer you sincere congratulations, sir. My acquaintance with Miss Delaney was indeed fleeting, but I have no doubt of your good fortune." The smoky gray eyes, one lid drooping, rested amiably on mine. "And please accept my felicitations, Miss Delaney."

"Thank you. I was quite startled to see you here, Mr. Lockhart. I imagined that you had left for England."

"The ship on which I have booked my passage leaves only once a month, so I have still a few days to wait." He glanced at Oliver and moved aside. "I won't detain you, sir. Please excuse my intrusion."

"Not at all," Oliver said with his usual politeness. "Your stay in Jamaica has been very short, but I trust you have found it enjoyable."

"Most pleasant. I wish I could stay longer, but I very much hope to return next year to complete a matter of business here."

"Visitors from England are always welcome," said Oliver. "If I can be of assistance in any way, please call upon me. I have one or two minor business interests and connections, both on the island and elsewhere in the West Indies."

Mr. Lockhart smiled. "That is a very modest claim, sir. I have quickly learned how high the name of Foy stands in Jamaica." He hesitated, then went on slowly, "There is a matter... possibly a very substantial matter, in which you might be interested." He made a gesture of apology. "This is not an appropriate moment, but if you have a free half-hour during the next few days a discussion might be to our mutual advantage."

Oliver considered. "If it is a business project I should prefer to see it set out on paper in the first instance."

Again Mr. Lockhart smiled, this time regretfully. "A sound practice, sir. But this is a matter I cannot commit to paper, for it is far too sensitive."

I expected Oliver to show surprise, but he was quite impassive as he said, "A project within the law?"

"Entirely."

Oliver rubbed his chin with the silver knob of his cane. "I

have to chair a committee meeting at the Jamaica Club at eleven o'clock on Tuesday next," he said. "If you would care to come along at noon, Mr. Lockhart, I shall be free. You will find the club on Hanover Street."

"Thank you. Until noon on Tuesday, then." Again Mr. Lockhart raised his hat to me and bowed. I noticed that it was a new hat, and not an expensive one. "Your servant, Miss Delaney," he said, "and I hope you will forgive my inadvertent intrusion."

My mind was busy wondering if the matter he intended to speak to Oliver about involved the scroll and the gold coin Daniel had given him. I had no idea what they signified, and had spoken of them to nobody, for I felt that Daniel wished it so. Now I decided that I would continue to say nothing unless Oliver spoke of them to me after his meeting with Mr. Lockhart. I said a few pleasant words of farewell to the man from England, then we moved on. When we had gone a little way Oliver said musingly, "It will be interesting to hear what Mr. Lockhart has to say for himself."

"Yes. He told me he had lived in China for some years, and I think his family had a business there. You know, he's quite droll in a way, Oliver. He keeps referring to himself as a favorite victim of a malicious Fate, and it's true that Jennie trod on his hat and broke it. On the other hand, Joseph was terrified of him and made signs against the evil eye."

"Very perceptive of Joseph," said Oliver with a smile. "Droll in manner Mr. Lockhart may well be when he chooses, but he's also a dangerous man."

I was startled. "Dangerous? However can you know that?"

He gave a shrug. "My dear, I recognize an adventurer when I see one. Now let us forget the gentleman for the time being and return to our seats. I have great hopes of Boy Blue winning the next race for me."

On Wednesday, when Oliver called to take me for a drive, I asked what had transpired at his meeting with Mr. Lockhart the day before.

He shook his head with a look of mingled amusement and regret. "A wildcat scheme, I fear."

"What sort of scheme, Oliver?"

My fiancé pursed his lips, frowning a little, and slipped the buggy whip from its socket. "Well . . . he is convinced there is a fortune to be made from coconuts here if only the crop were to be as fully exploited as it is in the southwest Pacific. Copra, vegetable oil, livestock feed, coir, toddy. It's an attractive theory, but in practice the capital outlay would never justify the return."

"I see." Those words of mine were meaningless. I had hardly paid attention to the latter part of what Oliver had said, because from the moment he began to answer my question I knew, though I could not have said how, that the answer was untrue. This was a shock, and made me feel uneasy for a few moments, then it dawned on me that most people would feel I had been inquisitive in asking about something that was none of my business, and no doubt Oliver had preferred to tell a white lie rather than snub me.

Sometimes during those days of our engagement we were alone together for a little while. If we were sure there could be no intrusion, Oliver would take me in his arms and kiss my cheek, my neck, my lips. This was very exciting, and I would find myself breathless, my heart beating ever faster. It seemed that little fires were being lit within me, and I knew a great but curiously nameless longing.

Twice at Oliver's suggestion he accompanied me while I went sea bathing. He was cordial toward Daniel, and amused by the tent in which I changed into my bathing dress. "Your Aunt Maude is quite right to call it a wigwam, Emma. We must build a small hut for you here, so that you can change in more comfort."

He strolled on the shore for half an hour, watching while I swam and floated in the cool clear water. Daniel used no bathing dress. He would come from his house or his workshop wearing trousers cut short above the knee, and simply let them dry on him when he emerged from the water. He had long since taught me to hold my breath so that I could swim for a little way under the water, and he had made me a pair of the goggles he used for diving. These enabled me to see marvelously well beneath the sea, and opened up a new world of great fascination and beauty for me.

In the last year he had taught me spearfishing, though I was not very clever at it. Daniel was an expert, and used a special spear made to his own design, a slender shaft of polished steel no thicker than my small finger, the end flattened and shaped into fine barbs before being brought to a needle point. He claimed that the steel handled better underwater than wood because it created less resistance.

Even though Oliver knew Daniel's reputation as a master diver, he was quite alarmed when we first vanished beneath the surface. Little Jacob's sister, Lily, standing guard by the tent, was able to reassure him that I was perfectly safe and had done this many times before. I was grateful to Oliver for indulging me in this particular pleasure of sea bathing, and felt determined to make myself the best possible wife for so kind a husband. It was to this end that a week before my wedding I spoke to Daniel about something that had been troubling me ever since the day Uncle Henry had informed me that Oliver Foy wished me to marry him.

Early on a Tuesday, when I knew Daniel would be at home doing his weekly cleaning, I drove to his house in our buggy, apologized for disturbing him, and accepted the glass of cool fruit juice he brought to me for refreshment in his little garden.

"Daniel, thank you," I said. "Can you spare a few minutes to talk to me?"

"Of course, Miss Emma." He sat down beside me on the cedar bench he had made, which was placed to look out over the village below and the sea beyond. "What do you wish to talk about?"

"Well, about being married. I've asked Aunt Maude, but she almost faints with embarrassment at any mention of what happens between husbands and wives, and how babies are made. I wish so much that your dear May was alive, because she'd explain everything, but as it is I've simply nobody to ask. I'm sure all the black children and coolie children know these things long before they're my age, but nobody has ever told me anything, and I do so want to know before I'm married."

Daniel sat with arms folded, gazing out across the Caribbean. "It is hard to believe that people who rule over a quarter of the world can be so stupid," he said quietly. "My mother once told me that the English do not approve of nature. I did not know what she meant then, but I have learned since." He turned to look at me, and his eyes were troubled. "Miss Emma, what you ask is something you must learn from another woman. It is not fitting for me talk to you of such matters."

"I know, Daniel, but who else can I turn to?"

He was silent for a few moments, then said, "Have you time to spare this morning?"

"Yes."

"Then I would like to drive you down to the village and ask Sheba to talk with you."

"Sheba! Oh, that's a splendid notion!"

I could not imagine why I had not thought of it myself. Sheba was May's sister, older by five years, a fat happy woman with six children and an amiable but idle husband who did casual work husking coconuts—when the spirit moved him, which was seldom. Sheba supported the family. She spent her mornings doing laundry for the Mesquitta Lodging House in Ocho Rios, and her afternoons working there as a kitchen hand and general maid. I had not seen her often, but remembered her as a very jolly woman with mischievous eyes in her black face and a deep hearty chuckle.

Daniel took the reins and drove us down to the ramshackle wooden house on the outskirts of the village. Sheba's husband was sitting on a broken chair in the sun, smoking a cigar, and fanning himself with a palm leaf. Three of Sheba's children, two boys and a girl, were playing some game with half a coconut and a few pebbles. Smoke rose from an unsteady-looking stovepipe chimney, and steam rolled from the open door and window.

"Wait here, please, Miss Emma," said Daniel. He got down and went into the house. Sheba's husband half opened one eye, then closed it again. The children stopped playing and stood gazing at me with solemn interest, but did not approach the buggy. Two minutes passed, then Sheba emerged from the house followed by Daniel. Her face and forearms were agleam with moisture, her long dress and white apron showing damp patches, but her fat cheeks were creased in a big smile of welcome, and her eyes were warm and merry.

"Mo'ning, Miss Emma."

"Good morning, Sheba. How are you? And all your family?"

"We're jes' fine. Now s'pose you tek them reins, Miss Emma, an' ol' Sheba come sit alongside so we go riding two—three minutes to a little quiet place along the road." She jerked a thumb over her shoulder. "Dan'l, he stayin' here till we come back."

"Thank you, Sheba." I slid across the seat and gathered the reins while she heaved herself up into the buggy and sank down beside me to a squeaking of springs.

"That way, Miss Emma." She pointed. I clicked my tongue and Rufus moved off at a walk. In less than a minute we were on a track that ran on the seaward side of the coast road, and in another three minutes, at a word from Sheba, I drew rein on a flat grassy terrace from which a low cliff dropped to the sea. Sheba settled herself comfortably in her seat with a little sigh, perhaps of contentment, for there were few moments of the day when she could sit down and rest.

"Dan'l says you don't know nothin' 'bout what happens when you git married, Miss Emma, an' you got nobody to tell you."

"That's right, Sheba." I turned a little so I could see her face.

She shook her head and sighed again, this time with wondering regret. "White people make like it somet'ing bad. Ain't like that no how, Miss Emma." Her cheeks creased in a smile, her eyes shone with mischief, and a chuckle made her whole body quiver. "You got a lovin' man givin' you nice love an' you givin' him nice love, it the bestest t'ing in the world. Jes' like livin' in heaven awhile. You believe me, Miss Emma. Like us black folk say, 'Marriage got teeth an' bite hot.'"

"Yes, I've had feelings which made me think it might be something very special."

"So now I tell you 'bout it. You was my sister May's sweet honey-baby, an' ol' Sheba real glad to help. Ain't nobody goin' to know what you an' me say here now 'cept us, an' that for true, so now we talk free." She smiled again, her fat cheeks rising so that her eyes were almost hidden. "On'y t'ing is, I got to speak plain words, and there's maybe t'ings 'bout a man an' a woman you ain't never learned no words for yet, so I got to speak names for them. But jes' you don't feel shy, Miss Emma, an' if ol' Sheba say anyt'ing you don't know what she mean, you jes' stop her an' ask."

"Yes, I'll do that, Sheba."

"So now we start wit' ezackly how the man is made different from us, an' what for the Good Lord make him so . . ."

On that small grassy terrace we sat with the buggy's hood shading us from the bright morning sunshine and we talked. For most of the time it was Sheba who spoke, her soft throaty voice easy and unhurried, sometimes breaking into a chuckle of delight as she explained mysteries to me. In the first minute or two I found myself flushing, more with surprise than embarrassment, but this soon passed, and when I broke in with the first of many questions I found no difficulty in speaking as plainly as Sheba.

It was more than half an hour later that we drove back to her house, to find Daniel playing cricket with the children, using a makeshift bat and a ball roughly carved from a piece of silkcotton wood. Sheba's husband watched, chuckling lazily at the squeals and scamperings of the children. Daniel came across and helped Sheba down from the buggy. Her husband called, "Where you been, woman?"

"Ain't nobody's business but mine, you ol' no-good man." She reached up to pat my hand. "You be happy, Miss Emma."

Two minutes later, as we drove away, I said to Daniel, "If I bring you a sovereign will you give it to Sheba for me?"

"There's no need, Miss Emma."

"Ask her to accept it if only to please me."

"Very well. Did Sheba tell you all you wished to know?"

"Yes, she explained everything." I shook my head and could not help smiling at my own state of wonderment. "I must say it all sounds very odd, Daniel. Very odd indeed."

On a warm June day tempered by the daily breeze from the sea that we called the Doctor, I was married to Oliver Foy by the Bishop of Jamaica, Dr. Nuttall, in the Parish Church of Kingston. The wedding was followed by a lavish reception at the Myrtle Bank Hotel. I was very excited, and also rather nervous at being the central figure on such an important social occasion, but Aunt Maude was a tower of strength and always at hand to guide or reassure me.

We were to spend a two-week honeymoon on Haiti, part of the island of St. Domingo and little more than a day's sail from Kingston. Oliver had borrowed a fine house on the coast south of Saint-Marc from a business acquaintance in Port-au-Prince, who had arranged for a full staff to be at our service. We were to travel accompanied by Oliver's valet, Ramírez, a colored man with Spanish blood, and two maids from Diabolo Hall who would in future be my personal lady's maids. Their names were Martha and Becky, both were a few years older than I and had been trained at other houses, so they were experienced in their work. I first met them a week before the wedding, at Diabolo Hall. They seemed pleasant young women with ready smiles, except in Oliver's presence. With him they were mute and awestruck. I thought I would be happy with them as my maids, but felt glad I would have little to do with Ramírez. He was a man of about forty who rarely spoke. His eyes had a dead look, and when they rested on me I had the feeling that there was contempt hidden in them.

We boarded a steamer at seven o'clock on the evening of my wedding day. Oliver had arranged for us to have separate cabins so that I might rest and sleep throughout the short journey. I much appreciated his kindness in this, for I found that the stress and excitement of the day had left me exhausted in body and mind. Next day toward noon we went ashore by tender, disembarking at a little jetty that served the fine house of timber and white stone standing on a low wooded ridge beyond the beach. Two carriages were waiting to take us up to the house. Our bedroom was large, cool, and splendidly furnished in the French style, with a private dressing room for each of us.

I enjoyed unpacking my beautiful clothes from the trunks, and could not sit still to let Martha and Becky do everything. I enjoyed the picnic lunch Oliver suggested, and the drive later between the beach and a green forest. I enjoyed remembering all that Sheba had told me, and was aware of excitement mounting within me, perhaps tinged with a little nervousness, as the day wore on.

I enjoyed the bath Martha and Becky prepared for me in the biggest hip bath I had ever seen, and dressing later in one of my lovely new dresses to dine with Oliver at a table so absurdly large for the two of us that I had to keep stifling a giggle.

I enjoyed the two glasses of champagne I drank during dinner, and Oliver's quiet but entertaining conversation. I enjoyed going to my dressing room later, sending Martha and Becky away, undressing myself and deciding which of my three exquisite nightgowns to put on before going to the candle-lit bedroom, climbing into the great bed, and waiting for Oliver.

After a little while my husband came to me, and it was then that the long and dreadful nightmare began.

4

IN THE WEEKS AND MONTHS THAT FOLLOWED OUR WEDDING
there were many occasions when I waited at night in our bedroom for my husband to come to me, but never again with
happy anticipation.

Sometimes I found it hard to believe that the outward appearance of our life together at Diabolo Hall seemed quite
normal to others, to my aunt and uncle, to the many friends
and acquaintances with whom we exchanged calls and mingled
on social occasions. I felt that no matter how I smiled and
dissembled, no matter that Oliver was outwardly as considerate
in his manner toward me as he had ever been during our engagement, all the world must surely see behind the masks we
wore and realize that he was a monster and I hated him.

It was stupid of me to feel surprised that nobody perceived
the truth. I had suspected nothing of Oliver's true nature myself
until it had been revealed to me, and I had had more opportunity
than most to know him. As long as I did not weep in company,
as long as I did not quite look at my husband when others were
present, it was unlikely that anyone would suspect my feelings,
and almost beyond possibility that anyone could imagine the
cause of them.

Humiliation and mental torment did not show on the skin, and pride kept them from showing on my face. As for physical hurts, Oliver was careful even in his most frightening moments never to mark me where it might show. I had no doubt that his man, Ramírez, not only knew how his master treated me but also took pleasure in the knowledge.

My own maids may have guessed something of the truth, but after the first night I never again allowed them to help me take a bath or dress, so they did not see the bruise marks of his fingers, the thin weals of the crop or broad ridges from the strap. The other servants, I was sure, knew nothing; not even Mrs. Ferguson, a housekeeper from whom few secrets could be kept. Our bedroom and dressing rooms were in the south wing, well separated from the staff quarters. I had never yet cried out under my husband's use of me, but even if I had screamed I would never have been heard.

Sometimes in the night, when Oliver had finished with me and was asleep, I would wrap myself in a blanket and lie on a rug in my dressing room because I could not bear to be in the same bed. Quite often, to my relief, he would be away for two or three nights, supposedly on business elsewhere. Ramírez always accompanied him. I soon suspected that his business had to do with women, for he always returned in a sated mood and would leave me alone for a few days. On one occasion I chanced to overhear a conversation between Ramírez and Martha in the hall outside our bedroom when they believed me to be somewhere downstairs, and this confirmed what I had suspected.

"Where you been wit' the master these t'ree days, John?"

"You mind your business, girl."

"Jest askin'. Becky say you go up to Moore Town to have lovey-lovey wit' them Maroon girls in the settlement there."

"You tell Becky she best keep close mouth. If she go round speakin' t'ings 'bout the master, he gonna ruin her for true."

"I don't care 'bout Mr. Foy going wit' the Maroon girls, John. I jes' sayin' how you t'ink you walk out wit' me when *you* go lovey-lovey wit' them?"

"It because I a man, Martha. Ain't for woman to tell a man what he do, so don't make me no trouble, girl. It me who fix everyt'ing for Mister Oliver right from when the ol' master die, so John Ramírez he a big man in the house. Big man wit' the master. You make me trouble, I talk to Mister Oliver an' you find you'self on some plantation pickin' coffee."

The voices faded as they moved away, but I could hear a note of fear in Martha's tone. I stood with comb in hand, looking at myself in the pier glass. Now I knew that my husband was in the habit of regular and secret debauchery with women up in the Maroon settlement, descendants of the early Spanish Negroes. The knowledge did not distress me, I was far beyond that. At first it seemed incredible that Oliver could have escaped gossip for so long if he was a libertine, but then it dawned on me that in all probability this practice was comparatively new for him.

His father had been a man of dominating character and a martinet. Perhaps it was only with Sir Anthony's death that Oliver had been able to give rein to his taste for debauchery, aided and guided by Ramírez. I had a strong conviction that he did not use his other women, the Maroon girls, as he used me. They would never have suffered it, even for gold. I was his chosen victim. Certain it was that he had a brutal and overpowering need for a victim. Perhaps this was because he had been subdued by his father's dominance for almost all his thirty-six years. Perhaps his natural instincts had become distorted in that time. Perhaps he had chosen me because I had no parents and he sensed that I could never appeal to my aunt and uncle. Perhaps he believed that in the oddity of my nature I would be a more satisfactory victim than most available young ladies, because I would not be so easily crushed.

But I was not concerned with reasons or causes or speculation. I only knew that I feared and hated my husband to such a degree that I was sometimes guilty of the dreadful wickedness of wishing him dead. Every Sunday we would go to church at Claremont for the morning service and sit side by side in the Foy pew. I would silently thank God that I had not yet been made pregnant, and beg that this should continue. Even the relief from Oliver's attentions I might expect from being pregnant would not compensate for the horror of carrying his child.

In my daily life I was allowed to do much as I pleased. As the wife of Oliver Foy I had many social duties, and I schooled myself to carry these out with meticulous care. For the rest, I would attend to whatever household matters Mrs. Ferguson brought to my attention, and spend my leisure hours as I chose. It was not in my nature to spend all my time at needlework and embroidery. Sometimes I would take one of the horses and go riding. If I was in pain after a bad night with Oliver I would not ride far but would find some small wooded dell and lie quietly in its shade, slowly coaxing my mind into emptiness so that I should not dwell on what the future held for me.

Because I desperately needed something to love, I spent much time working and supervising work on a large flower garden I had begun to establish on the north side of Diabolo Hall, away from the prevailing winds. Here I planned to grow all manner of flowers and flowering shrubs, hibiscus and angel's-trumpet, allamanda and jasmine, pandorea, begonia, Bermuda lilies, African violets, and roses. The laying out of the beds and preparation of the ground had been completed, and already planting had begun.

Oliver did not keep me short of money, so there was no difficulty about expenditure on my garden or on the books I would buy in Kingston to keep me occupied during whatever leisure hours were not filled in other ways. Except at night, it was not often that Oliver and I were alone together. In the evenings I would read or sew, or perhaps paint rather bad watercolor seascapes from memory. Sometimes Oliver would busy himself in his study with the management of the estate and the many business interests inherited from Sir Anthony. At other times he might spend the evening at his club in Moneague, which had premises in the hotel there, or at Hollymount House, the hotel near Ewarton, where he would meet men from Kingston and other parts of the island to discuss business matters.

On the rare occasions when we were alone together he would either behave as if I had ceased to exist or would talk as easily as if we were a happily married couple. At first I had tried to respond to this latter mood, perhaps with some faint hope that it would help to bring about a change in my plight, but soon I realized that these occasions always presaged a bad night for me, and were designed to lift my hopes so that he would have more pleasure in dashing them later.

Sometimes I feared I would go out of my mind, for when I forced myself to look into my future life as Mrs. Oliver Foy I knew that in the end it would become beyond bearing. Yet there was no escape. I could not run away. I could not return to Aunt Maude and Uncle Henry, for they would neither believe nor accept me.

I had seen Daniel only twice since my marriage. The first time, when he had asked how I was, I had lied to him out of pride and shame, smiling and saying that I was surely the most fortunate girl in Jamaica. He had given me a long look, but then I had quickly asked how his fine new boat was progressing, and we had talked of that for the rest of the time I spent with him. The second occasion was when Oliver was away for three days, partly on business perhaps, but I had no doubt partly for debauchery up at Moore Town with his Maroon girls.

It was Aunt Maude's birthday, and I drove to The Jacarandas in a buggy to take her a present and have luncheon there. I noticed that she studied me, and knew she was wondering if I might be pregnant, but to ask was beyond her. Though I tried hard to appear cheerful and pleased with life it was not a particularly successful occasion, and I felt both Aunt Maude and Uncle Henry were quite glad to see me leave soon after luncheon.

Instead of returning to Diabolo Hall I drove down to Ocho Rios, to the spot where Daniel's boathouse stood, and felt a rare glow of pleasure when I saw that the little steamer had been launched and was at anchor in the harbor, with Daniel on the foredeck painting the cabin housing, assisted by little Jacob. I soon attracted the boy's attention by waving my parasol, and in moments he was pulling toward me in the dinghy, heaving manfully on the oars.

I could hear his piping voice well before he was alongside the quay. "Dan'l say you like fo' him to come ashore, Miss Emma, or you like fo' to come see the boat?" He was beaming and panting as he drew nearer, and I moved to where stone steps ran down from the quay.

"I'll come and see the boat, Jacob."

The handful of villagers and fishermen nearby watched with mild curiosity, mainly because it had been some time since I had visited Ocho Rios and I was now Mrs. Foy. Most of them had been used to seeing me for many years as Emma Delaney, in company with May and Daniel, so it was no surprise to them that I should be stepping from the quay into the little boat that Jacob had so dexterously maneuvered alongside.

I would have been more comfortable in the riding breeches I had usually worn for sailing, but managed my skirts well enough, and at once Jacob turned the boat round and began pulling out to the steamer. As we came round the port bow he said, "Look good, Miss Emma!" and jerked his head with a sideways motion. Then I saw the name painted there. It was *Miss Emma*, and my eyes filled with tears.

Short wooden steps hung down from the break in the polished mahogany rail, and Daniel was waiting to give me his hand as I stepped onto the deck. "Welcome to your namesake, Miss Emma."

"Oh Daniel, she's beautiful. Have you tried her at sea?"

"Several times now." He wiped his hands on a cloth and ran his palm lovingly over the rail. "She is no swallow under sail, but she has a good heart, and works in friendship with sea and wind."

"And the engine?"

"Ah, that is a very happy machine. When *Miss Emma* moves under steam she is mistress of sea and wind, but she does not become too proud, for she knows that both her friends may sometimes be seized with madness, and grow very strong, to destroy all they can seize in their grip."

"I'm glad she's wise, Daniel. I would love to go out with you on her one day."

"That would be a great pleasure for me. If you permit, I will send a letter when I have completed all trials and finished all remaining work on deck and below. It will be very soon now."

"Yes, please do that. I shall have to bring one of my maids, and I expect she'll be seasick unless it's a calm day."

"Perhaps Mr. Foy himself might accompany you?"

I managed not to grimace, and said, "He's usually very busy, Daniel, but I'll certainly tell him about your boat. He might even be interested in buying it for one of his companies. It would be very useful for coastal work on a small scale, because it could ply between the little places where the Atlas steamer and the Royal Mail steamer can't put in."

Daniel nodded and looked along the scrubbed deck. "I would sail the length of the West Indies in this," he said softly. "From the Bahamas down to Trinidad. With a fair wind she will move like a sturdy buggy-horse. With a foul wind she will journey no less quickly under steam. She burns wood, so there is fuel to be picked up on any coast, and no island is more than a day's sail from the next." He had been staring out to sea, but as he fell silent his eyes focused on me again and he gave an apologetic smile.

I said, "You'd like to do that, wouldn't you, Daniel?"

He thought for a moment. "I have been lonely since May was lost to me, and sometimes I think it is better to be lonely at sea than on land. But I am a stupid old fellow to talk so much of myself and my boat. Are you well, Miss Emma? And Mr. Foy also?"

"Yes, thank you, we're very well." There was a little silence, then I said, "So she's a good sound craft?"

"Better than I could hope for, Miss Emma. I was diving to examine her keel and hull this morning, and everything down there is perfect."

"I'm so glad." My heart ached as I spoke. I would have loved to go down under the water with Daniel, drifting weightlessly in that beautiful other world, studying the hull of his fine little ship through the goggles that gave underwater vision, feeling the cool water enclosing my body and washing away all degradation. Daniel was looking at me with the same intent gaze I had caught before, and on impulse I said, "I'd like to talk to Sheba one day. Can you arrange it?"

He looked away, and I saw his jaw tighten as if my words held some hidden meaning for him. "Of course, Miss Emma. She works at the lodging house every afternoon, but you can talk with her any morning. Perhaps it would be more convenient if I brought her to my house to meet you."

I tried to appear quite casual as I said, "Yes, that would be very pleasant. I'll come next Tuesday morning."

For the next quarter of an hour Daniel showed me over the little steamer. I knew the workmanship was superb, for I had watched the building of her from the time the keel was laid, but now that she was afloat it was as if a life of her own had been breathed into her. The *Miss Emma* had been built for work, and her lines were not graceful, but to me she was a lady with sturdy good looks. Her single mast carried the mainsail and jib, with the jib hanked to the forestay. The smokestack was hinged so that it could lie flat when the boiler was not in use. A short companionway led down into the cabin, and from this a passage led to the tiny galley. The cabin was fitted with two bunks, and was so skillfully designed and furnished that it seemed quite spacious.

There was a small hold forward and another aft. The cabin, galley, after hold, and engine compartment were all connected below deck by a working passage to which there was also access from a trap in the wheelhouse. The engine itself was what Daniel called a steam reciprocating engine of the compound type. To me it was a rather frightening thing of shining steel pistons, mysterious wheel valves, and polished brass tubing, yet together with the boiler it occupied no more space than the upright piano in our drawing room at The Jacarandas. The

more I saw of the *Miss Emma*, the more I realized that Daniel
had created a marvel of compactness, with no inch of space wasted.

I said, "She's a wonderful little ship, Daniel. I'm so proud
you've called her after me. I can't imagine any greater compliment, truly."

"You are very kind, Miss Emma. I'm happy that you like
her."

We talked for a little longer, then Daniel rowed me back
to the quay and I set off in the buggy for Diabolo Hall. It was
a ten-mile drive and would take most of the afternoon, but I
was used to long drives and long rides. I let the horse move
at an easy pace, for I was in no hurry to return to the great
house that others thought of as my home but which to me was
a place of despair.

For the next few days, as was usual when Oliver returned
from a trip to Moore Town, I was not troubled by his attentions,
but this blessing was marred by an ever-increasing dread of
what would follow. On the Sunday we went to morning service.
Afterward, outside the church, we lingered as usual to chat
with friends and have a little conversation with Aunt Maude
and Uncle Henry. Oliver was as quiet, as amiable, and as
unassertive as ever. There could be no mistaking how highly
thought of he was in the community and how much his kindly
ways were appreciated.

I acted my part as his wife, just as I had done since we
were married, yet inwardly I felt in some strange way as if I
were disconnected from the world in which these other people
lived and had their being. Later that day, after we had taken
tea on the great terrace from which the distant haze of the
Caribbean could be seen, Oliver went to his study and I to the
pleasant room that had been used by Sir Anthony as a library.
During our engagement, when Oliver had shown me over Diabolo Hall, he had said with a laugh that I could consider the
five or six hundred books in the library as my own. I had since
taken him at his word, adding the books I had brought from
The Jacarandas and a few more purchased since.

This room and the sewing room were my two havens during
the day, where I could be on my own and free from the constant
strain of pretense. Today I planned to start listing the books
and putting some aside to take to Daniel. In years gone by it
had been his habit to read aloud to May for an hour each
evening, and he was still a keen reader. As I worked I found
myself growing steadily more tense and nervous, and soon I

realized that beneath my surface thoughts as I sorted the books, fear and shame were working like yeast within me. After a time I found myself standing quite still, a book unnoticed in my hand, staring into space and wondering with quiet desperation what in heaven's name I could do to make my lot bearable.

Then I was walking down one of Diabolo Hall's broad passages, my face feeling stiff and unnatural, my heart palpitating as I halted outside Oliver's study and tapped on the door.

"Come in."

He was sitting at a big desk, ornately carved in very dark wood, a number of papers spread untidily in front of him. His eyebrows lifted as I entered.

"Yes, Emma?"

"May I speak to you for a few moments, Oliver?"

Something stirred in the depths of his eyes. It was a dark gleam of pleasure, yet his frown deepened as he said, "You choose an inconvenient moment, my dear. I have work to do."

"Yes. Yes, I'm sorry to disturb you, but I'm feeling rather distressed and . . . I really must talk to you, Oliver. Please."

He put down his pen, swiveled his chair so that he faced me, leaned back with hands behind his head, lifted one foot to the other knee, and said, "Very well. About what?"

I was trying desperately to prevent my voice from shaking, but my efforts made it sound flat and unnatural. "Well . . . please, Oliver, I want to ask you to stop abusing me."

He looked incredulous, but I was meant to know that the look was simulated. "*Abusing* you? My dear Emma, how can you say such a thing? When have I ever uttered a harsh word?"

I struggled on, my heart sinking. "I didn't mean that, Oliver. Not verbal abuse. I meant the intimate things between husband and wife. I beg you to stop abusing me in that way. I'm sure I can be a very loving wife, and I want to be, but it's not possible when I'm degraded and . . . and punished. I can't go on, Oliver. I shall become ill."

"How *dare* you speak to me in this way, madam!" His voice was a whisper of fury and his face dark with apparent rage as he came forward in his chair and pointed a menacing finger at me, but the gleam of pleasure deep in his eyes was a small flame now. "How dare you stoop to discussing affairs of the bedroom! Such matters are not to be spoken of by any decent woman!"

"But I *must* speak of them, Oliver." My voice began to

falter despite my efforts. "Please . . . oh, please consider my feelings. Sometimes I fear I shall be driven out of my mind if you continue to . . . to use me as you do."

His face was a mask. "There is an excellent Lunatic Asylum in Kingston, my dear Emma, but I am quite sure you will never be an inmate of it. At the moment you are suffering from an attack of nerves. But you have a sturdy character and will soon learn not to be oversensitive, I am sure." He smiled suddenly, affectionately. "Now, I forgive you for your indiscretion in speaking to me in this way, and we will say no more about it."

He began to turn and pick up his pen, but somehow I stood my ground, though there were tears of frustration on my cheeks now, and my voice was hoarse. "Once more I beg you, Oliver . . . please try to understand my feelings. Perhaps it would help you to understand if you thought of your mother—"

Oliver's movements were always deliberate, but he came out of his chair with such swift ferocity that I fell back in fear. There was no pretense in him now, no hidden pleasure, only a shocking and venomous hatred.

"My mother?" he echoed in a soft dreadful voice. "Oh yes, I often think of her, Emma. I think of her, and I hope she is in hell. Did you imagine my father was a martinet? That was what the world thought, but they did not know my mother. Beside her, he was an indulgent man. She loved and admired him to distraction, and because I, the only child she was able to bear, was so different in looks and ways and character from my father, she *despised* me. As long as she lived she fought without pity to remake me in his image, and she failed. I found no freedom from her until the day she died."

Oliver was not looking at me now, but through me, as if staring into the past. There was a fleck of white at one corner of his mouth, and his voice had become a monotone. He fell silent, and slowly his eyes lost their glaze. After what seemed a long time he looked at me again and gave a sudden harsh laugh. "Oh yes," he said. "I have not forgotten my dear mother. Of that you may be sure, Emma." He leaned forward with a smirk of glee. "And since you are of a very spirited, very reckless character, I have now taken steps to protect myself. You may be sure of that, also."

"Protect?" I said muzzily. There was nothing left in me but gray despair. I now realized dimly what lay behind Oliver's desire to heap pain and humiliation upon me, but I cared nothing

for whatever cause drove him. I only knew that no appeal of
mine would move him. As for his talk of protecting himself,
that was beyond my comprehension.

He was taking a piece of writing paper from a drawer, and
now he handed it to me. "Read this, and mark it well, Emma,"
he said. "It is a copy of a sealed letter I have placed with my
solicitor to be opened in the event of my death."

As if in a dream I took the paper from him and tried to
force my mind into understanding the words it bore.

To the Commissioner of Police

*In the event of my death under strange or suspicious
circumstances I beg that every tolerance be shown to my
dear wife, Emma. Indeed, it is my wish that no investigation of the matter should take place.*

*I love my wife deeply, and it is not with anger but
with sorrow that I have become aware of the irresistible
desire that possesses her, a desire to become sole owner
and mistress of the Foy estates. With the exception of
this single mental flaw she is entirely rational and per-
forms her duties admirably. In many respects she is truly
devoted to me, and I pray that this aspect of her mind
will overcome the desire that lies in the darker side.*

*In any event, my love for her is such that whatever
may befall I wish only for her safety and happiness, and
to this end I make the request set out in the first para-
graph of this letter.*

Signed: Oliver Foy.

I had to read the letter twice before understanding came to
me, then I let it fall from my fingers as if it had been impreg-
nated with a blistering venom.

"You know that is all untrue," I whispered. "But you believe
I might find a way to do you mortal harm . . . so you have
concocted this story and accused me in advance, knowing your
request must be ignored."

He nodded slowly, smugly. "And I have made sure you
know of my precaution, Emma. That is the point."

I shook my head hopelessly. "If you believe I could plan
to do such a thing, then it is surely your own mind that is
diseased, Oliver. But at least it shows you are fully aware of
how dreadfully you mistreat me."

With my first sentence he began to show anger again, but with the second his face went blank as if he had closed his mind to my words. He picked up the letter, put it back in the drawer, sat down at the desk, and picked up his pen. "I'm sorry, my dear," he said amiably, "but I have rather a lot of work on hand, and I must deny myself the pleasure of continuing this conversation at the moment. I shall see you later, of course."

He began to write. I watched his bent head for a few seconds, then turned to the door in a daze of misery, wondering once more what was to become of me.

That night I resisted Oliver. The resistance became a struggle, then developed into a horrible brawl, a strangely silent brawl with only the sound of scuffling to be heard. I fought till I was exhausted, but Oliver was very strong, and in the end, sobbing with loathing, I was too feeble to deny him. Later that night, as I lay wrapped in a blanket on the floor, listening to the slow and measured breathing of my sleeping husband, I knew that my resistance had increased his pleasure.

On the Tuesday of the next week Oliver left immediately after breakfast for Kingston. As soon as he had gone I changed into my riding breeches and took Apollo from the stables, telling Solomon, the butler, that I would not be home for luncheon. It was unusual behavior for a married woman to go riding or driving unescorted, but not particularly unusual for Mrs. Oliver Foy to do so, since she was known to be less conventional than most. Solomon probably thought I would take luncheon at The Jacarandas, and I did not correct that impression.

Apollo was a good horse, and could go all day at a brisk trot with an occasional canter. We reached Daniel's house before noon, and as I turned the corner of it by the path leading from the road I saw Sheba sitting on the bench there, dozing in the sun. She roused as I dismounted, and Daniel came out with broom in hand. This was his day for cleaning.

Both greeted me with grave smiles, as if aware that my visit had some serious purpose. Sheba said, "You wantin' to talk woman talk, Miss Emma?" They still called me Miss Emma, never Mistress Foy.

I said, "Yes. And thank you for coming, Sheba."

"It pure pleasure, Miss Emma." She gave me a doubtful look. "Ain't on account you got a baby?"

"Oh, no. No, thank God."

Sheba nodded slowly, gave a heavy sigh, and looked at Daniel. "You fetch some nice glass o' sorrel for Miss Emma, then you give her horse to drink an' maybe nice rub so you leavin' me an' Miss Emma to our own a while, Dan'l."

"I have the drinks ready, Sheba." He went into the house and brought out two tall glasses of sorrel on a wooden tray of his own making, with legs that folded down to make a small table. He set this down by the bench, then took the reins and led Apollo away toward the little stream that went to form one of the eight rivers from which Ocho Rios took its name.

I was dry from the morning's ride, and sat sipping my drink for a while in silence before I turned to look at Sheba and said, "I'm in dreadful trouble, Sheba. I don't know what I can do."

Her face, usually so merry, was somber now as she said, "It because of Mr. Foy?"

"Yes."

"He takin' other women?"

I was surprised. "Why, yes. I thought nobody knew."

"Black folk know what white folk don't, Miss Emma. Mr. Foy like to play rooster wit' Maroon girls up to Moore Town, but black folk don't speak because if'n Mr. Foy don't like somebody then somebody gonna wish he never born."

"I see. But it's not just that he goes with the Maroon women. Sheba. I wouldn't care about that now, if only he would leave me alone. But he won't. And what he does to me is . . . awful."

Her fat round face creased with grief, and she shook her head. "Dear Lord save. You better tell ol' Sheba. Plain words, Miss Emma."

I did so, haltingly at first, but then in a dull monotone. When I had finished there were tears on Sheba's cheeks and she sat with arms across her chest, hugging herself and crooning a mumbled dirge. "Oh, Lord . . . bring mercy along dis poor chil' here . . . she got trouble, she got trouble . . . her man t'row away heaven to make bad hell for her . . ."

I grasped her arm and said, "Stop, Sheba, stop. It's no use behaving like that. I need help . . . advice." She looked at me with distraught eyes, then turned and called in a shrill voice to Daniel by the stream. He came walking toward me, leading Apollo, and when he halted I saw dismay in his face as he looked at Sheba, for she was a picture of despair.

"Miss Emma, she married to a beast-man, Dan'l," she said in a frightened whisper. "Mr. Foy, he got a big hurtin' devil in him."

I saw Daniel's shoulders slump. He looked down at the ground, then raised his eyes to mine. "From the beginning, Miss Emma?"

"Yes. I . . . I don't know how to stop it. I've nowhere to turn."

He said tiredly, "I was afraid from the start. I had heard about the Maroon women, and I felt there was something more. Something hidden. I did not know it was this."

"What am I to do, Daniel?"

He looked at me without hope. "I don't know, Miss Emma. I simply don't know."

It had been foolish of me to expect a miracle, for there could be no solution to my plight. If there had been one, I would surely have thought of it. I had considered speaking to Dr. Taylor. But what then? I could never imagine him daring to mention such a matter to Oliver, let alone remonstrating with my husband. As Oliver had said, the affairs of the bedroom were not subjects for discussion.

Sheba was speaking, partly to Daniel and partly as if thinking aloud. "That why she don't get no baby, 'cos her insides is scared and they ain't gonna take nothin' from that beast-man. Maybe Miss Emma she give me some gold sovereign to pay obeah man so he set real bad obi for Mr. Foy, then a *duppy* come in the night an' take him off. White folks leave window open in the night, so it gonna be easy for some big duppy to—"

Daniel said sharply, "Sheba, be quiet!" He looked at me apologetically. "She means well, Miss Emma."

"I know. Even your dear May half believed in duppies." These were evil spirits who prowled at night.

Sheba said, "Sorry, Miss Emma. Ol' Sheba jest a stupid woman. Ever'one know the obeah man can't lay no spell on white folk."

I said, "It's all right, Sheba," and put down my empty glass, trying to hold back tears of disappointment. I was angry with myself for thinking that because Sheba had helped me so greatly before, she could now, by some magic counsel, turn Oliver from what she called a beast-man into a gentle and loving husband.

I got up and managed to smile. "I'm sorry I've distressed you, Daniel, but please try not to worry. I'm sure my situation will improve, and I'd be glad if you and Sheba would put out of your minds what I've told you today."

"It will never be spoken of, Miss Emma," he said, his voice sad and low. "You may be sure of that."

"Thank you." I tried to put the subject aside. "Is all well with you, Daniel?"

"Why . . . yes, I think so."

Sheba sniffed. "He think so," she echoed. "Sometime he don't think what he doin' these day. You know a *shark* come near to catch him las' week when he gone way out on his boat?"

"Oh Daniel, no!"

He made an impatient gesture. "There was no danger. I had the *Miss Emma* out in deep water and was in the dinghy to study her trim when a shark became curious. When he began nudging the dinghy I used my spear to drive him away, but the barbs held more strongly than I expected, and when the shark made off he took the spear with him."

"Well, I'm glad it was no worse. Do be careful, Daniel. Will you have another spear made?"

"That is in hand already, Miss Emma."

"Good. And how is my namesake?"

"Oh, the *Miss Emma* is finished now. Complete in every detail."

"I hope you get a fine price for her."

"I do not think I shall be selling her." Daniel spoke distractedly, as if he found it hard to indulge in everyday gossip after what he had just heard. "Will you stay to take a meal with us, Miss Emma? Or to rest a little longer?"

"Thank you, but I must leave now."

He brought Apollo forward, helped me to mount, then diffidently reached up to take my hand. "Please, Miss Emma, be careful."

I looked down at him wryly. "Of my husband?" He nodded. "How, Daniel?"

"I mean especially in these next days. Three days, perhaps four."

I stared, puzzled. Sheba stood behind him now, forlorn and tearful. I said, "What do you mean?"

"There is strong weather coming. Very bad storm, perhaps a hurricane." He glanced toward the southeast, from which three times in my lifetime the frightful power of a hurricane had come close to the island. Usually only the western fringe of the terrible wind touched Jamaica, giving us storm weather, but older people remembered times when a hurricane had taken a slightly different path, times when the invisible monster had torn and battered and flogged the land without mercy, bringing death and havoc, destroying villages, flooding plantations, uprooting trees, and stripping the bark from others so that they died a lingering death.

I had never known Daniel to be wrong in predicting weather, and thought it was a gift that sprang from his affinity with sea and air, but he declared that he did no more than read signs that were there for all to see; the change in the nature and speed of the waves, the movement of cloud and variation of light, the change in the behavior of birds, insects, crabs, and even fish.

I said, "Why should I have particular reason to beware of my husband because of a hurricane, Daniel?"

He spoke slowly, still looking distantly away to the southeast. "When a man is possessed by evil passions, the time of a great storm may magnify those passions, and drive him with greater force."

"Do you mean . . . I could be in danger?"

"I pray that you will not be, Miss Emma."

I waited for a spark of fear to flare within me, but nothing happened. I felt only dull resignation. This in itself sounded a distant alarm, but I ignored it and said, "All right, Daniel. I'll try to be careful, and I'll come and see you again before too long. Good-bye for now. Good-bye, Sheba."

She wiped her cheeks. "Bye, miss. Ride good." That was a usual parting salutation among the black people.

Daniel said, "Thank you for the books you sent, Miss Emma."

"I hope you enjoy them." I touched heels to Apollo and moved away at a walk, not looking back, feeling the strange emptiness that was coming upon me more and more frequently as the days went by. Half an hour later, in Fern Gully, I saw Joseph coming toward me, half asleep at the reins of his empty donkey cart. As we passed, he saw me and knuckled his brow with a rather sheepish grin. I called, "Good day, Joseph," and rode slowly on.

Since leaving Daniel's house I had ridden with my mind blank, because there were no thoughts I could entertain that were not despairing, but the sight of Joseph brought back the small adventure of the broken-down cart and my encounter with Chad Lockhart. It seemed to have taken place in a different world, a world in which Emma Delaney had been another person entirely. I recalled my early annoyance with the stranger from England, then how his dry humor had amused me. I could still conjure up a mental picture of those smoky gray eyes, one with the drooping lid, which could make him look either droll or dangerous, and which had put Joseph in such mortal fear.

Perhaps outwardly I appeared much the same to other people today as I had appeared to Chad Lockhart then, but I knew that inwardly I was very close to some critical change in myself which could never be reversed. The alarm that had sounded distantly within me as I spoke with Daniel now sounded from a little nearer, but I was afraid to know its meaning, and twisted my mind away, letting Apollo carry me on at a steady walk as I withdrew myself from a world I could not endure but from which there was no escape.

The storm came three days later, heralding its approach with a brooding darkness that turned day to night. Throughout the island people hurried to make ready for the onslaught, barring doors and shuttering windows, securing cattle and horses under the lee of hills, using heavy ropes to lash down the roofs of barns and outhouses. There was nothing to be done for the protection of crops such as coffee, bananas, and cane, except to pray that the invisible monster would catch us no more than a glancing blow with his heel as he swept north across the tip of Cuba and on out into the Atlantic. In the coastal villages the fishermen would be hauling their small boats upriver, or sinking them well-laden with rocks in little bays, to save them being smashed into splinters.

I stood at the sewing room window looking out over a valley bathed in dark yellow gloom, and thought of Daniel Choong and the *Miss Emma*. She could not be sunk for safety, like the small rowing boats and dinghies, and she drew too much water to be hauled upriver, even if he could have found the labor for the task. Neither would she be safe in the boathouse, for the wind and sea could take this away as if it had no more substance than a dead leaf.

With the storm coming from the southeast, Ocho Rios would lie on the lee side of the island, and so would suffer less than the parishes of St. Thomas and St. Andrew, which would take the full brunt of the weather. Even so, Daniel's precious boat, which had taken him two years to build, would be in grave danger, and with a little chill of alarm I wondered if he might put to sea and attempt to ride out the storm in open water.

When Oliver and I sat down to dine that evening, the first howling squalls of rain had begun, and every few minutes the sky was torn by blue lightning. My head ached, and the very air seemed to throb with electricity. Oliver was affected by it, too. He kept his usual calm and leisurely manner, but I caught the gleam of excitement in his eyes, and he instructed Solomon to have a footman draw back the curtains of the tall window so that we could watch the fury in the sky.

I thought this was foolish. The island had not yet been struck by the hurricane, and this storm might grow no worse, but if the great wind came it could drive in any unshuttered window of Diabolo Hall, hurling shards of glass like daggers. I did not speak my thoughts to Oliver. He had not troubled me for several days now, and I had no wish to provoke him.

When we rose from the table he went to stand by the window, gazing out. Rain and wind lashed at the panes, bolts of lightning split the sky, and thunder rumbled like some menacing beast. Oliver stood with hands in pockets, shoulders braced back, almost as if challenging the storm. Unease began to creep through my bones, but I tried to thrust it away, and to forget Daniel's words of warning. Quietly I excused myself and went to the library, but after reading for half an hour my headache was worse and my eyes felt so hard and painful that I put the book aside.

Oliver was in his study. I tapped on the door, and opened it at his call. He was sitting at his desk, pen in hand, and looked up as I stood in the doorway.

"Yes, Emma?"

"I feel a little tired, Oliver, so I came to say good night."

"Very well, my dear. Good night, and sleep well."

He bent his head to his work. I closed the door and made my way along the passage to the great curving staircase of Diabolo Hall. As I mounted it I thought how aptly the house had been named—for me, at least. No doubt it had taken its name from Mount Diabolo, and I did not know why that peak had been so named. I only knew that I had entered Diabolo Hall with glad anticipation and found a devil in disguise there.

Becky had laid out my nightgown and turned down the bed. I undressed, put the nightgown on, brushed my hair, made two plaits of it, and turned the lamps low. For a few minutes I lay in bed listening to the storm, keeping Oliver out of my mind. I could not hope and could not pray to be spared his attentions, for to do so was to bring him into my thoughts as the cause of such hopes or prayers. It was better to wonder what death and

destruction the hurricane might wreak if it struck the island.
That was a cleaner and more bearable fear.

I fell asleep. When I woke the room was lighter than before.
I was lying on my side, and saw that the lamp on the table
near the grandfather clock had been turned up again. The hands
showed twenty minutes to ten, so I had not slept long. The
storm was still beating about the house, but seemed no worse
than before. I turned on my back and lifted my head.

The bed was large, without curtains or canopy. Oliver stood
at a little distance from the foot of it, slowly taking off his
jacket, his eyes fixed on me with a look I knew well and had
come to dread. A sudden gust howled past the house, rattling
the windows and fetching a menacing roar from the fireplace
as the chimney acted like a great organ pipe. I saw Oliver's
nostrils flare with a kind of responsive joy, and his eyes seemed
swollen in the lamplight.

He tossed his jacket aside and stood with hands on hips,
looking at me, then spoke in a harsh whisper.

"Strip," he said. "*Strip*, Emma!"

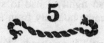

5

SLOWLY I SAT UP IN BED, AND AS I DID SO IT WAS AS IF A light shone in my mind to reveal a dreadful truth. Suddenly I knew with cold and terrible certainty that this was the moment of final choice. If I submitted to Oliver now, or suffered defeat at his hands as I had done before, then my spirit would be broken forever.

It might be that this was his ultimate aim, and that once he had achieved it he would thereafter use me only as an occasional toy. The notion held a repellent temptation, dark and seductive, for in it lay the promise of an end to fear and humiliation, the promise of peace through acceptance. And I, who had once been Emma Delaney, would become little more than a creature akin to that mythical being of voodoo . . . a zombie, one of the living dead.

Oliver moved round the bed, watching me as if fascinated by what he read in my face. He was between me and my own dressing room. I pushed back the covers, then suddenly lunged across the bed away from him, and ran for the open door of his own dressing room. He gave a short hard laugh and came after me. There was no time to slam and lock the door. As he reached it I was at the dressing table, snatching up one of the tall silver candlesticks that stood there.

I spun round and held it before me in both hands like a club, the unlit candle falling to the floor. A howling gust struck the window, and again the bedroom chimney roared like an animal. My jaw was locked so tightly I had to speak with clenched teeth, and my voice came hoarsely from a throat that seemed coated with sand.

"Keep away, Oliver!" I quavered. "Keep away from me, or I swear I'll strike you."

He stopped, eyes agleam with delight. "You *threaten* me, madam?" he said wonderingly. "You dare to threaten your husband? By God, you shall suffer for that."

"No!" The word was a whisper, and I felt tears running down my cheeks. "I will never let you beat me or degrade me again. Oliver. Never, never!" My voice rose and broke, but still the words came. "If you leave me in peace I will keep up whatever pretense you wish to the outside world, but I will not share your bed, Oliver. I will *not*! Have your Maroon girls as you will, but never touch me again."

He stood gazing with a strange, frightening blend of fury and delight, then sprang forward. I think he expected me to swing the candlestick up or to one side in order to strike, which would give him a chance to seize it, but in the anger and fear that possessed me I thrust straight at his face with the heavy base. The main force of the blow came from his own impetus. He managed to turn his head at the last moment, taking the impact on his cheek, but it sent him reeling back, dazed. Then he fell, and his head struck the rounded mahogany arm of an easy chair.

The wind screamed about the house, rain drummed viciously on the shutters. Oliver lay sprawled by the chair in a half stupor, a hand pressed to his cheek. Then his wandering eyes found mine, the stupor slowly faded, and what I saw in those eyes told me that my only hope now was flight, for otherwise I might never live through the night. In panic I plucked up my nightgown and ran to the door, dropping the candlestick as I did so. It could have taken no more than four or five seconds to snatch the key from the lock, slam the door, thrust the key into the keyhole from the other side, and turn it, but for half that time I could glimpse Oliver from the corner of my eyes as he came to his knees and then slowly to his feet, and in my terror it was as if those seconds were stretched into an eternity.

The door handle rattled furiously as I withdrew the key and threw it under the bed. Then came Oliver's voice, sobbing with dreadful rage, incoherent, calling on me to open the door, cursing and threatening with words unknown to me. I ran to my dressing room and dragged off my nightgown, panting like a running fox, heart racing with fear, thankful that Becky had laid out my undergarments ready for the morning.

Hands trembling, I pulled on the cellular combinations, fastening only two of the buttons. Vest, corset, and petticoat I ignored. As I opened the wardrobe I heard a heavy thump from Oliver's room, and my heart seemed to clench with fear as I realized that he was trying to batter the door down, perhaps with the easy chair. Panic urged me to flee as I was, but I made myself pull on riding breeches, shirt, socks, and riding boots, telling myself that the door was strong and solid, and that it opened inward, so it could not possibly be burst open by breaking the lock on one side or hinges on the other. Also, thank God, there was no bellpull in the dressing room.

As I ran through the bedroom, tying a scarf round my head, I could hear Oliver cursing between the blows he was delivering, but the door showed no sign of yielding, and the roar of the storm all but drowned his shouts. I caught up the small lamp beside the bed to light my way through the dark house. Except for Solomon, all the servants would have gone to their quarters long since, and he would have put out the lamps and followed as soon as Oliver retired. Two minutes later I was at the side door of the great kitchen, the door nearest to the stables. Here, several storm lanterns hung on hooks. I put down the bedroom lamp, lit one of the lanterns, and drew the bolts. The wind tore the door from my hands. Head down, I forced my way out, then had to use all my strength to close the door again.

A flash of lightning illumined the scene, and in it I saw trees bending, branches trailing in the wind, and glittering rain slanting down like thin rods of steel. Until this moment I had acted by instinct, without understanding what I was trying to do, but now, as I leaned into the wind and struggled toward the stables, I realized that I was going to Daniel Choong. If I reached him, I would beg him to take me away on the *Miss Emma*, away forever from Diabolo Hall and from the island where my life had become a nightmare. Such an idea was madness, of course, but I was beside myself with fear and could conceive of no other way of escape.

Again it was a struggle to open and close the stable door.

The horses were restless and uneasy, whickering in alarm as the thunder roared and rolled. Wind whistled shrilly through cracks in the timbers. While I was taking Apollo from his stall, great masses of straw rose from the floor as if by suction, and I heard a monstrous thump from above as the wind tried to lift the roof off the stables and almost succeeded.

I hung the lantern on a hook and began to saddle Apollo, muttering feverishly to myself as I worked. "Not too much haste . . . mustn't fumble . . . Oliver can't break out . . . oh God, please don't let him break out . . . help me, please. Strap through here . . . tighten the girth. Now the bridle. If he does break out, he'll be searching the house . . . he won't think of the stables . . . oh God, please don't let him think of the stables . . ."

At last it was Jone. I took down the lantern and began to lead Apollo out between the stalls. These were the household stables, where Oliver kept his carriage horses and one or two mounts for riding. The racing stables were a mile away near Rio Hoe. I had chosen Apollo because he was the best of the seven horses we kept at Diabolo Hall. Releasing his bridle, I unlatched the door carefully, first the top half, then the bottom, bracing myself for the effect of the gale. But as I lifted the second latch the wind gusted, hurling itself at the stables like a beast of prey. I gave a cry of horror as the door crashed into my arm and sent the lantern tumbling through the air. It fell on straw, and in an instant there was a blaze.

I was sobbing and crying, "No, no, no!" as I rushed out with Apollo and twisted his reins round the post by the mounting block. Within five seconds I was back in the stables, but by then there was no hope of putting out the fire, for the wind was driving it and feeding it with savage power. I ran from stall to stall, lifting the wooden bars, slapping each horse with all my might, shouting, pushing, urging them out. For perhaps half a minute they milled about in growing panic, and once I was sent sprawling amid their hooves but managed to roll away unhurt. As I came to my feet one of the mares, Ladybird, made a dash past the fire to the open door, and within moments the rest had followed.

I was so confused I scarcely knew what I was doing now, but I was frighteningly aware that Oliver would still be trying to break through the door, if he had not already done so, and that sooner or later the burning stable would be seen from the house. Curtains were drawn and windows shuttered everywhere, but the eerie fascination of the storm would surely bring inquisitive eyes to peer through cracks in the shutters from time to time, and soon the stables would become a beacon of fire, visible for miles.

The horses had scattered. I untied Apollo and began to lead him along the broad drive. This ended at iron gates set between pillars in the stone wall that hemmed the grounds on the east side of Diabolo Hall. I had not mounted yet, for I knew I would have to dismount to open the gates. I was now drenched as if I had been swimming with my clothes on. Shirt and breeches were clinging to me, and my boots squelched with water. We were twenty paces from the gate when I looked back toward the house. As I did so lightning flared continuously for long seconds across the black sky, and in its glare I saw Oliver coming toward me across the grass.

If it had not been that he was jacketless and wore a white shirt, I might not have seen him, for he was almost lost against the background of the house. But my eye caught the moving white shape, then found the featureless blur of his face above it, hair plastered to the brow by rain. The shirtsleeved arms were outstretched and curving forward, and because his legs were almost invisible in the darkness it seemed as if some fearful and faceless bird with thin white wings was swooping toward me. Then I saw that in one hand, held like a club, was something tall and silver... the candlestick with which I had knocked him down.

All this I saw as if it had been a tableau, a scene frozen on the slide of a magic lantern. Then the long flare of lightning was gone, and I was momentarily blind in the aftermath of it. A brief but earsplitting crash of thunder shook the ground, and I put my hands to my ears. Sight came back to me, and I saw the advancing figure again, close now, a menacing silhouette against the pale glare of sheet lightning reflected from a cloud.

I heard myself scream, and with the sound I glimpsed from the corner of my eye an impossible thing. The rain still drove down like thin steel rods, but one of those rods, swift and glittering, was traveling parallel with the ground, perhaps as high as my shoulder, passing from somewhere behind and to my left, flashing toward the awful shape advancing upon me.

It struck, and all light from the sky vanished. For long seconds there was blackness, then once more the pale sheet lightning flickered and danced in the dark world of the storm. Oliver lay on his back, feet toward me, arms asprawl, head tilted back so that I could see only his chin. From the center of his chest, rising from the sodden white shirt, there gleamed the slender and shining thing that was like the driving rain. But it was not rain. It was a slim steel shaft, with one end finely barbed and tapering to a needle point. I had seen one exactly like it many times, and used one like it occasionally, for this was Daniel Choong's fishing spear.

A hand touched my arm and he was beside me, another faceless figure in the night, but it could only be Daniel. I clutched at him, keeping Apollo's reins looped over one arm, and cried close to his ear, "*God help us, what have you done, Daniel!*"

His voice came to me faintly above the roar of the wind. "I believed he was about to kill you, Miss Emma."

"Yes." My teeth were chattering. I had little doubt that Daniel was right. He had taken my arm now, and was urging me back along the drive. I saw that as yet there was no glow of fire from the stables, perhaps because of the downpour, but wind and flame must soon overwhelm the rain. Daniel was shouting again. "You must go back to the house, Miss Emma! You will be safe now. Forget what you have seen, and do not worry about me. I shall be gone in my boat before dawn. I had planned to go, and have posted a letter of farewell to you."

My whole being was in a dark turmoil. I stopped short, pulling my arm free, cupping a hand about my mouth and putting my head close to Daniel's. I scarcely knew what I wanted to say, for all kinds of conflicting urgencies and emotions were flickering and flashing in my mind, even as the dark cavern of the sky was lit again and again by random flashes of lightning. "Yes, go quickly!" I cried, and gave him a little push toward the gates. "But I must go to Oliver. He—he may not be dead. I must fetch help."

I started in the direction where Oliver lay, some fifty paces away now and hidden by darkness. Daniel came up beside me and caught my arm. "No, Miss Emma—"

I was never to know what he might have said for in that moment there came a sight that was to engrave itself upon my brain like acid etching a picture into copper. A great bolt of lightning struck down from sky to earth, so close that the ground shook beneath our feet. We were sent sprawling, and Apollo would surely have bolted if I had not clung to the reins. But in the instant before we felt its force, I saw that the lightning bolt had chosen the spear rising from Oliver's chest as its path to the ground. Blue fire crackled about the steel shaft, and the air was filled with a strange smell of ozone. The fire encompassed Oliver, his whole body jerked and was lifted in the air by the enormous shock of the thunderbolt, arms and legs thrashing and twisting as if in some hideous, macabre dance. I did not see him fall again, for the impact of the discharge came like a great wind to knock me down, but as the fire-limned body writhed in the air I saw the steel shaft melt and shrink instantly to a shapeless lump, as if it had been tossed into a giant furnace.

Then I was lying on my face, being dragged across grass, clinging to the reins as Apollo skittered and backed in fear. The strain on my arms ceased. Daniel was there, gripping the reins with one hand, pulling me to my feet with the other. I was facing the house now, shuddering with new shock at what I had just witnessed. Dazedly I saw that the fire had exploded through the stable roof and was roaring defiance at the storm. The distant shapes of one or two loose horses, running in panic, were silhouetted against the light. And now there were other lights, storm lanterns carried by people coming from the house.

Some small part of my mind still capable of thought struggled to imagine what those people would eventually find. Oliver Foy, dead, with a fused fishing spear through his body. The horses loose and the stables burning. Mistress Oliver Foy out in the storm, dressed for riding, with the only horse not loose. Add to this the letter that Oliver had placed with his solicitor, full of false affection but deadly in its accusation, and it was grimly clear that I could not turn back now, that I could have no future as the widowed mistress of the Foy estates, even if I had wished to. And I did not wish to.

I peered through the rain at Daniel and clutched his hand, lurching a little as a gust of wind struck across the lawn. "Take me with you, Daniel, *please!*" I cried. "You're my only friend. For God's sake take me with you on your boat tonight, away from this awful place. There's nothing but misery for me here. I'd rather die in the good clean sea than suffer what will happen if I stay here."

I have only the vaguest recollection of what happened in the next few minutes. I know the storm was deafening. I believe Daniel tried to argue, and I believe I screamed at him. Then, some time later, I was mounted on Apollo and we were moving north on the road that would bring us by way of Fern Gully to Ocho Rios. The road ran downhill all the way and the wind was behind us now, driving the rain at our backs. Apollo moved at a steady, plodding gait. Beside me, Daniel sat hunched astride Feng Po, keeping the mule at a brisk walk. My mind was inert, and I realized dimly that all the fear and shock and horror I had endured in the past hour must have brought a kind of paralysis at last. For this I was thankful. I did not wonder how Daniel came to be on the grounds at Diabolo Hall, with his fishing spear, at such an hour and on such a night. I might come to know at another time, but it was of no importance. All the events of this dreadful night seemed to have been in some way inevitable, as if composed and set in motion by Fate.

Who was it who had once jested with me about being dogged by a malicious Fate? A man with smoky gray eyes . . . long ago in that other world I had known before my marriage . . . I could not remember his name.

There were pictures in my mind. A picture of Oliver Foy at the foot of the bed, with that chilling glint of delight in his eyes, staring at his wife and ordering her to strip. Another of him lying on the floor, a hand to his head, his wife holding the candlestick with which she had struck him, gazing down at him with dawning terror. Other pictures . . . a falling lamp and straw leaping into flame. Oliver Foy's wife sprawling amid the hooves of frightened horses. The faceless and monstrous white bird with thin white wings, swooping across the grass to destroy its prey.

But it was as if the woman in all these pictures, Emma Foy, who had been Emma Delaney, was not myself but another person. I was almost glad to feel the rain lashing at me and the wind chilling my body as we rode. Without these strong physical discomforts I might have felt I was experiencing a nightmare from which I must soon awaken, and I did not want to hope for an awakening that could never come.

It was well past midnight when we reached Fern Gully, and another ninety minutes before we came at last to the little harbor of Ocho Rios. The storm had not abated one whit, but we had suffered less during the latter part of the journey because the high ground behind us offered a measure of protection. No word had passed between us until we came past Daniel's house, and then I shouted, "Do you want to stop here to collect anything?"

He shook his head and leaned toward me. "Everything I wish to take with me is already aboard."

So it was true that he had planned to leave the island, even before he had risked the hangman's noose to save me on this fearful night. I found it hard to believe that my quiet and gentle friend Daniel Choong had killed my husband, Oliver Foy, less than four hours ago. It did not make me shrink from him. If I had held the spear at that moment I would surely have flung it at Oliver as he came loping toward me, silver club in hand. There would have been no thought of killing in my mind, only the desperate need to save myself, and I knew in my heart that the same thing could be said of Daniel. But a flung spear knows nothing of intentions.

The *Miss Emma* was riding at two anchors and was the only boat in the harbor. All the smaller ones had been hauled ashore and lashed down, or dragged up inlets, or sunk in protective bays. The wind was less noisy now than on the higher ground, but the darkness was intense except when bursts of lightning filled the sky. Here and there a gleam of light showed from a house, but every door and shutter was tightly closed against the storm, and there was little chance that anyone would see what we were about in the next hour or so. If they were not asleep they would surely be in bed, listening to the storm and hoping it would not become a hurricane.

I dismounted and turned Apollo loose before we reached the harbor, giving him a slap on the rump and telling him to go home. Daniel led Feng Po into his boathouse. Next day, when the *Miss Emma* was seen to be missing, Sheba would find the mule and either keep him or sell him. As for Apollo, I thought it likely that he would be home before sunrise, but if not he would be taken to Diabolo Hall by whoever found him.

I tied the plaits of my sodden hair behind my neck, and together we dragged Daniel's dinghy from the boathouse and down the short slipway to the sea. The heavy swell, driven by the storm, was setting across the bay, and the wooded islets gave some protection, so the journey out to the *Miss Emma* was not particularly hazardous. The rain itself, still teeming as if it would never stop, helped to flatten the sea, but was hampering when we came to clamber aboard, for we were half blind with water pouring down our faces and into our eyes.

As soon as we were safely on deck, Daniel bent several fathoms of line to the end of the painter and let the dinghy be carried well clear of the *Miss Emma* so that it would not be damaged by jostling against the bigger boat. The little wheelhouse gave a degree of shelter from the elements and allowed us to speak without shouting.

Daniel lit the binnacle lantern, then held me by the shoulders and looked into my face. His cap of curly hair was plastered to his head like thick black paint. Rain dripped from his chin and nose as it did from mine, and the dark slanting eyes were filled with misgiving. "You can still go back, Miss Emma," he said. "It is not too late. Sheba will take you in tonight, and you can return in the morning. There will be no more danger from your husband now."

I put my hands up and gripped his wrists hard, almost crying as I spoke. "No, Daniel, no, no, no! I'm part of it now. I can never pretend I know nothing. The police will take what is left of that spear from Oliver's body, and they will know it belonged to you. Nobody else has one like it. I can't bear to stay and endure all the questioning. I can't bear to let you go away alone. I can't bear to be left alone here myself. You and May were like parents to me, and there's nobody else I really care for, or who really cares for me. Please, Daniel—"

"Hush, child, hush. Be calm now."

I realized my voice had risen to an almost hysterical pitch, and I started taking deep breaths to gain control of myself. He gave me a little shake, then a wry smile. "Very well, Miss Emma. So now we must work. It will take an hour to get up steam, so for the moment we will hoist a rag of sail, just enough to give us steerage, and run before the wind." He glanced out of the wheelhouse window. "The seas are not so heavy that she will broach to."

Suddenly, strangely, amid the turmoil of the storm and of all that had befallen me in the past few hours, I felt calm and at peace. "Tell me what to do, Daniel," I said.

Working in darkness we hanked a small sail to the forestay. While Daniel lit the boiler fire, I worked the handle of the winch to haul up the bow anchor, and at once the *Miss Emma* turned her stern to the wind so that she pointed northwest. Daniel emerged from below with some rope, and together we fixed lifelines to rails, cleats, and any suitable securing points so that we would be able to move on deck more safely once at sea. When this was done he took the wheel and signaled for me to weigh the stern anchor.

In the instant that the anchor came free the boat leaped suddenly to life, thrusting forward with the wind. As Daniel had instructed me, I left the stern anchor dangling at two fathoms and immediately began to pay out a coil of stout cordage aft. Pulling this heavy warp would help to keep the stern from lifting clear of the water as the little boat pitched over the wave tops. At the wheel, Daniel held her steady as sea and wind took us with immeasurable power and carried us away into the night.

By the time I had finished my duties, joined Daniel in the lamplit wheelhouse, and forced the door shut against the wind, it was as if Jamaica did not exist, for as I glanced out of the port window I could see nothing but night. Daniel Choong, the *Miss Emma*, and Mistress Foy, who had once been Emma Delaney—we three were in another world now, and quite alone, and I was thankful to God for this.

Daniel had built the *Miss Emma* with a narrow passage leading from the foot of the wheelhouse companion ladder through to the cabin. In front of him as he stood at the wheel was the binnacle holding the compass, and to one side was a stout column with three levers projecting from the top of it for controlling the engine when the boat was under steam.

I said, "Do you want me to go below and stoke the boiler?"

He shook his head. "You are not familiar with the workings of the boat yet. I will see to the boiler myself very shortly."

I wiped water from my eyes with the back of my wrist, for my hands were filthy now, and said, "She's riding well, Daniel."

"Yes." He was holding the wheel lightly, as if coaxing the best from the boat rather than fighting to dominate it. "I think the storm will blow itself out in four or five hours. There will be no hurricane. Before then, when we have steam and when there is a lull, we will come about and sail under bare poles until it is safe to have the sea on our beam. Then we will set a course east-nor'east to take us through the Windward Passage."

"Where are we going, Daniel?"

He shook his head and gave one of his grave smiles. "Nowhere, Miss Emma. Nowhere and anywhere. I once said that in this boat I would sail the length of the West Indies. That is what we must do. But we have no destination. The *Miss Emma* is our only home."

I said, "I'm content for that to be so. What do you want me to do now?"

"Take the wheel, please."

I felt a little nervous, but Daniel kept his hands lightly on mine until I had the feel of the boat, then he took a jackknife from his pocket and opened it. "Don't be worried about handling her, Miss Emma. You are well capable," he said, and went out into the rain and the wind.

Somewhere above us the black storm clouds broke apart, allowing a shaft of moonlight to escape. Foam rolled along the sides of the boat as the waves swept beneath her, white foam, glowing with phosphorescence. I saw Daniel move to the rail just forward of the wheelhouse and start to haul on a line. It was clearly heavy work, and I realized he was hauling in the dinghy we were still towing. With the seas so high he could not possibly rig a whip to hoist it aboard, and in the dreamlike state of unreality that encompassed me I was wondering vaguely what he was about when I saw him hacking at the line with his knife. Moments later it was severed.

He moved from the rail, vanished down the cabin companionway, and emerged a minute later with something like a long, thick pole. It glinted in the moonlight, and I knew it was a heavy crowbar. Hooking an arm round one of the lifelines, he leaned over the rail and began jabbing and prizing at something on the hull. The clouds came together again, and he was lost to my sight.

Watching the foam as it creamed past, watching the compass, trying in vain to find some fixed point in the blackness ahead, it came to me that the name of the ship, *Miss Emma*, had not been painted directly on the hull, but on a finely carved board screwed to the timbers, and this was where Daniel had been working with the crowbar.

Two minutes later he returned to the wheelhouse, streaming with water. I expected him to take the helm again, but he made no attempt to do so, and took up a position just behind and a little to one side of me. "I cut the dinghy adrift and broke the name-board away from the hull," he said. "With the set of the tides they should be washed up on the north coast during the next few days, somewhere between Montego Bay and St. Ann's."

I moved the wheel a little, watching the rag of jib carefully, and said, "I don't understand why, Daniel."

"There's good reason, Miss Emma. If the dinghy and the name-board are washed ashore, it's to be hoped the authorities will believe the *Miss Emma* foundered, and that I went down with her." He shook his head slowly. "Heaven knows what they will imagine has become of Mistress Emma Foy. Nobody will dream that you have run away with me. Why should they?"

I said, "They might. Daniel. A little while ago Oliver left

a sealed letter with his solicitor, accusing me in the event of his dying an unnatural death." I recounted what the letter had said, and added, "Perhaps the police will think Oliver died by my hand, and then I ran away with you."

Daniel shook his head doubtfully. "It would not make sense. If you wished to acquire the Foy estates, you would not run away. I think it more likely that people will think you rode out in the storm to help recover the loose horses. That would be typical. You could have been thrown, lost your way on foot, and fallen down a sinkhole. That is the usual belief when the body of a missing person cannot be found." He glanced over his shoulder into the blackness. "Whatever they choose to believe, we have left them some strange mysteries back there."

Never was a truer word spoken, I thought. Ramírez would have taken charge by now, in the absence of both master and mistress of the household. The fire, fed by the wind, must surely have destroyed the stables. The loose horses, lingering somewhere nearby, would give proof that a human hand had caused the fire, either by chance or by design. In the light of day, Oliver Foy's body would be found near the gates, pierced by a twisted, lightning-struck metal shaft that could be traced to a half-caste Anglo-Chinese boatbuilder and diver. Oliver Foy's wife would seem to have vanished from the face of the earth. Her riding clothes would be missing. One of the horses, Apollo, would be found saddled but riderless somewhere between Ocho Rios and Diabolo Hall. The Anglo-Chinese would be found to have fled the island, risking the might of the storm. Few would imagine that he could survive its fury, and if the battered dinghy and name-board were washed ashore they would give credence to the notion that his boat had been sunk.

I felt a sudden almost guilty pang of sorrow as I thought of Aunt Maude and Uncle Henry, for whatever suggestions were put forward to account for my disappearance, everybody would believe me to be dead. I shrugged mentally. It was surely better for my aunt and uncle to believe this than to know the truth— that henceforward I would be living on a thirty-seven foot sloop with a Chinese coolie, wandering the length and breadth of the Caribbean like a vagabond of the sea.

Neither of us had spoken for a minute or two. I sensed that Daniel, at my shoulder, was assessing my ability as a helmsman. I had never handled a wheel before, always a tiller, but I was growing more comfortable every moment, for I felt that the *Miss Emma* was speaking to me through the spokes of the wheel, telling me her needs.

Daniel said, "Well done. I must leave you for ten minutes now." He turned and disappeared down the companion ladder.

I put all random thoughts out of my mind and concentrated on becoming one with the boat. Everything I wore was soaked to the last thread, and I stood in a pool of water, but from the beginning the storm wind had been warm and muggy despite the rain, and I did not feel cold as long as I kept my mind closed against the events of the night.

Less than ten minutes had passed when Daniel returned and took the wheel. He wore dry clothes now. "Go to the cabin and dry yourself, Miss Emma," he said. "I have put out spare trousers and a shirt of mine for you to wear. We shall have to share and make do until we can buy clothes for you, and we will not attempt that until we reach Guadeloupe. When you are dry and dressed, lie down and sleep until I call you. I have rigged a hammock, which you will find more comfortable than the bunk in such weather, and there are blankets if you need them."

I said, "Oh no, Daniel. I'll come back as soon as I'm dressed. I can make myself useful stoking the boiler or bringing you food, or taking the wheel while you—"

"Miss Emma, please." He glanced sideways at me with a little smile, but his tone was very firm. "There can be only one captain on a ship, even a ship as small as this."

For a moment I was taken aback. Deeply as I had loved May and Daniel, I had always taken it for granted that they would defer to me, for they were servants. But I had no servants now. Instead I had a companion, someone very much more than my equal, for I was utterly dependent upon him. I absorbed this realization soberly, and found no occasion for regret. Then I said obediently, "Very well, Daniel, I'll do as you say."

"Thank you, Miss Emma."

"I suppose we shall have to think about changing our names, and a new name for the boat, and . . . and all kinds of things."

"Yes." He took a hand from the wheel to rest it on my shoulder. "All kinds of things. But there will be plenty of time for that. Go and rest now. I will call you if I need help."

"You promise?"

"Yes. Look, there is a speaking tube here, and a whistle in the bulkhead alongside the starboard bunk."

I held his arm and pressed a cheek to his shoulder in a mute attempt to express my gratitude, for I was certain he had saved me from death that night. Then I went down the companion ladder and left him to fight the storm. When I had dried myself and put on some clothes, rolling up shirt sleeves and trouser legs that were too long for me, I climbed into the hammock, knowing that the happenings of the night would begin to churn in my mind, and that I had no hope of sleep. Yet within moments of my head touching the small pillow, and despite the endless pitching of the boat, I fell into a sleep so deep I might have been drugged, a sleep mercifully free from nightmares.

It was not always to be so. In the following weeks, and even months, there were times when I was carried back to Diabolo Hall in my dreams, there to suffer macabre pursuit through bedroom and hall, garden and stables, by the dreadful figure of Oliver Foy, grinning, a spear driven through his body, moving like one of the living dead animated by the power of the obeah man.

But on this night, the first of a strange yet curiously happy new life for me, I dreamed no dreams.

6

ON THE AFTERNOON OF MY TWENTY-FIRST BIRTHDAY I DRIFTED
slowly along the seabed of sand and rock at six fathoms, peering
through my underwater goggles, looking for lobster. I wore a
dark blue cotton shirt and calico trousers cut off and hemmed
above the knee for freedom of movement. Once I had been
unable to remain under water for as much as twenty heartbeats,
but now I could match Daniel in staying below for as long as
three minutes.

Attached to each side of the strap holding my goggles in
place was a small rubber bulb, as from a scent spray, with a
thin tube leading into each eyecup. The deeper I went, the more
air was squeezed from the bulbs into the goggles, and this
prevented the eyecups from being squashed against my face
by the increasing pressure of water. It was a simple but very
useful device, which Daniel had copied from the *ama* of Japan,
the fisherwomen who dived to great depths for shellfish and
edible seaweed.

The sea was beautifully clear, allowing the sunlight to penetrate easily to this depth. A little to one side I could see a
great distorted shadow on the bottom, the shadow of Daniel
swimming a fathom or so above me, watching for danger, a

steel-tipped bamboo spear in his hand. In all the hundreds of hours we had spent in and below the sea we had only twice seen sharks anywhere near us, for we were careful to spend several minutes looking for signs of them on all sides before diving in. Nevertheless, Daniel always insisted that we should take every precaution while in the water.

A slight movement caught my eye, and there to my right, nestling in a crevice, was a five-pound lobster, pale reddish yellow with blue-black spots. I flicked it out with the long-bladed knife I carried, scooped it into a short-handled net, slid the knife into the sheath strapped to my calf, then pulled the securing string of a net strung like a belt at my waist, so that the rocks it contained tumbled free. Without such weights it would have been an exhausting business to swim down through six fathoms and remain there with all the buoyancy of full lungs.

Now I came upright and began to ascend, not too quickly, just floating gently up with feet trailing, gradually exhaling all the time as Daniel had taught me, and as he had learned from the Sinhalese pearl divers in years gone by. Daniel rose with me and we broke surface together, half a cable's length from the boat and four times that distance from the palms and sandy shore of a small island half a day's sail from St. Kitts.

The sun was dazzling on our goggles, so we pushed them up to our foreheads as we swam slowly on our backs toward the boat that had been our home for almost three years. She was called *Casey* now, and I bore the same name. It was Daniel who had christened her, who had shaped and painted a new nameboard for her hull two days before we put into Basse-Terre on the French island of Guadeloupe, the first civilized landfall we had made after our flight from Jamaica, a full thousand miles away.

At that time I was still wearing some of Daniel's clothes and we were running south between the Virgin Islands and Anguilla, the northeast trades on our port quarter. The sea was calm that day, and the sun high in the sky when Daniel squatted on the afterdeck with a long board before him and a paintpot in his hand. I was at the wheel, but not enclosed in the wheel-house, for Daniel had so designed the steering that we had a deck wheel set a little forward of the wheelhouse, and we used this most of the time, only taking shelter when the weather was bad.

He stirred the paint, examined his paintbrush, and said, "What do you think of Casey as a name, Miss Emma?"

"A name for the boat?"

"Yes."

"Well . . . it seems a nice enough name. Is there any special reason for it?"

He smiled his slow smile. "You were christened Emma Catherine. The name Catherine has many different forms. One of them is Casey. I read this in a newspaper article about names long ago, in Hong Kong."

"I certainly didn't know it."

"I would like to call the boat after you, but in a way that only you and I will understand."

"You're very kind to me, Daniel."

He shook his head. "You are all I have, Miss Emma." He set the brush down, bent over the board, and began very carefully to outline letters with a thick black pencil.

I said, "I need a new name, too, and Casey will do very well. I've chopped my hair as short as a boy's, and I shall be wearing boy's clothes from now on, so it's good to have a name which could belong either to a boy or girl. I mean, whenever we're ashore, and you speak to me, people won't really know which I am."

He glanced up, and for the first time in many long days I saw a twinkle in his dark eyes. "Unless they are at a distance I think they will know you are a girl, Miss Emma. But yes, I will start to call you Casey now, and we must think of a new name for me, also."

I bit my lip. "Will there be a hunt for you, Daniel?"

He shrugged. "I am sure the Jamaican authorities will believe I have drowned, but they will follow the normal procedure of sending a description of me to all British possessions. We have no need to touch any British possessions, except perhaps at uninhabited parts of island coasts. In a year the whole affair will be forgotten outside Jamaica . . . and that is one place we shall never go to again."

I slipped a loop over the wheel and moved to trim the sail. When the task was done I went to stand beside Daniel, the breeze plucking at my oversized trousers and oversized shirt. "I don't suppose we shall be mixing with other people much," I said, "except when we're trying to earn a little money running small cargo from one island to another. Even then I think it best if I don't speak at all when others are about. My accent would make them curious."

"Not if you talk Jamaican creole, and you can do that just fine, Miss...Casey. I've heard you send May into fits of laughter with it many a time."

That was true. As I went to take the wheel again it occurred to me that I was already acquiring a face and hands made brown by wind and sun in a way no English lady would dream of allowing. Even now I could pass as a girl of Spanish or Portuguese descent, with a recent infusion of Northern European or American blood to account for my auburn hair. There were all kinds of odd mixtures throughout the islands of the West Indies, and my appearance would not attract particular attention as long as I did not speak like an educated young Englishwoman. But I could not pretend to be related to Daniel, for clearly I had no Chinese blood in me.

I said, "Daniel, if ever we have to explain how we're related, I think it's best if you allow people to believe I'm a creole girl you found on one of the islands and bought for yourself with a few sacks of copra from a drunken half-caste father. Something of that sort."

He concentrated on his work for perhaps two minutes in silence, then said reluctantly, "Yes. If men think you are my woman they will pay little attention to you."

"That's what I want, Daniel. No attention from men." I was suddenly trembling with aversion. "I'll talk some kind of creole, but only speak when I have to, and I'll call you...let me see. I'll call you Gubnor."

The use of the pidgin English word brought back a fragment of memory. On the road through Fern Gully, riding with Chad Lockhart of the strange drooping eyelid, I had quoted a native proverb: "Darg hab liberty watch gubnor." One day perhaps, I thought vaguely, I may ask Daniel about that Englishman, about the scroll in the bamboo, and the gold coin or medallion. Not that the matter could be of any importance now, for our world had changed. In future it would consist of sea and sky; wind, rain and sun; moon and stars; the occasional feel of the earth beneath our feet on island shores; the occasional commerce with people in small villages and minor ports; and our permanent home, the little boat called *Casey*.

This was to be our world for the future, and it could never touch the world of the stranger from England with the smoky gray eyes. So I thought. But I had forgotten Chad Lockhart's

claim to be the favorite victim of a sometimes malicious, sometimes whimsical Fate.

Daniel and I did not speak of that night of horror at Diabolo
Hall until many weeks later. By then we had followed the great
curve of the Leeward and Windward islands, and continued
west, with the coast of Venezuela beyond our southern horizon,
until we came to Aruba, the furthermost point of our wanderings. Here the Dutch ruled, though most of the people were
of native Indian stock. Here we sold a small cargo of coconuts
we had spent two full days picking on the uninhabited shore
of a small island of the Los Roques group. Daniel also found
work repairing canoes in the village where we sold our cargo,
and for this and the coconuts we were paid in gold. Not coin,
but two small nuggets worth a sovereign each, for the yellow
metal was mined on this rocky island.

From the village we moved to a sandy cove and beached
the little dinghy Daniel had bought in Guadeloupe to replace
the one we had abandoned. It needed recaulking, and this was
a task more easily done on the beach than on the deck of the
Casey. Daniel was teasing out the hemp while I made a little
fire to melt the pitch. His spear lay nearby, for we planned to
catch fish for dinner when we pulled back to the anchored
Casey. This spear was fashioned with a bamboo haft and a
head made by hammering a steel bolt into a flat, leaf-pointed
blade. In all the time that we were to sail the Caribbean, Daniel
never tried to make or have made a steel spear such as he had
used before. Perhaps he shrank from the memories it would
bring.

As I squatted by the fire, feeding it with oil-soaked lumps
of coir, I found myself saying, rather to my own surprise,
"How did you come to be at Diabolo Hall that night, Gubnor?"
I used his new name by habit now, even when we were alone.

He did not look up from his work with the oakum, but said
in a flat voice, "I had been to Kingston by train to collect the
new spear from the Naval Ordnance yard. They agreed to turn
it on their lathe in return for a small diving job I had done for
them. Coming back, the storm broke before the train reached
the terminus at Ewarton. We arrived late. I took Feng Po from
the livery stables where I had left him. The storm was very
bad. After a mile or two I decided to call at the servants'
quarters of Diabolo Hall, to ask permission of the butler that
I might shelter in the stables or one of the outhouses until the

worst was over. I thought he would not refuse, knowing I had for many years been in service to the family of the mistress of the house. As I came through the gates, I saw you . . . and him . . . Oliver Foy, coming at you with a club."

His voice faded to silence. After a little while I said, "The pitch will soon be ready, Gubnor. If you have another caulking iron in your toolbox, perhaps I could help with the work."

We never spoke of that night again.

By the time we completed our first voyage down through the West Indies to Aruba we had begun to settle into the way of life that was to be ours until it ended in disaster during our third summer. I learned that from the moment Daniel made up his mind to leave Jamaica he had been quietly selling everything he had no wish to take with him. This, together with money carefully saved over the years, meant that we were far from destitute.

In Guadeloupe, while I remained out of sight on the *Casey*, he went ashore and bought a small dinghy. He also bought a stock of clothes for me, returning with shirts and trousers, socks and boots, jerseys and waterproofs, all in boy's sizes. My underwear henceforward would consist only of short cotton drawers such as he wore himself, but again in a boy's size.

For the rest, the *Casey* had been marvelously well stocked when we left Jamaica, with everything stowed away in meticulous fashion. Food, water, and fuel were easy to come by. The sea was full of fish and shellfish, the scores of islands offered coconut palms with their fruit of so many uses, and in any village we could barter produce from elsewhere for whatever they had to offer, such as vegetables, fruit, cocoa, ground nuts, and grain for the four hens we kept in a sheltered coop on the foredeck.

We rarely sailed under steam, for it did not matter whether we took a day or three days to reach whatever island we decided to make our next landfall. Often we chose our destination according to the convenience of the wind, for we had no end in view but simply roamed like gypsies of the sea. Nevertheless, every few days we would lower the mainsail and lash the boom to starboard, fire the boiler, and run the engine for an hour or so, for Daniel held that machinery liked to be used if it was to give good service. He had constructed a system for drawing steam off the dry-tube of the boiler to a condenser, which gave us fresh distilled water to augment the supply from the four ten-gallon butts we filled from island streams whenever opportunity offered. This was another good reason for using the boiler regularly.

Our galley occupied an area not much larger than a card table, but since we kept to very simple cooking this was quite adequate. The lavatory was a tiny cubicle fitted with a commode seat above a metal pan, which could be flushed with seawater by working a small pump handle set in the bulkhead. Our bathtub was the sea itself during the first few weeks, but later Daniel rigged an ingenious system whereby the engine operated a pump that forced fresh water from one of our butts through a hose and into a suspended bucket with holes pierced in the bottom. We bathed daily in the sea, but once a week we would mount the hose-fed bucket on a whip over the afterdeck, set up a canvas screen, and take turns to enjoy the luxury of a freshwater shower.

On Daniel's advice I would always anoint myself with coconut oil from scalp to toes an hour before the weekly shower-bath, to prevent my skin from becoming dry and rough from so much exposure to sun, weather, and saltwater. This was good advice, for my skin remained smooth even though I became very brown, but I only followed it to please Daniel, for I no longer gave any thought to my looks. It seemed strange to remember that once I had worried about my eyebrows being heavy. The last thing I wanted now was to be in any degree attractive to men. It was certain we should have little contact with anyone other than natives during our wanderings, but I still carried the fear and dread Oliver Foy had instilled in me, and I never again wanted any man to look at me with interest.

Daniel allowed his hair to grow long, until it reached his cheekbones. He also grew a beard and moustache, keeping the beard trimmed to about an inch around his chin. Strangely, though his hair was black, the beard was grizzled. This gave him a fierce and sinister appearance that made me laugh—for by now time had passed and I was able to laugh again. I could not believe that anyone would recognize him from a description sent by the Jamaican authorities to other British possessions in the West Indies.

If I had ever imagined that my home would one day be a small steamer with a cabin half the size of our housemaid's room at The Jacarandas, and that I should be sharing this home with a man, I would have thought it impossible to preserve the decencies, yet this was not so. Daniel rigged a canvas curtain down the center of the cabin which ran on rings and could be pulled out as a screen if either of us wished to change our clothes. Usually this would only be when going to bed or getting up. During the day we mostly went barefoot, wearing only shirts and trousers, the latter cut short. We would go into the sea in these clothes, and let them dry on us when we came out, never really taking note of whether we happened to be wet or dry.

There were two bunks in the cabin. My nightgown was a man-size shirt. Sometimes we slept on the bunks. If the weather was rough, we would sling hammocks above the bunks for easier sleeping. When the night was balmy we slung our hammocks on deck. Whether we slept, or bathed, or answered nature's needs, we found it quite simple and no embarrassment to give each other whatever privacy was required, even in so small a home as the *Casey*.

There were times when we sailed through the night, if the fancy took us, working a four-hour watch in turns at the wheel. Usually we would heave to at dusk, putting out a sea anchor in bad weather or anchoring in an island cove. Such shelter was not hard to find, for as Daniel had once said in that other world we had left behind us, a boat could sail two thousand miles along the sicklelike curve of the West Indies and never be more than a short day's sail from land.

With only two of us aboard, there was never a time when we could feel that all repairs and maintenance had been completed, for on a ship like the *Casey*, constantly at sea, these were unending tasks. The standing rigging had to be examined constantly for signs of fraying, to be spliced or replaced if need be. Halyards, sheets, masts, rudder fittings, and all such equipment called for careful attention. A pin working loose from a rigging screw on a forestay or shroud could bring down the mast; a loose fitting on the transom could mean sudden loss of the rudder at a dangerous moment; our very lives depended on preventing such disasters, and to prevent them called for endless vigilance.

Sometimes we carried cargo, either from one small island to another or between coastal villages on the same island. Occasionally we carried for hire, but more often we were buying, selling, or bartering on our own account. Sometimes we sailed with empty holds. Whatever the case, we had always to be thinking of the trim of the boat, and this meant much work in distributing weight to get the best result.

I had always known Daniel to be a studious man, but I had

never realized how skilled he was until we began our new life on the *Casey*. His preparations for leaving Jamaica had been very thorough. He carried naval charts, a sextant, a telescope, and a chronometer. Over the years, working from time to time as a diver for the Royal Navy, he had sometimes bartered his services in return for instruction in the use of a sextant and in the science of navigation. Now he was able to make good use of those skills, and I was glad to begin learning them from him.

On leaving Aruba for the first time we made our way slowly east to the Windward Islands, clawing our way to windward close-hauled on a long tack, then coming round on a broad reach, which was the *Casey's* fastest point of sailing. Each day Daniel taught me more from his lifetime experience of sea and weather and sailing. He also instructed me, with limited success, in the mysteries of the steam engine. I learned the routine of simple maintenance, and how to dismantle and clean out the boiler, but I never truly understood what was happening when the machine crept slowly into motion, and I was always nervous of the shafts and rods and pistons, even when they were still and lifeless.

As week succeeded week and month succeeded month, the *Casey* wove her wandering course up through the Leeward Islands, round Puerto Rico, through the Mona Passage, and along the three-hundred-mile north coast of Hispaniola. We did not pass through the Windward Passage, for by unspoken consent we had agreed never to come within a hundred miles of Jamaica. Turning north, we threaded our way through the Bahamas, then came about to sail down the Florida Strait to Havana. This, in a sense, was the limit of our voyaging, for this was the tip of the West Indies crescent from which we would now retrace our steps down to the Grenadines and out to Aruba once more, though we could do so by a hundred diverse and wandering routes.

By the time we turned southeast from Havana to idle our way through the small islands hemming the coast of Cuba, I was a capable sailor and a proficient diver. From the beginning I found enormous pleasure in visiting the world that lay under the sea, a world full of beauty and excitement, but it was not for this that Daniel trained me so carefully. From time to time there was the opportunity to earn money or food or stores in some of the little ports by use of our diving skills, and at such times an extra pair of hands and an extra pair of eyes were invaluable. My underwater ability also helped to keep us well fed, in that I was able to share with Daniel the task of diving for lobster or the big queen conches.

Well-fed we were indeed, for the sea and the islands provided handsomely for most of our needs at the cost of no more than a little effort, while our boat and our skills enabled us to obtain whatever else we required either in cash or kind. In all the time we were together I was only once in dispute with Daniel, and that was regarding food. We had anchored in a sandy bay on the coast of Cuba one evening, close to a village, and during the night I was alarmed to hear the most pitiful sounds of sighing. I slid from my hammock and went to the rail.

The sounds were coming from the shore, quite loud in the still night air, and they were a heartrending blend of a sigh and a sob, as if some human soul were in torment. I was peering into the darkness when Daniel came up beside me, buckling the belt of his trousers. I turned my head to speak to him, so chilled by the wailing sighs that I spoke in a whisper.

"What is it, Gubnor?"

I saw the flash of his teeth as he smiled. "Turtles. The natives catch them and turn them on their backs. That way they remain alive for a long time, and the meat keeps fresh. We'll slip ashore and bring one back aboard. Turtle soup and turtle meat, Casey. They're both dishes fit for a king."

"You mean they're left to die *slowly*?" I wanted to put my hands over my ears to shut out the terrible sighing.

"Yes. But you mustn't judge the natives by civilized standards. We'll kill ours at once, and preserve the meat in salt."

I clutched the rail. "I'm not judging anybody, Gubnor. I can only think of those turtles. I mean . . . they're creatures I've played with under the sea."

That was true. On three occasions I had caught a turtle and been towed along before releasing it. They were by no means friendly and curious as I had found dolphins to be, but my stomach turned at the thought of them suffering slow death, and I even shrank from what Daniel was proposing. He said, "You have eaten slaughtered animals all your life, Casey. By what logic do you now say I must not kill a turtle?"

I closed my eyes tightly, trying to think. At last I said, "There's no logic in it, Gubnor, and it isn't a matter of principle. If I try to argue I can be tied in knots, because I have no argument. I only know I don't want you to kill a turtle. Perhaps it's because we have something in common with them, as we do with dolphins. We're all creatures who have to hold our breath under water." I pressed my hands to my cheeks and shivered. "Oh, I can't bear to hear that awful sound."

Daniel said, "A turtle given a quick death would be released from suffering."

"Yes, but . . ." I looked up at him in the moonlight. "There's something else we could do, isn't there?"

He laughed and touched my shoulder lightly. "It is sometimes good to be illogical, as long as we do not pretend we are being otherwise." He pulled off his shirt, stepped up on the rail and dived from it with scarcely a sound. I did not wait to put on my swimming breeches, but knotted the tails of my nightshirt between my legs and followed him.

Two minutes later we waded ashore and walked quietly up the beach. There were four turtles, and they were big ones. Without Daniel's help I would have been hard put to turn them over. As soon as we did so they began to move at a ponderous scuttle down the slope of sand, but when they reached the water, their own element, they were suddenly gone, vanishing with smooth grace into the moonlit sea.

We swam slowly back to the boat, and as we climbed aboard Daniel said, "Get dressed, Casey. We'll weigh anchor in ten minutes. I have no wish to be here when the natives find their turtle meat gone."

"I'm sorry, Gubnor. I spoiled your night's rest."

He squeezed water from his hair, and smiled. "If I never have a worse problem than that, Casey my dear, I shall be well pleased."

I found that the secret of true contentment in the life we lived was never to think more than a day into the future and never to think of the past at all. We had only three concerns; the weather, the boat, and our provisions.

An awareness of the weather became instilled in me, so that waking or sleeping there was always some part of my mind noting the smallest change of wind, the least alteration in the nature of the sea about us, and all manner of signs which might foretell what weather the next hours would bring. There was much to be learned simply by observation, but I also had Daniel to teach me. He was no longer the Daniel I had once known. Both in appearance and in what lay between us, all was now very different. Daniel had once been a servant. Now he was my friend and guardian, standing almost as a father to me in my thoughts, though in a way it would have been hard for any father and daughter to know the depth of companionship that came from living a life virtually cut off from the rest of the world, a life in which we had only each other.

We did not touch any British island until a full year after our flight from Jamaica. In this we were probably overcautious. One island took little interest in events on another island a hundred or a thousand miles away, and there was scant connection between the various British possessions, except for occasional visits by a ship of the Royal Navy.

Certainly nobody who had known Daniel Choong or Emma Foy would have recognized us, Daniel with black curly hair to halfway down his neck and a graying beard, me in a shapeless shirt or jersey, trousers, and boots, hair cropped short, not even to be easily identified as female. When we began to touch British territory, Daniel adopted an accent and called himself Harry Leng, pretending to be half American, half Chinese. Ashore, buying clothes or stores, he would do all the haggling while I lurked in the background with a conical straw hat shading my face.

If we had to speak to each other I would use any kind of patois or creole I had picked up, and I would pitch my voice deep and a little guttural. Often I was taken to be Daniel's son, or simply a hired hand, but when any storekeeper or port official realized I was female, Daniel would immediately make clear by his manner of address to me that I was his woman.

There was no need for us ever to have touched British ports, but Daniel thought it important for us to establish new identities throughout the islands. By the end of our first year, with a mixture of bribery and laborious forgery, we had ship's papers which declared that the *Casey* had been built five years ago at the Venezuelan port of La Guaira and named *Santa Maria*; that she had been sold to Harry Leng in Tampa two years ago and renamed *Casey*. We also had a supply of Bills of Health from a number of ports to prevent the *Casey* from being quarantined on arrival at a port where such a system was in force. Some of the bills were genuine, with only the date to be carefully altered. I was the expert with pen and ink and homemade rubber stamps, and I was rather shocked to find myself taking a mischievous delight in these shameless misdeeds.

As season followed season and we roamed the length of the Caribbean, our early fears faded. During the first months I had lived in dread that by some mischance we might be recognized, reported, arrested at sea by some British ship, and then taken back to Jamaica, where Daniel would surely be hanged for the murder of Oliver Foy. But by the end of our second year such fears had vanished, for our new identities were established.

Our days were full, and we were never afflicted by tedium. There was always a course to be worked out, a sail to be trimmed, an engine to be maintained, a home to be cleaned and kept in good order. There were always coconut palms to be climbed for their fruit, fish to be netted or speared, shellfish to be dived for, and small cargo to be loaded or unloaded.

With the turning of the seasons we met every kind of weather from windless calm to tempest. During the hurricane season we were sharply alert to all signs of coming bad weather, but twice we had to scuttle under sail and steam to run from the path of that destroying wind. Ordinary storms did not trouble the *Casey*, but a hurricane was a different matter. Even if she lived through it, she would almost certainly lose her masts and cabin housing. A wind that could pluck a tree from the ground was to be avoided, not defied.

Among our most precious possessions were the books Daniel had brought from his home. There were eighty-seven in all, including twelve volumes of Chambers's Encyclopaedia. Many were books I had passed on to Daniel, among them a set of Dickens and a handful of classic novels. The rest were textbooks on a number of subjects; history, seamanship, arithmetic, navigation, metalwork, woodwork, comparative religion, astronomy, and other equally varied matters.

One book, by a man called Edmond Hoyle who had died more than a hundred years ago, was about table games such as whist, chess, and backgammon. There were several card games for two players, and we often spent a leisure hour or so playing piquet or cribbage. Neither of us had played chess, but Daniel made a board and carved some chessmen, and with the guidance of Mr. Hoyle we taught ourselves to play. My game was never much more than elementary, but I believe Daniel would have become very good if he could have practiced against a worthy opponent.

In his youth in Hong Kong he had been taught the Chinese game of *mah tsiang*, which was played with tiles rather like dominoes but bearing Chinese characters. Together we made and painted a set of tiles so that Daniel could teach me yet another game to occupy our minds when we were at leisure.

In that time on the *Casey* we lived each day for itself alone, and I was more than content; I was happy. By the standards of English society it would have seemed an impossibly hard life for a girl gently brought up, but it did not seem hard to me, not when compared with the way most native girls had to work; and not when compared with the fear and misery of being the wife of a man such as Oliver Foy. I cannot remember being sad or downcast during that period of almost three years on the *Casey*. She was a brave, happy little ship, and after that first run down to Aruba, when we closed the door of the past behind us, there was often laughter to be heard as we went about any of the hundred tasks of our daily life.

Until my marriage I had always laughed easily, and now this blessing came back to me. Daniel, by contrast, had always been a quiet and controlled man, but he would often chuckle behind his beard as we enjoyed some joke together. I could even make him laugh outright by singing one of the old Jamaican folksongs I knew, using the mangled creole English.

> *Carry me ackee go a Linstead Market*
> *Not a quattie wut sell.*
> *O, Lawd! Not a mite, not a bite,*
> *Wat a Sat' day night ...*

My twenty-first birthday fell in the September that completed the third year of our sea-gypsy life. I had forgotten my birthday, Daniel had not. We were anchored off St. Eustatius, and when I came on deck in the morning I found my breakfast set on the folding table we used for games. Usually we ate sitting on canvas deck cushions, using low stools as tables, for greater stability. Today, on our games table, there was fresh bread Daniel had made during the night, slices of pineapple, a small dish of hard-boiled egg finely chopped and spiced with a Chinese sauce I especially liked, and a pot of excellent coffee.

It was not until he kissed my cheek, wished me a happy birthday, and held a folding canvas chair for me to be seated, that I realized what the occasion was. Later we sailed for St. Kitts, running goosewinged on a flat sea before a steady breeze. In the afternoon we anchored off a tiny island to dive for lobster. This was one of many small, nameless islands we had come to know during our wanderings, and the seabed around it yielded the finest lobsters we had yet discovered.

That night, at anchor off St. Kitts, we sat on deck cushions under the stars to enjoy our lobster supper. When it was eaten, and we had washed it down with a lemon and pineapple drink of our own invention, Daniel went below and returned holding something on his palm—a little satchel made from fine leather and with a pretty ribbon drawstring.

"We cannot let your twenty-first birthday go by without a birthday present," he said, smiling.

"Oh, bless you, Gubnor. You're so very kind." My eyes prickled with tears as I took the purse. Whatever it contained was both small and light, for when I held up the purse by its ribbon there was no bulge. For a few moments I dangled it in the light of the deck lamp, tantalizing myself by trying to guess what Daniel's present might be. At last I shook my head. "Is it hopeless for me to guess, Gubnor?"

He plucked at his beard, then nodded gravely. "I think so."

Carefully I eased the neck of the little purse open. When I tilted it over my palm something slid out, gleaming yellow in the lamplight, a golden disk, a charm of some sort, on a thick gold chain bracelet. I caught my breath in astonishment. We had sometimes been paid in gold in Aruba, but not in sufficient quantity to make a twentieth of what now lay in my palm, and although we lived well enough we had never earned money to spare over and above what was needed to feed and clothe us, and keep our home in good repair.

I peered more closely, and saw that the face of the gold bore a relief carving of a boat. Again I gasped, for when I turned it to catch the light I saw that the carving was a perfect miniature of the *Casey*, her sails drawing. Where on earth, I wondered, had Daniel managed to lay hands on the gold? Both chain and charm were of a deeper yellow than any gold I had seen on Aruba. Doubtless he had paid one of the goldsmiths there to make the chain, and perhaps also to cast the golden disk, but he must have provided the gold for it, and I was quite sure that Daniel himself had made the carving, working at night while I slept.

There was something about the charm . . . golden, circular . . . that touched a chord deep in my memory, but I could not identify it. The notion that perhaps the disk had not been cast but had once been a coin came into my mind. If this were so, the coin was bigger than a sovereign, and I could not imagine what it might have been, for I knew of no other gold currency in the Caribbean. I thought of the many stolen hours Daniel must have spent at night, filing the face of the coin smooth, then slowly carving away the gold with a fine stylus to leave the shape of the *Casey*.

There were tears on my cheeks now, and my throat had closed so that I could not speak. Clutching the charm bracelet in my hand I knelt by Daniel, put my arms about his neck, and pressed my face into his shoulder. After a few seconds I sat back and was able to say, "Thank you, Gubnor. It's the most wonderful present I've ever had."

He shook his head. "A very small return for the years of companionship you have given me, Casey dear. Very small. And now let us both drink to your health."

I laughed, and we raised our pewter pots of lemon and pineapple mixture. If I had been other than I was, if I had been a girl of quick intelligence and the fine sensitivity of instinct to go with it, I would surely have felt some dark presentiment at that moment. But I felt only warmth and contentment. Nothing came to me on the wind or on the waves or from the stars to tell me that a dreadful end to this chapter of my life was very near now, and that the charm I held in my hand, fashioned and given with so much love and friendship, would act upon me like a curse, like the evil-impregnated mommet or curse-doll of the obeah man, delivering me into the hands of the living dead.

7

WE DRANK TO MY HEALTH AND I SETTLED BACK ON THE DECK cushion, leaning toward the lamp. The reverse side of the charm felt as if it bore slight ridges, and when I turned it over I could faintly make out a coat of arms.

"You made it from a gold coin, Gubnor?" I asked wonderingly. Daniel nodded, and as he did so I was able to identify the vague recollection that had stirred in my mind. "Oh, now I remember. It's like the coin you gave Mr. Lockhart that day—" I stopped short, for without thinking I had broken our unwritten rule never to speak of the past. Apologetically I said, "I'm sorry."

Daniel shook his head. "There is nothing to be sorry about, my dear." He spoke absently, as if his thoughts were far away. "I have sometimes felt I would like to tell you of what lay behind Mr. Lockhart's visit. It has no importance now, but . . ." He lapsed into a long silence, then resumed as if unaware of having stopped. "For almost thirty years now I have carried a burden of guilt, and perhaps it will help if I share this secret." He reached out and put his hand on mine for a moment, smiling. "Share it with my deputy daughter, my friend, my shipmate."

A chill touched me, and I said, "Only tell me if you want to, please Gubnor. I'm not curious."

"I think it is time," he said. "Do you remember what the young man told you about me?"

"Well..." I forced my mind's eye to look back into a past I had closed a door upon for the last three years. "He said your real name was Ma Ho and that you had ruined his family and brought his father to disgrace and death, but I told him that was ridiculous. You couldn't possibly have done such a thing."

Daniel leaned back against the cabin housing and sighed. "Thank you, Casey, my dear. But I fear Mr. Lockhart spoke the truth."

I groped for words, and could find none to say. Daniel stared at the moon and went on, "His father was founder of the Lockhart Trading Company. It was a very big company, both in Hong Kong and Shanghai, second only to Jardine Matheson. The father, R. J. Lockhart, was a true merchant venturer. Wealthy, but with his fortune always at risk. And then, one day, his two acres of warehouses in Hong Kong, and an even larger area in Shanghai, were destroyed by fire with all they contained. That was bad, but worse still was the fact that R. J. Lockhart himself was accused of having responsibility for the fires."

I sat up straight, staring. "But why?"

"There are two answers to that question," Daniel said, and I heard a deep weariness in his voice. "The first answer is that he was in severe financial difficulties and was perpetrating a fraud on the insurance company concerned. That is what the prosecution said at his trial. The second answer, and the true answer, is that he was accused of this crime of arson because the whole affair had been carefully arranged to make him appear guilty."

"Carefully arranged? But by whom?"

Daniel was silent for a little while. At last he said, "Do you know what a tong is, Casey?"

"A tong? Singular? No, I don't know the word."

"It is a Chinese secret society, like the Mafia of Sicily or the Camorra of Italy. The Lockhart family offended a powerful tong in some way, perhaps in a matter of business. The leaders of the tong decided that the Lockhart Trading Company must be destroyed. For this it was necessary to destroy R. J. Lockhart also. Plans were made and orders were issued. Two very junior members of the tong were instructed to cause the fires and then to confess to the insurance company assessors that R. J. Lockhart had paid them money to burn down his warehouses in Hong Kong and Shanghai. I was one of those two junior members."

I put my hands to my cheeks. The gold charm, forgotten in these past minutes, hung from my fingers and I felt its coolness against my skin. "*You*, Gubnor?" I whispered.

Daniel rubbed his eyes with the heels of his hands, as if to ease an ache in them. "I had worked as a clerk in the Lockhart Hong Kong warehouse for five years," he said. "During that time there were several occasions when I spoke with Mr. Lockhart himself, and I liked him, Casey, I truly liked him. When I was first summoned before the tong leaders and given my orders, I said I could not do such a bad thing to my employer. Then they described the things that would be done to my mother if I broke the oath of obedience I had taken on joining the tong four years before."

I felt cold with horror. "Why did you join, Gubnor? Why?"

He looked down at his hands. "I was a boy of seventeen when I was offered the chance. I cannot pretend I even hesitated. To be part of a secret society was a wonderful thing for a young man such as I, struggling to support four younger half-brothers and half-sisters, so that my mother need not ply the only trade she knew. The tong would protect me, protect my job and family. I was too young to realize the price I might have to pay, too stupid to see the reality that lies behind the idea of the tong. They deal in torture and death, and they are without mercy. So I obeyed their orders, and I was one of the two who caused the fires and who later made a false confession to incriminate Mr. Lockhart."

I moved to sit beside Daniel against the cabin housing, slipped my hand through his arm, and leaned my head on his shoulder. There was nothing I could say. The young Ma Ho had been faced with two evils, and had chosen what to him was the lesser.

"We were assured that we would receive only a light sentence for having confessed," he said, his voice barely audible above the soft lapping of water about the hull. "I served only one year. The tong paid my mother enough money to keep our family for three years, when the last of them would be old enough to work. Mr. Lockhart was tried and found guilty of arson and fraud. His company was ruined, his family disgraced.

He was sentenced to seven years penal servitude, and died after only two years, still protesting his innocence."

There was a silence on the *Casey* except for the many small creaking boat-sounds from timbers and rigging. I could well have felt that on this night of my birthday I had been plunged from happiness to misery by Daniel's tale, but for once I had no thought for myself. Eyes closed, I was feeling myself in the skin of a half-caste Chinese boy who wished harm to nobody, but who had brought disaster and death to a man and his family.

I said, "What happened to Mr. Lockhart's wife and children?"

"His wife was quite a young woman. There was a little girl of five and a baby boy of one year. He was the Lockhart you met in Fern Gully, twenty-two years later, Mr. Chad Lockhart. His mother was a brave woman. She remained in Hong Kong with the children, and worked as a buying agent for an American company there. I believe she was helped in this by the influence of an American doctor who had been a friend of her husband. She must have had few enough friends, for she would be an outcast to all the English community. She came to visit me while I was in prison..."

Daniel hesitated, and I felt him shiver. After a few moments he went on, "She knew her husband was innocent. Knew I had given false evidence. She came to beg me to tell the truth and clear her husband's name. I...I could not speak to her. I sat mute, unable to say a word. And when she left, saying she would fight till her dying breath to expose me for the liar and perjurer I was, I told the prison governor that I would not agree to see her again. It was unbearable, Casey."

I said in a shaky voice, "Poor lady. And poor young Ma Ho. What happened when you came out of prison?"

"My family had gone. There was a Chinese merchant from Macao, who had regularly made use of my mother's services when on visits to Hong Kong. He was sufficiently enamored of her to take her back to Macao with him, I suppose as a concubine, together with the children. As an ex-convict I did not wish to jeopardize her position, so I did not attempt to rejoin my family. But I did wish to leave Hong Kong and to break away from the tong. I took work as a stoker and went on a cargo boat to Manila. After that I worked at several trades in different places. I think you know all that part of my life, for I have told you stories of it since you were small. At last

I came to Jamaica . . . and was greatly blessed to have the good fortune of meeting May there, and later marrying her."

Daniel fell silent. My cheek against his shoulder, I watched the mast moving against the stars with the gentle swaying of the boat, and thought about the strange sad story he had told. At last I said, "I'm so glad you were able to have those years of happiness with May. Do you know how Mr. Chad Lockhart managed to find you after so long?"

"I cannot be sure. I know that even from boyhood young Mr. Lockhart dedicated himself to clearing his father's name. He told me so, on the day he came to Ocho Rios, and I think it was through my family that he found me. Once every year until my mother died, eight years ago now, I wrote a letter to her. She was a prostitute, but she bore me, fed me, clothed me, and secured a place for me at a mission school. I loved her, Casey. Perhaps when the young Chad Lockhart grew up he tried to seek out those who had incriminated his father, to make them confess they had given false evidence. Perhaps he traced my mother to Macao and discovered from her family there that I had written from Jamaica." I felt Daniel shrug. "How he found me does not matter. What is strange is that for two years I had been trying to find him."

I sat up and looked at Daniel. "But how, Gubnor? And why?"

"How? By writing to the bank in Hong Kong which had handled the affairs of the Lockhart Trading Company, asking if they could tell me the whereabouts of R. J. Lockhart's family. They did not reply. I then wrote to the solicitor who had defended R. J. Lockhart, and was given an address for Mr. Chad Lockhart in Shanghai. I wrote there, and almost a year later the letter was returned by a person at that address who said that Mr. Chad Lockhart had occupied the house previously but had returned to England two or three years ago. All this had taken a very long time, for the post between Jamaica and China is not swift. It was a great courtesy of the person in Shanghai to write, but he gave no address in England for Chad Lockhart. I was wondering what to do next when you came riding down from Fern Gully that day, warning me of a man from England who claimed I was his enemy."

Daniel got to his feet and moved to the rail. As I rose and followed him he said, "When my May died, I felt free to try to discharge some of the burden of guilt that lay upon me. I wrote out a detailed confession, and had my signature to it witnessed by a solicitor and his partner in Kingston. I wanted to send this to the son of R. J. Lockhart, so that he could clear his father's name"—Daniel's voice fell to a whisper—"and so perhaps free me at last from the memory that still haunts me, the memory of that brave lady who came to plead with me in prison."

I said, "Was the confession written on that scroll in the bamboo case I saw you give Mr. Lockhart that day?"

"Yes. And that was another reason why I made ready to leave Jamaica. British justice is sometimes slow but usually sure. In time I would have been taken back to Hong Kong to answer for what I had done."

There was a long silence. After a while I turned to Daniel and held out the bracelet and charm on my palm. "Put it on my wrist for me, please, Gubnor. I shall only wear it on special occasions, but today is my birthday, after all."

He smiled, gave a sigh of relief, then passed the chain round my wrist and carefully fastened the clasp. "It is good to have spoken at last," he said quietly. "Try not to think too badly of me, Casey."

"I could never think badly of you. Never." I lifted my wrist and watched the charm dangling from the chain. "Was this once a gold coin, Gubnor?"

He hesitated, then said, "Yes. A Spanish eight-escudo gold coin. A doubloon."

I had seen such a coin once or twice before. In the days when the buccaneers sailed the Caribbean, and when Henry Morgan turned from piracy to become governor of Jamaica, gold pieces of eight and silver pesos were common currency from Mexico to Peru and from Panama to the Bahamas. A few were still bought and sold each year in Jamaica, as curios, for the native boys would occasionally find one or two amid the sunken ruins of the old Port Royal.

I said, "Is this one of the old coins?"

"Not very old. It was minted in seventeen ninety-four. In a good light you can see the date on the reverse, together with a coat of arms and the name of Charles the Fourth of Spain."

That date was over a hundred years later than the earthquake of 1692, which had destroyed Port Royal, so the coin could not have come from the submerged ruins. I said, "Was it a coin like this that you gave Chad Lockhart, together with the scroll in the bamboo case?"

"Yes."

I waited for Daniel to go on, and when he remained silent I found myself wondering where he had obtained the coins, why he had given one to Chad Lockhart, and what he had said when he gave it. Since they spoke in Chinese, I had no idea what passed between them, but I could not ask such questions. It was for Daniel to choose how much of his story he wished to tell me. I rested my hands on the smooth, close-grained rail in front of me, still a little warm from the day's heat, and I looked out along the silver carpet the moon had laid across the sea to the far horizon.

Some time later Daniel said, "It is better that I do not tell you where the coins came from. I was able to identify them by reading old records preserved in the library of the Institute of Jamaica. They are very particular coins, and I had four of them. One I gave to Mr. Lockhart, two I melted down before giving them to a goldsmith to make the chain and clasp of your bracelet. The fourth I used for the gold charm. I filed the obverse completely smooth, and I engraved the *Casey* on that face."

I said hesitantly, "I don't want to be inquisitive, but may I ask you why it's better for me not to know where they came from, Gubnor? I know you wouldn't have stolen them, so it seems a strange thing to say."

"To know what they are and where they came from could be dangerous, Casey dear." He turned, leaned against the rail, folded his arms, and sighed ruefully. "Perhaps I am wrong. Perhaps another day I will think it better to tell you. I wish I were a wiser man. So often I find myself not knowing what to do for the best."

I moved to put my arms around his neck and give him a hug. "You're the wisest and best man I've ever known, Gubnor." As I stepped back I was suddenly overcome by a great yawn, which I could not smother. Daniel laughed, and when it had passed I said, "Oh dear, I'm sorry. I suddenly feel so sleepy. I think I'll just clear away the supper things and then go to bed."

"Don't do anything, Casey, I will see to the clearing up. Off you go now, and I will sling your hammock here while you get ready for bed."

"Are you sure you don't mind?"

He smiled and shook his head. "I feel wide awake, and very happy. A weight has gone from me."

"I'm so glad, Gubnor." I held up my wrist. "Thank you for such a beautiful birthday present."

It was next morning, on St. Kitts, that Daniel went ashore to buy vegetables and returned without his usual smile of greeting for me.

"A man has been inquiring about us, Casey," he said as I helped him lift the sack from the dinghy.

After so long a time our fears of discovery had faded almost completely, and my heart jumped with sudden shock. "What sort of man?" I said anxiously. "Not someone from the Colonial Service?"

"No, I'm sure it wasn't." Daniel climbed aboard and patted my shoulder reassuringly. "If the matter was official, the commissioner here would have sent for me."

"The man didn't ask after us by our old names?"

"No, no, no. Nothing like that. He did not even seem to know our present names."

"Then I don't understand how he could inquire about us. Is he still here? Who told you of him, Gubnor?"

"The storekeeper, Mr. Tanner. He said there was an Englishman here a few weeks ago asking about a small trading steamer run by a Chinaman and his woman. The man arrived on one of the island steamers and left with it when it sailed next day."

My fear began to abate a little, and I breathed more easily. "Did Mr. Tanner tell you anything else about the Englishman?"

"Only that he was a gentleman, not a trader, and that he was about fifty years old with a beard like mine, but his was red and gray instead of black and gray. Mr. Tanner did not know his name, and I gather he was not very communicative."

"Well . . . it doesn't sound too threatening, I suppose. But it's strange. Why should he be looking for us?"

"I do not know, my dear. Perhaps there is a job for which we and the *Casey* are particularly well suited, and this gentleman heard of us vaguely by word of mouth. We are quite well known throughout the islands, even if our names are not."

That was true. The boat, and Daniel, and my shapeless form lurking in the background were familiar sights in many places now, but the village natives did not use our names, and of the white people we dealt with there were few who bothered to remember them; they generally referred to us as the Chink and his girl. As we hauled the dinghy aboard I said, "Mr. Tanner knows our names. What did he tell the Englishman?"

"He said a half-Chinaman called Harry Leng and his coolie woman traded round the islands in a steamer called the *Casey*, but that it was hard to say where we could be found at any particular time. We might be a mile or a thousand miles away."

I gave Daniel a hand to settle the dinghy on her blocks. "Are you worried, Gubnor?"

He thought for a moment, then smiled and shook his head. "I was at first, because it came as a shock. But the more I think about it the more I feel it is impossible for anyone in the world to suspect that Harry Leng and his woman were once two other people."

I felt my anxiety fade. What Daniel said was true, and I knew he would not give me false reassurance. For all that, the incident kept coming to my mind in the next few days like a small shadow, bringing with it a feeling of curiosity in which there was a tinge of unease. I think it was the same for Daniel, though we never spoke of it.

Perhaps with another month and another thousand miles behind us the small shadow would have vanished, but we were not to be allowed that time. A far greater shadow was creeping toward us, thrown by the cruel disaster that was soon to strike with such dreadful power.

Two weeks later, sailing south from St. Vincent with half a ton of coconuts we had promised to provide for a trader on St. Anthony, there came a moment shortly before sunset when we looked at each other and knew that dangerously bad weather was brewing. The waves rolling in from the Atlantic had slowed their rhythm and were lifting high. There were curious bars of cloud on the horizon to the east and southeast, and occasional squalls of heavy rain swept across the sea.

Daniel was at the wheel. I had just come from the galley with two mugs of coffee, and as I handed one to him I said, "Do you think there's a hurricane coming?"

He looked for a long time toward the eastern sky, and seemed to be sniffing the air. "I'm afraid so, Casey," he said at last. "But it won't reach us for another twenty or thirty hours."

We sipped our coffee, both pondering the same question. St. Anthony lay twelve hours hard sailing from our present position, and offered fair shelter from a hurricane. We would have time to unload our cargo, sail round to the lee side of the little island, and find a secure anchorage there before the great storm struck. But if we wanted the best shelter available we should alter course now and sail southwest for seventeen or eighteen hours to reach La Faucille. Originally colonized by the French, this island had been British now for more than a century. It was shaped like the blade of a sickle, a long thin curve with its back to the southeast. This convex coast was of high rugged cliffs, from which the land sloped down for a mile to the inner coastal curve of beach and woodland, where a population of two or three thousand lived in pleasant villages and a single town called Tavistock, which was also a port.

I said, "Will there be time to unload at St. Anthony before sailing west for La Faucille and Tavistock?"

Daniel thought for a while, then said, "It is just possible, but it would be taking a very grave risk."

"I thought so. But if we go direct to Tavistock for shelter it might be a long time before we can get back to deliver the cargo to St. Anthony, and we're not the only boat trading between the islands."

Daniel nodded. "Also, Mr. Latham buys only during the first week of the month. We do not want to be left with the cargo, so we will deliver the coconuts and shelter at St. Anthony. It is only a little less secure than La Faucille." The decision was made, and I thought it was the right one. No foreboding warned me that a strange quirk of Fate was to make our decision meaningless.

We did not heave-to that evening, but sailed on through the night, snatching what sleep we could by catnapping in turns, for the wind was shifting and we were constantly trimming the sails to make the best speed we could. At dawn a dull red sun lifted above the horizon to bring ominous leaden glints from the clouds in the eastern sky. Ninety minutes later we came into the bay at St. Anthony.

Here, all preparations were being made for a hurricane. Shutters were going up at the windows of the cottages, small boats were being hauled up the slipway or sunk in the sandy bay, and everything movable was being taken indoors or lashed down. No sooner had we tied up at the wooden jetty than Mr. Latham, who owned the store there, came hurrying along with two native boys and a mule cart to receive our cargo.

We had dealt with Mr. Latham on several occasions. He

knew Daniel as Harry Leng, and knew me as Casey, but it had not been until our third visit that he realized the young person in the cap, cut-down trousers, and loose shirt was female. A brisk man with a blunt manner, he had exclaimed in astonishment, "Good Lord, that's a woman, Leng!"

Daniel had shrugged indifferently. "Coolie girl," he replied in the rough, American-accented voice he always used when we were ashore. "Indian momma, white poppa. I buy her cheap in Puerto Rico." Mr. Latham had simply nodded, his momentary surprise evaporating. He was not particularly interested in a pair of sea gypsies he had dealings with perhaps twice each year.

Now, as usual at such times, while Daniel and Mr. Latham were concluding their business on deck I was keeping in the background and making myself useful at the same time. We had rigged a whip to a boom over the hold, and I was below, filling the net sling with coconuts for the native boys to hoist and swing out to the cart.

I estimated that it would take four hoists to clear the cargo, and was loading the net for the third time when I heard the sound of a new voice, an English voice, from the deck just above me. I took no notice, but a few moments later Daniel appeared by the hatch, looking down. "Get up on deck, Casey," he said. "The boys can finish unloading."

I was puzzled, but made no answer and went up the ladder. On deck I stood in a slovenly way with head bowed a little, thumbs hooked in my trouser pockets, gazing at the scene on the jetty with a dull-eyed lack of interest that in no way reflected my true feelings. Daniel stood with Mr. Latham by the break in the rail where a short gangway had been laid. On the jetty, a man lay on a stretcher with a gray blanket covering him to his shoulders. He had dark hair and a stubble of beard. At first I thought he was a lightly colored native, then realized his skin was white but deeply tanned by sun and weather, like my own. Beneath the tan was a pallor of sickness. His face was damp with sweat, his eyes were closed, and he lay as if utterly exhausted.

On the gangway stood another man, thin-faced and with sandy hair, about forty years of age, wearing a crumpled black cotton jacket and a clerical collar. Hovering near the stretcher were two natives. I assumed they had carried the sick man to the jetty, but could not imagine why.

Daniel jerked his head toward the man on the gangway and

spoke to me in the usual brusque way that our roles demanded. "You listen good along this feller, Casey." He looked at the man. "Now say it again."

The clergyman blinked, his wispy hair fluttering in the building wind. "You wish me to explain to this boy?"

Mr. Latham said, "She's a girl, Mr. Cruse."

Daniel nodded. "My woman. You tell her, mister. Ain't just my life you want to gamble."

The man in the black cotton jacket looked at me with a harassed air. "I am the—er—Reverend John Cruse," he said, "and I am a missionary sent from England by the Methodist Church to bring the gospel to some of the smaller of our West Indian islands. Do you understand what I am saying, Miss—er . . . Mrs.—ah . . . young lady?"

I nodded dourly. Mr. Cruse continued, "I am gradually visiting the islands, trying to establish a meeting place in the main town of each. This is a preliminary step, of course—"

Mr. Latham broke in impatiently. "Better come to the point, Mr. Cruse."

"Quite so, quite so." The clergyman waved a hand toward the man on the stretcher and went on hurriedly. "As I have explained to your—er—to Mr. Leng here, this man on the stretcher is an American gentleman who came to St. Anthony on the monthly steamer from Grenada. He must have been infected with yellow fever, for he fell sick almost immediately. My wife and I took him into the cottage we have rented here, and arranged for a native woman to nurse him. At one time we thought he would die, but as you see he is recovering from the fever. Unfortunately, in the past forty-eight hours Mr. Redwing appears to have developed a highly inflamed appendix. Oh dear, I wonder if you understand that word . . . ?"

I looked at Daniel. He tapped his stomach with a finger and grunted, "Piece of gut gone bad in belly belong him." I nodded, and looked at Mr. Cruse again, wondering what he thought we could do for the poor man on the stretcher.

Mr. Latham spoke quickly to me, probably because he found the clergyman long-winded. "Mrs. Cruse, she's trained in nursing, see? She says this bad thing in the belly is going to keep swelling up till it bursts, and then the man will die. He needs an operation. Needs a special doctor to cut him open and take the bad bit out. Understand? Haven't got a doctor here. Only place they might help is on La Faucille. Convent there. Nursing order of nuns. They run a hospital serving quite a few islands—

when the patients can be got there. Don't know to what extent they can handle surgery, though."

Mr. Latham went on speaking, then Mr. Cruse joined in, but I scarcely listened, for now I knew what was wanted of us, and I felt a chill of fear. The man on the stretcher, Mr. Redwing, as the clergyman had called him, needed urgent surgery. His only chance for this was on La Faucille, and even then the chance was small. We knew the convent and the attached hospital there. On one occasion we had carried medical supplies from St. Vincent, when the island steamer broke down. I did not think it likely that they had the skill or equipment to remove an appendix, but presumably if it was not removed the man would die.

There was only one way in which he could be taken to La Faucille today, and that was aboard the *Casey*. But whether by sail or steam we would need between eight and ten hours to fetch the island. The question was, could we reach it before the hurricane struck?

I emerged from my frightening thoughts to hear Mr. Cruse saying, ". . . this surgeon from England is touring certain civil and military hospitals in the West Indies by arrangement with the Colonial Office to give instruction in new methods. I am sure I detect the hand of God in the most blessed fact that Mr. Carradine happens to be instructing at the hospital on La Faucille just at this time."

His words robbed me of the best excuse I had for claiming it would be pointless to attempt such a journey, and my fear deepened. Daniel stood with arms folded, eyes half closed, apparently pondering, but I knew he was watching me. This was a decision he would not take without my agreement. Mr. Latham said, "It'll be touch and go, Leng. Six to twelve hours before that hurricane strikes, that's what I reckon, and I favor the shorter time."

The clergyman said in a low troubled voice, "I cannot urge you to risk your lives. I can only say that I believe this man will certainly die if he does not receive attention within the next twenty-four hours. Perhaps I could also say that Mr. Samuel Redwing is a businessman of some substance, since he is investing considerable time and money in the search for natural fertilizer throughout the islands. Therefore he will be more than happy to pay handsomely for—"

Daniel cut him short with an angry slicing movement of the hand. "I don't trade for a feller's life," he growled. "You said your piece, Mr. Vicar, now leave it there while the woman thinks."

"By all means, Mr. Leng, but . . . forgive me, but are you sure she has understood?"

"I'm sure." Daniel was still watching me, and I had the curious feeling that other eyes were also upon me. My fear was very great. I loved the sea, but I knew it could be seized by a wild and monstrous rage, and in such a mood it was utterly without mercy. My gaze went to the man on the stretcher. He was gaunt from the sickness he had endured, but I felt his was a face that might smile easily. He was in his early forties, I judged, and would stand almost six feet tall. With a little start I realized that his eyes were not fully closed, and that he was looking at me from under his eyelids. This was the other gaze I had felt upon me.

I moved to the gangway without quite knowing why. Mr. Cruse gave me a look of surprise and stepped aside. I took two steps to the jetty and went down on one knee beside the sick man. As I did so I heard Daniel say slowly, "Could you have Casey stay here with you and your wife till I get back, Mr. Cruse?"

Before the clergyman could answer my head snapped round and I said loudly in my coolie voice, "No! No, Gubnor. I neber gon' stay 'longside dis prayin' *bockra*." Bockra was the creole word for white man. I went on more quietly, "We both gon' go, we both gon' stay, please. You leave me t'ink a minute."

When I looked down, the American gentleman's eyes had opened a little wider and were watching me. The whites were yellow and the eyes held pain, but I saw a hint of puzzlement and interest in them also. I was certain he had been conscious and aware throughout the whole of the conversation, which meant that he now knew his only chance of life lay in my hands.

His lips, dry and cracked, twisted slightly to form the ghost of a smile. "Hallo, Casey," he said in a croaking whisper.

I said in the gruff voice I had used before, "Mo'ning, mister."

We looked at each other. After a moment or two he gave a feeble shake of his head and said, "It's a poor gamble, little lady."

Now it was too late. In those few seconds we had exchanged a look and less than a dozen words, but it was enough to make

him a real person to me, not simply an unknown man on a
stretcher. I stood up and looked at Daniel. "I neber gon' sit
about watch 'im allalong die, Gubnor. Dis woman say we gon'
try takum along La Faucille."

8

WE SAILED HALF AN HOUR LATER, WITH MR. REDWING strapped to the stretcher and the arms of the stretcher itself roped to cleats screwed into brass plates set in the deck of the cabin. These securing points had proved a boon to us in bad weather when we wanted to make all fast.

The after hold was carrying as many rocks as Mr. Latham's native boys had been able to load in the time available. We needed this ballast to keep the stern down. Mr. Cruse's wife had provided us with some laudanum to ease the sick man's pain, and we had prepared the boiler furnace with tarred wood so that we should have steam quickly available if the time came when we needed it. Both wind and sea would be behind us on this voyage, but if the wind became too strong for sail we might have to rely on the engine.

Running free with the wind directly abaft was not our best point of sailing, but over the years the *Casey* had become a part of us; we knew her every whim, and could judge to an inch the amount of canvas needed and the trim of sails to get the best from her. The frequent gusting and shifting of the wind meant constant work, and most of this fell upon Daniel, for I was at the wheel. For a long time now, Daniel had held that

I was a more sensitive helmsman than he, and could coax an extra fraction of speed from the *Casey*. There may have been a little truth in this, for certainly I had grown to "feel" her needs through the spokes in my hands and the timbers beneath my usually bare feet.

For the first three hours we ran under almost full sail, but the wind grew suddenly vicious, forcing us to reef the mainsail to prevent constant yawing. After another hour we took in the mainsail completely, set up the smokestack, and fired the boiler to get up steam. The squalls had turned to constant rain now, and I was soaked, for I was standing watch at the deck wheel, not in the shelter of the wheelhouse. This was by my own choice. I did not mind being drenched, and from where I stood Daniel and I could call to each other more easily as we worked the little ship.

Every hour since leaving St. Anthony, Daniel had gone below to see that all was well with Mr. Redwing, and now it was time for him to look at the sick man again. Instead he came to the wheel, rain streaming from his beard, and lifted his voice above the steady howl of the wind. "Hot coffee before it becomes too rough to manage, Casey. Put some rum in it, and see if the patient can take some."

I nodded and moved away, then paused and looked back. "Is it safe for him to drink?" I shouted. The deck was heaving strongly now, so that one moment I was looking down at Daniel and the next looking up toward him. He gave an exaggerated shrug of his shoulders and called, "Mrs. Cruse said he must not eat anything if he is to have an operation. She did not forbid drinking, and the poor man is pinched with cold. Rum and hot coffee might help."

I went down into the comparative quiet of the cabin and knelt beside Mr. Redwing, peering down at him in the gloom. It was midmorning, but the sky was so dark it could well have been dusk. His eyes were closed as if in sleep. I dried my hands on the blanket, then felt his brow. It was clammy, but not excessively hot. His eyes opened, and as I started to speak it was only at the last moment that I remembered to use my half-caste native voice.

"Gubnor say how's yo' feelin', mister?"

He studied me curiously for a few seconds, then said slowly, "I've been listening to you . . . for quite a while now, honey. And you're not what you seem. A West Indian half-caste girl doesn't call out in an educated English accent I can't imitate,

'We'll have to lower the mainsail any minute now, Gubnor. Can you manage, or shall I lash the wheel?'" Mr. Redwing smiled feebly. "There were plenty of other examples."

I felt a wave of alarm, and was angry at my own stupidity, but I tried to hide my feelings and looked blank as I said, "Me no catch dat t'ing you say, mister. Gubnor say me carry you some coffee wit' rum for drink good." I got up and went through to the galley. Daniel had set the engine to work now, and with steam piped from the boiler I quickly made a pot of strong coffee and laced it with rum. I had never overcome my dislike of this strong spirit, and even the smell offended me, but we occasionally used rum to warm our blood in bad weather conditions.

I half filled a large pewter mug to avoid spilling, and carried it up to Daniel. He was in the wheelhouse now and took the steaming drink gratefully. "How is the patient, Casey?"

"All right, I think. But he knows I'm not what I pretend to be. He's heard me calling out in my own voice all morning."

Daniel grimaced. "I did not think. It is the first time we have had anyone else aboard. Just keep pretending, Casey, and if he speaks of it to me I will say he must have been delirious."

I went below again to take a mug of coffee to Mr. Redwing. When I loosened the strap that kept him from being thrown about he found himself too weak to sit up, and I had to help him. Twice I heard him catch his breath with pain, and when at last I managed to get him sitting upright he leaned heavily against me, his head resting against my shoulder, muttering curses under his breath.

"Hell's . . . teeth. Like some damn baby . . . devil take it . . ."

Apart from Daniel, this was the first man I had actually touched since the dreadful night when I had fought against Oliver Foy in our bedroom at Diabolo Hall. Somewhere deep within me a cold spark of repugnance stirred, and I had to smother it quickly by telling myself that all men were not tarred with the same brush, and that few indeed could be so cruel and bestial as Oliver.

Mr. Redwing's panting eased a little, and he said, "Sorry, Casey. Excuse the language."

I helped him hold the mug with my free hand and said, "Yo' talk t'ings I neber catch, mister. Drink now." He began to sip the rum-laced coffee. Twice we spilled a little down the front of his shirt with the pitching of the boat, but most of it he managed to drink gratefully. When the last drop had gone he rested his head against me once more and said in a croaking voice, "Thanks, honey. And listen . . . if you and that good man up there on deck have a secret you want to keep, don't worry about me having a loose tongue. Sam Redwing never let a friend down yet." He tilted his head back and gave me a feeble grin, then tried to imitate my creole speech. "Yo' catch dat t'ing I say now, Casey?"

I looked blank and helped him to lie down again, then refastened the strap. In the few minutes I had been below, the storm had grown markedly worse. I wiped the sweat from Mr. Redwing's face, moved into the galley to drink my own coffee, then went up on deck again. Rain and a curious yellow darkness made it impossible to see more than a stone's throw from the boat. At the wheel, Daniel was fighting to hold the *Casey* on course. The wind was beginning to scream in a way I had never known before, and I felt my stomach tighten with fear.

Another four hours at least to La Faucille. It would be easy to miss the island completely; it would be easy to run into the great wall of cliffs that formed the southeastern coast. If we managed to avoid both, and passed close to the north or south extremity, we would then have to turn in order to fetch Tavistock, on the lee side. But in another four hours the seas would be too mountainous for us to turn without being capsized by a beam sea.

An hour later, in a sudden terrifying squall, the foresail was torn away just as we decided to take it in. Daniel fed steam to the engine, the propeller bit into the sea, and for the next two hours I took the helm in the wheelhouse while Daniel stood hunched beside me, a hand on the throttle lever. Each time the *Casey* pitched over the crest of a great wave, the screw came momentarily out of the water. Freed from pressure, it would spin at such speed as to cause the whole engine to shudder. There was danger of the shaft or piston rods breaking unless Daniel closed the throttle valve at such moments.

The wheel jerked and lunged in my hands like a live thing, and I was so desperately weary from the struggle that I could not tell the exact moment when I knew we must surely be doomed; that we had gambled and lost. There was nothing to be done now but fight to the end. Either we would be destroyed against the cliffs of La Faucille, or we would be swept past the island and destroyed later. Certainly we could not turn into the lee of the island, and neither could we live through the hurricane without shelter.

There came a time when I found Daniel knotting a line around my waist. I realized my eyes had been almost closed for some time now, and that I had been keeping the *Casey*'s stern to the seas by feel. Some freak of light had brought better visibility, but the sea and the wind had become twin demons of destruction, roaring and shrieking as they clawed at the little ship.

Daniel was shouting in my ear. "Land, Casey! La Faucille! Going to hit the cliffs... can't steer clear now. Try for Alligator Gap. Understand?"

I stared through the rain. The *Casey*'s bow went down, the engine screamed as the screw left the water, and I saw the long convex curve of the cliffs that waited to kill us. Our course had been good. Too good. We were going to strike almost at the midway mark of the long sickle of land that was La Faucille. We would never reach the little town, with the convent and hospital, that lay on the far side only a mile from the cliff top.

Numb with the combination of noise, violent movement, and exhaustion, I tried to grasp what Daniel was saying. Alligator Gap? Yes... on previous visits to the island we had chosen that name for a freakish V-shaped split in the otherwise solid wall of rock that formed the southeastern coast. It came roughly in the middle of the long rampart of cliffs, at a point where they dipped to a height of perhaps fifty feet, and the freakish effect had been caused by alternating layers of hard and soft rock. Over thousands of years, the softer rock had been worn away, leaving great projections jutting horizontally from each side of the gap, like teeth in the open jaws of an alligator.

Slowly I realized what Daniel meant us to attempt. Enormous waves were lifting the *Casey* and carrying her forward, passing beneath us, then hurling themselves against the cliffs. If we could steer for the gap, if we could ride in on a giant wave for the last half cable length, and be poised on its crest when we reached Alligator Gap, then we might by a miracle be tossed into those jaws of rock and left wedged upon the great stone teeth. The ship would be wrecked, half crushed in those jaws, but if they held her thirty or forty feet above normal sea level we might have a chance of survival.

If... if... if. But there was no other hope.

The engine screamed again as the screw came out of the water. Something would break before long, but that had ceased to matter. In two or three minutes the *Casey* would die, but

her tortured engine would hold out long enough for us to make
our puny attempt to cheat the sea of her prey.

Daniel leaned down with his head close to mine and shouted,
"Take the deck wheel, Casey. I'll join you there. Wheelhouse
might break away when we hit." The same thought had occurred to me. I nodded, waited for him to get a grip on the
wheel, then went lurching out on my trailing lifeline and clutched
at the spokes of the deck wheel. A few seconds later Daniel
was with me, pressed close behind me, his arms passing on
either side of my body to reach the wheel. The engine was still
giving a little steerage way, but the set of the sea was trying
to turn us to port, and the time had come when only our
combined strength could keep the Casey's stern to the waves,
for the backlash coming from the cliffs was plucking at her
now.

A great wave lifted us and sent us flying forward. I kept
my eyes on the foam that drained like white blood down the
teeth of Alligator Gap. Our bow was in line . . . if only we could
hold it so . . . if only the crucial wave came at the right moment.
We were in a trough, and the dreadful ramparts of stone were
hidden. I thought for a moment of Mr. Redwing, lying strapped
on his stretcher, and wondered if Daniel had told him how
close we were to the end.

Our stern lifted. Up . . . up . . . we seemed to be gliding backward up the slope of a tremendous wave, and suddenly there
was nothing but a great dark valley of sea below us and the
gray cliff wall ahead, with the wind screaming like a creature
in agony all about us. We were rushing forward, poised on the
broad crest of the giant wave now. The wheel was trying to
break my hands. We were leaping at the gap, high . . . too high,
above the topmost of the stone teeth . . . we would slide back
down the reverse side of the wave and . . . but no. The great
crest broke against the teeth below, the Casey dropped like a
falling boulder, the smokestack flew high over my head, the
shriek of timber and steel being torn apart rose even above the
triumphant howling of the storm demons, and the whole world
shattered about me.

There was a time of darkness, then something stirred in the
depths of my being. I was asleep, and did not want to wake
because I knew I would wake to nightmare. Noise beat all
about me, and instinctively I held my breath for long seconds
as I was suddenly engulfed by water. Fearfully I forced myself

to awaken into the nightmare. I was lying face down, timber beneath my cheek. Something held me pressed to the deck, something that cut into me cruelly from thigh to shoulder as it passed obliquely across my back.

A line. Yes, a lifeline. But it could not be mine. I held my breath as another wave engulfed me. The bigger waves were reaching the wreck of the *Casey* as she lay perched on the topmost teeth of Alligator Gap, plucking at her, trying to tear her down.

Daniel! I cried his name aloud and struggled to rise, but the rope holding me down was as unyielding as a bar of steel. I could not lift myself a fraction of an inch, and could not squirm from beneath it. Another wave struck, and the deck beneath me quivered a little. When the wave fell back I shook the water from my face, opened my eyes, and found myself looking down into a dark void. It was seconds before I could grasp what had happened. Then I realized with a kind of dull sorrow that the whole of the stern of the *Casey* had broken away. I was lying with my feet toward the deck wheel, my head on the very edge of the splintered deck timbers, where our little boat had been sheared apart as if by some monstrous blunt ax.

Below me lay the sea, a wild dark creature battering at the lower teeth of Alligator Gap. Sometimes it was well over sixty feet below me as it drew back to leave a deep trough, sometimes it was less than ten feet below as it came in for a new assault; and sometimes, perhaps once in every minute, a bigger wave would engulf me.

Daniel! Again I called his name, fighting to fill my lungs against the relentless constriction of the rope that pinned me, helpless as a butterfly. This time I heard a faint answering call. Impossibly, it seemed to come from below me.

I stared down, refocusing my eyes, and saw him swing into view only six feet beneath me amid a spume of breaking wave. He hung from the lifeline fastened in a bowline about his chest, one hand grasping it above his head. The other arm hung limply, and in the dull yellow light I could see it was covered with blood. Now, for the first time, I realized that the rope holding me down and cutting so mercilessly into my back was Daniel's lifeline. It ran from a securing point by the base of the deck wheel, and carried his full weight. I could feel pain where it had sunk deep into my thigh, and much sharper pain where it crossed my collarbone and dropped down over the broken timbers.

In the moments before we struck, when I had believed us to be surely doomed, fear had suddenly left me, but now it returned to choke me as I struggled wildly but in vain to free myself. A gust of wind had swung Daniel out of sight beneath me, but now he came into view again, face turned up toward me, calling, *"Casey! Can you hear me?"*

"Yes Gubnor! Yes!"

"Can you ... winch working ... haul me up?"

I had no idea if our hand-winch had been torn away or wrecked, but in any event I could never get to it. I was sobbing with fright as I shouted down at the top of my voice. *"I can't move, Gubnor! Can't move! Your lifeline is pinning me down!"*

A wave crashed all about us, but this time the remains of the *Casey* did not shift. When the sea drew back I shouted again. *"Did ... you ... hear ... me?"*

He shook the water from his eyes and looked up. *"Yes. I heard."* Perhaps the wind was abating a little, for his voice came to me more clearly now.

I craned my neck to peer down as I called desperately, *"Can you climb up?"*

"No. Arm broken."

Oh, dear God. We were trapped. When the sea at last plucked the *Casey* down, we should die, but that meant we might be a hideously long time dying. I called, *"Tell me what to do, Gubnor! Please! Tell me what to do!"*

He lifted his face, and my heart pounded with sudden hope as I saw his teeth show in a smile. *"Find your lifeline and draw in the slack, Casey. Then hold on firmly."*

I groped with one hand, found the lifeline at my waist, and gathered it in until it became taut. Daniel swung out of my view, then into it again. He had something in his hand, but I could not see what it was. Head bent, he put the hand to his mouth for a few seconds, then lowered it to his side, and looked up.

I shouted above the wind and rain, *"I've done what you said, Gubnor."*

"Good girl. After the next big wave, move quickly. You are almost at the cliff top, and I think you can climb the slope."

"No, you don't understand! I can't move!"

"Do as I say, Casey. Do not fail me. After this big wave coming now—be ready!"

The mountain of water came rolling in upon us and broke. First came the shock of its striking, then the plucking and tugging as it creamed back down the sloping deck, like an animal trying to sink claws into an escaping prey. Daniel appeared below me, leaning back as he hung from the rope. He lifted his good hand and I saw the glint of steel. Horror seized me. Now I knew what he held. It was the jackknife he carried on a spring clip attached to his belt, and he had lifted it to his mouth to open the blade with his teeth.

I screamed, *"No, Gubnor! No!"*

He looked up, calling to me in a loud deliberate voice. I heard the words, but did not take them in, for they seemed to have no part of the dreadful thing he was about to do in the hope of saving my life. He repeated the words. *Reef... Heart...? Tell...?*

My mind could register nothing but what was about to happen, and I shrieked again, *"No, Gubnor! Please! No!"*

"Remember, Casey!" He set the blade against the line above his head. *"Please do your best. Now... go!"*

On the last word his hand made a slashing movement with the well-honed blade, once, twice... then he was falling, vanishing into a deep dark trough only seconds before a towering new wave curled forward and broke with a thunderous roar, burying him under countless tons of seething water as it hurled itself into the great stone teeth of Alligator Gap.

I was free and on my feet, gripping my lifeline, following it back to the securing point, sobbing with shock and sorrow. I would gladly have lain there to let the next wave take me, but Daniel's dying words were in my ears, driving me on. *Do not fail me...*

What remained of the *Casey* rested on the topmost teeth of the narrow gap, canted over to one side and sloping down from bow to stern. The lower gunwale was on the port side, resting against a slope of smooth but creviced rock that slanted up for some fifteen yards to the cliff top on one flank of the gap. It was a steep slope, but not too steep for me to climb.

I wriggled out of the lifeline noose and had one leg over the gunwale when I remembered Mr. Sam Redwing. Without making any conscious decision I found myself clawing my way back across the deck and down into the cabin. The roof of the housing had been ripped away, and one side was stove in. For a moment I thought some freak action of the waves had snatched the sick man away, but then I saw him, still strapped to the stretcher and almost submerged beneath the water that washed about the deck. It was draining away through a hole in one corner, and I realized that if the teeth of Alligator Gap had not driven right through the *Casey*'s bottom, Mr. Redwing would have been drowned by the water taken aboard whenever one of the big waves swamped us.

I was no longer afraid. A numbness had gripped my mind, blotting out all emotion and leaving only enough freedom of thought for me to do whatever might have to be done. For this I was thankful, and prayed that it would continue. If I began to think of Daniel I would break down completely, and that would be to fail him.

I waded through the water and knelt beside the stretcher. Mr. Redwing's eyes were closed, and I thought he was either dead or unconscious, but when I put a hand on his chest to feel for the heartbeat, he opened his eyes and looked up at me with vague disbelief.

"Casey?" His lips formed the word. The scream of the storm had fallen to a steady howl, and when I leaned down I could just hear his voice. His eyes moved to look beyond me as I began fumbling to release the ropes securing his stretcher to the cleats in the deck. He said, "Where's . . . Gubnor?"

I shook my head. The wet ropes were stubborn, and time was against us. I moved to the shattered locker at the foot of my bunk and took out the sheath knife I wore strapped to my leg when diving. Some part of my mind must have been thinking ahead, for I also hung my goggles round my neck, and spent a few precious seconds fastening the knife to my calf. I was about to turn away when my eyes caught something small and pale brown lying on the tangle of spare clothes. This was the leather bag in which I kept the charm bracelet Daniel had given me. My mind a blank, I thrust the little bag into my pocket and turned back to Mr. Redwing.

Another big wave struck, and the *Casey* shifted again, but no water reached the cabin. I registered dully, without much caring, that the seas must have become a little less mountainous. With the knife it was the work of a moment to cut through the securing ropes of the stretcher. I lifted my voice and said, "Can you move? Enough to climb a steep slope?"

His head rolled from side to side, and I put my ear down near his mouth to catch his words. "No good . . . too damn weak . . . even lift my head . . ."

I had suspected as much, and this was why I had not cut

the strap holding him to the stretcher. I called, "Wait. I'll be back," then waded through ankle-deep water and out on deck. Though the wind had eased a little, the rain was pounding more fiercely than ever, and I was glad to slip my goggles into position. The deck locker by the winch was broken, but the contents had not scattered. Working steadily, not allowing haste to make me fumble, I sorted out a block with a twin pulley, another with a single pulley, and a fifteen-fathom line. Two minutes later I was scrambling up the slippery rock face that slanted up from the port gunwale, fingers and toes seeking crevices, the tackle slung on my back.

I was strong for a girl, my life aboard had ensured that, but I knew I would never have the strength to haul Mr. Redwing up the slope on his stretcher. However, by using a jigger I could exert three times my own strength. This was something I had learned as a sea gypsy, and this was what I now planned to do. I was not thinking of Daniel, I dared not, but within me was an awareness that he had lost his life in trying to save the life of a stranger, and I could not bear to let that sacrifice be in vain.

A big wave poured over the boat while I was on the cliff top securing the single-pulley block to a spike of rock there. Rain lashed at my face like small knives, but through my goggles I saw the *Casey* lurch and slip a little. I made fast one end of the line, sheathed my knife, and went slithering down the slope again, helped by the three lines of tackle that now reached down from the top. When I knelt by Mr. Redwing he beckoned feebly, and I bent my head to hear against the bellow of the storm.

"Get out, Casey!" he croaked. "For God's sake get clear. She can't last much longer."

I forced myself to smile at him, though I doubt that he could see it with the rain beating on his face. "I'm going to drag the stretcher out now," I called, "and I've rigged blocks and tackle to haul you up the slope. Understand?"

His lips moved. I leaned down again and heard whispered words, the same words he had first spoken to me on the jetty at St. Anthony. "It's a poor gamble, little lady."

I put my hand to his cheek for a moment, trying to make a gesture of reassurance, then took the handles at the head of the stretcher and began to drag it up the three steps leading to the deck. I had expected trouble here, but the uptilted bow reduced the incline of the steps, and with two or three steady heaves I brought Mr. Redwing out. The most difficult part was then to lift the head of the stretcher high enough to rest across the gunwale, but I managed it at last, and cut a short piece of line to secure the stretcher handles to the hook on the block with twin pulleys, which lay in readiness at the foot of the slope.

Again I clawed my way up the slippery rock. At the top I took the free end of the line, found a good position for bracing myself, and began to haul. Slowly, foot by foot, the stretcher edged over the gunwale and began to climb the slope, its short U-shaped iron legs slipping easily over the rock, for the streaming rain acted as a lubricant. Three minutes later I was able to secure the line, reach down to grasp the handles, and haul the stretcher onto the flat ground of the cliff top.

For a moment I thought of casting about for some kind of shelter . . . a cave, an overhang of rock, anything to keep the worst of the storm from us for a few hours while I could think and gather strength for what had to be done next. Then I remembered that if I brought Mr. Redwing to the hospital too late for surgery he would die, and Daniel's sacrifice would be to no purpose.

In a remote way I knew I was very tired, but I would not allow myself to accept this. I could not afford to be tired yet. I moved away from the stretcher, keeping parallel with one edge of the V-shaped cleft forming Alligator Gap. The part of my mind that was not frozen, the part able to reason, told me that this was a strange freak of nature that must have attracted attention from the islanders over many years, and perhaps therefore some sort of path might exist, running up across the island from Tavistock, a mile away on the other side. If there was such a path, it might make an impossible task possible.

There was. Even in the poor light and driving rain I could see fifty yards of it forming the first leg of a zigzag. It was a narrow path of rough pale stone, running between wild plants and shrubs, with an occasional tree bending before the wind. If it zigzagged all the way my journey would be two miles rather than one, but at least the slope would be less acute, and I would be more easily able to manage the stretcher.

Ten minutes later we were a good fifty feet below the level of the cliff top and gaining a measure of protection from the wind. The rain still teemed, but I was glad of that, for the water helped to ease the legs of the stretcher over the rough path. I had made myself a harness of rope and used Mr. Redwing's blanket for padding, since it was completely sodden and of no further use to him. Like an ox dragging a plow, I plodded slowly down the path with the stretcher behind me.

It troubled me to be towing Mr. Redwing feet first, for I knew he must be getting badly bumped and joggled, but I had to have the front end of the stretcher raised a little from the ground, and I could never have kept it lifted if he had been head first behind me, for the weight would have been too great.

Sometimes the going was bad, and I had to stop and maneuver my burden very slowly. At other times the rock was so smooth I had to take care the stretcher did not keep banging against the back of my legs. After half an hour I was completely exhausted and knew I would have to stop, yet some time later I emerged from a sleeplike trance to find myself still trudging on, leaning into my harness. Somehow I managed to withdraw into that blessed blankness again, and this happened several times, but each time was shorter than the last, for my neck and shoulders were aflame with agony, and this kept bringing me to my senses. The rain that beat upon me was welcome now, for its coolness gave a little easement.

I lost all sense of time, but I suppose it must have been between two and three hours after leaving the cliff top that I lifted my head to see the shape of rain-swept buildings ahead. I recognized the spire of the little church at Tavistock, the line of small houses, and the larger bulk of the combined convent and hospital of the third-order Dominican Sisters, but no living thing moved in the heavy twilight of the storm.

A dull satisfaction came upon me, followed by quick alarm as I suddenly found it increasingly difficult to set one foot before the other. I began to count the steps I took, but found myself lying on the ground, weeping as if my heart would break, sobbing, "Gubnor... Gubnor..."

His voice sounded in my head. *"Do not fail me."*

There was a time of huge struggle, then I lurched against a big wooden door set in an arch of stone. This was the main door of the hospital. Daniel and I had come here to bring medical supplies when the regular steamer had broken down. I found the chain of the bellpull, and began to tug at it... again, and again, and again.

There were faint sounds from beyond the door. A bar was lifted, a big handle turned. The door opened a little way, and in the light of a lantern I saw a man in a priest's brown robe bracing himself to hold the door against the bludgeoning wind.

I remembered him now . . . Father Joseph, from the church here. He had come to the quayside especially to greet us when we brought in supplies for the hospital, and had chatted with Daniel at some length during a later visit. Beyond him stood a nun in a dark habit and a middle-aged gentleman in a frock coat, with thin fair hair and a long, lean face.

I took a step forward into the opening, dragging the stretcher behind me, and fell to my knees, turning to point to Mr. Redwing. "Appendix," I said in a flat voice that seemed to come from someone else. "Appendix . . . allasame belly-debil . . . dat bockra got belly-debil . . . belly-debil . . ." I kept jabbing a finger, pointing in rhythm with the words.

My voice failed and I fell sideways in the harness that held me. The world swam. The bearded face of Father Joseph was close above me, peering down, and I heard him speak in a voice sharp with astonishment. "It's Harry Leng's woman from the *Casey*! Dear Lord in heaven, just look at her shoulders . . . they're *raw*!"

I said, "Gubnor tol' me come . . ." Then the darkness I longed for swooped down to enfold me, and there was nothing more.

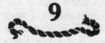

9

THERE WERE TIMES WHEN I EMERGED A LITTLE WAY FROM THE darkness, enough to be distantly aware that gentle hands were tending my pain-racked body, but always I sought to burrow back into oblivion again, for my sleeping mind knew that the time of awakening would bring only heartbreak and fear. Yet there came a moment when the thrust of wakefulness would not be denied.

Against my will, my eyes slowly opened. Without moving my head I saw that I was in a small room with white walls and an open window with a fly screen, through which I could see clear blue sky.

Daniel! Memory pounced with merciless claws. A great sob rose in my throat and I turned on my side to bury my face in bandaged hands and weep . . . weep from my very soul for the good brave man who had been my beloved companion. A cool hand rested on my brow as if in blessing, and a woman's voice said, "There, child, there. Weep as you will, it brings ease to the sorrowing heart." A little pause. "Here is a handkerchief to hold to your eyes, dear. Try not to wet your bandages. Do you understand?"

I fumbled for the handkerchief, held it to my eyes, and

continued weeping. After several minutes when the spasm had passed, I lay limp with exhaustion, breath shuddering, trying to collect my thoughts. I had not shed my last tear for Daniel, that I knew. There would be times when memory of him would catch me by the throat and I would weep again for my lost friend, but the Daniel I knew would not have wanted me to give myself up to mourning him. I remembered the patient courage with which he had set himself to face a new future when he had lost May, and knew I must try to follow his example.

A new future... ? Fear gripped me with cold fingers. I was alone now. I was Casey, with no other name, a coolie girl without a home or work, without money or a protector. What kind of future could there be for me? One thing was certain, there could be no going back. I could never become Emma Delaney again.

I turned on my back, wincing a little from the pain in my shoulders, and opened swollen eyes. A tiny middle-aged nun with a pretty face sat beside the bed now, smiling sadly down at me. "We're all so sorry for this tragic event, Casey," she said. "Mr. Redwing told us the whole very brave, very sad story."

Mr. Redwing. It was hard to believe I had forgotten him till now. I said in my coolie voice, "Gubnor tell me dat Yankee-man got debil in belly. Tell me big word *appendix*. Tell me big bockra doctor-man wit' prayin' ladies belong dis place can take out belly-debil. Maybe I neber bringum quick time 'nuff. Maybe belly-debil killum dead now?"

She shook her head. "No, Casey, you brought him to us just in time. We have a special doctor with us, and he operated within the hour to take out the appendix... the belly-devil. Mr. Redwing is rather weak because he almost died of yellow fever before the appendix trouble, but he's alive and making a good recovery now. Can you understand when I speak like this, dear? Mr. Redwing says you're quite clever at understanding English, even though you don't speak it very well."

I nodded. "Me catchee dose t'ing you say." I closed my eyes for a moment. So at least I had prevented Daniel's sacrifice being wasted. Mr. Redwing had survived, and it seemed he had kept silent about his belief that Harry Leng's coolie woman was not what she seemed to be. I was grateful to him for that and knew it must have been by choice and not by chance, for if he had told about the journey from St. Anthony, the coming of the hurricane, and the wrecking of the *Casey*, then he must have spoken to the doctor or the sisters at some length since his operation. Certainly he had been in no fit state to do so before. Remembering the way I had dragged him across the width of the island from the cliff top to Tavistock in that merciless storm, I marveled that he had lived through the ordeal.

I opened my eyes and said, "How much time I bin 'sleep, prayin' lady?"

"Two whole days, Casey. But Mr. Carradine is pleased about that. He said your whole system needed complete rest. He's also pleased at the way your shoulders and hands are healing from the rope abrasions. He says both you and Mr. Redwing must have very strong constitutions. Mr. Carradine is the special doctor I told you about, but he's called mister instead of doctor, because he's a surgeon. I'll fetch him now and arrange for you to have some broth. I'm sure you must be hungry. By the way, you must call me Sister Agnes, not praying lady." She got to her feet and patted my arm. "I shall be very pleased to tell Mr. Redwing that you're awake at last. He hasn't stopped asking about you since he came round after the operation."

She smiled again and moved to the door, a little doll of a lady, barely as high as my shoulder, the long habit hiding her feet so that she seemed to glide on wheels. I lay gazing at a crucifix on the wall, thinking quietly of Daniel, talking to him in my mind as I had once long ago talked to the portrait of my Grannie Elliot.

You asked me not fail you, Gubnor. And I didn't, I truly didn't. I saved myself, as you wanted, and I was able to save Mr. Redwing, too. I don't know if you remembered about him, but if you had, then I know you would have wanted me to do my best. But there was something else, Gubnor . . . something you said just before you . . . before you cut the rope. I was so afraid, so horrified, I didn't take it in. I'm sorry. Thank you for all you did for me. I'll never forget. I don't know what will become of me now. It's going to be very difficult, but whatever happens I won't feel sorry for myself, I promise you that . . .

I must have fallen into a doze, but no more than ten minutes could have passed when the door opened and Sister Agnes came gliding in followed by a man wearing a white jacket with short sleeves, carrying a leather bag. I recognized the long, lean face, for I had glimpsed it briefly in the moments when

Father Joseph had opened the hospital door to me. Sister Agnes said, "This is Mr. Carradine, dear. He's come to have a look at you."

I said nothing. Mr. Carradine put his bag down on the locker beside the bed, took out a stethoscope, hung it around his neck, pulled down one of my lower eyelids and peered closely, then picked up my wrist in strong bony fingers, all the time talking slowly, with a strong Scottish accent and in a continuously flowing monologue, but as if speaking his thoughts aloud rather than addressing me.

"A fine hot squirmy appendix you brought me, girlie," he said with much rolling of r's. "And none too soon, either, but thank God you've opened your eyes at last for that confounded Yankee has been pestering me about you since the moment he came round, not that I blame him, mind, for how you brought him off that wee boat and across the island I'll never know, not that it would have done him much good if I'd not been here to snip that useless bit of gut out of him, I sometimes wonder what the Almighty was thinking of when he stuck that in the human body—oh, forgive me Sister Agnes, no offense intended—will you loosen the ribbon of this nightdress, please, so I can listen to the girlie's heart? Thank you. H'mm. H'mm. As I said before, she's the healthiest young animal I've ever come across. Strange body coloring for a coolie woman, wouldn't you say? She's pale as any northern European on the parts that haven't been exposed to weather, and the hair and eyes don't suggest a black or yellow parent, h'mm? I'd say some white fellow must have fathered her on a half-white woman, so the Caucasian blood is dominant, a tragedy to my way of thinking. You can fasten the nightdress again now, Sister, she's a handsome girlie, beautifully made, and with a good strong character to have saved that Yankee fellow as she did. Put her in decent clothes and maybe she could pass for a lady, yet she'll never be aught but a poor ignorant savage." The droning rise and fall of his voice ceased for a moment. He fixed me with a stern eye, then suddenly spoke directly to me and twice as loudly, almost shouting. "You feelie muchee better now?"

Oh Gubnor, how we would have laughed at that together.

I looked at Sister Agnes and said, "I neber catch what dis bockra say."

"He's asking if you feel better now, Casey."

I looked at Mr. Carradine again and nodded. "Dis woman

wanna say big t'ank-you along what you done, mister." As I spoke the door opened and a native girl in a white smock came in, carrying a tray with a small earthenware bowl and a spoon.

"Ah, the broth," said Mr. Carradine, closing his bag. "Let her have as much as she'll take, Sister, and see there's plenty of liquid for her to drink—fruit juice, water, milk, whatever she fancies. More broth this evening, and tomorrow we'll start her on solids. I'll be off now." He drew breath as if to shout at me again, then changed his mind, gave me a rather hurt look, and stalked to the door.

I had no appetite, but under Sister Agnes's coaxing I managed to finish the bowl of broth. When I was done, she sponged my face and left me to rest. That night I cried again, grieving for Daniel, but when I slept it was a good sleep and free from bad dreams. Next day I was hungry, and ate well. Sister Agnes brought me a message from Mr. Redwing, thanking me for saving his life and saying he hoped to be allowed to visit me soon. In the afternoon Mr. Carradine came to see me and told Sister Agnes that the bandages could come off my hands and shoulders next day.

I slept less easily that night, perhaps because I was well rested now. Memories of those last moments when Daniel had given up his life kept coming vividly to my mind, and when I managed to shut them out they were replaced by thoughts that frightened me. Soon the day would come when I could no longer remain at the hospital, and how I would live then I could not imagine.

Next morning, after breakfast, Sister Agnes brought me a raffia bag. In it were the clothes I had been wearing on the day of the hurricane, my shirt, cotton drawers, and short trousers, together with a small bundle wrapped in a piece of cloth.

"We've patched and mended your clothes as best we could, dear," she said apologetically, "but I'm afraid they suffered badly in all that happened."

I thanked her and unwrapped the piece of cloth. In it lay my diving knife in its sheath with the leg-straps, my diving goggles, and the washleather bag holding my charm bracelet. Until this moment I had completely forgotten thrusting the little bag in my pocket as I made preparations to hoist Mr. Redwing up from the deck of the *Casey*. I held the bracelet to my breast and wept silently for a little while, then put it away and placed everything back in the raffia bag. The thought came to me that this now contained all my worldly possessions. I caught a troubled look on Sister Agnes's face, which made me wonder if the same thought had occurred to her.

It doesn't matter, Gubnor. I'll find some way to earn my daily bread. Better this than the life I led at Diabolo Hall. Better anything than that.

Sister Agnes took the bandages off my shoulders and hands, exclaiming with delight at the way the abrasions had healed, and later I had a visit from Mother Paul, who was the reverend mother of the little convent, accompanied by Father Joseph. From them I learned that the hurricane had eventually torn down the wreckage of the *Casey* from Neptune's Fingers, which was their name for Alligator Gap. Fishermen had seen some flotsam and broken timbers from her floating off the coast there, but had not found Daniel's body. I was glad to know that he slept his long sleep in the sea, but I could not help weeping again. Reverend Mother and Father Joseph were both very kind and said prayers by my bedside, offering thanks that I had been spared and also been given strength to save the life of another.

Later Mr. Carradine called on his daily rounds, and I lay pretending not to understand one of his long monologues addressed to nobody in particular. In it he made reference to the fact that in three days' time he would be catching the monthly steamer and moving on to the hospital at St. George's, on the island of Grenada. In a way I was not sorry to hear this, for I had been troubled by the way in which he had speculated about my origins.

Toward noon I was sitting up in bed, feeling restless, and wishing I could dare to ask for a book to read, when Sister Agnes came bustling in, rather excited, and began making sure my borrowed nightdress was properly fastened at the neck. "It's Mr. Redwing, dear," she twittered. "He's just outside in a wheelchair, and Mr. Carradine has given permission for him to visit you for a little while."

I felt sudden anxiety, without quite knowing why. "Please, you tell dat Yankee-man I gon' sleep, Sister Agnes."

"Good heavens, that would be a *lie*, Casey! We can't have that."

"I neber gon' make talkee-talkee along dat bockra. I jus' coolie woman."

"Oh, you *must* see him, dear. For all our sakes. He's such a forceful gentleman, and he's wearing everybody out with demanding to see you. He's even worn Mr. Carradine out, can you imagine that? Besides, it would be so unkind if you didn't allow him to thank you. There, you look very nice, and you mustn't worry, because I'm sure he'll do all the talking."

She went gliding out, giving me no further chance to protest, and a moment later returned pushing Mr. Redwing in a wheelchair. This was the first chance I had had to see him properly. His straight black hair was rather long, and brushed back behind his ears. The stubble of beard had gone, and he was clean shaven. His cheeks were a little hollow, his eyes perhaps more sunken than was natural, but the pallor behind his tanned face had gone now, and his gaze was very clear. I was too uneasy to study him and looked down quickly, but in that brief moment of seeing him brought in I had the impression of a man who had been through a great ordeal but was now in swiftly growing health.

He said quietly, "Hallo, Casey."

I mumbled, "Mo'ning, mister."

"I'm glad to see you looking so well."

I made myself meet his gaze. He sat by my bed wearing a white cotton nightshirt of some kind, a thin blanket over his knees. When I had spoken to him briefly on the jetty at St. Anthony I had thought him to be in his early forties, but now I felt he could be no more than thirty-four or thirty-five. He had a broad face, not handsome, but with very steady eyes and a hint of impassivity that reminded me a little of Daniel. Remembering that he was American and his name was Redwing, I wondered if he might have Red Indian blood in him.

He turned his head and said, "Sister Agnes, would you be very kind and leave us alone for ten minutes? I have to thank Casey, and I'm concerned about her future, but she's kind of embarrassed at the moment, and she might find it easier to talk if we were alone."

Sister Agnes blinked. "Oh, dear. She really should be chaperoned while you are visiting her, Mr. Redwing."

He smiled. "Sister Agnes, you and your sisters have taken wonderful care of me and I love you all dearly. But if you don't allow me a private talk with Casey, I'm going to turn very awkward, very uncooperative, very troublesome—"

"Oh please, no, Mr. Redwing!"

"Sister Agnes, I'm in no condition to start any improper conduct."

"Oh, Mr. Redwing, really! You shouldn't speak so in front of her."

"Forgive me." His smile faded and his voice wavered a

little. "Then please remember that this girl deliberately staked her life to save mine. Not once but twice. First when she told Harry Leng that they must risk the hurricane, and again when the *Casey* was wrecked, and she stayed to get me off before the boat was torn down from the cliffs. I haven't cried since I was a child of five, Sister Agnes, but I feel close to it now, as a grown man, when I think what this girl dared and achieved for a total stranger. Can you really imagine I might do anything to hurt her?"

"Oh, of course not, Mr. Redwing. It's just that . . ." Sister Agnes paused and seemed to come to a decision. Looking about her conspiratorially she whispered, "Well, ten minutes then." She crossed herself, muttered something under her breath, glided to the door, and went out, closing it behind her.

I sat with my hands in my lap, looking down at them. After a moment or two Mr. Redwing said very softly, "Please trust me, Casey. You can, honey, that I promise. You need a friend now. Please let Sam Redwing be that friend."

I did not know what to say. He went on in the same soft voice, "Casey, will you please just look at me while I say what I want to say to you?"

I lifted my eyes to his and waited. He said, "I know you're frightened. I know you're not what you seem to be, and I don't figure Harry Leng was, either. I don't think you were his woman, and I've wondered if you might be his daughter, but you'd have more Oriental characteristics if you were. I'm not going to ask what secret you're hiding, or who you really are. Sure I'm curious. Anyone would be. But if you don't want to tell me, then I'll never ask. Believe me, Casey, the debt I owe you, and the respect, the admiration, and . . . yes, the affection I feel for you, are all a whole lot bigger than my curiosity."

He paused as if gathering his thoughts, and we remained looking steadily at each other. After a moment he went on, "I owe a debt to Harry Leng, too. He gave his life for me. Whatever he was to you, I think he was all you had, and I think his first concern now would be your safety, which makes it my first concern too. So here's a simple question, honey. What's the best way I can help you?"

I closed my eyes, torn by indecision. It seemed I was a poor judge of men, for I had thought Oliver Foy to be a decent and kindly man until he taught me otherwise. Could I place any trust in Mr. Redwing?

What shall I do, Gubnor? He seems to mean what he says,

but I'm such a fool. Wait, though...I've just thought of some-
thing. He tried to make me leave him when we were wrecked
in Alligator Gap. A bad man would never do a thing like that,
surely? And I'm going to be in such difficulties if I don't accept
his offer of help...

It was almost as if Mr. Redwing could follow my thoughts,
for I heard him say, "It's no gamble this time, little lady."

I opened my eyes and said in my own voice, but very quietly
so I could not be heard beyond the room, "You're very kind,
Mr. Redwing. Yes, the man you knew as Harry Leng was all
I had, but I wasn't his woman and I wasn't his daughter. I
won't tell you our real names, or why we took on new identities.
That's something I don't want anybody to discover."

He sat back in his wheelchair with a sigh of relief. "I knew
it," he said wonderingly. "I knew you were gently born. And
you're English, aren't you—No, don't answer that, I shouldn't
have asked, it just slipped out because of your accent." He
glanced at the door. "Look, we haven't many minutes left, and
there may not be another chance to talk alone, so let's get back
to the question. What's the best way I can help you?"

I spoke slowly, trying to gather my thoughts. "Well, I think
I would like to get right away from the Caribbean...and I
shall need to earn a living, but I haven't any skills to offer.
There can't be much demand for a girl who can only swim and
dive and handle a boat. Oh, I can write a legible hand, and I
suppose I could keep house quite well, because I've run a
household—" I broke off abruptly, conscious that I had given
some small clue to my past, but Mr. Redwing waved a hand
and said, "I've already forgotten it, honey. Go ahead."

"Well, do you think...would it be possible for you to find
employment for me in service, somewhere in America?"

He frowned. "Sure I could do that," he said reluctantly,
"but I don't live there myself because most of my business
interests are elsewhere, and I wouldn't be able to keep an eye
on you." His mouth tightened. "Besides, what kind of man
would I be to let the girl who hauled me out of that deathtrap
go into service?"

"But Mr. Redwing—"

"Sam. While we're alone, please make it Sam. I'm not a
man to ask favors, but I'm asking you to do me the big honor
of accepting my friendship, Casey."

My eyes filled suddenly with tears, but they were not tears
of sorrow. I said, "Thank you. I'm glad to have you for my

friend . . . Sam. But I won't let you keep me, and I don't see any alternative to my going into service to earn a living, at least to start with. I don't know what the fare to America is, but I could pay you back a little at a time—"

"Now hold it there, Casey, hold it right there," he broke in sternly. "Independence is fine, but don't let it get to be an obsession. I'm deeper in debt to you than I can ever repay, so it's unkind, honey, it's truly unkind if you turn down whatever small thing I'm able to do in return."

I put a hand to my head. "Yes. Yes, I'm sorry, Mr Redwing. I mean, Sam. I always longed to repay the man you knew as Harry Leng, but I never could."

"Right. So we won't argue about things like fares, and money to rig you out with clothes, and so on. Now let's think—" He stopped short, catching his breath and striking his brow gently with the heel of his hand. "I'm a clown!" he breathed. "Why didn't I think of it straight off? I must still be thick-headed from the chloroform." He looked at me eagerly. "Casey girl, would you be happy to go to England?"

My eyes widened. England . . . the country of my birth, and four thousand miles from Jamaica. Surely there could be no better place to hide from my past. I said, "Oh, yes! Can you really find me work there?"

"No trouble. I've been based in London for the last few years, and I know a real good employment agency." His eyes twinkled suddenly as if at some private joke. "I'll write to the lady who runs it, she's by way of being an old friend." He thought for a moment, frowning. "I hope you'll let me tell her the little I know about you myself, Casey. I mean, simply that you're an educated girl but that no questions are to be asked about your past. Can I do that?"

"Won't it . . . put her off?"

He shook his head firmly. "No. It might help her to find you a better position. After all, you can't go on pretending to be a half-caste coolie girl once you're in England."

I was feeling confused, and could not imagine what life would be like for me in England, but I had decided to put my trust in Sam Redwing and I knew his last words were true. My long masquerade was ended now, and I would have a new role to play. After barely a moment's reflection I said, "Whatever you think best for me, Sam."

"That's great." He glanced at the door again. "We'll have Sister Agnes back soon, but that doesn't matter, I can fix everything now. Just leave it to me. I'll be seeing you again, but I bet we'll be chaperoned next time, so I'll do the main talking and you do your belly-debil talk."

I blinked in surprise. "How did you know I called your appendicitis that?"

"I heard you, Casey. I heard you gasping and gabbling when they opened the hospital door to us. I never lost consciousness that day from the time the hurricane caught us till the moment they put me to sleep for the operation." His voice fell to a whisper. "I remember it all, Casey girl. I remember you hauling me up from the deck to the cliff top, and dragging the stretcher down that rocky path, hour after hour through blinding rain and hellish wind. And in all that time I knew ... I *knew* there was never a moment when you thought of leaving me." He edged his wheelchair a little nearer. "May I take your hand a moment, honey?"

I was puzzled, and felt myself flush a little, but lifted the hand nearest to him and offered it. He took it very gently in one of his own big hands and simply stared at it with a kind of wondering air for long seconds. Then he leaned forward, brushed the knuckles with his lips, and laid it carefully down on the bed. "Proud to be your friend, Casey," he said softly. "Proud to be your friend."

It was less than a minute later when Sister Agnes returned. "Well, I hope you've finished your little chat, Mr. Redwing," she said chirpily. "And I hope you'll be a better patient now you've seen for yourself that Casey is getting on so well. She'll be allowed to get up for a little while this afternoon, and in another day or so she'll be right as rain. But you must have plenty of rest yourself, Mr. Redwing, so say bye-bye to Casey, and off we go."

"Yes, Sister Agnes," he said with a meekness that made her eye him suspiciously. "Good-bye for now, Casey."

"Eat good, mister," I said. "Don't you go catchee no more debil in dat belly belong you."

He almost laughed, but managed not to, and grinned at me unseen by Sister Agnes. "I'll remember what you say, Casey girl. Believe me."

I cannot think the sisters were able to persuade Sam Redwing to rest very much that day, for by next morning a great deal had been arranged. When Sister Agnes woke me she told me with much excitement that I would be leaving on the monthly steamer in only two days' time to catch a ship from Grenada for England. One of the older nuns, Sister Clare, was being sent back to England for her health, and I was to make the journey under her care.

Mr. Carradine had declared me well enough to travel, and he would be on the steamer with us as far as Grenada, where he was to demonstrate new methods of surgery in the hospital there. Mr. Redwing, I was told, would require another week or two of convalescence before he would be fit enough to travel, and so he would be taking the next steamer from La Faucille a month later.

I was quite dazed by the suddenness of all this, but at the same time I felt relief that I should soon be far away from the Caribbean. I had known three years of peace and happiness with Daniel on the *Casey*, but there was nothing left for me here except the possible danger that some day, somewhere, I might be recognized. Afloat on the *Casey* I had been almost invisible. Few eyes had ever seen me. But the *Casey* had died with her master.

In the afternoon, dressed in my patched and darned clothes, I was allowed to visit Sam Redwing in the small room he had been given in the west wing of the little hospital. He looked tired but was in good spirits and writing busily on a pad as Sister Marie ushered me in.

His face lit up. "Casey, it's good to see you. Have they told you about going to England?"

"I catchee some t'ing Sister Agnes tol' me, mister. Gubnor teach me 'bout big island he call England wit' big white Queen. You send me dat place fo' work?"

"That's right, Casey." He glanced at Sister Marie, who had taken a chair by the window and was hemming a worn pillow-case. "You'll be going on a ship with Sister Clare to London. Reverend Mother has made arrangements for her to live in a convent there, but you'll be met off the boat by a lady who runs an employment agency in a place called Blackheath, near Greenwich, quite close to where your ship will dock." He flickered an eyelid at me. "Do you understand what I've just said?"

I nodded. "Some word dis woman no' savvy, but me catch good 'nuff, mister."

"I'm sure your English will improve if you practice talking with Sister Clare during the voyage. Now, the lady in Black-heath will take charge of you and find work for you in the kitchen of a big house. A kitchen—like the galley on the *Casey*, where you cook things, but much bigger."

"Yes, mister."

Sister Marie glanced up from her needlework. "I think she's really a very intelligent child, Mr. Redwing," she said. "Given time to settle down and pick up the language, she might easily rise to be a parlor maid, or even a lady's maid."

"I'm inclined to agree, Sister," he said solemnly. "Now, what about clothes? She must have a reasonable wardrobe, and she'll need all sorts of bits and pieces—brush, comb, handkerchiefs, handbag, toiletries, it's quite a long list."

Sister Marie said patiently, "Will you please stop fretting, Mr. Redwing? Father Joseph's flock in Tavistock includes over ten white families, and there are just as many in Mr. Fenshaw's flock of Methodists. Casey's exploit has made her quite famous here, and we've been assured she will have plenty of discarded clothes to choose from, as well as all the little accessories she'll need as a young woman instead of a . . ." she glanced at me over the top of her spectacles as if trying to find the right word. "Instead of a sailor-girl."

"Well, that's fine. I'll write a letter of thanks to both gentlemen to read out to their congregations. But do remember, if money's needed there's plenty available."

"You've told me that three times, Mr. Redwing."

He grinned. "I like to make sure." Turning to me again he tapped the pen on his pad. "This is a letter to the lady who will meet you, Casey. I've asked Mr. Carradine to see that it catches the Royal Mail steamer from Grenada, so it will get to England well before you do. Your ship is slower and calls at St. Lucia and Le Havre on the way to London."

I wondered how Sam Redwing had been able to obtain money here on La Faucille, but did not think this was the kind of question a coolie girl would ask. It was not until later, when Mr. Carradine was talking with Sister Agnes in my room on his evening rounds, that I learned the answer. It appeared that when we took Sam Redwing aboard at St. Anthony he had been wearing a waterproof money belt around his waist next to the skin. It held a few sovereigns, but it also held a letter of credit from the Westminster Bank in London to the value of one thousand pounds. This was good almost anywhere in the world, and certainly in a British colony, so he had spoken the simple truth in saying there was no lack of money.

I saw my new friend twice more before leaving La Faucille,

and each time Sister Marie was with us, so we could not speak freely. The first of these meetings came next day, and I felt very strange because I was wearing shoes and stockings, underwear, and a dress. It was hard to believe I had ever worn such clothes without discomfort. Later, on the steamer, I was to be in trouble with Sister Clare when I unwisely let slip that I had stopped wearing the drawers provided. After her shocked reprimand I promised to wear them in the future, and did so, but I cut off most of each leg so that they were like the short drawers I had worn on the *Casey*.

The dress in which I was presented to Sam Redwing for approval was the best of three I had been given, but it was still a rather poor fit. I suppose Emma Delaney would also have thought it dowdy and unfashionable, but I was no longer Emma Delaney. I was a coolie girl being taken to England to go into service there, and as such I was dressed better than I had any right to expect. Sam Redwing looked me up and down. I saw his lips tighten, and for a moment I feared he was going to speak angrily to Sister Marie. Then he seemed to think better of it and said without enthusiasm, "Thank you, Sister. I guess it'll take a little while for Casey to get used to female clothes."

"Oh, she'll soon settle into them, Mr. Redwing, I'm sure. And she'll look much nicer when she's allowed her hair to grow long, of course."

"She'll always look like a million dollars to me, Sister."

"I beg your pardon?"

"Just an American expression. Does she have everything else she needs?"

"Oh yes, I'll show you the list later, Mr. Redwing."

"Thank you, Sister. By the way, I want her to have a purse with some money in it."

"Oh, but Sister Clare will have charge of whatever funds are needed. I don't suppose Casey would quite understand how to use money."

"I think she would. Harry Leng was a trader. In any event, I can't have her leave here penniless, even with Sister Clare to look after her, so we'll make sure she has a sovereign or two in her purse, please."

Sister Marie sighed resignedly. "Very well, Mr. Redwing."

He looked at me, and I saw a touch of laughter in his eyes. "Another thing. She needs a surname. She can't go to England simply as Casey."

Sister Marie said, "We thought her name should be Casey Leng."

I started to shake my head. Harry Leng had never existed, and I did not want to carry that name. I would have been proud to carry Daniel's true name, but this was impossible. All I could take with me was the name he had given me at the beginning of my new life, Casey. It was as if Sam Redwing sensed my feeling, for I had barely shaken my head when he said, "Casey Leng? Oh, surely not, Sister. Since the relationship was without benefit of clergy, it would hardly be proper for Casey to assume the name of Leng, as if he had been her husband."

Sister Marie looked startled. "Oh dear, we hadn't thought of that. Perhaps I had better discuss it with Reverend Mother and Father Joseph."

"No need," said Sam Redwing with a smile. "I've chosen a name for her. If she's to work in England, then what she needs is a nice, simple, anonymous sort of name. Like Brown. Casey Brown is a splendid name."

"Well . . . if you say so, Mr. Redwing."

"I do, Sister. It's a fine Anglo-Saxon name."

"Really? I think Brown is quite nice, but I've always felt that Casey was a rather unusual name for a girl."

"She's an unusual person," Sam Redwing said simply, then looked at me. "Have you understood what I've said about your name, Casey?"

I nodded. "I catch dat name good, mister. Plenty English feller dey callum Brown."

"That's settled then." He waited until Sister Marie turned to open the door, then quickly winked at me.

I saw him briefly again the next day, half an hour before I was due to leave the hospital with Sister Clare and Mr. Carradine for the steamer, which had tied up at the jetty that morning. With Sister Marie present, I started to thank him in my clumsy creole phrasing for his kindness to me, but he stopped me with a quick gesture. "It's nothing, Casey. Nothing compared with what you did for me. Now, enjoy the trip and try not to worry about anything. The lady from the Blackheath Domestic Agency will meet you and Sister Clare when you dock, and she'll take care of you from then on. I shall be coming to England myself as soon as I can manage it, so I'll look you up. I mean, I'll come and see you wherever it is that you find a position in service. You understand?"

"I catch all dat t'ing you say, mister. Dis woman hopin' you gon' feel everyway better soon."

"I'll be fine." He put out his hand, and I moved to take it. The charm bracelet I had put on my wrist jingled faintly. The only other possessions that remained from my three years as a sea gypsy were now packed in the well-worn suitcase I had been given—my diving goggles and sheath knife, a shirt, short trousers, and cotton drawers.

Sam Redwing looked up from the bracelet and said, "From Gubnor?"

I nodded, my throat closing suddenly so that I could not speak. He seemed to decide against another question, and held my hand firmly for a few moments, looking into my eyes. Then he said, "Good-bye. And thanks again, Casey girl."

Twenty minutes later I boarded the boat on which I was to begin my journey to a far country and a strange new life. I expected it to be the hard life of a girl in service, and was determined that in time I would find ways to better myself. I did not know that Mr. Sam Redwing had his own plans for me, or that Fate was already weaving a startling pattern with threads from my past.

10

I CANNOT PRETEND THAT I ENJOYED THE VOYAGE TO ENGLAND, for I had too much time to think. During the short journey on the small island steamer to Grenada the sea was unusually rough. This did not trouble me, but both Sister Clare and Mr. Carradine were confined to their cabins by sea sickness, as were most of the twenty-odd passengers aboard. I spent the greater part of each day sitting on deck, wishing I had something to do. I had not fully realized till now how constantly busy we had been on the *Casey*, and it seemed unnatural to be making no decisions and exercising no control over the craft that carried me.

On reaching Grenada we left the steamer, Mr. Carradine to go to the hospital at St. George's while Sister Clare and I stayed at a convent for two days until the time came to board a larger steamer called the *Avon*, a cargo ship that also carried passengers, plying between London and the West Indies. Sister Clare and I had a small cabin with a dividing curtain. In the dining room we shared a table with two business gentlemen. They seemed to be uneasy in the presence of a nun, and were certainly put out to find themselves at table with a half-native girl from the islands, though they did not complain in front of Sister Clare.

It soon became known that the brown-faced girl in the ill-fitting clothes was a coolie girl being taken to England to go into service there, and this ensured that none of the passengers attempted to pass the time of day with me. Sister Clare was kindly toward me, but for most of the time was rather distrait because she lived in constant fear of the ship going down. I felt very sorry for her.

Every morning and evening I had to pray with her in the cabin for half an hour. This was silent prayer, and I found it difficult to fill the time. After thanking God for blessings received I would ask forgiveness for my sins. This was a subject in which I could rarely be specific, and I tended rather apologetically to leave it for God to decide what I had done wrong. Then I would pray for Daniel's soul, for my Aunt Maude and Uncle Henry, for Sam Redwing, and for the sisters at the hospital on La Faucille, not forgetting Sister Clare. This would take no more than five minutes, and to pray for the poor and distressed everywhere did not greatly extend that time. I could never bring myself to believe that God would be impressed by repetition, and when I could think of no more to say I would apologize and simply recall happy moments from the past as I knelt by my bunk with hands clasped and eyes closed.

Sister Clare slept a great deal when we were neither eating nor praying, so I was often alone. This gave me too much time in which to grieve for Daniel and to worry about what would happen to me in England.

I'm sorry, Gubnor. I know you would just want me to remember you with love, and not keep weeping in my heart. It would be easier if I had something to do, or even somebody to talk to, but until I'm in England I daren't let it be known that I can speak anything but creole. So I can't get into conversation, even if anyone was willing to talk to a coolie girl. Perhaps I could tell Sister Clare that you started teaching me to read and that it would help me just to look at a book and pick out letters and words. They have a small library on board . . .

I had seen *Oliver Twist* in the library and hoped Sister Clare might give me something of this sort. Then I could find some out-of-the-way corner in which to read secretly while pretending just to turn the pages. I suppose it was only natural for her to pick out a children's book consisting of one very short story, printed in very big type and illustrated with line drawings. It was about a small girl who kept forgetting to say her prayers, until one day her pet rabbit, of which she was extremely fond, escaped from its hutch and ran away. Distraught, she prayed fervently for it to come back safely, which it duly did that same night, and thereafter she never forgot to say her prayers. I did not find it an engrossing story.

As the *Avon* made her way across the Atlantic our course took us steadily into more northern waters. We crossed the twentieth, thirtieth, and fortieth parallels, and the weather grew cooler. I was not troubled by a cold wind and gray skies. Even in the Caribbean there had been many a night when Daniel and I had worked our little ship while soaked in spray and with a strong wind to chill us, so I was well inured to the vagaries of weather.

What troubled me now was apprehension. Had I been a fool to trust Sam Redwing? How would I fare in England? Was there really a lady who ran a domestic agency and who would find work for me? All that had happened in recent days seemed suddenly remote and unreal to me, and I felt very much alone. Sister Clare was small comfort when I asked the name of the lady who would take charge of me when the ship docked.

"Her name, dear? Well, now that you mention it, I don't think Mr. Redwing told me her name. No wait, yes he did. It was Liza... Liza something. But she will have received his letter, and he said she would meet us when we disembark at the Royal Albert Dock, so there's nothing to worry about." She blinked. "Well, I *suppose* there's nothing to worry about, but I don't quite know what we shall do if the lady isn't there. Oh dear, you've quite upset me, Casey. Two sisters will be there to take me to the convent in Ealing, but we shall be all at sea if Mr. Redwing's lady isn't there to take charge of you."

I said in the semipidgin speech I had allowed to improve a little during the voyage, "Mr. Redwing, he tol' me dat lady got workplace she call Black-heat' Do-messic Agent."

"Ah, the Blackheath Domestic Agency? Yes, I believe he did mention that name, so perhaps we can find it if the worst comes to the worst, but I think we must both pray hard that the lady will be there, Casey. And please practice your pronunciation, dear. Say *that*, not dat. Tongue between teeth. Let's try it together. *That*. Again. *That*. Very good."

Seventeen days after leaving Grenada the *Avon* sailed through the Strait of Dover and rounded the Isle of Thanet to come into the Thames Estuary soon after dawn. I was on deck at that hour, as usual—a habit from my years on the *Casey*—and I had been watching our progress on the big map beside the purser's office ever since we had sighted Lizard Point the day before.

I remembered hardly anything of England from my childhood, yet oddly enough the sights I saw as we moved up the river seemed in no way strange to me. It was as if my blood carried a kind of memory in it. There was little beauty to be seen in these lower reaches of the great river as we approached London. Factory chimneys belched smoke. A mist hung over the marshes at Halfway Reach. Huddled houses beyond the muddy banks were dark with city grime. Small boats, steamers, barges, and craft of every kind moved busily about the gray waters, and not one I saw was as trim, as clean, or as freshly painted as we had always kept the *Casey*. Yet I sensed that for all the squalor of these poor areas on the eastern side of London, here was a city with a warm heart.

My own heart lifted a little with sudden hope. Life in service would surely be hard, but in time I would work my way to something better. A month ago I had lost everything—my friend, my home, my way of life. Mingled with my grief had been the dread that without the *Casey* on which to hide myself away there was a far greater chance that someday, somewhere, I might be recognized as Emma Delaney, who had become Mistress Emma Foy. This was a huge fear, but now it had been taken from me. I was four thousand miles from Jamaica and from all who had known me in the dreadful days when I had been the wife of Oliver Foy.

As I stood at the rail and watched our approach to the Royal Albert Dock I felt I had much to be thankful for. Then I looked down at the water and my blood chilled suddenly as a floating piece of cordage caught my eye. For a moment I could not understand what had happened to me, then memory seemed to explode painfully in my head.

A dream . . . a nightmare I had suffered two nights before, broke through the merciful veil of oblivion and was with me again in all its horror. I could not imagine now why it had not woken me that night, or why I had not remembered it vividly next morning. Perhaps my inner self had tried to protect me by hiding it from me, but the sight of that floating rope had been too powerful a reminder.

In my dream I had been swimming underwater with my spear, seeking a fish for supper. Then Daniel had appeared, swimming toward me. He was wearing his goggles and his face was quite normal, but all the rest of his body was a skeleton, with the severed lifeline trailing from his waist.

I was almost out of my mind with horror and wanted to flee, but could not because this was Daniel and he was calling to me urgently. In my dream I did not seem to realize that it was impossible for him to speak underwater. I heard his voice, but his words were unclear. Whatever he was saying he seemed to repeat it, as if trying to be sure I understood, and all the time the skeleton body was coming closer and closer to me.

I suppose the nightmare must have ended in the way most dreams do, by fading away or being replaced by another dream. In the morning I had felt low and troubled, but all recollection of the horrible dream had vanished till now. I clutched the rail, and a memory came flooding into my mind. I recalled the moments when Daniel had hung at the end of the lifeline that pinned me helplessly to the *Casey*'s broken deck. Through the beating of rain and the howl of wind, even as he made ready to give up his life, he had called to me in a strangely emphatic way. I had heard the words, but they had not registered on my reeling mind, for I had been shattered by horror.

Now my forehead was damp with perspiration and my teeth were chattering as, with a great effort, I thrust away the recollection of both dream and reality, unable to bear such memories. A hand plucked at my arm and Sister Clare was beside me, her face pale and anxious. "Why, there you are, Casey, I've been looking everywhere for you, child! We shall be getting off soon, so we must make sure we've packed everything."

We had combed our little cabin and ticked off lists of our few possessions twice already since morning, but poor Sister Clare was still fearful that we might forget something. I managed to smile at her and said, "Belong what name you t'ink we neber pack everyt'ing, Sister Clare? We neber forget nothin'."

"We did not forget *anything*, dear," she corrected, then peered at me. "Are you all right, Casey? Goodness, you do look peaky. I expect it's the excitement. Come down to the cabin and we'll say a last prayer that Mr. Redwing's lady is there to meet us. Oh, and the sisters from Ealing, too. I hadn't thought of that before, but we really should have put them in our prayers. Come along, dear, there's just time if we hurry."

A porter with a trolley led the way from the Customs shed, trundling our two suitcases and Sister Clare's trunk. It was a

day in mid October, with thin white clouds half veiling a watery
sun, but I did not feel cold, I was in a fever of nervousness.
Other passengers from the *Avon* were being greeted by friends
or relations who had come to meet the boat.

Our porter said, "Cab or tender, ladies?"

Sister Clare clutched my arm, looking about us frantically.
"Oh dear, I'm not sure. We are to be met here, you see, but
—ah, there they are!" She almost squeaked with joy as two
nuns came fluttering toward us, and next moment they were
introducing themselves to Sister Clare and welcoming her to
England.

I hung back a little, gazing slowly around, then found my
eyes held by a lady who stood by a carriage some twenty paces
away. She was rather plump, with a round pretty face, hair the
color of dark honey, and large blue eyes, which looked out
from under the wide brim of an elegant velvet hat with ostrich
feathers. I judged her to be in her late twenties. She wore a
mulberry red jacket and a black skirt, from beneath which
peeped black kid shoes with a three-button strap. She was no
taller than I, yet despite this and her more rounded figure she
gave an impression of cool elegance as she stood with one hand
resting on the handle of a long-stemmed umbrella, looking
toward me.

I realized I was staring rudely and was about to look away
when to my utter astonishment the lady slowly and deliberately
closed one eye, opened it, then came sweeping toward us.
Again I felt bewilderment, for both in manner and expression
she exuded a haughtiness in total contrast to the long wink she
had given me. "Sister Clare?" she said on a rising note as she
drew near, ignoring me completely now and addressing my
companion.

Sister Clare turned and gave a gasp of relief. "Ah, you must
surely be Miss—ah—Mrs.—ah—Liza . . . the lady to whom
Mr. Redwing wrote concerning Casey?"

"I am Liza Faith," came the reply in condescending manner.
"Miss Liza Faith, principal of the Blackheath Domestic Agency.
Yes indeed, it was to me that Mr. Redwing wrote regarding a
young person seeking a position in service here." I had rarely
heard such a beautiful speaking voice in a woman, but her
manner as she took a lorgnette from her handbag to look me
up and down was dauntingly lofty. For the first time I felt
aware of the unattractive figure I must cut with my half-grown

hair, my brown face, and my ill-fitting clothes. As befitted my position, I dropped my eyes and made a small curtsy.

The lady said, "This is she?"

Sister Clare said eagerly, "Yes, Miss Faith, this is Casey Brown, and a very good girl she is, I assure you. I understood from Mr. Redwing that you would be taking charge of her now."

"Quite so," said Miss Faith in the same cold yet musical voice. "She may share a bed with my kitchen maid until I have found a position for her. I am sure Mr. Redwing would wish me to thank you for escorting the child to England. Where is her luggage, pray? That suitcase? Nothing more? Then I'll wish you and your friends good morning, Sister Clare. Porter! Porter! The small suitcase, if you please. Take it to my carriage over there, the town and country carriage with the yellow stripe along the side." She waved a languid hand at me. "Say good-bye to Sister Clare, girl."

I muttered, "Yes, madam," and turned to Sister Clare. "Bye, sister. I sayin' big t'ank-you."

She kissed me on the cheek. "Good-bye, dear. And practice hard with your pronunciation."

Miss Faith said, "Quite so. Now follow me, Casey." She turned and moved after the porter, gracious and unhurried, using her tall umbrella like a staff of office.

I said, "Very good, madam," and followed a pace or two behind.

A coachman opened the carriage door, took my shabby case from the porter, and slid it under a seat. Miss Faith mounted the step nimbly enough and gestured for me to enter and sit facing her. The door closed. She sat with head bowed a little, the brim of the hat almost hiding her face, hands resting on the carved ivory handle of the umbrella. A few moments later the carriage moved off, rattling over the dockside cobbles.

I found my hands were clenched tightly in my lap, and made a great effort to unclench them. My head buzzed with random and apprehensive thoughts. Would this cold and disdainful lady really find work for me? How long would it take? Would she provide for me in the meantime? What would the kitchen maid be like—the one whose bed I was to share?

We turned into a broad busy road, and as Miss Faith lifted her head to reveal her face I saw another woman entirely. Her lips were parted in a smile, the blue eyes were full of mischief, and her whole appearance was as warm now as it had been chilly before. Even as I stared she tossed her umbrella aside and leaned forward.

"Was I convincing, Casey dear?" she said with bubbling enthusiasm. "Sam said in his letter that I *must* support your pretense of being a coolie girl until we were well away from the nuns. Wasn't I simply *horrible*? But you did understand, didn't you? That wink was to let you know." She gave a splutter of laughter. "How did you like the lorgnette? Wasn't that a splendid idea? I shall act out the scene again for Sam when he comes home." Her smile vanished suddenly, her lips trembled, and her eyes filled with tears. "He's quite out of danger, isn't he, Casey? There's no doubt he will recover?"

I was utterly confused, and for the moment could only answer this strange lady's last question. "Why . . . yes. Mr. Redwing was making good progress when I left."

"Thank God for that, though it's better than the wretched man deserves, rushing about the world on harum-scarum ventures." She gave a sigh of relief, then smiled her warm and friendly smile once more.

I said uncertainly, "Excuse me, madam, I wonder if I might ask—"

"*Don't* call me 'madam,' for heaven's sake, dear. My name is Liza."

"But . . . you are the lady from the Blackheath Domestic Agency?"

"Yes, of course."

"Well, I understood that you might find a place for me in service—"

She leaned back, and her laughter was as musical as her lovely voice. "Oh, pish and tush! Sam never had the slightest intention of seeing you go into service."

My head was swimming. I said, "I'm sorry, I don't understand."

She leaned forward again and took my hands in hers. "Of course you don't," she said gently. "So now I shall explain. Sam Redwing and I grew up together. Our families were close friends. He was six when I was born, so I have known him all my life. He is as precious to me as my brother," she said, her eyes twinkling ruefully, "and equally irritating. Well, a week ago I had a long letter from him. It had come on the mail boat from Grenada and was *pages* long. In it he described all that happened from the time he was taken ill on St. Anthony."

The carriage lurched as we swung round a corner, but Liza

Faith only held my hands more tightly. "I must have read his letter twenty times," she said, her voice shaking a little, "and I have lived through the ordeal with him in my imagination. Dearest Casey, you lost your good friend and almost lost your own life in saving Sam Redwing. For that you will always have my friendship and devotion, if you will accept them."

I sat gazing stupidly into that pretty round face, fragments of thought spinning about my mind like leaves in a whirlwind. Many times during the voyage I had speculated apprehensively on what my lot would be when I arrived in England, but I had never dreamed of being made welcome, much less of a welcome such as this. I found that tears were running down my cheeks, and although I tried several times to speak, the words remained trapped in my throat.

I closed my eyes and, as if from a distance, heard Liza Faith's voice. "Oh, you poor dear, what you must have gone through. But all's well now, I promise." I felt her move to sit beside me, then her arm was about me as she drew my head down to rest on her shoulder. "There, now. Don't try to speak yet, Casey, just have a nice little cry and you'll feel better soon. Here's a handkerchief."

It was like being a child again, with May Choong holding and comforting me. I found that to lay down my fears and burdens for a while, and give myself up to that comfort, was a relief beyond measure. Liza Faith chatted on, gently patting my shoulder. "Oh, just wait till I see that stupid man. How could he send you here in those awful clothes? Still, I suppose you had to keep up the pretense of being a coolie girl. Oh, now listen, Casey dear. I'm wildly curious, of course, any woman would be, but I promise there will be no questions about you. Sam made that very clear. You're our friend Casey Brown, and if anybody wants to know where you come from, just refer them to me and they'll be sharply told to mind their own business. Ah, we're just going into Blackwall Tunnel now, dear, so it's no use my talking for a while . . ."

Her voice was lost as the sound of wheels on cobbles echoed and re-echoed about us. With my head pillowed on that soft shoulder, and with long apprehension swept suddenly away by relief, I could easily have fallen asleep at that moment, but I made myself open my eyes. We were in a lamplit tunnel, filled with the noise of our own and other carriages. It was a long tunnel, and I discovered later that it ran under the River Thames to Greenwich. After two or three minutes I made a great effort to pull myself together and sat up, drying my eyes and clutching Liza Faith's gloved hand.

The tunnel ended, and we came up a slope into feeble sunshine once more. My companion said, "We'll soon be home now, dear. Are you feeling a little better?"

I turned to smile at her. "Yes, very much so. I was only weeping from relief. I can't thank you enough for the kindness of your welcome."

"Oh, pish and tush. I've been looking forward to this ever since I got Sam's letter. It's my most exciting moment for years."

"Please forgive me if I seem stupid, but I'm still confused, Miss—I mean, Liza. Did you really mean you wish me to call you that?"

"Of course, dear. Whyever not?"

"Well, I . . . I don't quite know what is to happen now. I expected to go into service somewhere. That's what Sam —Mr. Redwing said."

"Please call him Sam. He only said that for the benefit of the nuns, Casey. He was helping to maintain your coolie-girl identity."

"But I have to find work of some kind. I've nowhere to live, and nothing except my few belongings and two sovereigns he insisted on giving me before I left."

"You have a home," Liza Faith said simply. "My brother and I occupy a house by Greenwich Park, and when Sam is in England he lives with us. There's plenty of room for you, Casey. I've had a nice little bedroom made ready."

For a moment I could not speak. Then: "Oh, but you can't take me into your home like that! I'm a stranger to you, and you don't know about me, I mean about my past, and—"

"Casey, you gave Sam Redwing his life. That is all I need to know." She looked at me with grave blue eyes, then her face was suddenly lit by laughter again. "Oh yes, Sam said in his letter that you were a very independent person, but you need not feel we're offering charity. You see, my brother has his own affairs to attend to, and I have my domestic agency to run. We have no staff living in, just two daily maids who divide the day between them, and a woman three mornings a week for rough cleaning. This means I have to keep house and cook, which takes time I can ill afford, and to tell the truth I'm really not very good at it."

My heart lifted. I could scarcely believe my wonderful good

fortune. "Do you mean I could come to you as cook-house-keeper?"

"Well yes, but not as staff. You could be one of the family and help me run the agency, and I would so love to have a friend."

I looked at her wonderingly. "Surely you have many friends?"

She laughed, but without rancor. "Oh, far from it, my dear. For a lady to run a domestic agency is almost like her being in trade, so other ladies are a little chary of befriending her. Besides, my brother's profession is one that raises eyebrows rather than wins friends, and we tend to be regarded as somewhat Bohemian. Will you come and live with us as my friend and companion, to keep house and cook, and to help at the agency if you have time? There will be a salary, of course, so you will have money of your own, but I'm afraid it will be quite small, because for various reasons we live rather frugally."

She stopped to draw breath, and smiled at me hopefully. The carriage was climbing a steep hill now, and as I looked out of the window I could see in the distance, several miles away to the west, a great dome that could only be the cathedral of St. Paul's. I felt weightless, as if I were drifting below the surface of a sunlit sea. Turning to look into Liza Faith's warm blue eyes I said, "Did Sam Redwing ask you to do this for me?"

She shook her head. "He told me all that had happened, and simply asked me to take good care of you until he returned."

"Surely that was asking a great deal of you?"

"My sweet, a man with whom you have spent your childhood, be he friend or brother, will make the most outrageous demands on you as a matter of course. But in this instance I'm most grateful to him, or rather I shall be if you accept."

"Oh, dear. I can scarcely believe I'm not dreaming. And I'm a little afraid. When did you decide to offer me a home, Liza?"

"I've thought about it ever since Sam's letter arrived, but I didn't decide until . . . oh, at least twenty seconds after I'd seen you there on the dockside."

"That was . . . very impulsive."

"I know, dear, but I have an excellent instinct. If you're worried on my account we can agree that this is a trial period until Sam comes home."

"Yes, I would want you to feel free to change your mind.

There's something I should tell you, though. I learned some plain cooking when I was younger, and I've cooked for two in the galley of the little boat I lived on for several years, but I'm a very ordinary cook."

"That's splendid, because I'm a bad one. I'm sure my brother and Sam will be delighted. Well, what do you say, Casey? Will you come and share our home as a friend?"

I closed my eyes for a moment and let out a long slow sigh as I allowed myself to believe at last that all this was truly happening. "Yes," I said, "oh, yes please. I can think of nothing else in the world I would rather do."

The house lay within a stone's throw of Blackheath and on the west side of what I later learned was Greenwich Park. It was called Heathside, and stood three stories high, with a large basement kitchen and a small walled garden.

As soon as we arrived Liza introduced me to a maid called Amy. She was young, with an impudent face, and from the way she eyed me as she took my shabby suitcase I realized I would quickly have to establish my authority with her if I was to be a satisfactory housekeeper. This did not trouble me. I was poorly dressed and had the look of a gypsy girl, but I had not been Mistress Emma Foy with a small army of servants for nothing.

"Just put the case in Miss Brown's room, Amy," said my companion. "She will unpack it herself." Then to me, but for Amy's benefit: "My dear, I do think they might have found better clothes for you after you had lost all your belongings in the shipwreck, but never mind. We will arrange a complete wardrobe for you without delay."

Amy blinked and looked at me more carefully before turning away with the case. Liza murmured, "It's true about the wardrobe. I have orders from Sam to fit you out with whatever clothes you need, and at his expense. No argument, Casey dear. Even in strictly material terms you risked and lost a valuable boat to save him. Now, shall I show you round the house first, or would you prefer to rest?"

I shook my head, aware that I was constantly smiling from the happiness that now spread through my whole being. "I'm not tired," I said. "Not a bit tired."

"Splendid. Come along then. I've told my clerk to take charge at the agency for the whole day, so you and I can spend it together. This is the dining room, it's small but quite pleasant.

Later today we'll take a boat up the river to Charing Cross, then a cab to Oxford Street to do some shopping. You'll need shoes and underclothes, of course, and one or two ready-made dresses and a suit to see you through until my dressmaker can run up some nice things for you. Now here is the sitting room, it looks out onto the garden, you see..."

My new friend chattered on happily as she took me round the house, and I found myself responding in a way that surprised me. Vaguely it occurred to me that I had not talked with another woman for over three years, and perhaps a hidden need was now emerging in the presence of this warmhearted and generous lady.

By the standards of Diabolo Hall the house was tiny, but by the standards of the *Casey* it was huge. I found myself attracted to it at first sight. The kitchen was sensibly equipped and laid out, and I felt I could manage well enough there, particularly when I had time for a little practice with a cookery book at my elbow.

The small walled garden was delightful, and Liza told me she took care of this herself with occasional help from a boy who came in to do any digging or heavy work required. On the first landing were three rooms and a combined bathroom and water closet. One room was an office or study, the other two were bedrooms for Liza's brother and for Sam Redwing whenever he was in England, which generally amounted to six or seven months in each year. The next floor had a similar arrangement of rooms, including, to my surprise, another bathroom and water closet.

"We had it put in soon after we came to the house ten years ago," said Liza. "To share a bathroom with men, unless one is married to at least one of them, is irritating beyond measure. The small room here is my office and sewing room, though heaven knows I do little enough sewing. This is my bedroom beside it. I have to climb an extra flight of stairs, but it's much better to be up here without the clatter of men rushing about past your door at all hours. Besides, there is a much better view."

It was true. From the window I could see again the distant dome of St. Paul's, also the famous twin towers of Tower Bridge, together with a silhouette of much of the great city of London. Liza's bedroom was as pretty and as unaffected as she was herself. Across the landing was a spare bedroom, simply but pleasantly furnished, and this was to be mine. My suitcase stood beside the dressing table, where Amy had placed it.

Liza said, "I do hope you'll be comfortable, Casey." I looked about the room, then out of the window toward the river, and my heart sang.

Oh Gubnor, whoever could have dreamed I would be so lucky? I've just realized this lady is so much like your dear May, a happy person with a warm heart. Now I can start a new life here without fear of anyone ever discovering who I used to be, and not as a scullery maid but as a family friend . . .

I said, "One day you must ask Sam to describe the cabin on the *Casey*. Then you'll know just how comfortable I shall be in this beautiful bedroom, Liza."

"Good. Now take your hat off and let me look at you. H'mm. Yes. Given a few weeks for your hair to grow and for that gypsy brown face to fade to its natural color, you'll be quite a beauty. It's really most unfair on an old maid like me, but never mind. I'm past hope myself, so I shall enjoy seeing men making eyes at you."

"Oh, no!" I said quickly. "No . . . I—I don't want anything like that."

She looked at me curiously for a moment, and seemed about to ask a question, then changed her mind and patted my cheek gently. "All right, my sweet. If you want men kept at a distance, leave it to Liza. Now, suppose you take half an hour to settle in, wash your hands and face, and tidy yourself? Then we'll drive down to the pier in the gig. Oh, by the way, that town and country carriage isn't ours, I hired it today, just to impress your Sister Clare. Are you sure you won't be too tired for a trip to town?"

I thought of the thousands of hours I had stood watch on the *Casey* by day and by night; of wrestling with wet canvas in a fierce wind; of loading or unloading up to two tons of cargo; and of all the small struggles I had known that made up one great battle for survival. "No, Liza," I said, and smiled. "I'm sure I won't be too tired."

"Very well, dear. I think you'll find all you need in the bathroom. Just call me if there's anything else you want. Oh, and there's hot water in the tap. We have a boiler in the basement to give a constant supply."

She left me then, and I went to the bathroom to wash and tidy myself. I had no better dress to put on, so I unpacked and put my few belongings away in the wardrobe and chest of drawers, then stood by the window, gazing out with dreamy contentment. After a little while I thought I would tap on Liza's door to let her know I was ready to go. It was as I crossed the landing that I heard a door open and close on the floor below. I assumed it was Amy, and was startled when a man's voice called up the stairs, "Liza, are you there? Why are you at home today?"

There was something about the voice that made my nerves twitch with alarm, yet it was an amiable voice with no hint of bad temper. I realized the man could only be Liza's brother, who must have been in his bedroom when we paused briefly on that floor. For a moment I hesitated, embarrassed, then moved to stand at the head of the stairs, looking down. There was a window behind me, across the landing, so I could have been little more than a silhouette to the man below. He stood with a foot on the first stair, looking up, and as I saw his face the floor seemed to lurch beneath me like the deck of the *Casey* in a high sea.

Time spun backward, and I was Emma Delaney again, riding through Fern Gully beside a man who was my friend's enemy, a man with smoky gray eyes, a thin white scar across his right temple, and a right eyelid that drooped so that the eye was half closed.

11

CHAD LOCKHART SAID, "GOOD LORD, I FORGOT. LIZA WAS meeting the *Avon* today. You must be Sam Redwing's mystery girl, Casey Brown."

My throat was like sand and seemed to have shriveled so I could barely breathe. It was impossible to speak. My head whirled and I remembered how Chad Lockhart had spoken of being a favorite victim of an often malicious Fate. Today, surely, I was the victim. I was three years and four thousand miles from Fern Gully now, yet Fate had brought me into the home of the only soul in England who could recognize me. A moment ago I had been unbelievably happy. Now, in seconds, despair had torn that happiness to shreds.

Chad Lockhart was mounting the stairs. "Good morning," he said. "Or is it just afternoon? I'm Chad Lockhart, Liza's brother. I've read Sam's letter, of course, and I really don't know how to thank you for what you did."

He was nearing the top of the stairs now, and I stepped back a pace or two. I had changed since our encounter in Jamaica, my hair was short and my face tanned by sun and weather, but I knew with weary resignation that he could scarcely fail to recognize me as Emma Delaney, if not at once, then within a matter of minutes. "Welcome to England," he said with the pleasant smile I well remembered. "I do hope you will be—" He broke off, tilting his head to one side with a mildly baffled air as he studied me. In my despair I felt my too-heavy brows come together, and knew they would twist in the comical way I had ceased to worry about for the past three years. No doubt it was this quirk of expression that made recognition almost immediate.

He caught his breath and his eyes widened for a moment. "Good God," he said softly, "it's Emma Delaney. No, Emma Foy."

The door of Liza's bedroom opened and I heard her come out, but I was still looking into Chad Lockhart's eyes and finding a quick wariness there. Liza said, "Chad, you're quite outrageous. Normally you sleep till well past noon, and I was going to introduce you to Casey after we'd bought her some decent clothes, but here you are bouncing around before you're wanted. I really don't know how I put up with you. Now let me introduce you. Casey dear, this is my brother Chad, and you might as well know at once that he's a professional gambler, but don't worry, he's not at all dangerous. Chad, this is Casey Brown from nowhere, and I don't need to tell you what we owe her."

"Indeed not," he said slowly, and put out his hand. "Welcome to our home, Casey."

As if in a dream I took his hand, released it, and said in a wavering voice, "Thank you, Mr. Lockhart...I thought your...your sister, Liza, mentioned a different name...Liza Faith."

"Oh, Faith is her other name," he said vaguely, as if his thoughts were very much elsewhere.

"He means it's another Christian name," said Liza, buttoning the jacket of a less impressive suit she had changed into. "Liza Faith Lockhart, and I use Liza Faith professionally as principal of my domestic agency. It has such a nice reliable sound to it. Good heavens, Casey, is something wrong? You look so drawn and shaken." She came to put an arm round me and stared indignantly at her brother. "What have you been saying to her?"

Chad Lockhart pursed his lips and touched the scar above his temple. "Nothing to give offense, I assure you, Liza."

"Now you're being sly! I can always tell when you touch your forehead like that." She turned her head to give me a puzzled glance, then looked at her brother again. "What is it, Chad? Do you know something about Casey? Oh, but you couldn't or you'd have told me before. Unless... good heavens, is it possible that you *recognize* her?"

Chad Lockhart laughed. "My dear imaginative sister, how could I possibly recognize Casey?"

My head felt empty, my tongue numb, and I said in a slow, thick voice, "Thank you, Mr. Lockhart, but it won't do." Liza's arm was still about me, and she was holding my hand. I turned my head toward her and said, "Your brother and I met in Jamaica some three years ago, Liza, and he knows my true name. I hoped to leave my past behind, but that is out of the question now. I feel bound to tell you all that has happened. Then you can decide..." my voice faltered, "you can decide if you wish me to leave your home."

Chad Lockhart said, "I'm sorry. It would be better if I had not recognized you, but there was no chance of that."

"Be quiet, Chad," his sister said sharply. Then, to me, and very gently, she said, "Nothing can change what you did for Sam. Are you sure you wish to open the past to us, Casey? You need not, and Chad will never reveal your true identity, of that you may be sure."

"I must speak now, Liza. I must."

"Very well. Chad, you will take Casey down to the sitting room and give her a very small brandy and two or three biscuits to eat with it. There must be no argument. I shall join you in a few moments with some coffee. Amy should be making it now, I told her we should like a cup before setting out on our shopping expedition to London. Off you go."

She followed us downstairs and continued down to the kitchen. Chad Lockhart took me into the sitting room, saw that I was seated, then brought from the sideboard a little brandy in a glass, and a dish with some digestive biscuits.

"Sip it very slowly," he said, and sat down in an armchair, legs extended, chin cupped in hand, contemplating me with somber interest. "We'll wait for Liza before you begin," he said, "but tell me one thing. Your friend on the *Casey*, the man Sam called Harry Leng in the letter he wrote to us—was he really Daniel Choong?"

I nodded, and gave a little cough as the brandy caught my throat. "Yes. That was Daniel."

"I see." He was silent for a few moments, then smiled the wry smile I well remembered from the day when he had helped me with Joseph's broken cart. "It seems Fate is still inclined to play her capricious games with me. I never dreamed that the Casey Brown of Sam Redwing's glowing letter, that mysterious young woman who pretended to be a coolie girl and who saved Sam from death in a hurricane, would prove to be the young lady whose acquaintance I made some three years ago in Fern Gully."

Before I could answer, the door opened and Amy came in with a tray of coffee, followed by Liza. "Put it down here, please," said Liza. "Then carry on with the first floor rooms until it's time for you to go. And be sure that when Meg arrives for the afternoon you tell her she is not to disturb us here. Do you understand?"

"Yes, ma'am." Amy cast a curious glance at me, then hurried from the room. Liza sat down and poured coffee. Her brother got up to pass me a cup and take one for himself.

"Now," said Liza, settling back in her chair and giving me a cheerful smile of encouragement, "tell us all about it, Casey dear."

I said slowly, "Well... as your brother knows, my name was once Emma Delaney, and I lived with my uncle and aunt on a prosperous estate in Jamaica, not far from Ocho Rios..."

When I began to speak I thought my story would be very long in the telling, but this was not so. The first part needed only touching upon, for Liza had been told of her brother's chance meeting with me, and how I had ridden ahead to warn my friend Daniel Choong of his coming.

When I spoke of my marriage to Oliver Foy I was again mistaken in thinking I would be embarrassed or find myself groping for words. Perhaps the brandy helped, but I told this horrible part of my story briefly and simply, without emotion: "From the first night I discovered that Oliver was a depraved man whose greatest pleasure was to beat me and degrade me in every way. I cannot be specific in your brother's presence, Liza, but he used me monstrously. He was also a libertine who enjoyed bouts of debauchery with the Maroon women of Moore Town."

Liza was sitting up in her chair now, her face pale, lower lip caught in her teeth, blue eyes wincing with shock. Chad Lockhart stood up and moved to the window, looking out upon the small garden, hands clasped behind his back, body rigid.

I said, "There came a time when I knew I must withstand my husband or be broken forever, to become a creature in total submission to him . . ." Strangely calm, as if speaking of somebody else, I told how I had fought and been beaten, then how I had fought again, and threatened, and struck him down with the silver candlestick. I told how I had fled out into the tremendous storm, certain that he would kill me once he laid hands on me.

The longest part of the story was in telling of the fire in the stables, and of the moment when the dreadful figure of Oliver Foy had come stalking through the storm toward me, silver club in hand, to be impaled on the fishing spear flung by Daniel, and then, if not already dead, to die seconds later as lightning melted the spear in his body to a shapeless lump of metal.

I said, "Daniel's boat, *Miss Emma*, was ready, and he said he would sail at once despite the storm. I begged him to take me with him. I could not bear to face the investigation into Oliver's death, for I was terrified I might incriminate Daniel. Nobody would have believed the truth, that my husband was a monster who would have killed me in a passion of fury for withstanding him. So we rode down to Ocho Rios through the storm. We set sail, and we survived. The *Miss Emma* was renamed *Casey*, a variation of my second name, Catherine. I took the same name so I could pass for a boy at a distance, and Daniel Choong became Harry Leng. We sailed the Caribbean for three years and were very happy. Then came the day when we were going to shelter at St. Anthony from a coming hurricane, and found Mr. Redwing there, needing an urgent operation."

I thought for a moment and remained silent. There seemed nothing else of importance to say. When I looked at the grandfather clock standing against the wall I saw to my surprise that the time was twenty minutes past twelve o'clock. I had told the strange story of the past three years of my life in little more than a quarter of an hour.

Liza said in a whisper, "Oh, dear God. You were only seventeen when you married that evil man. You poor child."

Chad Lockhart turned from the window, his eyes as cold and gray as a sea mist. "It's as well Oliver Foy is dead," he said quietly. "Sam Redwing has Cheyenne Indian blood in him, and his gratitude counts no cost. He would have sought the man out and killed him."

Liza shivered. "Let us not speak of such things, Chad."

There was a long silence, then Liza suddenly shook herself as if to throw off haunting thoughts and looked across at me with a smile. "Casey dear, I know it must have been a shock for you to find Chad here, but in the end I'm sure you'll be glad to have told us everything and got it all off your chest."

Her brother said, "I imagine Casey will wish to tell Sam when he comes home."

They both looked at me, and I said, "Oh, yes. Yes, of course I would want him to be told now, but ... do you mean you wish me to remain in your home? Daniel was my dear friend and companion, and I still love him as if I had been his daughter. But I know what happened in Hong Kong long ago. He told me of the awful thing the tong forced him to do, and how it ruined your family and caused your father's death, so I can understand that you might want to have nothing to do with me."

Liza said a little sadly, "We no longer feel enmity toward the man you call Daniel Choong. Even my brother, who all his life has been obsessed by the disaster we suffered, no longer feels vengeful toward him. We spent much of our lives in Hong Kong and China, and we know the power of the tongs. Your friend was no more than a tool in their hands, and besides, he did his best to make restitution."

I said, "You mean the confession he gave to Mr. Lockhart that day?"

"Yes. The scroll in the bamboo case. And please call my brother Chad." She glanced across at him. He stood by the window, looking out again, head bowed slightly in a brooding stance. Liza said, "I mentioned Chad's obsession just now. It used to be a double obsession, for from the time our mother died he had only two purposes in life, beside which nothing else mattered. The first was to restore the good name of R. J. Lockhart, our father, by establishing his innocence of the crime for which he was imprisoned. This has now been achieved, thank God."

I broke in impulsively. "Oh, that's wonderful! Was it Daniel's confession?"

Chad Lockhart answered without turning from the window. "Yes. It took a year and a half for the Hong Kong courts to authenticate and then accept the confession, but they did so in the end, and a posthumous pardon was granted."

"I wish Daniel could have known. He would have been very glad."

"By the time the Hong Kong authorities sought him through the Colonial Office he had long been reported dead. But a solicitor in Kingston had witnessed the confession and swore an affidavit that it was genuine."

Liza said, "Chad's second obsession, the one that remains, lies in a determination to repay every penny to the creditors who suffered when our father's company was made bankrupt, but I fear this will take him rather more than a lifetime." She stood up briskly, went to her brother, and stood on tiptoe to kiss his cheek. "It's a good thing I love you, Chad dear." She turned to me, her pretty face animated and unshadowed again. "Of course you must stay with us, Casey. Nothing has changed. Emma Foy ceased to exist three years ago, and you are another person, Casey Brown." Without pause she continued, "Now, it's rather late for us to think of taking luncheon in town, but fortunately there is a pleasant hotel only a few minutes away across Blackheath. Chad, you shall drive us to the Cavendish and give us luncheon there, then take us down to the pier for the half past two boat."

He turned from the window, his drooping eyelid lifting in surprise. "You're surely not going on a shopping expedition after all this upheaval and excitement? Aren't you both exhausted?"

"No dear, I am stimulated, and if you think about Casey you will realize she is not the sort of girl to be easily exhausted. Why are men so stupid? Useful, of course, but stupid. Never mind, we shall go and put our hats on while you fetch the gig."

As Liza took my arm Chad Lockhart laughed, and his face was suddenly filled with amiable good humor. "The gig will await you in five minutes, ladies," he said. "Or perhaps I should allow more time if there are hats to be put on."

The hotel stood on the hill leading down into Blackheath Village, not far from a church of gray stone with a tall spire that dominated the south side of the heath. I was uneasy about my poor clothes, but Liza, who was clearly well known at the Cavendish, informed the head waiter that I was a dear friend from America who had been shipwrecked. She did so in a carrying voice for the benefit of other diners, and I noticed that frowns of disapproval changed to sympathetic glances in my direction.

I had thought myself too flustered and overwrought by all that had happened to have any appetite, but when a dish of splendid roast beef was set before me I suddenly found myself ravenous. I had not eaten in any sort of style or in a public place for over three years, and I made a very special effort to recall old ways, for I dreaded doing anything that might make Liza feel ashamed of me.

Chad Lockhart had put aside the brooding quietness with which he had listened to my tale, and made an excellent host. He and Liza carried most of the conversation, and as if by unspoken agreement they refrained from asking me any questions now that we were in a public place, and instead talked of general household matters and of Liza's domestic agency. I learned that they had come to England from Hong Kong ten years ago, on the death of their mother. Chad had been sixteen then, and Liza twenty. With a tiny capital she had started the Blackheath Domestic Agency while Chad had earned a little by keeping books of account for several professional men —mainly lawyers and doctors.

"Much as I detest paying him a compliment," said Liza, "I must confess that he was always a brilliant mathematician. Even as a boy in Hong Kong he dealt with dreadfully complicated accounts as if they were less than child's play. He should have taken a degree and become a teacher"—her brother winced and laughed at this—"but we couldn't manage that, and in any event it wouldn't have been at all to his taste." She rolled her eyes resignedly, and I remembered with something of a shock that when she first introduced him to me she had announced casually that he was a professional gambler.

I had seen that the furnishing of their home was adequate but not expensive. The same was true of their attire, and Liza had said plainly that they lived in a fairly frugal fashion. I found it strange that a man of seemingly limited means could be a professional gambler. It was surely an ill-chosen occupation for a man with an obsessive wish to repay large sums to creditors of his father's bankrupt company, and I could not imagine that it was generally regarded as a respectable occupation.

Chad Lockhart was saying, "I'm usually in town of an evening, but I always dine at home on Sunday, and I shall look forward to sampling your culinary skill, Casey. As Liza will confirm, her cooking is well-intentioned but unpredictable."

"It's true," Liza agreed. "I can do exactly the same thing on two different occasions and get completely different results. Do you find that, Casey?"

I said, "Well, no, but I'm not very experienced." I paused for the waiter to serve us with blackberry and apple pie, then lowered my voice so I should not be heard beyond the table. "The woman who was my nannie taught me plain cooking. When I grew up and she left, I used to go to her house quite often, and practice making simple dishes."

"I'm sure you'll manage splendidly, dear. Chad usually sleeps well past noon, then he gets up and has breakfast, if you please. But at least that's nice and simple. I usually pop back from the agency and make him bacon and eggs and kidneys, with toast and coffee, but I hope you'll be doing that for me once you've settled in. Can you drive the gig?"

Chad said, "She's a very able horsewoman, and I hope she'll keep you under a tight rein when she begins to help at the agency, Liza." He gave me a smile. "It's a successful agency without being very profitable, and that's because my sister is too kindhearted. Most agencies take the first month's wages of a person for whom they find a position in service, but Liza—"

"Oh, you're a hardhearted brute, Chad," she broke in. "You spend your time hobnobbing with the wealthy gentry and never see how difficult life is for an illiterate child hoping to go into service as bootboy or scullery maid."

"My darling, I've every sympathy with them and I do know how desperate they can be. I was washing bottles after school in Hong Kong when I was twelve, to help us survive."

"Until I found out and took you home by the ear!"

"Nevertheless, we've both known extreme poverty. I can understand you sympathizing with the people you find work for, but why do you have to be so waspish with clients seeking servants?"

Liza's eyes sparkled with mischief. "I'm only like that with the pompous ones. Anyway, whatever you say, the agency has never yet failed to make a profit." She turned to me. "Enough to keep us in reasonable comfort, and pay the rent, and allow Chad to do what he has to do. The rent is smaller than it should be, but that's because the house belongs to Sam Redwing and he insists we're doing him a favor by looking after it for him."

I said, "Oh, I didn't know it was his house." I remembered that Mr. Cruse, on St. Anthony, had told us the sick American gentleman was of some substance, and later Sam Redwing had supplied funds for my passage to England from a letter of credit for a thousand pounds. I wondered what his profession was, and how it came about that he had grown up with Liza and Chad Lockhart, but I did not voice those questions. Time would answer them, and for the moment I was more concerned with trying to remember all that May had taught me about cooking, to add to what I had learned for myself in the tiny galley of the *Casey*.

We left the hotel restaurant at fifteen minutes past two o'clock, in time for Chad to drive us across the heath and down through Greenwich Park to catch the boat from the pier on the half hour. Without realizing it, I must already have decided to trust myself and my future entirely to Liza, for as the gig carried us across the green heath I was filled with a carefree tranquillity. My anxieties of the past weeks were forgotten, and I found myself looking all about me to take in my surroundings, eagerly absorbing my first new sights and sounds of the country I barely remembered.

There were some boys playing cricket near a big pond, using a board propped against a stick as a wicket. Further on, two urchins were racing over the grass, broken boots flapping, struggling to get a homemade kite to fly. Two soldiers strolled at a steady pace, each with a young woman on his arm. Several carriages, large and small, moved on the roads that crisscrossed the heath. We turned into Greenwich Park, and drove past the Royal Observatory. I remembered that somewhere close by was marked the line of the Greenwich Meridian, the line of zero longitude from which the east to west charting of the globe had begun, but still I asked no question. I was content to wait, to observe and absorb, and to let all things come to me in due time.

Beside me, Liza reached across and patted my hand. "Look at me for a moment, Casey," she said. I turned my head to do so, and after a second or two she smiled. "You're not afraid any longer."

"No. Was it so very obvious?"

"I don't think most people would have known. I'm gifted or cursed with a very sensitive perception. In any event, that look in your eyes has gone now, and I'm so happy."

Chad saw us aboard the river steamer, agreed to meet us there again at six o'clock, and drove away. I was enchanted by the thirty-minute journey up the River Thames, and kept turning around in order not to miss anything on either bank as we made our way beneath Tower Bridge and London Bridge, then on into King's Reach, to pass under Waterloo Bridge and come at last to Westminster Pier. Here Liza hailed a hansom cab, and in another twenty minutes we were alighting in Regent Street.

For me, the next two hours passed in a dreamlike daze as we went from shop to shop. Liza was quite wonderful. Where the shop assistant was polite and helpful she was amiability itself. But let some woman turn up her nose, be it ever so slightly, at the shabbiness of my secondhand clothes, or frown at the sight of my cut-down drawers, and Liza would become another person, blue eyes frosty, tongue sharp as a knife, crushing in her manner.

"It is a great advantage," she said to me as we emerged from a dress shop where we had bought two dresses, "to have had experience of shopping in Hong Kong and China. One cannot bargain here, as is the custom there, but one learns to act convincingly to achieve the best results. Oh dear, I'm still talking in my haughty style, as I did to that wretched woman just now." She giggled, then turned to level a warning glance at the boy she had hired to carry our parcels for us in a little handcart. She was later to pay him twice the price agreed, much to his delighted astonishment.

I had always thought Kingston to be a large and crowded city. Now I realized from my river trip that Kingston could have been lost in a small corner of London, and that it was sparsely populated by comparison. The pavements here were crowded with people, the roads with horses and carriages of all kinds. When Liza decided she had acquired a sufficient wardrobe for me for the time being we were in Piccadilly, but to take a cab from there was pointless, because nothing was moving. A knifeboard bus had collided with a dray at Piccadilly Circus, and all traffic was held up until the road could be cleared. Horses and carriages stood so close that we had to push the animals' heads aside as we crossed the road. With our little boy trundling his cart ahead of us, we made our way down into Pall Mall. Here Liza poached a cab from a gentleman who had just hailed it, by rolling her eyes at him with pathetic appeal and putting a hand to her head as if in an extremity of exhaustion.

"We ladies must use what few advantages we have," she announced as we rattled off toward Westminster, our parcels, including two hats in large boxes, piled on the seat opposite. "Men are unconsciously selfish creatures, Casey, and if you spoil them they will take it entirely for granted. I've always been careful not to spoil Chad, and I do beg you to follow my example. At the same time I detest women who govern their menfolk. It has an unmanning effect. I have never told Chad what he should or should not do, no matter what I may have felt." She sat thinking for a moment, then added, "And I've been the same with Sam Redwing."

There was a note in her voice I could not quite interpret, and I looked at her quickly, but she was gazing out of the window as if her thoughts were far away, and I could not read her expression.

Dusk had fallen and the lamps were lit when we disembarked at Greenwich, a boy from the boat carrying our parcels. Chad raised his hat to us, and his pleasant smile of greeting seemed as much for me as for his sister. He handed us into the gig, loaded our parcels aboard, and in five minutes we were home.

The afternoon maid, Meg, had made tea, which we drank thankfully, then between us Liza and I made a simple dinner for the two of us with grilled lamb chops, cauliflower, brussels sprouts, and potatoes Meg had set to boil when Chad left to meet us at the pier. As we ate, I asked about dinner for Chad, and was told he would dine at his club that evening, as he always did except on Sundays.

By eight o'clock Meg had cleared the dining table, washed up, and left to go home. Liza and I were in the sitting room with cups of coffee when Chad came down from his room. I had heard the water running in his bathroom, and now I saw that he was freshly shaved and wearing a very fine gray suit with a shirt I judged to be handmade.

"I'm off to the station, Liza," he said. "Will you be here tomorrow or is Casey to be in charge?"

"I'll send Casey back from the agency to do your breakfast. Chad dear. She knows where everything is in the kitchen now, and she wants to start working at the agency without delay."

"Splendid. I'll see you tomorrow evening, then." He bent to kiss her cheek, then turned to me. "And I shall see you some time after midday, Casey. I hope you'll be happy with us."

I said, "You can't imagine how I feel." Tears came suddenly to my eyes. "It's like . . . like waking up in paradise. I'm sure your sister is the most wonderful person in the world."

Liza said, "Oh pish and tush."

Chad shrugged. "I suppose she has her points," he conceded with a doubtful air.

When he had gone, Liza looked at me curiously and said, "I don't believe you've asked a single question yet, Casey."

I gave her a dreamy smile. "I'm just so content to be here. And I don't want to be inquisitive."

"Oh nonsense, dear. If you're to be one of the family it's best that you come to know all about us. That will happen gradually, of course, or perhaps not too gradually because I'm an unstoppable chatterbox, but for the moment I'll explain about Chad. He'll be walking to Greenwich station now to catch a train for Charing Cross, then he'll go to his club and play cards for money until the small hours, breaking off to dine at some time during the evening. When the night's play has ended he will catch an early train from Charing Cross and arrive here at about six o'clock. He will go straight to bed and sleep till perhaps half an hour past noon."

I put down my coffee cup and said, "I see. So he will want his breakfast at about one o'clock?"

"That will do splendidly. Now let's go to your room and sort out your new clothes. I must say they all fitted marvelously well for ready-mades." She gave a sigh. "How I wish I had your pretty shape. I'm sure I ate only half as much as you at luncheon, but every ounce I consumed will turn to flesh. Oh, never mind. I think you should try on that blue dress again, Casey. I have a fancy it may need a tiny alteration at the waist."

Two hours later, after enjoying a hot bath, I said good night to Liza, closed my bedroom door, took off my new dressing gown, put on my new nightdress, closed the tap of the gaslight as Liza had shown me, and lay down between fresh cotton sheets on my comfortable bed.

For the first time since the hurricane had left me alone in the world I was without anxiety about the future. I had a vague intention of lying in the darkness and slowly reviewing the wonderful day that lay behind me, but sleep came upon me, swift yet stealthy, to carry me down into dreamless depths.

In the following days my only moments of sadness were when I thought of Daniel. For the rest, I rose each morning looking forward eagerly to the day's work ahead. By the end of the first week I knew that Liza Lockhart had no hidden side to her character. She was quite simply as kind and as lovable as she seemed. I got on well with Chad, perhaps because he at once set an informal pattern by treating me as if I were a younger sister. I also came to learn a great deal about him in those first few days, yet I was never sure that I really knew him, for I felt there were depths in him I could not readily fathom.

Each morning I rose well before seven, made my toilet, then went down to the kitchen and cooked a good breakfast for Liza and myself while she used the bathroom. The range would be out but still warm, and there was a gas ring to give immediate heat for frying. We would sit down to eat at half past seven, and be dressed and ready to leave the house when Amy, the morning maid, arrived at eight o'clock. After we had left, Amy would light the range, rake out the boiler, which remained alight all night, and refill the hopper with coal. Then she would begin clearing, washing up, and the general cleaning of the house.

By ten minutes past eight, Liza and I would arrive at the Blackheath Domestic Agency. This stood on the short hill below the church, and had once been a shop. Behind the rather dark glass frontage, men and women who had registered with the agency, seeking work in domestic service in all grades from butler to scullery maid, would sit in rows on benches for hour after hour, clutching their references and hoping to be sent out to a prospective employer for an interview. In the main they were cheerful and philosophical folk, though strict in maintaining the differences of position among themselves, so that conversation was between equals only, footman to footman, kitchen maid to kitchen maid.

The agency was opened at eight o'clock each morning by Mr. Potter. He had spent most of his life overseas as a clerk in the Colonial Service, and was now an elderly man living in a room above a shop across the road, glad to earn a few shillings a week by copying out letters, drafted by Liza, in his beautiful copperplate handwriting for two or three hours each day. Every morning when we arrived and passed between the benches of waiting people I remembered how lucky I was not to be sitting there myself, hoping for work as a scullery maid.

Liza's office was at the back. The room was spacious, the light good, the furniture secondhand but adequate. Here she would study advertisements for staff in newspapers and send out letters of application for people in her books. There was incoming mail to be dealt with, records to be kept, new applicants to be interviewed, references to be taken up, and personal callers to be attended to.

At twelve o'clock I would take the gig, drive home across the heath, and go through the house with Amy to see what had been done and what still needed doing. Meg, the afternoon maid, was a timid girl and very biddable, but Amy was of the kind to test my mettle, as I had suspected, and she did so on the third day. She could not know that I had dealt with Jamaican servants, and I was no longer the shabby creature she had first seen when I came direct from the ship three days before.

I told her coldly that I was Miss Lockhart's housekeeper and intended that the work should be done as I wished. There were, I pointed out, a dozen girls waiting at the agency who would be glad to replace Amy if she wished to give notice. I think it was not so much my words as my manner that startled her into the realization of having made a bad mistake. Every vestige of impudence vanished in a moment, to be replaced by earnest assurance, and from then on she worked well for me without further trouble.

After an inspection of the morning's housework I would go to the kitchen and make two sandwiches, one to take back to Liza. By the time I had done this I could usually hear water running in the bathroom above, and would start to prepare Chad's breakfast. His toilet was quickly made, for he left bathing and shaving till later in the day, when he went off for the night's gambling. By one o'clock he would come down to the dining room and exchange greetings with me as I put his breakfast and the morning paper before him.

"That looks very nice, Casey," he said on the first morning, when I was more than a little nervous. "Are you going to have a sandwich and a glass of milk, as Liza usually does?"

I said, "Yes, that's all I want at midday, thank you. I'll take a sandwich back for Liza, and we can get milk for her from the dairy across the road, she said."

"Good. Well, bring your sandwich and milk, and sit down with me for ten minutes while you have it. Liza always does."

"Well . . . are you sure?"

"I'm quite sure I don't want you to go and have your luncheon in the kitchen."

When I had brought my sandwich and a glass of milk he said, "There hasn't been much chance to talk yet. Tell me about Sam. How was he when you left him?"

"He was rather weak, and trying to do too much too soon, especially for me. But Mr. Carradine said the operation had gone very well, and I think the weakness was mostly the aftermath of yellow fever."

"And the ordeal of the hurricane."

"Yes, that too."

"Thank you for saving him. You were very brave."

"No. I was frightened from the start."

"Of course. There can be no bravery except in overcoming fear. Casey, I'm glad you're here, Liza needs a companion."

"I'm already devoted to her, Chad. It seems so strange . . ." My voice trailed away.

"Yes?"

"I'm sorry, I was about to pass a personal remark, I sometimes say things before I've thought properly."

He smiled. "Then you haven't changed. I seem to remember you apologizing for the same defect when we met on the road. But please make your personal remark, you have my dispensation."

"It was just that Liza is so pretty, so capable yet with such a lovely nature, I can't imagine why she isn't married."

Chad sighed. "Yes, I think it's a great waste, and so does Sam. It's partly because she spent years mothering me when I was younger, but not entirely so. Liza has had offers, one or two from very decent chaps. I don't know why she's always refused them."

I realized I had drifted into discussing Liza in her absence, and that was the last thing I wanted. I finished my milk and stood up. "I must be going now. Just leave everything for Amy to clear when you've finished, please."

"Thank you for an excellent breakfast."

In the first day or two at the agency I was of little use except to run errands and copy out some letters, but by watching Liza and asking questions I quickly learned the rudiments of the business and was able to be of increasing help. At the beginning of the second week Liza set me to interviewing some of the applicants, and after a nervous start I managed quite well with this, for I quickly discovered that they were far more nervous than I was. Quite often ladies seeking staff would call at the agency to make inquiries, but I was not put to the ordeal of attending to them.

"You can come to that later, dear," Liza said cheerfully, "when you look a little less like a girl sailor. I've done the best I can with your hair, and it looks quite nice, but it's still very short. Once it's grown long enough to put up, and once you've lost your brown face, we'll see how you get on with the ladies. Now don't be alarmed, your background gives you the natural manner of gentry, and that's what matters."

Our days were full, for except at weekends we rose early and worked through till five o'clock. I would then leave the agency to do any shopping required and make preparations for dinner, returning at six in the gig to collect Liza. Usually we finished dinner at half past seven o'clock, so the evenings were not long. We would do some mending and sewing, read, discuss the day's work, gossip together, spend a little time chatting with Chad before he left for the night, and sometimes spend an evening washing our hair and trying to beautify ourselves with a great assortment of creams and lotions Liza possessed.

"We must make the most of it before Sam comes home," said Liza one evening. We were sitting in the kitchen, having some cocoa before going to bed. She was peering at me through a mask of yellow cream, her hair tied above her head like the neck of a sack, and my own appearance was similar except for the hair. "With a man in the house," she declared, "one can only beautify behind closed doors, which is so much less fun."

On Saturday the agency was closed at one o'clock. Saturday afternoon and Sunday provided our leisure time. We paid no calls, but would walk in Greenwich Park, take a trip on a river boat, or visit one of the many museums or historic places with which the river abounded. I enjoyed every hour of my new life, and would sometimes briefly lie awake in bed after a busy day, marveling at my good fortune.

On Sundays we would sleep late, spend the day in leisurely fashion, and attend evensong at Greenwich Church. Chad rose at his usual hour but was with us for the afternoon and evening. I was a little nervous about this on the first Sunday, but found there was no need to be. Whether his manner was assumed or not I was unable to tell, but he treated me with much the same amused affection that he showed toward Liza. This set me very much at ease, for which I was grateful.

After two weeks Liza asked me to take over the agency books of account. It was simple bookkeeping and presented no difficulties for me. Once I had studied the books I realized the truth of what Chad had said on my first day, for although the agency thrived, the profit was small because Liza took only a small commission. By the time all costs of placing a kitchen maid, for example, had been set against her week's wage that we received for our services, there was sometimes a loss. But I would not have wished Liza to change her ways. As she pointed out, the agency made enough to help keep us fed and sheltered in a way that much of the world would have envied. We had both lived in faraway places that had taught us the truth of this.

I did not at first know what contribution, if any, Chad made in the home, but since Liza handed over to me all responsibility for housekeeping from the third day, I quickly found that she and her brother shared the household expenses equally. At the time it struck me that Chad could scarcely be a losing gambler if he was able to pay money regularly into the housekeeping account; on the contrary, it seemed he must be something of a winner, at least in a small way.

I was right in a sense, but hopelessly wrong in my assumption of the scale on which he gambled, and I did not dream of the effect this was soon to have upon my life.

12

THE THIRD SATURDAY AFTER MY ARRIVAL IN GREENWICH WAS Chad's birthday. Liza had persuaded him to stay at home for the day, and she and I made secret plans to celebrate the occasion. With great daring we had bought three tickets for the early evening performance at Barnard's Music Hall, only five minutes' drive away, near what I referred to as the northwest entrance of Greenwich Park. Liza called it the lower entrance, because it lay at the bottom of the hill. She was amused by my way of referring to places and directions in terms of compass points, which meant nothing to her, but I had lived by the compass for three years, and was always unconsciously aware of wind, weather, and direction, even on land.

After the music hall show we planned to return home for a special birthday dinner of Surrey capon with braised celery, roast potatoes, parsnips, and sprouts. I was now sufficiently at home in the kitchen to be able to prepare all the vegetables and set the capon to roasting slowly so that everything would be ready for table within an hour of our return from the music hall.

To begin the meal I had made a dish of mixed seafood, one I had devised during my years on the *Casey*. Greenwich was a splendid place for seafood, brought fresh upriver daily, and I had earned much praise from Liza and Chad for my fish and shellfish dishes. I had yet to acquire any skill with desserts, and so I planned to serve cheese and biscuits instead. As a special treat we had spent six shillings on a good bottle of champagne.

There was a hint of winter in the air that day, and we returned from an afternoon walk across the heath with glowing cheeks. When we had taken tea together Chad went to his study with strict orders from Liza that he must not come near the kitchen but must be ready to drive us to a secret destination at six o'clock. Liza and I put on aprons and began to prepare the dinner, Liza being wholly content to work under my instructions. As we busied ourselves with all that had to be done, I found it hard to believe that this had been my home and these my friends for little more than three weeks.

While we worked we chatted, as usual. "I'm sure your hair will be long enough to put up well before Christmas," said Liza, "and it's going to look beautiful. Such a lovely color, Casey."

"Thank you, and it's kind of you to say so, but I wish I didn't have such funny eyebrows. They're too heavy. Do you think I should pluck them?"

"You'll do no such thing! They suit you, dear. I'm not sure why, but they're just right for your face, and I love the way they go squiggly when you're thinking."

"Oh, that's just what I hate about them. Are the parsnips ready, Liza? Thank you. I'm so excited about this evening. You know, a week or two before the hurricane I had my twenty-first birthday, and I was diving to a six-fathom bottom with Daniel to get a lobster for our supper. Doesn't that sound strange now? But it was just an everyday matter for me then."

"I love hearing about your adventures with the *Casey*," said Liza. "It doesn't upset you to talk about them now? I mean, about Daniel?"

I shook my head. "I still have moments of grief, but I don't mind talking of Daniel. I sometimes speak to him in my mind, and tell him how lucky I am and how kind you and Chad and Sam have been to me. I know it seems silly, but I started to do it when I felt very much alone and without friends."

"It doesn't sound in the least silly to me, my sweet" Liza said firmly. She cocked her head as there came the sound of a brisk *rat-tat-tat* from the front door. "Ah, there's something for us in the evening post. I'll go and see what it is."

She returned a few moments later with a letter. "It's from Sam, bless him. He must have managed to send it on the next steamer from that little island. Have I time to read it, or is there something you want done?"

"No, everything's going nicely. You read your letter."

She sat on a wooden chair by the kitchen table and opened the letter. "Well, it's not as long as the last one. That was all about the hurricane, and how you had rescued him, and what he wanted us to do. This is only two pages. Now let's see..." She was silent for a minute or two, then gave a happy sigh. "He says he's quite well again, and this letter will catch the mail steamer so it will arrive seven or eight days before he does himself." She gave a little laugh. "He says apart from pidgin English his only conversation with you lasted little more than ten minutes and he had no chance to say all he wished to. He hopes you've settled in happily, and he's quite sure both Chad and I will think you're wonderful—"

"Oh Liza, don't!"

"It's what he says, dear. I shall have to tell him how awful you are. Ah, he's sailing on the *Derwent*, which is due in London on the morning of the tenth. That's a Saturday, isn't it? Yes, next Saturday. How lovely. We won't open the agency that morning, so we can go to meet him. My goodness, what a difference he'll see in you. Oh, it really will be so nice for you to meet him again looking a well-dressed and attractive young lady."

I set the capon in the roasting jack and said, "I think I shall feel rather shy. In fact, I know I shall. Do please keep the conversation going, Liza. I won't know what to say."

She smiled. "Sam Redwing is an American, and nobody can remain ill at ease in his company for long. I don't think I realized you know so little about him, but of course you've only ever exchanged a few words. Our families were neighbors in Hong Kong, and we grew up like brother and sister. How many potatoes will you want, dear? About eight? They're quite a nice size."

"Do nine, just to be sure. You were saying about Sam?"

"His father was a doctor. I don't know why the family came to Hong Kong, but Sam's grandfather was a Red Indian, and I think perhaps American society frowned on the idea of a half-redskin doctor being married to a white American wife. She was a sweet lady, and Sam's father was the kindest of men. They died together in a boating accident off Hong Kong, about ten years ago."

"Oh, that's very sad."

"Yes. They were like a second mother and father to me. When I was small Sam used to come into our house almost every day to play with me." She giggled. "We squabbled endlessly. He always wanted to play soldiers and I wanted to play nurses. He wished I had been a boy, of course, but he just had to make the best of me because there were no little boy neighbors. Chad was born when I was four, and then a year later came the crash, when father's firm collapsed and he was sent to prison."

I said, "Oh Liza, I'm so sorry about... about all that."

"It's long past now, dear. Except for Chad." She thought for a moment, rather sadly, then gave a little shrug and continued. "I was too young to grasp what was happening, of course, but we promptly lost all our so-called friends, except for the Redwings. I think poor Sam fought half the boys in the school he attended, just in our defense. He always had a black eye or swollen nose during those awful weeks. My mother was quite remarkable. When the trial was over she set up a small office in Kowloon as a manufacturers' agent, and slowly built it into a paying concern."

I thought of white society in Jamaica. It would no doubt be very similar to white society in Hong Kong, so I could guess how Mrs. Lockhart and her children would have been regarded. I said, "You must all have found it very hard, Liza."

"Oh, we got used to it, and there was always Sam and his parents, they never faltered in their friendship. After our father died, Mother became... oh, I don't know. She lived only for her work. It became an obsession. That was when Chad and I were more or less taken over by the Redwings. Certainly we lived more in their house than in ours, right up to the time Mr, and Mrs. Redwing died."

I said, "You must have been quite grown up then."

"Oh, yes. I was twenty and Chad sixteen. Our mother died in the same year, so I decided to sell the business and come to England. Sam said he would join us, and in fact he bought this house with what he inherited from his parents, then went dashing off on some business venture, just as he does now."

"I don't think I know what his business is."

"That's not surprising, Casey. In some ways Sam is still a

redskin, but in others he's very much a Yankee, full of ideas and enthusiasms, very hard working and not afraid of risks. I think he was out in the West Indies looking for deposits of guano. It's a very valuable fertilizer, and he did well with a venture in guano around some islands off Peru."

"He must be quite rich, then."

"That depends. Sam is never really poor, but when he's rich his money is tied up in business. If a venture succeeds, he sells up and puts his money into something new, and if it doesn't succeed he gets another idea and starts all over again. Now, is there anything else we have to do?"

I looked at my cooking plan and at the pots of prepared vegetables. "No, we've done all we can for now. There's only the table to be set, then we can go and get ready."

As we were laying the table in the dining room a thought occurred to me, and I said, "Liza, when Sam is here and Chad is usually away all night, isn't that rather awkward for you? I mean, people are so strict about ladies being chaperoned."

She looked at me, her blue eyes brimming with mischief. "We acquired a reputation as Bohemians right from the start, dear, and that's really quite useful, because people *expect* Bohemians to be shocking. Truth to tell, we didn't give the matter much thought. Sam regards me as he would a sister, and it seemed quite natural for the three of us to settle in here. I don't quite know what the neighbors think, and I don't much mind. We get on with them well enough on a formal basis, and I've always been too busy to make close friends. The church people are surprisingly nice. I believe they suspect that nothing improper is going on, and are vaguely aggrieved on that account, because they feel Bohemians *should* be rather scandalous."

I laughed as I folded a table napkin to a fleur-de-lis pattern. "Oh dear, they'll be even more indignant now there are two females here to chaperon each other."

Soon after six o'clock we left the house and drove down to Barnard's Music Hall. I felt sure Chad had guessed the nature of the surprise we planned for him, but he affected to be astonished when we joined the straggling line of people making their way into the theater. They were a cheerful crowd and very mixed, costermongers and seamen, parlor maids and their suitors, shopkeepers with their wives, and a sprinkling of gentry. All seemed eager to enjoy themselves, to laugh at the comedians and shed a tear with the ballad singers.

The evening's entertainment could not have been described

as uplifting. It was loud, jaunty, and sometimes vulgar, yet very skillful in its own way, and I enjoyed it immensely. One of the turns was a young woman who danced and sang dressed as a sailor. She was billed as a male impersonator, and Liza nudged me when she came on, muttering, "You're not the only one, Casey!" which gave us both a fit of the giggles.

As soon as we arrived home I begged Liza and Chad to sit by the fire, chat with each other, and take a glass of sherry while I finished cooking the dinner. I was nervous now about how everything would turn out, and wanted to be alone in the kitchen. Less than an hour later, very thankful and somewhat red-faced with effort, I had everything in hot dishes on the table and was able to call them to the dining room.

It seemed to me that the capon was a little too well done, but both Chad and Liza vowed they preferred it that way and praised me extravagantly for the dinner. I had bought ice packed in sawdust from the fishmonger for cooling the champagne, and there was merriment when Chad thumbed the cork out with a loud *pop*! and tried to get the foaming golden liquid into our glasses without spilling any. I drank a glass and a half myself with the dinner, and felt as if I were floating.

Later, when I had served coffee, it was time to give Chad our birthday presents. Liza's was a sovereign case in engine-turned silver. I had only learned about Chad's birthday a week before, and had given much thought to it. I still had the two sovereigns given to me by Sam Redwing, but I planned to return these to him. With the housekeeping money, I was given an extra pound for myself each week. This was so generous a sum that I had shed tears and argued when Liza first informed me of it, though my protest had been in vain. I knew that if I spent too much on a present for Chad it would embarrass him, so I had bought a gentleman's handkerchief in fine linen and sat up late in my room one night to embroider very carefully his initial in one corner.

As a little joke when presenting her birthday gift, Liza moved to where Chad sat at the end of the table and went down on one knee like a sultan's handmaiden. He laughed and rolled his eyes up for a moment. "Not very convincing, my darling. Casey knows well enough that big sister rules me with a rod of iron."

"Don't call me big, dear," Liza said plaintively as she stood up. "It's much too true."

"Nonsense." He unwrapped the sovereign case, exclaimed with delight over it, then stood up to kiss Liza fondly.

She beckoned to me. "Come along, Casey. Make your presentation." Chad looked surprised. Perhaps because I had drunk some champagne I felt unselfconscious, and I followed Liza's example, dropping a deep curtsy as I handed the little package to him.

"Well, thank you Casey, but you really shouldn't have done this," he said, smiling. "Now let me see..." He opened the package, examined the handkerchief and embroidery with apparent admiration, and thanked me again.

Liza said impatiently, "Well, for heaven's sake give the girl a kiss, little brother. After all, she's like one of the family now."

I felt myself flush, and for a moment was almost vexed with Liza. Chad cocked his head and looked at me from under a drooping eyelid, though whether his gaze held mockery or reluctance I could not tell. He gave a little laugh as if making up his mind, reached out to take my hands, then leaned forward and kissed me first on one cheek and then the other. "You've given me a splendid birthday, Casey, and I'm very glad to have you with us," he said.

Liza sniffed. "Rather formal, but perhaps you'll do better next time, Chad. Now, as a special treat, Casey and I are going to withdraw to the sitting room and leave you in peace to smoke a cigar and finish the champagne, but don't be more than twenty minutes, then we shall have time for a game of *mah tsiang*. Perhaps we could begin to teach Casey."

"Oh, but I play it!" I exclaimed. "Daniel taught me. He made a set of little tiles, like dominoes but engraved with different colored dragons and symbols for seasons and winds and flowers. Is that the game you mean?" Liza and Chad smiled at each other. "You really are an unexpected treasure, dear," said Liza. "Whoever would have thought it possible that an English girl from the West Indies would know how to play a Chinese table game. Sam will be delighted." She took my arm and we went through to the sitting room, leaving Chad to his cigar and champagne. As Liza closed the door she said, "I was unforgivably interfering just now in telling Chad to kiss you, but please don't be angry with me."

I shook my head and smiled. "I was rather taken aback, but I could never be angry with you."

"Tell me, did it trouble you at all? I mean, did you feel distressed when Chad kissed you?"

I put a log on the fire and looked at her with some bewilderment. "Why, no. It was . . . well, it was very nice and friendly."

She sat down in an armchair with a sigh of relief. "Oh, that's splendid. I did it on impulse, you see, because I've been worried. Your dreadful experience as Oliver Foy's wife could very well make you hate men in general, or at least feel repelled by the slightest contact with them, and that would be such a pity."

I took the chair on the other side of the fireplace and said, "I felt a hint of that when I was first looking after Sam, but it quickly passed. I think I regard Oliver as having been a monster rather than a man. I expect I went rather pink when Chad kissed me, but that was embarrassment." I smiled. "Why do you say it would be a pity if I had disliked it?"

"My sweet, you're young and attractive. One day a suitable young man is going to want you very much for his wife, and if you liked him, I would be sad to think you had been put off by what happened to you before, so I'm glad it isn't so. I don't want you to become an old maid on the shelf like me."

"Oh, Liza, don't say that. Any man would be so lucky to have you for a wife. I'm sure you gave up years to looking after Chad when you were my age, and I know you've had offers because Chad told me so."

Looking into the fire, smiling a little, she said, "Well . . . I didn't accept them."

I waited for her to continue, but when she sat gazing absently at the flames I said after a while, "Anyway, I have no thoughts of meeting a man and getting married. I'm much happier as I am."

"Oh, nonsense, Casey dear." She sat up straight and frowned at me. "You were made to be married to the right man." Her eyes suddenly widened and she put a hand to her mouth. "Dear Lord, I hope you didn't imagine I was matchmaking just now! You might well have done, but please don't think that. You needn't have the slightest worry that Chad will start to court you, dear. He'll never marry." She shook her head a little ruefully. "Never."

I wondered how she could be so certain, but felt it was not for me to ask. "It didn't occur to me that you might be matchmaking," I said, "so please don't worry about it. Shall I fetch the *mah tsiang* board and tiles, so we'll be ready when Chad has finished his cigar?"

"Yes, dear, you'll find them in a leather case in the right-hand drawer of the cabinet there."

When I had set the case on a small inlaid table and opened it, I suddenly remembered that on this evening I had intended to wear my gold bracelet. It was my only piece of jewelry, and until now there had been no special occasion on which to wear it. Several times during the day I had reminded myself about the bracelet, but I suppose when the time came to dress for the theater I had been so anxious about the dinner preparations that the idea of wearing it slipped completely from my mind.

I felt that in a way I had been unkind to Daniel, and decided I would at least wear his lovely gift to me for what remained of the evening. Excusing myself to Liza, I ran upstairs, took the bracelet in its little bag from a drawer in my dressing table, put it on my wrist, then hurried down again to show it to Liza. Tears came to her eyes when I recounted how Daniel made the charm for my twenty-first birthday. "And was this your little boat?" she said, peering at the engraving. "Oh Casey, did you really sail for three years on such a craft? Seeing this makes all the stories I've coaxed you into telling me seem so much more real. What a strange life it must have been."

"Yes, I suppose so. It didn't seem strange at the time."

"Next summer we must go to the seaside, so you can show me how you swim underwater. Did you know that two or three years ago Chad and Sam learned to dive? I mean, diving in special suits with great helmets. They spent two months under instruction from Siebe and Gorman, the firm that makes these diving suits."

I stared in surprise. "But whatever for?"

"I don't know, dear. It must have been one of Sam's speculative ventures, I suppose, though I must say it's the only one Chad has ever taken part in. They were rather secretive about it, I remember, but whatever their reason for learning to be divers, nothing ever came of it, so I imagine it was one of Sam's projects that failed before it started."

I gave a shiver. "I'm sure I would be frightened in a diving suit. I'd hate it, with my head enclosed in a helmet, breathing air pumped down a hose. And you wouldn't be free to swim and float and drift just as you please."

"You make it sound wonderful, Casey."

"It is, Liza, it really is, once you've learned how to hold
your breath for long periods without feeling panicky. It's almost
like being able to fly."

A minute or two later Chad joined us and we settled down
to play a game of *mah tsiang*. It was normally a game for four,
but Liza and Chad knew the variation Daniel had taught me
for two or three players, and I soon realized they were experts.
We had been playing for only a few minutes when Chad exclaimed softly as I reached out to place a tile.

"That bracelet, Casey—you weren't wearing it before."

"No, I meant to but forgot. I was telling Liza just now that
Daniel made it for my twenty-first birthday. Or rather, he had
the chain made by the native goldsmiths on Aruba, and made
the charm himself. It bears an engraving of the *Casey*."

Chad took my wrist gently. "May I look closely?"

"Yes, of course."

He fingered the small round charm, holding my wrist close
to his eyes, studying first one side and then the other. I glanced
at Liza, who pulled a comical face and gave an exaggerated
shrug to indicate that she did not know why Chad should be
so interested. He lifted my wrist a little, holding the charm to
the light so that he could look at it obliquely, and sudden
memory came flooding to my mind.

The *Casey* was engraved on the obverse of what had once
been a gold coin, and Chad was looking at the reverse now,
which carried the coat of arms and date. It was a coin rather
more than a hundred years old, a Spanish piece of eight escudos. A doubloon, Daniel had said, minted in the reign of
Charles IV of Spain.

I caught my breath and said, "Oh, I'd forgotten! It was once
a coin, a piece of eight. Daniel had just four of them, and two
were melted down to make the chain. But the fourth he gave
to *you*, Chad, that day above Ocho Rios, when he gave you
the scroll with his confession."

Chad nodded and laid my hand on the table. "I thought so,"
he murmured, and his face was quite without expression. "Did
he tell you where the four coins came from, Casey?"

"No." I hesitated. "No, I don't think so."

The half closed eye seemed to look through me. "Surely
you must know whether he did or did not?"

Liza slapped down the tile she was holding and stared indignantly. "Don't be so brusque, Chad! Whatever has got into
you?"

"I'm not being brusque, Liza." His voice was quiet, and he still looked at me. "It's a reasonable question."

"Well, I didn't like the way you asked, and I can't see that it's any of your business."

I said, "Please, Liza. If Daniel gave a coin to Chad, then it must be his business. And I know it seemed stupid for me to say I didn't *think* Daniel had told me where the coins came from. I don't understand why I said it, except that it seemed . . . well, seemed to be the right answer in some way. But that's silly." I met Chad's gaze. "The truth is, Daniel never told me where they came from. He almost did, I think. He was very much in two minds about it, and perhaps if he had lived he might have decided differently. But at the time, on my birthday, he felt it was better for me not to know, because the knowledge might be dangerous."

There was a little silence. Liza said in a subdued voice, "Have you any idea why, Casey?"

I shook my head, still keeping my eyes on Chad, wanting him to see the truth in them. "No, Liza. None at all."

The frost melted from his gaze, he gave a small sigh, a wry smile, and became a different man, the amiable and leisurely man I had come to know and like over these past three weeks. "If I was brusque, I'm sorry," he said, and patted my hand. It was as if he were speaking to his sister.

Liza said, "Do you still have the coin Daniel gave you, Chad? Do *you* know where it came from?"

"Yes. Yes. And no." He began to sort through his tiles, studying them.

"What does that mean?"

"It means yes I still have the coin. Yes I know the place it came from. But no, I don't know where that place is."

"Oh, don't be ridiculous!"

He smiled at her. "It's true, darling."

"Then don't be mysterious. Tell us the place the coins came from."

He thought for a moment or two, then shook his head. "I'd prefer to leave things the way Daniel left them."

Liza wrinkled her small nose. "Wretched men. You're all the same, always nursing secrets. Well, are we going to play or not?"

He grinned. "It's your turn, Liza, we're waiting for you. Come along now."

She glared and pointed a finger. "All right. But I know one

thing. That grin means you've just suffered a big disappointment, little brother. I can read you like a book."

He sighed and inclined his head. "That's why I'm careful never to play any game for money with you, little sister."

Next morning Liza sprang a surprise on both of us. It was a cold but bright November day, and at breakfast she announced that Chad and I were to go horseback riding on the heath.

"I've arranged for a boy to bring two nice horses from the livery stables for a couple of hours, and I have some riding breeches for you to wear, Casey. They're ready-made, but they should fit well enough because Mrs. Howard had all your measurements for making the suit and the dresses."

Chad and I looked at each other with smiling bewilderment, then at Liza. "I'm sure we shall enjoy it," he said, "but why this sudden enthusiasm for horse riding, and why aren't you included?"

"They frighten me," she said. "I don't mind driving a horse from behind, but the thought of sitting on one makes me feel quite faint with fear. I don't think I'm the right shape. But you like riding, Chad, and I know Casey used to ride a lot in Jamaica, so I decided the exercise would do you both good."

"I usually walk for an hour by the river every morning before catching the milk train home," said Chad. "You're the one who needs exercise. You're a bit plump, darling."

Liza sighed. "The fact that you're right doesn't make you any the less loathsome for saying it. Why don't you accept that I'm the shape God made me, brother dear? I shall get no fatter and no thinner, whether I eat like a bird and go bicycling all day, or eat like a gourmand and sit in a rocking chair."

I said, "You're beautiful, Liza. I think you're just right for the person you are."

"Flatterer."

"No, truly. Anyway, thank you for arranging about the riding. I shall love it. But what will you do yourself this morning?"

"Oh, I shall follow you in the gig and watch for a while, unless it gets too cold. Then I'll come home and do some sewing or read my book." Like me, Liza was an avid reader and at present was engrossed in a strange fantasy of Mr. H. G. Wells called *The Invisible Man*.

I thoroughly enjoyed the riding. From what I knew of Chad's past I thought he might not be very experienced, for it seemed he would have had little opportunity to ride, but in fact he proved to be a good horseman. It transpired that when he and Liza and Sam Redwing had come to England, Sam's first business venture here had been to buy livery stables at Woolwich, employing Chad to deliver, collect, and exercise horses as required. It had been a moderately profitable venture of which Sam had grown weary after six months, but during that time Chad had spent most of his days driving and riding.

Blackheath was a good place for a gallop, and I was happy to feel the wind tingling on my cheeks, but for the most part we walked or trotted, with an occasional canter. Chad made a pleasant riding companion, for our living under the same roof had quickly brought us to the point where we felt no need to make polite conversation. We talked as the mood took us, but were quite content to ride for a while in companionable silence.

At mid morning we turned into the park and rode past the Royal Observatory. Here I asked that we might stop for a moment to look at the long strip of solid brass set in the cobbles to mark the Prime Meridian, the imaginary line of zero degrees that was the starting point for the navigation of every ship that sailed the world's seas. I could never bear to pass by without pausing to pay my respects, and always felt a little quiver of excitement at sight of it.

As we moved away, Chad and I began to speak at the same moment: "Do you remember—"

We broke off, laughing, and I said, "You first."

"I was going to ask if you remembered how cross you were with me that day in Fern Gully, when you found I had been watching you struggle with the cartwheel instead of helping you."

"Yes, of course I remember. And you said something about not wishing to deprive me of the chance of success."

"So I did."

"It's funny, but I was just going to ask if you remembered how Jennie, my mare, put her foot through your hat while we were getting the wheel on Joseph's cart."

Chad's smoky gray eyes sparkled as I turned to look at him. "I hope I succeeded in hiding my dismay," he said. "I could ill afford a new hat at the time."

"So I suspected. It's rather late, but I'll apologize again." We rode on for a while, then I said, "It's strange, really. You spoke that day about Fate being a lady who likes to play tricks on you, sometimes malicious and sometimes just whimsical, yet you follow a profession that seems very vulnerable to tricks of Fate." I stopped, frowning. "Oh dear, I'm sorry, I was thinking aloud again. It's unpardonable of me to make such a comment."

He laughed. "I'm not offended by your comment, Casey dear." He occasionally used Liza's way of addressing me in those terms, and it always warmed me. "The fact is that the lady has only a very limited influence on my kind of gambling. I rely on mathematics, not luck."

We were riding along the bottom of the hill that ran down to the northern edge of the park, with the beautiful Queen's House of Inigo Jones on our left. I thought about Chad's last words, then said, "I'm not sure I understand that."

"I play whist, mostly. Poker sometimes, when I can find fellow players, though it's more popular in America than here. There's a measure of luck in all games, but in card games of skill it plays a small part compared with memory and mathematics."

"Why mathematics?"

"Because if you have a head for it, you can work out the precise mathematical chances of two or more different lines of play, and then choose the most favorable. Luck is a minor element and tends to even out over a long period, but if you play to better mathematical chances than your opponents, you're bound to win. Even Lady Fate can't stop you."

"Suppose your opponents are even better mathematicians?"

"Then I should lose. But don't think me immodest if I say I've yet to meet anyone better. Most gamblers are highly superstitious and equally unscientific. They rely on luck."

I remembered the occasional whist drives held at The Jacarandas to raise funds for the church. "It must be very hard work," I said. The words expressed only half the thought in my head, but Chad must have guessed what I left unspoken.

"You mean for small returns?"

"Well, I did think that, remembering Aunt Maude's whist drives, but at least I didn't say it, so I need not apologize this time."

"Casey, you're unfailingly refreshing." He was silent for a few moments, and when I glanced at him I could see his amusement as he rode with hat tilted back on his head. "My winnings average rather more than five thousand a year," he said rather ruefully. "I've yet to find a more profitable way of exercising my small talent."

I reined in and swung round to look at him, feeling my eyes go wide with astonishment. "Five *thousand*? But that's a huge sum, Chad. Oh dear, you shouldn't have told me, it's really not my business. But . . . but why let Liza run her agency when you could live splendidly with a staff of ten on such an income?"

"I retain only a modest amount for our living expenses," he said. "The rest goes to pay debts."

"Debts?"

He tilted his hat forward to shadow his eyes, and gave a nudge to his horse. I saw that his face had become impassive before I turned my horse to move on beside him. "Debts," he repeated without emphasis. "When my father was bankrupted and jailed, my mother spent the rest of her life working to pay all creditors in full. In fifteen years she barely scratched the surface of that task. Before she died, I promised to continue the work until it was completed."

I put out a hand to touch his arm and said, "Don't talk about this if it upsets you, Chad. And forgive me if it's my fault we stumbled onto the subject."

"No, Casey, no," he said almost impatiently. "It's not your fault in any way, and in fact I'm glad of the chance to explain a little about the way we live. I know Liza won't have told you much about me because she feels it's not for her to do so, but I think it's time now."

"Only if you want to tell me, Chad."

"I do, though there's not a great deal to tell. I saw my mother work like a slave all my life until she died when I was sixteen. Before she died I made her two promises. First, that I would never give up trying to clear my father's name, and second, that I would never give up trying to pay off his creditors. Liza and I came to England, and for the next few years it was all we could do to make a living, but at last I felt able to leave Liza for a while and work my passage back to Hong Kong and Shanghai."

I said, "Was Liza on her own?"

"Yes. Sam was in New Guinea, I think. Then he joined me in Shanghai for a time."

"Why did you go back, Chad?"

"To trace the two witnesses who had given false testimony against my father. One had died. The other had disappeared abroad when he came out of prison."

"That was Daniel. He never forgave himself."

"I know. And I know how he was compelled by the tong's

threats against his mother, he wrote it all out in his confession. I spent a year in Hong Kong and Shanghai altogether, and failed in my task. Before I left for England I hired a Chinese inquiry agent in Hong Kong to trace Ma Ho—Daniel's real name. I should have done so before. This man had the wit to trace Daniel's mother to Macao and then learned that letters had been arriving from Jamaica once every year for many years. He sent me this information, and . . . that's how it was I came to Jamaica."

We were climbing the steep grassy slope of Observatory Hill now. Three ragged children came tumbling and rolling down in a flurry of arms and legs, a favorite game for urchins on that hill. I said, "So you found Daniel, he gave you his confession, and that meant you had kept your first promise. I'm glad now, Chad, but I was quite frightened of you at the time. Later, after we met again at the race track, Oliver said you were a dangerous man."

He gave me a quizzical look and said gravely, "I expect he was exaggerating."

I smiled. "I'm not so sure. Joseph behaved as if you were Baron Samedi, the voodoo King of the Dead."

"Ah, yes. He made signs against the evil eye, I recall."

As we turned along the top of the hill I said, "Chad, when will you complete your other promise? I mean, paying off the debts?"

He looked up at the sky. "It's hard to be precise. I pay annual interest of five percent, and that takes almost half my income."

I blinked. "Half? I don't understand."

"It's quite simple, Casey. I owe fifty thousand pounds."

13

I SAT STUNNED AS OUR HORSES WALKED STEADILY ON. THE sum was almost too great for me to imagine. Chad said casually, "The debt was rather more than that when I first assumed responsibility for it. At present I have to find two thousand five hundred every year simply to pay the interest due. That leaves only about the same amount to make repayment of capital."

I was out of my depth in financial matters of such size, but after laboriously working out the figures in my head I said, "Does...does that mean it will take you twenty years to clear the full amount?"

"Not quite. As the debt is reduced, so will the annual interest be reduced, which means that each year I can pay off a larger part of the capital."

"But even so! Oh, Chad..."

"That's what Liza says. Or rather, she used to. She never speaks of it now."

"Has Sam not been able to help you?"

"Casey dear, there's no point in transferring a debt from creditors to a friend, and in any event Sam's ventures have never yet made him a great fortune. He's always optimistic that one day we'll go into some venture together and become rich overnight, but I doubt it. I'm too cautious to put my faith in Sam's enterprises."

"You think gambling is a cautious way of making money?"

He grinned. "It is for me. The Chinese are great gamblers, you know, but I used to win pocket money from them even as a boy. When I came back from the Far East I decided it was the only profession I was competent to follow. Liza lent me money for a decent suit, plus a little more to bribe a couple of penurious members who proposed me for a decent club, and so I became a gentleman. After that it was just a matter of playing in the kind of company whose stakes I could afford, until I accumulated enough to stand a run of bad luck at higher stakes in richer company. And so on."

I said, "Are the stakes very high?"

He shrugged. "At whist I usually play at stakes of five pounds a trick and fifty for the rubber. You can win or lose a hundred or two in an evening at that level. At poker I play draw poker, blind opening, and table stakes."

"It's like a foreign language to me, Chad."

"Yes, I suppose it is. I was just describing one of several varieties of poker. It's a game at which I've won as much as a thousand in an evening, and lost as much as five hundred when the cards ran badly. But in the long run, luck can never beat a good card memory and calculation of odds."

We came to the top of the hill and moved on toward the gate leading out to Blackheath. After a while Chad said, "Your eyebrows have squiggled together. What are you thinking, Casey?"

"Oh . . . perhaps I'd better not say."

"Why not?"

"You might think I was criticizing."

"And you're not?"

"No."

"Then I won't think so."

"Well, I believe I was thinking that it seems a shame to spend so much time doing something that has no value. It seems a waste."

"Oh, I agree. Don't misunderstand me, I find the occupation very stimulating. There's always pleasure in exercising one's mental faculties, and I enjoy what I do. But you're quite right, it's a worthless way to spend one's life. Unfortunately it's the only way I can earn sufficient money." He gathered the reins. "Come along, let's canter."

We set heels to our mounts and rode in silence for a few minutes, crossing the heath to the Dover Road, then on to the stretch called Washerwomen's Bottom. As we slowed to a walk and turned north again I said, "What would you like to do if you could choose?"

He smiled his self-mocking smile. "I'd like to publish books."

"Write them?"

"No. Publish them. I'd like to publish educational books, because I'm sure most books in that category could be done very much better."

There was sudden warmth in his voice, and when I looked at him I saw the spark of enthusiasm in his eyes, a surprising contrast to the usual cool gaze. He went on, "Even while I was still at school I discovered that most experts are poor writers. They're often vague and ambiguous and inexact. They have no skill in conveying their knowledge to others. But a man or woman with a gift for words can take the thoughts of the expert and present them in such a way as to be easily understood."

I remembered our books on the *Casey*. One had been a primer on the science of navigation, but the text was appallingly obscure. I recalled wrestling my way through it sentence by sentence in an effort to comprehend the muddled instructions. "How would you find the writers to put the knowledge of the experts into simple form?" I said.

Chad looked at me in surprise. "That's part of the challenge. It's like a treasure hunt, choosing a subject that needs a first-class textbook, finding an expert to provide the material, finding a writer to make good sense of it, making sure they don't end up fighting like cat and dog. And at the end, a really fine book. I can think of nothing more satisfying."

I could not help smiling at his enthusiasm, and said, "Why don't you do it?"

"Ahh . . ." He sighed a long sigh. "Publishing is a gentleman's profession and requires a lot of money, particularly for a new venture. I'd be very happy to try it, except that whatever money I have is committed elsewhere for the next twenty years."

It was next morning that Liza and I first encountered the man she was to dub Casey's Butler. Our waiting room was unusually full, and we were both interviewing new applicants for work in service, taking down details of name and address, age, experience, and references. Although we had only the one office, Liza and I worked without distracting each other, and were very formal if we had occasion to exchange a few words, always addressing each other as Miss Faith and Miss Brown.

I finished noting particulars of a girl seeking a position as parlor maid, and asked her to send in the next person as she left. A few moments later there was a tap on the door and a tall man entered. He wore a morning coat suit of iron gray worsted, well made and of good quality. In one hand he carried a silk hat, and over the same arm was folded a Chesterfield overcoat. He was perhaps fifty, with a square face and rather penetrating blue eyes. His hair was thick and short, chestnut red in color but tinged with gray, and his beard was cut in the style favored by the Prince of Wales.

If I had not glimpsed him sitting among the other servants when I went to the door earlier, I would have taken him for a gentleman seeking to engage a valet or perhaps a housekeeper. As it was, now that I saw him properly and could note the quality of his dress and the manner of his bearing, I could only assume that he was a very superior butler or personal manservant. Such men could be quite well dressed and bear themselves with dignity, but in my brief experience I had never seen any servant like this one.

I noticed that Liza was distracted for a moment from the cook she was attending to, for she gave me a somewhat startled glance. Feeling rather uncertain of myself, I pointed to the chair beside my desk and said, "I am Miss Brown. Please sit down and tell me how we may help you."

"Thank you, Miss Brown." He had a mellow, pleasing voice, quite unlike the artificially refined accent I had heard one or two senior servants use. He sat down, rested his hat on his knees, and looked at me very directly with what seemed a curiously profound interest. "I wonder if you could assist me to find a position as a butler?" he said.

"Well . . ." I reached for one of our application forms and picked up my pen. "Let me set down the particulars, and then we can see. Your name, please?"

His name was Richard Brown, his age, forty-nine, his address was on a road in Blackheath I did not know. I wrote all this down, then said, "What experience have you had?"

"None, Miss Brown," he replied apologetically, "but I am very willing to learn."

Liza finished with her cook and sent her out, but did not

ask for the next person to be sent in. Clearly she was curious about this man, and perhaps also interested to see how I would deal with him. I finished writing "No experience" on the form, and said, "Do you mean you have served as a footman before but never as a butler?"

"No, Miss Brown, I mean that I have no experience of working in service before." He was watching me with an expression I could not fathom, but I could have vowed there was humor in it.

I put down my pen and said, "Then what sort of experience have you acquired in your previous employment?" I had made no comment on the fact that his name was the same as mine, for it was one of the most common in England, but I was trying to avoid using it because I felt that too much repetition of Miss Brown and Mr. Brown would sound foolish.

"I have had quite wide experience," he said. "You see, I was a soldier for many years."

Since he had not spoken my name this time, I felt I could use his, and said, "I'm not sure that what you learn as a soldier would equip you for domestic work, Mr. Brown."

I was about to ask if he had been a batman in the army, but as I paused he said gently, "Colonel."

"I beg your pardon?"

"Colonel Brown, not Mr. Brown. It is a point of no particular importance, but—"

I interrupted, my voice rising with indignation. "You are a *colonel*?"

"Why yes, Miss Brown. A retired colonel."

I flashed a look of astonishment at Liza, and saw that she was struggling not to laugh. Turning to the man again I said sharply, "I think you have been wasting my time, sir!"

He looked troubled. "If that is so, please forgive me. Do you feel it unlikely that I could obtain a position as butler?"

"I think it impossible, and I greatly doubt that you wish to do so, since you have the good fortune to be a gentleman."

He nodded pensively. "True. But a gentleman is permitted to be eccentric, surely? That is a great English tradition, and I do believe I might find it both interesting and enlightening to work as a butler. Albeit for a short time, perhaps."

He lifted his eyebrows, smiling, and to my surprise I found myself smiling in response as I shook my head. "I don't think you would last very long, Colonel," I said "and since I have the reputation of Miss Faith's agency to consider, I'm bound to tell you that we cannot accept you on our books." I crumpled the form I had begun to fill in.

"What a pity," he murmured, and glanced toward Liza. "But perhaps you ladies would allow me to give you tea one afternoon?"

Liza laughed then, and said, "Really, Colonel, that is not at all a proper suggestion."

His blue eyes twinkled. "An eccentric may make such suggestions without impropriety, Miss Faith. And perhaps we could give substance to the occasion by discussing my purchase of a small interest in your agency. I am seeking fresh activities now that I have taken early retirement."

"I'm sorry, Colonel." Liza was still smiling. "I don't think we could cope with an eccentric partner."

"Ah, I am hoist by my own petard. But will you ladies do me the honor of coming to tea with me? The address I gave is of the Lansdowne Hotel, where I now live. The lounge is comfortable, and they serve very nice cucumber sandwiches. Or we could go to a tea shop if you prefer."

I had left the matter in Liza's hands now, and was rather enjoying the outlandishness of this unusual gentleman's behavior. It was almost with regret that I heard her say, "Thank you, but we must decline, and we must also ask you to allow us to carry on with our work. We are business ladies, you know."

He rose at once. "Yes, I must not detain you further, but since we are not too distant neighbors, perhaps we shall meet again. Good-bye, Miss Brown, and thank you for your kindness. Goodbye, Miss Faith." He bowed over our hands in turn, and went quietly out.

Liza and I looked at each other, then burst into smothered laughter. When she could speak, Liza said, "Oh, what an extraordinary man! I've never known such a thing to happen before. It must be you, Casey, you seem to attract peculiar happenings. But he seemed quite a nice gentleman, didn't he? I can't imagine there's any harm in him."

"No . . ." I said slowly. "I think you're right, Liza. But I have a feeling that Colonel Brown is not quite what he seems to be."

The story of Casey's Butler was told to Chad that evening, with Liza making a great joke of my expression on discovering that the would-be butler was a colonel. Chad was amused. "You should have agreed to take tea with him," he said. "If we don't do something to maintain our Bohemian reputation now and again, we'll gravely disappoint the neighbors."

I saw Colonel Brown on two occasions during the rest of that week. The first time was as Liza and I drove to the agency one morning. He was out on the heath, riding a splendid gray mare, and came cantering across as he saw our gig, reining in to wait for us, and raising his hat as we passed. According to the ladies who wrote about etiquette in the magazines, he should not have done this and we should have ignored him since we had never been introduced, but without consulting each other we both smiled and inclined our heads and wished him good morning.

The second occasion came two days later, when I was shopping in Greenwich before returning at six o'clock to collect Liza from the agency. The lamps had been lit, for dusk was falling, and as I crossed the road I came upon Colonel Brown, leaning on his cane under a gas lamp, talking to our vicar from Greenwich Church. They both greeted me, and Colonel Brown said, "You have a heavy basket there, Miss Brown. May I carry it to your gig for you?"

To refuse would have seemed churlish. I thanked him, we wished the vicar good evening, and together we walked to where I had left the gig by the Naval College, only fifty yards away. When Colonel Brown asked, very pleasantly, not after Miss Faith but after Miss Lockhart and her brother, I realized he must know more about us than I had thought, but he made no attempt to engage me in conversation or press his company upon me. When we reached the gig he put my basket in, handed me up, and wished me a courteous good evening.

I might have wondered more about this rather strange colonel if I had not been otherwise preoccupied, but during the past few days I had become increasingly nervous about meeting Sam Redwing again. This was foolish, and I thought Liza and Chad might laugh when I told them of it, but in fact they were both sympathetic.

"It's very natural," said Liza. "You first met him in your own little world of the *Casey*, when you were supposed to be a coolie girl, and you've hardly exchanged more than a few words with you as your real self. Now you're to meet him in a different world and as a different person, so of course you feel shy. Dear Lord, when I think of what you went through with your husband it's a wonder you can bear even to look at a man. Any man."

It was Friday evening. Chad had just come down freshly shaved and bathed, and was sitting with us for a few minutes before leaving to catch the train for his usual night's gambling.

"The real reason why Casey is nervous about meeting Sam again," he said thoughtfully, "is very simple. She saved his life, and as she may already have noticed, Sam is a romantic. He's going to overwhelm her with thanks all over again. He's going to tell us every tiny detail of how Casey rescued him, and he's going to make a great heroine of her."

I exclaimed, "Oh, no!"

Liza said, "But what she did *was* heroic, Chad."

"I agree, darling, but Casey doesn't think so and she's going to be greatly embarrassed." He grinned and got to his feet. "Now I must go, but I shall play truant again tomorrow so I can come with you to meet Sam off the boat."

He kissed Liza, gave me a smile, and wished us both good night. When he had gone I said, "You know, I think Chad was right. I'm worried that Sam might make a great fuss of me."

Liza looked up from a glove she was mending. "I'm afraid he will, dear. Sam's sense of gratitude is quite unstinting. You know, you and Chad have something in common. Each of you has saved Sam Redwing's life. With Chad it happened ages ago, but as far as Sam is concerned it could have happened yesterday."

Greatly intrigued, I put down my own mending and said, "Tell me about it, Liza."

"There are some details I don't know, but they had an encounter with pirates when Chad was just turned fifteen."

"Pirates?"

"Oh, not Spanish main type of pirates with the skull and crossbones. But there are still Chinese pirates who sail the coastal waters in junks, from Kiungchow right up to Shanghai, ready to pounce on little ships slow enough to be grappled and boarded. They take any valuables or cargo, sometimes the craft itself, and often kill their victims out of hand. It's rare for them to come close inshore by Hong Kong because of the navy, but they're very daring, and they sometimes snap up a prize at dusk. Well, that's what happened to Sam and Chad. They had been out fishing one day on the ketch Sam's family owned at the time, with a crew of three Chinese. Coming back, they were a mile offshore when a junk came out of the dusk and grappled them. A dozen pirates were hauling on the ropes to bring the boats close enough to board."

I shivered. "Oh Liza, what a dreadful moment."

"Yes. Enough to freeze the blood. Sam had a pistol and fired twice, but then somebody threw a club of some sort. It hit Sam on the head and knocked him half senseless. The crew ran below to hide, and three pirates jumped from the junk to the ketch, all with big Chinese swords. Chad hit one with a belaying pin as he landed, knocking him back into the sea. The man dropped his sword on the deck, and Chad must have snatched it up. He won't ever talk about what happened, but Sam saw most of it. He says he came out of his daze and lay there on the deck, able to watch everything but quite unable to move a finger. The blow on the head seemed to have paralyzed him for a few moments."

I said, "So Chad was alone against the two pirates?"

"Sam says the first thing he saw was Chad standing astride him, and there was a dreadful clashing of steel with little sparks flying in the dusk. Then Chad gave a terrible cry and seemed to hurl himself at his attackers. He was never big and muscular, but always very wiry and very quick. Sam thinks he wounded both pirates quite badly, judging from the blood on the deck afterward. In any event he drove them right back over the side, and then slashed the grappling ropes. Somebody threw a sword, and the tip just sliced Chad above his eye, the one that droops now. But he was able to snatch up the pistol Sam had dropped and fire another four shots as the ships drifted apart. I suppose the pirates had had enough, because they sailed off into the darkness, and that was the end of it. But Chad has had that funny drooping eyelid ever since, and Sam never fails to send or bring him a little present every year on the anniversary of that day. He's a remembering man, Sam Redwing."

I tried to imagine the horror of the scene faced by that young boy. It seemed to me that he must have been possessed by a kind of berserk anger to have driven off two desperate men armed with swords. When I said as much to Liza she looked pensive. "I don't know, dear. It's not like Chad, really. Perhaps it was more a matter of him being very determined." She looked at me with blue eyes full of affection. "Rather like you."

"Me?" I was startled.

"Dragging a sick and helpless man on a stretcher across a Caribbean island in a hurricane?"

"Oh, but I just didn't stop to think, Liza."

"You had more than enough time to think, but I won't argue with you. Sam can do that."

Next morning we hired a growler to take us to the Royal Albert Dock. The great noise of the iron-tyred wheels on the cobbles as we clattered through Blackwall Tunnel reminded me vividly of the day I had stepped ashore from the *Avon*, full of trepidation, expecting at best to find work as a scullery maid, only to be met by Liza Lockhart, who had given me a new life happier than any I could have imagined. Sitting beside her now, I pressed her arm in silent gratitude as we passed through the lamplit tunnel.

The *Derwent* had docked a little early and was already tied up alongside when we arrived, but it seemed an age before the gangways went down and disembarkation began. Liza was flushed with excitement, I was as nervous as I had expected to be, and Chad leaned on his cane with his usual tranquil air.

Suddenly Sam Redwing was there, striding toward us with hat in hand and carrying a small suitcase, an even taller man than I remembered, tanned by the voyage and looking in excellent health now, lips parted in a grin of huge pleasure. I edged back a little so I should not intrude upon his greeting with Liza and Chad. As he drew near he simply dropped both hat and case to the ground, swooped upon Liza, grasped her at the waist and lifted her in the air with a whoop of delight.

"Liza, honey! It's good to be home." He put her down and kissed her heartily. "I'm always afraid I'll come back one day to find some beau has married you and carried you off."

She was laughing, tears in her eyes, straightening her hat. "That's the day pigs will fly. Welcome home, Sam."

"Thanks, Liza girl. And how's Small Fry?" He gripped Chad's hand and delivered a joyous punch to the shoulder. "Still winning, you paleface dog?"

"I'm making ends meet." Chad's manner was quieter but I felt his pleasure was just as great. "Are you fully recovered now, Big Chief?"

"I'm as good as new, and we know who to thank for that." He leaned sideways to see me, for I had hidden myself almost completely behind Chad. "Ahh . . . Casey. Let me have a look at you." He moved forward and reached out to take both my hands in his, gazing at me wonderingly. "Lord, I scarcely know you, honey. Your hair's longer, your face has lost that gypsy tan, you're wearing real nice girl's clothes, and you look pretty as a picture. Gee, you're *smaller* than I thought. How in the name of Old Nick did you get me off that boat?" His hands tightened and he glanced at Liza and Chad. "With a block and tackle, up a cliff, in a hurricane."

I felt the color rushing to my cheeks at his flattery and said quickly, "I'm so very happy to see you well again, Mr. Redwing."

"Sam, please. Remember?"

"Yes, I'm sorry. I'm feeling shy and confused, but I want to thank you with all my heart for sending me to your dear friends, Liza and Chad. They've looked after me as if I were their sister."

Sam nodded slowly. I had glanced toward Liza as I spoke. Her eyes were on Sam, and when I looked back at him I found him staring at me with strange intensity. A moment later he released my hands, laughed, and turned to gather up his hat and suitcase, saying, "Let's all go home." But in that brief moment when I was under his gaze I had felt a sharp qualm of unease. I could not have given the cause, but it seemed to spring from a sudden presentiment that some strange trouble I could not identify was about to fall upon me.

14

DURING THE RIDE HOME AND THE LIGHT LUNCHEON I HAD prepared for us there was much talk and laughter. Though it had rained quite a lot during the week, on the day of Sam's arrival the sky was clear and a wintry sun warmed the air. Before tea that afternoon we all went for a walk through the park to the river. This was by Sam's wish, for he declared that he loved Greenwich, and though he often left it he always longed to be back.

I felt at one with him in this, for even in the short month I had lived here I had acquired a deep affection for this little part of London. I loved the feeling that history lay in the very cobbles we trod, and in the banks that held the river. I could stand as if in a dream, looking down from the park at the beauty of the Queen's House, and of Wren's colonnaded Royal Naval College beyond, peopling them in my imagination with figures from the past. And yet I enjoyed the modern bustle of the place, so different from anything I had known in Jamaica.

By day the streets seemed full of cries from every kind of street seller, the knife-grinder and chair-mender, the man with a tray of ginger cakes and the women with packets of fresh herbs. There were stalls of shrimps and winkles, cockles and mussels, whelks and eels. There was the muffin man with his bell and the hokey-pokey man with his ice cream. For entertainment there was the barrel organ man, or a fiddler with a monkey on a chain, or a trio of minstrels working their way back to London after appearing at some country fair.

I hoped that our afternoon walk in the fresh air would clear away the shadowy unease in my mind, but this was not to be. Later, while I prepared dinner and Liza unpacked Sam's scanty luggage acquired en route, Chad told Sam the truth about my identity, revealing that I was the girl he had met in Jamaica, and recounting all that I had said concerning my marriage to Oliver Foy, his death at Daniel's hands, and our running away together on the *Casey*.

I knew nothing of this until I went to join them in the sitting room, having done all I could in the kitchen for the time being. Liza had finished her task before me and was already there. When I entered the room Sam was pacing with arms folded tightly across his chest, shoulders hunched, as if struggling to hold in the dangerous anger that glinted from eyes narrowed to dark slits. Liza was saying, "Please calm down, Sam dear, there's nothing to be done now"—she looked at me for support—"and you'll upset Casey if you go into a rage like this."

He stopped pacing to glare at her. "Don't tell me not to get angry, Liza!" I was shocked at his manner, but then recalled that he had been Liza's playmate in early childhood, and they had grown up as closely as brother and sister. He flung out a hand toward me, almost choking on his words as he continued: "This . . . this swine of a man, Foy, he has a wife like Casey there and he . . . he maltreats and degrades her? You bet I'm in a rage!"

Chad sat gazing moodily into the fire. As Sam finished speaking Liza shot me another look of appeal, and I screwed up my courage to intervene. It was not my place to do so, and it might offend Sam, but it was clearly what Liza wanted, and there was nothing in the world I would not do for her.

I said, "Sam, I would be very glad if—"

He turned toward me and broke in on my words. "I wish to God I'd known you then, Casey. I wish I'd known about *him*—"

I interrupted in turn, and very sharply. "Sam, I'm not a coolie girl to be talked down. By your courtesy and generosity I'm Casey Brown, of this household. Will you listen to me, please?"

He stiffened, and from the corner of my eye I saw Chad look up. I went on, "Oliver Foy is dead. It all happened more than three years ago, and I want nothing better than to forget it and never speak of it again. I had a very happy life on the *Casey*, and my life here has been very happy too, so I'm not to be pitied. This is the day of your homecoming, Sam. Please don't spoil it for us by anger."

Sam Redwing stared at me for long seconds, then his face cleared and he nodded gravely. "All right, Casey," he said softly. "All right, Casey girl. Whatever you say."

I was troubled by the intensity in him, and to lighten the atmosphere I said in my coolie voice, mixing Chinese pidgin learned from Daniel with the West African creole of the English-speaking Caribbean islands, "Dis woman stop ten-piece minute wit' you bockra, after go housecook for make plenty good kai-kai."

Everybody laughed. Sam clapped his hands together and said, "That's how she talked to me all the time at first." Chad got up and held a chair for me, saying, "If you can spare ten minutes, sit down and tell us about Caribbean pidgin. We know housecook means kitchen and kai-kai means food, but what's bockra?"

"It just means a white person." I was thankful to Chad for helping to change the subject, and hoped it would distract Sam, for even though he had relaxed now I could feel his eyes still on me as I moved to sit down. For a moment I was able to catch a glimpse of Liza in the looking glass above the sofa. She was gazing at Sam, and unaware that anyone's eyes were upon her. On her pretty round face there was an expression that startled me, for in it were mingled happiness tinged with sorrow, and longing tinged with a kind of wry hopelessness.

As I turned to take the chair I saw Liza in reality, and already the look had gone, but it remained printed upon my mind like a photograph. At the time my head was too full of jumbled thoughts to interpret what I had seen, and it was not until I lay down in bed that night, after a busy, exhausting, yet happy day, that I abruptly sat bolt upright with shock as realization burst upon me.

It was so simple and so clear. Liza was in love with Sam Redwing. I thought it likely she had been in love with him for a very long time, and I was utterly certain that neither he nor Chad had any idea of her feelings. Sam had known her since the day she was born. I knew, from the times when Liza and

I had chatted about the past, that in childhood he had played with her, teased her, pulled her pigtails, fought for her, and in general behaved like an older brother. And now, all these years later, his way with Liza was just the same; but at some point during those years, Liza's comradely affection for her childhood playmate had turned to deepest love. I doubted that this was recent. In all probability it had happened during her teens, for I suspected that Sam Redwing was her first and only love, and this was why she had never married.

I lay down again slowly, beset by a turmoil of thoughts and feelings. My heart ached for Liza. I was impatient, almost angry with Sam for not having fallen in love with Liza and married her long ago. I warned myself never to let Liza guess that I knew she was in love with him, for since her feelings were not returned this would be humiliating for her. And I felt within me a great foreboding as I recalled the way Sam had kept looking at me.

I did not want to flatter myself, but I had little doubt that he was intrigued by me, probably because of the drama of our meeting and the mystery that surrounded me. Now that he knew the truth, I hoped he might find me less intriguing, but my fear was that his feelings toward me might be of a very much stronger nature.

The next day was Sunday, and in the evening we all went to church at St. Alfege's, Greenwich. Sam was reluctant, claiming that he was just a heathen redskin, but Liza swept his protests aside. "Whenever you're at home you come to church with us on Sunday, and you're not to start backsliding now, Sam. I've enough to do without worrying about your soul."

"My soul? I don't think I've got one, honey."

"Nonsense, it's just well hidden. If we keep trying, we'll come across it sooner or later."

Colonel Brown was in the congregation that evening. Liza nudged me as we rose for the second hymn, pointing surreptitiously to our left, and I saw the tall bearded figure in one of the side pews, a row or two in front of ours. When we left after the service the vicar buttonholed Sam for a few moments to welcome him on his return, and as we paused just within the porch the colonel passed us, giving a little bow as he wished us good evening. Liza and I responded. Chad returned the bow, and then, when the colonel had passed out of earshot, he murmured, "From the description you gave, Liza, I imagine that must be Casey's Butler."

On the drive home Liza recounted the story of the eccentric colonel for Sam's benefit. "I'm sure he only pretended to be seeking a position as butler so he could strike up an acquaintance with Casey," she said with a giggle. "He has a very odd way of looking at her, you know, as if he were making a profound study of our Miss Brown."

I said, "Oh Liza, it's not just me. He has that penetrating look for everyone, I think. Perhaps it's because he was a soldier." At that moment I was not so much concerned with Colonel Brown as with the way Sam kept gazing at me as we sat facing each other in the carriage, and I found myself constantly looking out of the window to avoid meeting his eyes.

All through that day there had been times when I felt myself to be under something of a strain. Sam was happy to be home, and Chad equally glad to see him there, declaring that his return restored a proper balance to the household. But I could not help being alert to the way Liza looked at Sam when she did not know anyone was watching her, and I could not help being very much aware of Sam Redwing's interest in me. The combination of these two factors gave me moments of great anxiety, and it was a relief to know that I would be back at my usual tasks next day, dividing my time between the house and the agency.

"Your routine won't be very different with Sam home, Casey dear," said Liza that evening as we finished a game of *mah tsiang* before going to bed. "He can have breakfast with us in the morning if he's up in time, otherwise he'll have to put up with whatever he can persuade Amy to cook for him, poor man." She turned to Sam. "You usually spend your days in town, pursuing this scheme or that, so you can either have luncheon there or have whatever Casey happens to be getting Chad for breakfast. Then, if you're good, you can have dinner with us, providing Casey doesn't mind cooking for three."

Sam smiled at me. "I don't want to put her to any trouble."

I said, "It's no trouble at all, but my cooking is sometimes a little suspect."

He grinned. "Not as bad as Liza's, I bet."

I frowned at him. "Don't be unkind."

He looked surprised. "Liza doesn't mind. She knows she's a poor cook."

"Liza has the agency to run. She can't do everything."

Liza said, "You're lovely and loyal, Casey, but I don't suppose I would cook any better even if I didn't run the agency."

She looked at Sam. "Are you rich or poor at the moment, Sam dear?"

He considered. "Sort of middling. I'm O.K., you might say."

"You're what?"

"O.K. It's a word they use a lot in America. I was there again for a while before going down into the Caribbean. It means all right. Yes. Fine. In good order."

Chad said, "How do you spell it?"

"It's just the two letters. O and K."

"Then why does it mean the various things you said?"

Sam lifted his shoulders in a shrug. "Search me. I never found anyone who knew." His eyes sparkled suddenly. "Hey, talking about cooking, there was a bit I missed out when I was telling you about the hurricane, how Casey heaved me up and got hot coffee down me, right in the middle of it—"

I said, "Oh no, Sam," and stood up. "You talked about that day all through dinner, and if you're going to start again then please wait till I've gone to bed. I'm embarrassed when you make so much of it."

He looked hurt for a moment, then nodded as if confirming something to himself. "Sure. I'm sorry, honey." He turned to Liza: "I'll tell you another time. You were asking just now if I'm rich or poor. You need some money?"

She shook her head, smiling. "No. If you're rich you'll probably be at home for quite a long time before you plunge into some new venture. If you're poor you'll soon be away again. I just wondered which it was likely to be."

Sam laughed. "Same old Liza. You know, Casey, way back when she was five years old she always wanted to know what I was going to do next."

Liza said placidly, "Only because you're such an idiot, Sam, and if you have something too wild in mind I try to dissuade you."

"Well, I'll be selling out my interest in that fertilizer project. It means taking a small loss, but that won't break my back. And I'll be looking for something new, but it won't be abroad, it will be right here." He looked at me. "I don't aim to go away again for a long time."

It was good to plunge into work at the domestic agency next day and forget the shadowy anxieties that prickled within me. Liza was a little quieter than usual, and I wondered if she was preoccupied by much the same thoughts as were in the back of my mind. Shortly before noon I went off in the gig to do some shopping, then continued to Heathside to make breakfast for Chad. Sam had come down for early breakfast that morning, and I hoped he might be out for luncheon, but he was waiting to help me alight as I drove in, and ready to follow me to the kitchen and chat, but I said firmly that I would make mistakes if I tried to cook and talk at the same time, and I must have the kitchen to myself.

I was a little troubled at the notion of serving him another breakfast rather than luncheon, and decided I must arrange matters differently in the future. Twenty minutes later I sent Amy to tap on Chad's door and tell him that breakfast was about to be served. He was always ready, for he had told me that by listening for the sound of the gig arriving on the drive beneath his window he could judge when I would call.

At one o'clock Chad came into the dining room with Sam as I was setting the chafing dishes on the sideboard, and he wished me good morning with his usual amiable manner. I said, "Good morning, Chad dear. I'll just fetch the coffee and then I must hurry back to Liza."

Sam looked disappointed. Chad lifted an eyebrow and said, "You usually keep me company while you have your milk and sandwich."

"I know, but you have Sam to keep you company now, and we're so busy at the agency today. I can't leave it all to Liza." There was some truth in what I said, but not a great deal. My main concern was to avoid being in Sam's company whenever I could. The notion that he might fall in love with me, might want to court me and even propose marriage, was frightening. I liked and respected Sam Redwing very much, but knowing as I did that he was the love of Liza's life, I could not begin to think of him as other than a friend.

Strangely enough, I did not fear courtship by a man because of what Oliver Foy had done to me. The years as a sea gypsy seemed to have cleansed me from the stain of all that pain and humiliation, and to have freed me from any revulsion toward men that my husband had implanted in me. I did not believe that marriages were made in heaven, though I had cause to know that some could be made in hell. I thought it likely that I might have made a satisfactory marriage with any one of three or four young men I could recall from among the families I had known in Jamaica. After the horrors I had experienced, I felt I could wish for nothing better than simple kindness in a husband, and I was sure Sam Redwing could be relied upon for that. But I did not want a husband, and above all I did not want Sam to court me, for I would feel guilty of betrayal.

It seemed to me that until now he had been a bachelor without thought of marrying. While this was so, Liza could perhaps bear to love him without response. But if he fell seriously in love with me, with a stranger from across the world whom she had taken into her home, it would surely be heartbreaking for her. I could not speak out. I could not tell him of her love and urge him to open his eyes and see her not as the grown version of his childhood playmate but as a lovely woman whom a man should be grateful to cherish. That would surely be an unforgivable intrusion, and a fruitless one. I could not speak to Liza. Could not apologize for the fact that Sam felt for me what she yearned to have him feel for her. That would be a cruel humiliation.

Of one thing I was very sure. Rather than hurt Liza I would go away, simply disappear quietly one day by taking a train to a distant town and finding work in service. I did not know how I could bear to do this now, but I knew I would do it if need be.

As I drove back to the agency I prayed that I was mistaken, and that out of conceit I was imagining Sam to be attracted to me. Liza looked surprised to see that I had brought my lunchtime sandwich back to eat with her, together with sufficient milk from the dairy for the two of us. Our desks in the office had been pushed together facing each other, and as I sat down at mine I sought for a way to prevent any talk of Sam and his return home. Nothing came to mind, and in desperation I did something I had always been careful to avoid before. I asked questions about Chad.

"Liza, did Chad mention that while we were out riding last week he told me how he's gradually paying back the bankruptcy debts?"

She smiled and shook her head. "No dear, I made a point of leaving it to him to tell you whatever he wished, but I'm glad you know."

I unwrapped our sandwiches, put them on two plates, and passed one across to Liza. "It seems a dreadful burden for you both," I said. "A lifetime burden. I don't know much about these things, but it seems strange to me that such debts can be inherited."

Liza made a wry face. "They can't, my sweet. Creditors are paid so much on the pound, and that's an end of it. But not as far as Mama was concerned. She had a fanatical sense of honor, and worked herself into an early grave paying back a tiny fraction of the debts."

"Oh, I'm sorry. Yes, Chad told me about that. But if the debts aren't inherited, why has he carried on trying to repay them?"

She was silent for a few moments, her eyes blank with remembering, then she said in a rather tired voice, "He was sixteen, which is a very impressionable age, especially for a boy. On her deathbed Mama made him promise never to rest until he had cleared Papa's name and paid all debts." She looked at me, and her clear blue eyes were moist with tears. "To exact a deathbed promise can be a very wicked thing, however well intended. When Chad was younger I argued violently with him, trying to make him see that he should not be bound by such a promise, for it was given under dreadful duress. How can a boy refuse his mother as she lies dying? Oh, it was so unfair, Casey."

I said, "Yes, and such a terrible burden. I marvel that he isn't a jaundiced and ill-humored man. Could he not be satisfied with having cleared your father's name?"

Liza sighed. "No, dear. That promise sank steadily into his very being until it became . . . well, an obsession, I suppose. I know he can never free himself from it now, not until he has discharged his task. This is why he will never marry. He has nothing to offer a wife and children while he must carry a millstone of debt for half a lifetime to come. Sam has argued with him, too, but Chad is quite immovable, and so we try no more. I hate to quarrel with my brother, and so I accept that he must obey the devil that drives him in whatever way he thinks best, and I simply try to give him my love and support."

I felt my heart go out to Liza, and in that moment my determination to do anything rather than hurt or humiliate her was strengthened. I said, "He told me that what he would really like to do is publish books."

She smiled and rubbed a tear from her eye impatiently. "Yes, he would do it very well, I think. But never mind. I suppose few of us are lucky enough to have whatever we want most, so we must make the best of what we do have." She put aside her empty plate and glass, and turned the pages of a notebook. "Now, Mrs. Farrow will be calling at three to run her eye over our references for a cook and a parlor maid. Will you deal with her, Casey? She can be rather trying, and I'm in a funny mood today. I might be too impatient with her."

I said anxiously, "You're not feeling unwell?"

"Oh heavens, no."

"Liza, I haven't upset you in any way?"

"Not for a moment, and don't look so round-eyed with alarm, Casey dear. I'm quite all right. It's just that I'm always at sixes and sevens for a day or two when Sam comes home and throws the household into confusion."

"He is rather...overwhelming. But you don't mind, do you? I expect you're used to him."

She gave me a whimsical look. "It's no use minding with Sam. You take him as he is or not at all. I learned that when I was five."

Next day Sam bought a gig for himself. During the week he spent two afternoons in London and the rest of the time haunting me. When I left the agency at noon to make Chad's breakfast, Sam would be waiting to drive me home and bring me back. On one of those days I felt I was being doubly haunted, for I came out of the agency to find Sam sitting on the bench by the church in conversation with Colonel Brown. It was a cold day, not at all the weather for sitting out, and as Sam drove me home after I had exchanged greetings with the colonel he said, "That's a tough old buzzard. Just finished a ten-mile walk, he was telling me."

I said, "He certainly seems very sprightly. How did you come to be chatting with him?"

"Oh, he just came walking across the heath, sat down, and introduced himself." Sam grinned. "He didn't mention having applied for a job as butler, but said he was known to you and Liza, and that he'd seen us in church. Seems a nice friendly sort. He was telling me he's spent most of the last twenty years abroad, and only came back to England recently." Sam turned his head to gaze at me with warm eyes. "Well, how are you, honey?"

"About the same as I was when you saw me at breakfast, Sam. I'm fine, thank you."

"Settling down happily now? Enjoying your new life?"

"Oh, very much. You've all been so kind. Now please watch the road, Sam, or we'll run into something."

Twice that week Sam appeared at the agency in the afternoon, wishing to take us to the tea shop across the road for a pot of tea. We refused and shooed him away, for we were genuinely busy. I pretended to believe that it was Liza's company he sought rather than mine, since they were lifelong friends, and I did everything possible to avoid being left alone with him, but each day I became ever more conscious that he was strongly attracted to me.

If Liza was in any way aware of this she gave no sign, and treated me as affectionately as ever, but by the end of the week, though I struggled to keep a bright countenance at all times, I was in despair. Sam had not yet begun to court me, but I was sure he would do so soon, or, being the impulsive man he was, might even propose to me. I would refuse, of course, but there could be nothing secret about such a matter. Liza would know, and thereafter would carry the knowledge that even if one day Sam turned to her as other than a friend, she would be no more than second best. The thought of this was more than I could bear, and it made me go hot with a curious kind of shame.

On Sunday morning I woke early and lay in bed trying to think what I should do. I knew that if I simply disappeared from Heathside Liza would miss me greatly, yet I could think of no other way to protect her. And if I went, could I go without leaving some sort of message? But what could I say? The problem was still unresolved when I got up, washed and dressed, and went down to make breakfast.

At three o'clock that afternoon, for the second time in my life, I received a proposal of marriage. But not from Sam Redwing.

15

On Sundays we dined at one o'clock, and either Amy or Meg would come for an hour in the afternoon to earn a shilling by washing up. At three o'clock on the second Sunday after Sam's return I inspected the kitchen, made sure that all plates and cutlery had been put away in their proper places, gave Amy her shilling, and told her she could go home.

Sam and Liza were playing a game of draughts in the sitting room. I had been invited to play the winner, but had excused myself on the grounds of having domestic matters to attend to. I was going up to my room to tidy myself, and had reached the first landing when Chad appeared in the door of his study and said, "Could you spare me a few minutes, Casey?"

"Oh." I was a little puzzled. "Why, yes. Of course."

He stood aside for me to enter, held a chair for me to be seated, and said, "Do you mind if I close the door?"

In most households this would have been quite out of order, but ours was a far from conventional home, and I had no qualms about being alone with Chad. I said, "No, I don't mind. What is it, Chad? A secret?"

"Not really." His manner was pensive as he took the big chair behind his desk and swiveled it to face me. "May I ask you one or two personal questions? They may seem impertinent, but there's good reason for them."

"Well...yes." I felt a twinge of unease. "I haven't done anything wrong, have I?"

He shook his head. "Casey, remembering your experience of marriage, do you think it's likely that you will wish to marry again?"

Taken completely by surprise, I stared into the smoky gray eyes but could read nothing in them. Had he noticed the nature of Sam's interest in me, I wondered, and was he making an oblique reference to it? If so, why? I tried to stop speculating, and gave thought to his question. There was only a very brief pause before I said, "I have no wish to marry again, Chad. There was a time when the thought would have made me shiver. That's long past now, but it's still unlikely that a day will come when I shall wish to marry. I'm very happy as I am."

"Thank you for a clear answer," he said politely. "Now a second question. I have to ask if you feel able to trust me completely, Casey, and I beg you to be utterly candid in your answer. I shall take no offense if you tell me you have reservations."

I was almost beyond surprise now, and scarcely wondered at his question. "I'm not quite sure in which way you mean—" I began, then broke off and gave an impatient shake of my head. "Oh, but that doesn't matter. Yes, I trust you as I trust Liza and Sam."

"Thank you," he said again. "Now, do you remember that a little while ago I explained to you how I make money by gambling, in order to pay the family debts?"

"Yes, I remember very well. You spoke of having a memory for cards and an ability to calculate mathematical chances, so you didn't depend on luck."

"That's right. But I have a problem. First, there is a limit to the number of men in my club who play cards for high stakes, and some of those who do are becoming a little disinclined to play against me, though I can always find plenty willing to partner me at the whist table."

"Because you win consistently?"

"Yes. Don't misunderstand me. I'm not suspected of anything shady, but I am beginning to be regarded as a professional gambler, which isn't entirely acceptable among gentlemen." He smiled. "I am indeed a professional gambler, of course, but I can well do without being marked as such. It would therefore be better if I adopted a more casual approach, and played only three nights a week at my club instead of six, but that will reduce my income by half."

I stared at him in dismay. "Oh Chad, that means it will take... I don't know, years and years longer to clear those horrible debts. I know it's not my business, but surely you've done enough? I don't think there can be any legal or moral obligation on you—"

He lifted a hand quickly to stop me, his face expressionless. "I promised," he said simply. "For better or worse I promised, and there's an end to it."

I looked down at my hands clasped in my lap and said, "I beg your pardon. It wasn't for me to speak."

"There's no need to apologize." His voice was friendly, and when I looked up he wore that faint smile of self-mockery I had come to know so well. "All is not lost," he went on. "I've been planning for some time to find a way of playing for higher stakes than my club permits, and this calls for a somewhat different arrangement."

I said, "Can you risk higher stakes? I know you told me that the mathematical chances defeat luck over a period. But can you withstand a long run of bad luck?"

"I have sufficient reserve to stand the worst possible attack Lady Fate can launch," he said, "and also to cope with those occasions when the cut of the cards gives me an unskilled partner. Which reminds me, I was playing with a most excellent partner the night before last, a new member of my club and an acquaintance of yours."

I was surprised. "Of mine?"

"Yes. Your namesake, the eccentric colonel, sometimes known in this household as Casey's Butler."

"Good heavens, is Colonel Brown a gambler?"

"Not really, just a very accomplished player who's rich enough to sit at high-stake tables if the fancy takes him."

"Is he as good as you?"

Chad smiled. "Well, not quite, perhaps. But this is all by the way. The point is, Casey, that higher stakes than I play for now will increase my earnings proportionately, and help me discharge my task the quicker."

"Yes, I understand that."

"A club isn't the best place for what I have in mind. There are some very rich people who like to play cards for high stakes, but who find clubs too public for their taste. They don't like to be gossiped about. Now, for some time I've had in mind the possibility of running a very small establishment in a private house in central London, where a few selected people known to me could meet and play for high stakes. Not a club, but a private residence, with three or four card rooms and not more than one table in each room, to avoid distraction."

I was following Chad closely, but at the back of my mind I kept wondering what these plans could have to do with me. He went on, "There would be a small dining room, and staff sufficient to provide an excellent service, without charge, of course. I would invite guests to play there twice a week, with play ending at midnight. This will help to take away any impression of my house being a high-class gambling den"—he gave a lopsided smile—"even though that is what it will be. On other days I shall play at my club, as usual."

I said, "Won't such an arrangement be a great expense? Surely it will cost a lot of money to rent a suitable house and provide staff?"

Chad smiled. "You have a practical turn of mind I much admire, Casey, and that's the sort of question I hoped you would ask. In fact the cost won't be too great. I've found a suitable house I can rent for three hundred a year in St. James's Square, an ideal location. Staff will only be needed two days each week, from noon till midnight, and I've found a married couple with a daughter to live on the top floor as caretakers. They can keep the place clean and properly serviced during my absence, for I propose to continue living here in Greenwich. Total expenses will come to less than a thousand a year, and even allowing for that I anticipate doubling my income. That is, if the one remaining problem can be solved."

I had not taken my eyes from his face as he spoke, and now I voiced a random thought that came unbidden to my mind. "Chad, do you enjoy gambling?"

He looked at me wonderingly, as if I had surprised him, then shook his head. "You're the first ever to ask. Even Liza and Sam take it for granted that I do. In fact I've little but contempt for gambling. I enjoy the challenge of the game itself, the mental gymnastics, the logical deductions, the memorizing, the calculations, but I would as readily play for matchsticks as for money. I happen to be skilled at it, so I use that skill for a purpose, there's no more to it than that."

"Well, I wish you the very best of good fortune in your new venture."

"There's still a problem to be solved before it can begin."

"Oh yes, I forgot. What is it?"

"I can't invite people to play cards at my home unless there is sufficient background to make it a home. On my own, I should be regarded as Chad Lockhart, gambler. Also, since I shall be playing myself, I can devote little time to acting as host. I shall need somebody to control the staff, help me welcome my guests, make sure that everything possible is done for their comfort, keep an eye on their needs during play, supervise the dining arrangements, ensure that cabs are ready to take them home, and at the same time provide a pleasant and homey domestic background. In short I need a hostess, Casey. I need a wife."

I said, "Yes, I see what you mean, but who—" I caught my breath and felt my cheeks go pale. For long seconds I simply stared at him, unable to speak, my mind in fragments.

"It would be a marriage of convenience," he said gently. "No more than that, I promise. We would continue to live here just as we do now, except that on two days each week we would go to the house in St. James's in the afternoon to have everything ready for, say, six o'clock onwards. On those two nights we should sleep at the house and return in the morning. Separate rooms, of course."

I drew breath to speak, scarcely knowing what I intended to say, but Chad went on quickly, "I hope you're not offended at my suggestion of a marriage in name only. The task I have to complete debars me from marrying for the usual reasons, and your past experience deters you from taking a second husband, so I hope you will find nothing offensive in what I ask. If in the fullness of time you found someone you wished to marry, it would be simple to have our marriage annulled. The fact that we had never lived as man and wife would provide ample grounds for this, and I would support your claim."

I was shaking my head and my face felt warm now, but strangely enough I was quite untouched by embarrassment. I said, "Oh please, Chad, don't go so fast. I'm not offended, but when you talk of us being married and then of an annulment in the same breath I—I feel I'm going to laugh, but I'm afraid you might think I'm laughing at you instead of me, so I try to suppress it and that makes my face go funny."

He leaned back in his chair and laughed himself then. "Thank God you still say what you think and still know how to smile at yourself, Casey. I'll try to do the same, so let me put this very simply and without being solemn about it. I've asked if you will enter into a marriage of convenience with me and I've explained how it will help me. But will it help you? Well, I can't claim that it will help you as much. I can only say that you will have financial security and I shall treat you with every courtesy. Perhaps, for you, there may be a further advantage. You're an attractive young woman and you may soon find yourself the object of quite proper but unwanted attention from young men. As my wife, you would not be troubled by that problem."

He stood up, moved to the window, and turned to face me, hands behind back. "I'm sorry I couldn't put this to you gradually, Casey, it's not that sort of question. You probably feel somewhat dazed, but will you please think about what I've said, and let me have an answer as soon as you've made up your mind?"

I had already made up my mind, and was ashamed of myself for being about to refuse an appeal for help from a friend who had shown me every kindness. I liked Chad Lockhart and trusted him. I had nothing to lose by accepting his proposal. But I was frightened out of my wits at the thought of playing hostess to the wealthy gamblers at the house in St. James's Square. As I sat seeking a gentle way to refuse, I became aware of some particular thought plucking at my mind for attention. I tried to push it aside, but it would not yield, and recognition flared suddenly within me.

Chad had said that as his wife I should be spared the problem of young men wishing to pay me attention. My slow wits had only just registered that it would solve the much more particular problem that had been driving me to distraction. Only a few hours ago I had almost come to the conclusion that I would have to leave Heathside to prevent the cruel irony of having Sam Redwing, the man Liza loved, declare his love for me.

I said abruptly, "Wait, Chad, wait. I'm thinking." He folded his arms and leaned against the wall by the window, watching me curiously. Because I had newfound friends it had been some time since I had talked to Daniel in my mind, but I did so now.

Would it be wrong, Gubnor? I suppose it would in a way, if we promise to love each other when that's not really true. But I think we love each other in the way of good friends, and perhaps that's enough. Chad can't marry for love, and I don't want to share any man's bed, so perhaps we can make a marriage based on friendship. And it would mean I needn't go away from this home I've found. I don't know how I could bear that, but I know I would do it rather than hurt Liza . . .

Chad said tentatively, "Casey dear, you've been glaring at me for the last minute with the most menacing frown."

"Oh, I'm sorry." I shook my head as if I had just emerged from the sea and was shaking water from my hair. "I was just thinking hard."

"Then you can't have rejected the notion outright. I expect you're concerned as to whether Liza can manage without you for two days each week."

"Well, I hadn't quite reached that yet, but I was going to."

"Let me reassure you. She would miss you on those days, but work at the agency wouldn't suffer because the whole thing is better organized now. I would pay for a part-time clerk if need be. As for dinner on those evenings when you would not be here to cook, I'm sure Liza could manage, or she and Sam could dine out at my expense. I'm confident there would be no serious problem."

I thought he was probably right. With a little ingenuity I could manage the housekeeping side well enough, and I could think of nothing that would please Liza more than an arrangement that would help Chad to pay off the family debts in perhaps half the time she had expected. It was also true that if I refused Chad, and so had to leave Heathside altogether, Liza would lose my help completely.

I stopped thinking and stood up. "Yes, Chad," I said. "I'll marry you under the conditions you've suggested."

His eyes lit up with pleased surprise. "Oh Casey, I'm so glad. I really had very little hope." He came toward me, took my hands, and lifted one to touch his lips to the knuckles. "I suppose we'd better go and tell the others?"

"Yes." I gave a nervous laugh. "I wonder what they'll say."

"Let's find out," he said, smiling, and moved to open the door for me.

Sam looked up at once as we entered the sitting room, his eyes warm as they touched me. On the other side of the small table Liza frowned over the draughts board. "He's going to get another king," she informed us. "Sneaky redskin."

Chad closed the door behind us and took my arm. "Pay attention, you two," he said. "Remember that scheme I told you about last spring? The idea of a house where selected wealthy gentlemen could play cards for high stakes?"

Liza's head came up quickly, hope in her eyes. "Is it going

to be possible, Chad? You've not spoken of it again, and I was afraid you found it too big a problem."

"No, I've been working on it, little sister. I have an option to take a lease on the house, and I have the service and catering arrangements made."

Sam leaned back in his chair, hands thrust in pockets, legs stuck out in front of him, grinning. "But you have to find the lady, Small Fry," he said. "You need a combination of wife and hostess to create a respectable domestic atmosphere, we all agreed on that."

Chad nodded, smiling. "So we did, Big Chief. And since I don't consider myself available for other than a marriage of convenience, you produced three candidates in a month, all stupefyingly unsuitable."

"They weren't too bad," Sam said with a touch of indignation. "A little well worn maybe, but—"

Liza said, laughing, "Sam dear, they were awful. I don't know where you find such lady friends."

"They weren't exactly friends, Liza. The point is that when you're looking for a woman to marry Chad on a strictly commercial basis you're bound to have a very limited field."

"But the problem has now been solved," said Chad.

Sam's eyebrows shot up, and he chuckled. "Solved? That's great, but who's the lady? Who's going to make you look a respectable husband while forgoing the joys of your fond embrace . . . ?" While he was speaking his eyes had turned to me, at first full of humor but then abruptly stricken as his voice trailed to silence.

Liza spoke in a startled tone. "Casey?"

I said anxiously, "Do you mind, Liza? Will it be all right?"

She stood up and came toward us, blue eyes troubled. "Chad, how could you? It's not fair to her."

I said quickly, "Wait, Liza. Chad didn't try to persuade me, and I'm not making any sacrifice. I've no thought of marrying properly again, and by doing this I can perhaps help to halve the time it will take for Chad to clear all debts, so I'm well content. I'm only worried because I shall be away for the best part of two days each week, and I feel I might be letting you down with the agency and the housekeeping—"

"Oh, pish and tush, girl!" She shook her head impatiently and took my hands. "Now look at me and tell me—is this what you want?"

I was only too glad to avoid Sam's gaze, and looked into

Liza's eyes as I said, "As long as you don't disapprove, this is what I want."

She gave a lovely smile and I saw tears come into her eyes before she gathered me in her arms. "My sweet, I'm very pleased." She made a dismissive movement of her head. "Off with you, you two men. Take yourselves for a drive, or a walk. It's stopped raining and the exercise will do you good."

I heard Chad say, "Whether she's right or not we'd better do it, Sam. Let's take both gigs, and I'll give you a race round the heath. There's just time before dark."

If Sam replied I did not hear him, and I kept my face pressed to Liza's shoulder so that I should not see him. I heard the sound of feet slowly crossing the floor. A door opened. Chad said something. A door closed. Liza heaved a sigh and stepped back, looking at me with her head on one side. "You're sure, my darling?" she said.

"Oh, very sure, Liza."

"Well, I had a feeling that Chad was up to something, but I never dreamed it was this."

I said, "I'm sorry if it came as a shock, but I didn't know myself until just now." I wondered if she had noticed Sam's response, and added, "I expect Sam was surprised, too."

"Oh, he must have been aghast. He's a confirmed bachelor, and although he talks in a very worldly fashion about Chad making a marriage of convenience, I imagine he's quite shocked at the idea of his friend actually getting married. Men like Sam are often impractical. Now come and sit down so we can talk about the best way for you to act as hostess to wealthy card players."

"Oh yes, please," I said fervently. "I'm so frightened about that."

We were still talking eagerly half an hour later when Chad returned. Dusk had fallen as he came into the sitting room still wearing his topcoat, hat in hand, fresh color in his cheeks from the sharp November wind. Liza said, "Where's Sam?"

He gave a smiling shrug and began to take off his coat. "The last I saw of him he was flying up the Dover Road toward London in his gig, uttering those shrill Cheyenne whoops of his."

I felt a wave of anxiety. "Where do you think he's gone, Chad? Will he be all right?"

Liza said placidly, "Don't worry, dear. Sam is occasionally seized by a mood that sends him galloping off at random like a wild horse. He may come back in the next ten minutes, or we may get a telegram from Greece next month to say he's gone into the olive oil business."

"Or from Italy to say he's making a fortune in sardines," said Chad. "You never know with Sam." He went out to hang up his hat and coat, then returned and stood with hands held toward the fire. "I thought we might marry about a week before Christmas, if you agree, Casey. That will allow time for the banns. After Christmas we can use the days when you're not at the agency to make all preparations at the St. James's house, so that we're ready to invite our first guests by the middle of January."

Liza said, "There's almost no activity at the agency immediately after Christmas, so I shall close it down for a week, then I can come to town with you and help with all that has to be done."

I said thankfully, "Oh, bless you, Liza."

"I echo that," Chad agreed, and moved to bend and touch his cheek to hers. "And will you make the wedding arrangements, little sister? Very quiet, of course, with just the four of us. I'm hoping Sam will be back, and will stand as my best man. As for registration, I think Casey had better be set down as an orphan, parents unknown. Sister Clare could support that if need be." He looked at me. "Would you mind?"

I shook my head. "No, I'd prefer it. I don't want to have any hint of my past written down."

Liza said, "We shall need a man to give Casey away."

"Do you think Mr. Potter would do it?" I suggested.

Chad looked puzzled. "Potter?"

Liza said, "Old Mr. Potter who helps with our clerical work. Yes, I'm sure he'd love to do it. He's very fond of Casey and makes a great fuss of her." She regarded her brother sternly. "Chad, it's understood that you release Casey if at any time she asks you to do so?"

"Of course. I've assured her of that."

The evening was spent discussing all the many aspects of Chad's new venture and making what plans we could. It was odd to think he would soon be my husband, in name at least, but I did not feel awkward or apprehensive. My main feeling was one of huge relief that I need no longer live in hourly fear of Sam Redwing beginning to court me openly for all to see.

Sam did not come home that night, nor the next. Liza and Chad showed no concern, but I began to worry deeply, for I guessed that on this occasion his sudden disappearance was not caused by some impulsive whim but by the announcement of my engagement to Chad.

I went to bed on the Tuesday night feeling very troubled. At two in the morning I found myself suddenly awake, and knew that some unusual noise had disturbed me. It was much too early for Chad to have returned from his club. I lit the gas, put on my dressing gown, and went out into the hall. There was no sound from Liza's room, but this did not surprise me for I was more easily roused than most. My years at sea had made me sleep like a sailor, with one eye open, alert to anything that went beyond the normal expectation of sound or movement.

My first thought was that Sam had returned, and when I listened carefully I could hear a faint scuffling sound from the landing below. I went back to my room, lit the candle in the candlestick beside my bed, then went out and down the stairs to the landing where Chad and Sam had their rooms. In the sphere of light thrown by the candle I saw Sam Redwing crawling slowly on hands and knees toward his door.

I ran to him, put down the candlestick, and dropped to my knees beside him, an arm across his shoulder. "Sam!" I whispered in alarm. "Are you hurt? What's wrong?"

He turned his head sideways and looked at me with a baffled air from half closed eyes that were red and sunken. "Why... it's li'l Casey," he mumbled in a slurred voice. "Jus' going t' bed, Casey girl. Ol' Sam jus' going t' bed."

"Sam, you're *drunk*!" I said in a shocked whisper.

He screwed his mouth to one side, opening and shutting it in what I realized was an attempt to wink, then he gave up and said, "You bet. Drunk O.K. Drunk 's a goddamn lord."

"That's enough!" I whispered fiercely. "Don't you dare swear in front of me, Sam Redwing. Now stand up. Come along, I'll help you. Stand up, and I'll get you to bed. That's right. Lean on me. And don't you *dare* make any noise!"

I almost yelped aloud myself as he trod on my bare foot, but managed to bite back the cry. With a struggle I opened his door, helped him through, sat him down on the bed, then went back to fetch the candle before lighting the gas mantle in his room. I could smell whiskey on him, and cheap scent. He wore the same shirt as when I had last seen him, but it was very grubby now and had rouge marks on the collar and front. I did not want Liza to see that, and began to take off his jacket as he sat swaying before me.

"Come along, Sam," I whispered. "Pull yourself together." I dragged the jacket away and threw it to one side. "Now I want that shirt. No, don't keep toppling forward on me like that. Hold my shoulders while I see to the buttons."

"Want Sam's shirt?" he croaked obligingly. "Sure, honey. You take it . . . take anythin' . . . bes' girl in the world, my li'l Casey . . ."

"Hush, Sam! Be quiet!"

"You know somethin', li'l lady? Casey . . . she's bravest girl . . . whole world. You know that?"

"Is she, Sam? Well, never mind about her just now, pull your arm out of this sleeve. That's better. And keep your voice *down*." I was half wrestling with him, and he was lolling from side to side as I tried to get his shirt off.

"Fell in love wi' li'l Casey," he mumbled dolefully. "You know that? Fell in love . . . deep as Grand Canyon. Want . . . marry her. Too late now. Mustn't . . . mustn't tell anyone. Shhh . . ."

I pulled the shirt away. "No, we mustn't tell anyone. Now lie down, Sam. No, no, the other way. That's better." I pushed a pillow under his head, then went to the foot of the bed and began to unlace his boots. I was wondering if I should bring him strong coffee and wash his face to try to sober him, but his head suddenly fell sideways and his breathing became deep and slow with sleep. He did not wake as I took off his boots and spread the eiderdown over him. Turning the gas low, I picked up the candle and went down to the kitchen, carrying his shirt and jacket.

There was hot water in the tap. I spent five minutes scrubbing out the rouge marks from his shirt, and another five sponging his jacket with warm water containing a few drops of disinfectant to destroy the smell of scent. I went back upstairs, put his shirt in the laundry basket that stood in the men's bathroom, hung his jacket over the back of a chair in his bedroom, then turned out the gas and went back upstairs to my own room, hoping that Sam would not remember my part in his homecoming.

There was no sound from his room next morning as I went down to prepare breakfast, and no signs that might have told Liza he was home again. Since I was trying to hide the manner of his return from her, I said nothing about what had happened during the night. When Amy arrived I gave instructions for a morning's work that would keep her away from Sam's room, then went to harness Sandy in the gig for our drive across Blackheath to the agency. I saw nothing of Sam's gig or horse in the small stable, and decided he must have left them at a livery stable somewhere in London. Judging by the state of his clothes, he had come home to Greenwich by boat, and a far from clean one.

At noon, when I returned to make breakfast for Chad, I saw Sam waiting for me at the open front door as I drew the gig to a halt. He looked pale and his eyes were still a little red as he came to help me alight, but he wore clean clothes and was freshly bathed and shaved. I said, "Hallo, Sam, it's good to see you back. Does Chad know?"

He shook his head, then winced slightly. "No. He's still asleep. I guess."

"I doubt it. He's always down for breakfast by the time I have it ready."

"Can I talk to you please, Casey? About last night?"

We were in the hall now, and as he closed the door I said, "Oh. You remember, then?"

He held his head and nodded. "I remember enough."

"Where's Amy?"

"On the top floor cleaning your room and Liza's."

"All right, come down to the kitchen and you can talk while I work."

He followed me down and sat straddling one of the kitchen chairs, looking very uneasy as I took off my hat and coat and put on my apron. "I'm sorry about last night, Casey," he said. "I'm ashamed of being drunk, but thank you for looking after me."

I was determined to keep the conversation lighthearted if possible, and said with a smile, "Dis woman no savvy bockra talk."

He stared down at the floor. "You're a very kind girl, Casey, but I can't take the easy way out of this. You're to marry Chad, and that being so I said things last night I shouldn't have said. Remember?"

I busied myself cutting rind from some rashers of bacon. "Yes, but you weren't yourself, Sam. I didn't take it amiss. Would you like some breakfast?"

"Oh God, no. No thanks, honey. Look, since I said what I did last night, can I ask you one thing? Can I ask if you knew I was . . . was in love with you?"

I put some fat in the pan and said slowly, "I knew you believed yourself to be so."

"Believed? You mean believed wrongly?"

"Wait. Let me get everything started cooking or I'll make mistakes. You could fill the kettle and cut some bread ready for me to toast."

There was silence for perhaps three minutes. In that time I prayed for the right words to come to me, then I took a chair and sat down facing Sam across the scrubbed kitchen table. "Will you listen to me and really try to take in what I'm saying, Sam dear?"

He eyed me warily. "I'll try."

"Please do. Please open your mind to the notion that you may see me in a false light. You're a romantic person, Sam. Very romantic. That's not wrong, or silly. I like people with romance in their hearts. I think I would have been a romantic myself if Oliver Foy hadn't destroyed something in me."

"Not destroyed, Casey, no. You're still—"

"Please, Sam. You promised to listen. Now, I'm sure you remember how we met, and all that happened between then and the time when Mr. Carradine operated on you for appendicitis. You remember me on the *Casey* in that hurricane, you remember what happened to Daniel when we were flung into Alligator Gap, and you remember how I hauled you up from the boat and across the island. You were helpless and could do nothing, so you saw me as a sort of heroine, and this was magnified enormously because even at the time you realized I wasn't the coolie girl I appeared to be. That made me very interesting to a romantic man like you, Sam. You were almost obsessed with a determination to know me better, so you persuaded me to admit that I was a gently born English girl, and then you set out to help me. Thank God you did. I can never thank you enough, and I say that with all my heart. But you put me on a pedestal. You made me Casey Brown, the heroine. And you mistook hero-worship for falling in love."

He drew breath to speak, but I stopped him with a quick gesture. "No, we're not going to argue it back and forth, Sam. We're never going to speak of this again. All I ask is that you think very hard about what I've said. Take away the hurricane and La Faucille, take away the mystery of the coolie girl, just put me here in Heathside as the ordinary person I am, and you wouldn't be particularly smitten by me, I'm sure." I started to get up from the table but continued casually, as if adding a self-evident afterthought, "Especially when you've always had Liza to compare anyone else with."

I saw him blink in a puzzled way, then he gave a small shrug, started to say something, stopped before he had spoken, and spread his hands with a resigned smile. "You've gagged me, Casey. All I can do is apologize for making an exhibition of myself last night. Did you tell Liza?"

"No." I was busy at the range now. "It's not for me to carry tales, and I wouldn't want to hurt Liza."

"Hurt her?"

I looked over my shoulder at him. "She's your lifelong friend, Sam, but she isn't a man, she's a woman. Do you imagine she would think well of you if she knew you had gone off on a two-day debauch of whiskey and women because you fancied yourself crossed in love? You've hurt yourself by losing some self-respect, and it would hurt her just as much."

He rested his head in his hands. "You're a hard hitter, Casey girl," he muttered. "Maybe she'll guess anyway."

"Why? Have you done this before?"

He looked up, a flicker of painful humor in his eyes. "I'm thirty-six and no plaster saint, but I've never been off on a bout of dissipation like this before."

"Then I don't think she'll guess. I've washed the rouge off your shirt and used disinfectant to kill the smell of whiskey and that awful scent on your jacket."

"Oh, dear God," he groaned. "Well . . . thanks again, honey."

"Go out walking all afternoon before Liza sees you. That should get more color to your cheeks and less to your eyes, Sam dear."

"Holy smoke." He started to laugh, winced, and said, "Maybe I could have some coffee if you're making some for Chad?"

"Yes, I've put plenty in the pot for both of you." As I spoke I heard a foot on the stairs leading up to the hall, and Chad called down. "Casey, have you seen Sam?"

I lifted my voice a little. "Yes, he's down here with me."

A moment later Chad appeared, buttoning his jacket. "I thought I noticed signs of the wanderer's return in our bathroom just now." He looked at Sam and grinned. "You've been imbibing firewater, Big Chief."

I wasn't quite sure what he meant, but said, "Will both of you please get out of my kitchen and wait in the dining room? I'll bring your breakfast up in five minutes, Chad. As for Sam, he's just tired."

"But of course," Chad said solemnly. "Come along, Sam old chap, you can lean on my arm if the stairs are too much for you."

When they had gone I sighed with relief. It was good that Sam had spoken, for he had given me the chance to put into his mind the notion that what he felt for me was false hero-worship rather than love. I hoped this was true, but in any event the air had been cleared.

A little later I sat at table to have my sandwich and glass of milk while Chad ate breakfast and Sam drank strong coffee. Nothing more was said about Sam's odd disappearance. In desultory fashion the two men were discussing the relative merits of what I gathered were two different ways of playing poker, draw poker and stud poker. It was all incomprehensible to me, and I was wondering if as Chad's wife and hostess I ought to learn at least a little about the main card games, when Sam said, "Is that enough lunch for you, Casey, just one sandwich?"

"Oh, heavens yes, it's plenty. I have a good breakfast and dinner. If I eat luncheon as well, I'll get fat."

Sam nodded and poured himself more coffee. "Liza only has a sandwich, too," he remarked, more to Chad than to me, "but she stays kind of plump."

Chad nodded. "Always been a bit podgy though, hasn't she?"

"Oh, sure. I guess it's just the way she's made."

I could feel anger burning within my chest, and struggled to keep my voice casual as I said, "It's not very nice of you to discuss a subject like that behind Liza's back."

Both men looked surprised. Sam said, protesting, "You've got it wrong, Casey. We'd say just the same thing if Liza was here now. We've often pulled her leg about being kind of fat, haven't we, Chad?"

"Often," Chad agreed. "Right back to when we were boys."

"But you're not boys now and I hope you'll never do it again!" I said fiercely, heedless that my voice was shaking. "Liza *isn't* fat, she's just very nicely covered, and even if she *was* a little plump it would suit her marvelously, because she has a sweet round face that's pretty as a picture, and the most wonderful eyes, and lovely hands, and in fact she has a very *nice* shape, and the kindest heart you could wish for, and she moves *beautifully*. Will you two never realize how lucky you've been, having her to look after you all these years?" My voice rose. "One day a man will come along with his eyes open, and he'll see her true worth and marry her. Then you'll be sorry! But she'll be free of two men who can think of nothing better than to keep telling her she's podgy or plump or fat! Now excuse me, please."

I put down my half-eaten sandwich and moved to the door, hands trembling, aghast at my outburst yet not regretting a word of it. There was a dumbfounded silence until I opened the door, then Chad's voice said quickly, "Wait, Casey. Please."

I stopped and turned. Both men were standing, watching me. There was another silence. They looked at each other, and it was as if some tacit understanding passed between them. Both heads turned toward me again. Chad said, "We acknowledge our fault. We won't repeat the offense. And we humbly apologize."

I was as much shocked at myself as I had been angry with them, and shook my head uncertainly. "No . . . no, Chad. You and Sam don't owe me an apology. I was speaking for Liza, and I was carried away."

Sam said slowly, "You spoke well for her, Casey. I guess we've always taken her for granted."

I felt embarrassed now, and said awkwardly, "Well . . . I must go."

Chad spoke in a quiet voice. "Don't leave us in anger, Casey."

"Oh, I'm not. I—I know I flared up, but that's over now."

He smiled gravely. "I hope you flare up again if ever you find us similarly obtuse."

I very much wanted them to know that I spoke truly in saying my anger had passed, for the easy friendship that had grown up between us was too precious to be marred by doubts. I said, "I'm at fault myself in exactly the same way, Chad. I've just realized that in the short time I've been here I've come to take you and Sam for granted. When I spoke angrily just now I spoke without fear that you might turn me out of the house, because I knew I had no cause to fear, but if I had spoken like that to Oliver Foy he would have thrashed me unmercifully."

I saw Sam's nostrils flare, and in Chad's gray eyes there was a sudden measureless chill. "Oh, don't look like that," I went on hastily. "It's all long past and done with. I'm just taking myself to task for seeing the mote in your eyes and not the beam in my own, and now I must hurry. Good-bye for the moment, and I'll see you both this evening."

I closed the door behind me before any more could be said. In the hall I put on my hat and coat, picked up my gloves and the little bag containing Liza's sandwich, then went out to the gig. As I drove across Blackheath I reflected that what I had said regarding Oliver was only half true, for he had needed no excuse to brutalize me. I recalled wondering what it would be like to be married to Oliver Foy, and the dreadful shock of discovery. Memory of it sent a sudden shiver through me.

Impatiently I pushed such thoughts aside. I was another person now, Casey Brown. Soon I would be Chad Lockhart's wife, in name at least, and this would take me still further from the girl who had been Emma Delaney and then Mistress Emma Foy. Nothing from that other world I had once known, long ago and far away, could reach out from the past to touch me now, for I was another person.

16

I WAS MARRIED TO CHAD LOCKHART ON THE FRIDAY BEFORE Christmas Day, which fell the following Tuesday. The ceremony was performed at St. Alfege's Church in the afternoon. I did not wear white, but was in a sweetly pretty dress of pale blue, which Liza said admirably set off my auburn hair, now grown long enough to put up in an attractive style.

Mr. Potter, from the agency, gave me away with great dignity. Sam Redwing, as best man, was more nervous than anyone present. Our only guest was Liza, but Chad had paid for the church organist to play for us so that the empty silence should not be too daunting. Afterward, in the vestry, my husband kissed me briefly on the lips, Liza embraced me with all her usual affection, and Sam kissed me on the cheek, as did Mr. Potter.

Walking down the aisle on Chad's arm to leave the church, I realized with astonishment that another guest had been present, for there in the back pew I saw a head of hair much like my own in color but tinged with gray. Colonel Brown rose as we approached. He wore a gray morning suit and carried a gray top hat and a silver knobbed cane. We acknowledged his bow, passed on, and waited for him in the porch with Liza and Sam.

He emerged after a few moments, buttoning his overcoat and looking a little diffident at finding us awaiting him. "My felicitations, Mrs. Lockhart," he said rather gruffly. "And congratulations to you, Lockhart, my dear fellow. Hope you don't regard my presence as an intrusion, but I've listened to the banns these last three Sundays, and felt I'd like to be here for the occasion." He half smiled. "Felt I owed it to Mrs. Lockhart for her kindness in dealing with an eccentric old fool at the domestic agency, and to you, young man, for that splendid evening of partnership at the club recently."

Chad said, smiling, "You're not intruding, Colonel. It's very neighborly of you to have come along."

We all murmured words of agreement, and Sam said, "There's no reception, but we're going to open a bottle of champagne at home, if you'd care to join us."

There was pleasure in the penetrating gaze Colonel Brown turned on Sam. "A thousand thanks, but I wouldn't dream of it. You'll enjoy yourselves far more without a stranger to entertain. I wish you and your husband every happiness, Mrs. Lockhart." He bowed over my hand, then over Liza's. "Congratulations again, young Lockhart. A pleasure to renew your acquaintance. Redwing, haven't seen you on that bench on Blackheath lately." He shook hands with Chad and Sam, clapped his hat on his head, lifted his cane in a final salute, and strode away.

We exchanged smiling glances. Sam said with a chuckle, "Can you imagine him being interviewed for a butler's job? He'd have the lord of the manor tugging a humble forelock to him."

All through that day I had to keep reminding myself that this marriage of mine was simply a matter of business convenience, for from time to time I felt quite emotional from a blend of happiness, thankfulness that I would not have to run away, and a kind of warm yearning for I knew not what.

That evening we dined at a good restaurant, then returned home to play a game of *mah tsiang* before going to bed. There was no moment of embarrassment. I simply wished everyone a general good night, then as usual went down to the kitchen to put everything in readiness for the next day's breakfast and to list any shopping needed. As I went up to bed Chad and Sam were still talking in the sitting room.

I was in my dressing gown brushing out my hair when Liza tapped and entered at my call. "Casey, I couldn't go to sleep without coming to see if you were all right. It's been such an exacting day, and you've looked marvelously calm and at ease, but I'm sure you must be limp with exhaustion. Why don't you sleep late tomorrow while I see to the breakfast? I'm sure it would do you good."

"No, no, I wouldn't hear of it, Liza dear. I want everything to go on as usual, and I'm really not tired."

She sighed and sat on the corner of the bed. "Well, if that's what you want. You do have remarkable energy, I suppose it comes from being a sailor. I wanted to ask you, are you happy about today? No regrets?"

I put down the hairbrush and turned to her. "None at all, I promise. I know it's an unusual arrangement but it suits Chad, and I can't think of anything better for someone like me. It's going to be lovely, having a sister."

She nodded wistfully. "Yes. Lovely for me, too. I think you will have to behave a little more like a real wife with Chad in public, dear. Just in small things I mean, like taking his arm, greeting him with a peck on the cheek, brushing a thread from his lapel, straightening his necktie. If you don't do little possessive things like that, it will look rather odd. And the same applies to Chad."

"Yes, I suppose so. We'll have to practice, but I'm sure we'll soon fall into the way of it."

"I'll speak to Chad." She got up and bent to touch her cheek to mine. "Good night, Casey. Sleep well."

When I woke on the morning of Christmas Eve and drew back my curtains I could not believe my eyes. The earth had turned white overnight.

Snow! I had never seen it before, or at least had no childhood memory of it. Even before washing and doing my hair I threw on some clothes and ran downstairs to our little garden, almost dancing with excitement as I made great footprints in the velvety whiteness, catching up a handful to press to my lips and taste, marveling at the beautiful lacework of snowflakes clinging to every branch and twig of the silver birch in the far corner.

Later, as we sat to breakfast, the others were much amused by my great excitement. I was teased as a simple coolie girl, and responded with comments in the papamiento speech of the Dutch islands—a mixture of French patois, Spanish creole, and old Dutch and English. In the evening we went carol singing with a party from the church. Chad and Liza had good voices, Sam and I had poor ones and so were given the task of holding lanterns on sticks so that the singers could read the words.

It was a happy Christmas for me, though there were moments when I remembered Daniel and felt my eyes swim with tears. Then I would comfort myself with the thought that if he could have seen me he would be overjoyed at my good fortune. We exchanged presents, ate a lot more than usual, drank a little sherry and port wine, and played pencil-and-paper games in the evening. The moment I enjoyed most was on Boxing Day, when we were able to go ice skating on the Prince of Wales's pond on the heath, and Liza proved to be a most graceful and elegant skater while the rest of us took more than one tumble apiece.

The remainder of that week was spent in making ready the house Chad had leased in St. James's Square. It was in a good state of decoration and had been let furnished. The previous tenants had been a family of seven, plus servants, and most of the furniture was well suited to Chad's purpose, for it was of high importance to have the atmosphere of a home and not a club. Despite this, a great deal still needed to be done in the way of organization.

There were alterations to be made in the kitchen so that it would be capable of providing a variety of meals and snacks at short notice. Certain rooms had to be rearranged for card playing. There were staff to be interviewed and later rehearsed in their duties, card tables and comfortable chairs had to be brought in, toilet facilities to be arranged for the guests. In some rooms the light was inadequate and had to be changed. There seemed endless matters to be dealt with, but we worked well together. Sam often disappeared for a few hours on business of his own, but he was invaluable in that whatever was needed he always knew somebody who could provide it or do it quickly.

Every day I spent some time in the room that was to be my bedroom, being measured or fitted for the dresses I would need as Chad's wife and hostess. I was thankful to be kept busy, for whenever I had leisure enough to think, I became frightened that I would be a dreadful failure in the role I was to play.

The following week Liza and I returned to work at the domestic agency. She had said she could manage without me, and that for me to work three and a half days a week with her and two nights with Chad in town would be much too arduous, but I would brook no argument over this, and in the end Liza yielded. It was arranged that I would work in the mornings on Tuesdays and Thursdays, when I was to play hostess in the evening, but that I would not start work at the agency on Wednesdays and Fridays until after luncheon.

By the end of the first week in January most of the work had been done and I had grown accustomed to being addressed as Mrs. Lockhart. In public Chad and I fell quite easily into the way of behaving as if we were truly husband and wife, while in private we continued just as before. On the second Tuesday of the month I was able to go through the house and make sure that it was prepared in every detail for all domestic purposes. In the afternoon a small army of women, sent from the agency by Liza, cleaned through the house from top to bottom, and I was busy supervising them when I was called to deal with a carter who had two large crates to deliver. This surprised me, for I was not expecting them.

"Do you know what's inside?" I asked the carter.

He gave a heavy sigh, and clicked finger and thumb at his assistant. "Delivery note, Walter."

Walter, an unhappy man with crossed eyes, fumbled in his pocket and produced a pink piece of paper, which he handed to the carter. "Delivery note, Perce," he said.

Perce unfolded it, studied it, then looked at me. "Twelve gross of playing cards, missus."

"Twelve *gross*?"

"That's what it says 'ere, missus."

"Wait. Just wait here, please."

I hurried away to find Chad. He was in one of the card rooms, brooding over the position of a table. When I told him of the carter he laughed. "That's right, Casey dear." We were in public, so he patted my arm affectionately. "Twelve gross will do to start with."

"You really mean it? Twelve times one hundred and forty-four packs of cards?"

"Well, at whist a new pack is broken open for every rubber. And at poker any player can call for fresh cards at any time. It's to prevent all possibility of cheating. When gentlemen play for high stakes they like certain rules to be observed." He smiled. "They trust one another, of course, but as Sam will tell you, there's an American saying which goes, 'Trust your fellow man, but always cut the cards.' That's why we have no mirrors near the card tables, and why you'll find that no reflecting object is ever placed on the table. It also explains why I've said that neither you nor any of the servants must approach a table while a hand is being played."

He slipped his arm through mine and we walked to the door. "As for the cards themselves, certain ungentlemanly folk have been known to mark selected cards with a thumbnail. That's why the cards are changed frequently, so let's go and have them deliver twelve gross of packs. Our soirées must always be utterly above suspicion."

On the second Thursday of the month we held a dress rehearsal. The guests were a dozen out-of-work actors, hired by Sam through a theatrical agent of his acquaintance. When first assembled they were inclined to regard the affair as somewhat comical, but Chad quickly called them to order, his voice cool and sharp, favoring them with that side of his face on which the drooping eyelid could make him look so sinister.

"Those of you gentlemen who have no wish to earn your guinea and your dinner this evening may leave at once," he said. "The rest of you will remember that you are hired to play the part of guests, not giggling schoolboys, so kindly give the matter your professional attention."

He paused. There was an embarrassed mutter of apology and shuffling of feet, but nobody accepted the invitation to withdraw. Chad said, "Very well. You will now leave the house and return in twos and threes, at intervals over the next half hour. You will be received first by my butler and then by my wife and myself, or possibly by my wife alone. You may make up your own tables for play, and where there is any problem of making up a four for whist, my wife will unobtrusively help by making introductions. Please use your own names. The butler will announce you, and my wife will remember who is who."

Standing by Chad's side in one of my new dresses, I managed not to flinch at those last words, though my mouth was dry and I offered up a silent prayer. He went on, "Those of you who play whist or poker are welcome to do so. Those of you who can't will please play whatever card game you are able to. Whenever you wish for refreshment during the evening, please ask—but never when a hand is being played. There is a dining room with five tables, which can seat you all for dinner, but I suggest you go in small parties at different times, since this is the more likely procedure. The menu may be studied while you are at the card table, and orders may be placed. Is all this quite clear to you? Good. Then when next you enter this house you will be wealthy gentlemen visiting a private home to play cards for high stakes, which is not an occasion for heavy drinking or roistering. Please play this role with sincerity and decorum."

The first hour was a great ordeal for me. Because I was acting a part I felt foolish as well as inept, but gradually we all seemed to fall more easily into our roles. It helped to keep reminding myself that this would be a part I would play again and again in the future. There were small problems that evening, both in the kitchen and at the tables, but we learned from these, and nothing disastrous befell.

When midnight came and the actors left with their guineas, I dropped into a chair opposite Chad at the table where he had been playing, and let out a long sigh of relief. "Oh, thank heavens you planned this rehearsal, Chad. Was I very bad?"

He smiled and flicked over one of the cards scattered on the table. It was the queen of hearts. "On the contrary, you were very good." He tapped the card. "You even won the actors' hearts, and they normally love nobody but themselves." He studied me curiously. "You were a little stilted at first, as I knew we all would be, but weren't you frightened?"

I rolled up my eyes in a grimace. "Out of my wits, almost."

"You never show it, Casey. I've never seen you show fear."

"If so, it's not because I'm brave, whatever Sam may say." I rested my arms on the table, my chin on my hands. "I expect," I said slowly, sleepily, "that I've learned to hide it. I've known quite a lot of fear . . . some at sea, but mostly at Diabolo Hall. At sea it helps you keep your head if you don't show it, and at Diabolo Hall I would have been broken completely if I had allowed it to show."

He picked up the queen of hearts and looked at it idly. "It doesn't trouble you to speak of that now?"

"No. Thanks to you and Liza and Sam." A yawn surprised me, and I hastily smothered it. "Oh, excuse me."

He stood up. "I don't wonder you're tired. It's time for bed."

"Yes. I sent the kitchen staff off at eleven-thirty, but I'll just go and see they left everything in order. The Birchalls can clear up everywhere else tomorrow morning."

The Birchalls were the caretakers Chad had engaged, who lived on the top floor, a family of husband, wife, and a fifteen-year-old daughter. Mr. Birchall was an ex-sergeant of the Cold-stream Guards, an utterly reliable man who commanded his family as if they had been privates in his platoon, a situation both wife and daughter seemed to accept quite happily. The service they gave was excellent.

When I left the kitchen I found Chad waiting for me at the foot of the stairs. We went up together, then along the passage to the back of the house where our bedrooms lay opposite one another. As we paused there I said, "Chad, if we caught the train that leaves at twenty past six, we would be home in time for me to make breakfast for Liza and Sam."

"Oh . . . I don't know. It means a short night's sleep for you."

"I've rarely had more than four hours at a stretch for most of the last three years, and I can have a nap after breakfast."

"Well, if you're sure."

"Yes, I'd like to do that."

"All right." He smiled and turned to his door. "Good night, Casey. Thank you for doing so well tonight."

"I'm glad you felt I did. Good night, Chad."

My husband went into his room, and I went into mine.

When six weeks had passed it became clear that Chad's new venture was to be a success. I had expected to feel great anxiety on the first night, but from the moment our gentlemen guests began to arrive, something within me seemed to respond to the challenge. It made me think of times when I had planted my bare feet solidly on the deck of the *Casey* and held a steady course against a boisterously shifting wind. At the end of the evening Chad praised me far more warmly than I deserved, but truth to tell I was not too displeased with myself for having managed rather better than I had feared.

By the end of the sixth week, when we had held a dozen such soirées, I could look back and realize I had really made a great fuss about nothing, for my duties as Chad's wife and hostess were quite simple and undemanding. Most of my work, such as it was, went on behind the scenes and consisted of making sure the kitchen staff and other servants performed their duties smoothly and well. Since all had been carefully chosen, it was really not an onerous task to supervise them.

As guests arrived, Chad and I would receive them as if we were host and hostess at a dinner party, a musical evening, or some similar occasion. We would offer a glass of sherry or port, and make conversation for a while until there were enough gentlemen to begin play, then Chad would invite them through to one of the rooms set out for cards. Usually he held back from making up a table himself until two games were already in progress, but sometimes one of the early guests would urge him to join a game. Then I would be left to receive those coming later, and to make excuses for my husband. Since all guests came to play cards, none took offense if Chad was unable to receive them.

These were not club members, but guests who came at Chad's formal invitation, and so they were carefully selected gentlemen whose behavior could be relied upon. Several were titled, all were rich, and all were avid cardplayers, though not all were good players. The same faces appeared regularly, for this was a limited circle, and I quickly fell into the way of greeting our guests with what I hoped was a manner welcoming without being effusive, for it was vital that they should never feel we were seeking their attendance as if they were customers.

"Good evening, Lord Marsham, how nice to welcome you again," I would say. "You're looking very well indeed. I fear my husband has succumbed to Colonel Reid's persuasion and is partnering him in a rubber at the moment. Do please excuse him. As you see, Sir Charles and Mr. Ashleigh are taking a glass of sherry with me. You have all met, of course? Yes, so I thought. Would you care to join us here and gossip for a few minutes while waiting for a fourth for whist, or have you a fancy to take a seat at the poker table this evening?"

I never actually drank my glass of sherry, and I rarely had to make conversation for long. On two occasions there was an uneven number of gentlemen wanting to play whist, and this involved some rotation at the tables, with players sitting out, but to the extent that I had to make conversation it was not arduous. Chad had given me a list of some forty possible guests, with an indication of their various interests, and I found that asking questions and listening to answers was a good way to become well regarded as a hostess.

About once every hour I would visit each of the three whist rooms and the one poker room, to remind the gentlemen unobtrusively of my presence. No doors were ever closed, so it was easy for me to time a visit for a moment when a hand had just been played. Then, before anyone could rise I would insist that they remain seated and ask if I could send a footman to take note of their wishes for refreshment at the card table or dinner in the dining room. It was a curious and unconventional evening's entertainment, but I believe this in itself held some attraction for the kind of gentlemen who came to the house in St. James's Square.

I was intrigued to catch glimpses of Chad at the card table. Some men showed excitement, disappointment, triumph, or exasperation, according to their fortune or lack or it. Chad always wore the same amiable and rather dreamy expression, as if his thoughts were elsewhere. I mentioned this to Liza and Sam at dinner one evening, when Chad was out playing cards at his club.

Sam laughed. "That's how he looks when he's concentrating, honey, and believe me there's no one better at it than Small Fry. He's remembering every card played, and making deductions from every card played, so by the time a hand's halfway through he knows just about what everyone's holding. Same with poker. Every time the dealer picks up an exposed discard and puts it at the bottom of the pack, Chad can keep a count of those cards right through the pack till they're dealt again, isn't that right, Liza?"

She smiled and nodded. "It gives him a big advantage. I've seen him pick up a pack, run quickly through it, then recite the order of the cards without looking."

Sam chuckled. "Used to do that when he was a kid. That's how it is he can keep his losses small, even when he cuts a poor partner and the cards are running against him. Give him a decent partner or decent cards and he'll win. Give him both and he'll have the shirt off your back in no time. The pity of it is, he doesn't give a tinker's cuss for the money, except to the extent it helps pay off those ancient debts."

It was true enough that Chad was indifferent to the winnings or losses of the day. During our first twelve evenings he twice had small losses, once on the second evening, but when I showed concern at this he only shrugged. "Just part of the mathematical pattern, Casey. There were no bad players here, but I drew the least able of partners and was dealt with the poorest cards. To be only twenty pounds down on the evening is quite satisfactory." At the end of the sixth week his winnings were fifteen hundred pounds after all expenses of rent, catering, and staff had been paid.

Apart from the two days a week spent on this new venture, life for me continued much as before, except that Liza decided not to open the agency for half a day on Saturdays in the future. She claimed that this was because so little business was done on a Saturday morning, but I felt sure she had done it for my benefit, since she held a quite unfounded belief that I was working too hard.

To my great content, Sam no longer eyed me adoringly and neither of us ever spoke of what had been said that day after his drunken debauch. I was thankful to find there was no sense of awkwardness if we happened to be alone together, and felt I had been right in thinking his passion for me had sprung simply from seeing me in a heroic light.

The only thing to mar my sense of well-being was that in the first eight weeks of the year I suffered on three occasions the same horrible nightmare that had come to me two nights before my arrival in England, the dream in which Daniel's skeleton came swimming toward me underwater and seemed to be trying to tell me something. On both occasions I woke in the midst of this horror and felt shaken for hours afterward. It would have been a relief to tell somebody about it, but in the light of day I shrank from inflicting such a gruesome tale upon my friends.

In the middle of March, following an exchange of telegrams. Sam went to Spain. He returned three weeks later, full of zest, to inform us that he had sold his share in a cork manufacturing business at an unexpectedly good profit. In response to what I now realized was a customary question from Liza as to whether he had returned rich or poor, he announced that he had used most of his profits to buy a share in a sherry producing concern and was therefore not rich but only O.K.

It was soon after his return, on an evening in early spring, that Chad tapped on the door of my room in the house at St. James's Square and called, "I'm going down now, Casey."

This was part of what had become our routine. Each Tuesday and Thursday we made the short train journey up to London, reaching the house by three o'clock. Chad would then make sure that everything concerning the card playing and gambling was in order while I went over the selection of dishes to be offered that evening by our cook, Mrs. Fielding, and also saw to it that all cleaning, laundering, and other domestic matters had been properly carried out.

By four o'clock all would be done and we would go to our bedrooms, each of which was provided with a hip bath. The reliable ex-Sergeant Birchall would have put big copper jugs of hot water in readiness. After my bath I would do my hair carefully, choose whatever dress I wished to wear for the evening, and be ready to go downstairs by soon after five o'clock. Chad was usually ready a few minutes earlier, and would tap on my door before going down. I never failed to enjoy these London days, from walking to the station with Chad, talking of all kinds of things on the train journey, making the house and ourselves ready for the evening's guests, right through to the pleasant half hour of waiting before they arrived.

From the beginning Liza had wisely said that we should have a time of quiet domestic companionship together to create the right atmosphere for receiving our guests, and we had made a habit of this, sitting in the drawing room with a pot of strong tea, which we drank with lemon and no milk, sometimes reading a newspaper or magazine, but more often simply talking. It was on the second Tuesday in April that something different happened. I was ready a little early and wrestling to fasten the rather stiff clasp on my charm bracelet, when Chad tapped as usual. I called, "Wait, Chad, I'm just coming," and went to open the door.

He smiled at me as I came out into the passage. "The green dress. That's my favorite, Casey. You look splendid."

"Thank you, Chad dear. I think it's the one I like best, too. Could you fasten this for me, please? I'm having rather a struggle."

"Ah, Daniel's bracelet." He took it from me and looked at it pensively. "You usually wear it only on special occasions."

"It's Daniel's birthday. The ninth. I wanted to put it on for him."

"Yes, of course you would."

I held out my wrist, and as he looped the bracelet around it he smiled suddenly. "This reminds me of that day when we put the wheel back on the cart, and afterward you fastened my cuff links for me."

The same memory had come clearly to my mind at the same moment, and in that moment time seemed to stand still. I was conscious of Chad's fingers touching my wrist, of his bent head close to mine, of his wiry body carrying the excellent suit he wore with easy elegance, of his cool voice, smoky gray eyes, and drooping lid, of the leisurely manner that hid a ferocious obsession with a deathbed promise made long ago.

I watched his fingers bringing the two parts of the clasp together, and a small fierce glow was born in the center of my being, a glow that spread like a leaping flame through the very fibers of my body. The touch of his fingertips made me feel weak with yearning, and I knew a desire I had never known and never thought I would feel, a desire that Sheba had tried to describe to me on a day in Ocho Rios, when we sat looking out over the sea as she told me what marriage should mean.

I wanted to take Chad's face in my hands and kiss his lips, wanted to put my arms about him, wanted to feel his arms holding me pressed close to him. I had never dreamed that such feelings could come to life in me after the misery I had suffered at Oliver's hands, but I was startled at how strong and raw they were.

Head swimming, it dawned on me with a sense of shock that I was in love with the man who was my husband. Somewhere within me I knew that the shock sprang not from the happening but from the realization of it. I had been falling in love with Chad over a period of time I could not measure, but had been blind to it until this instant.

He pressed the clasp together and lifted his eyes to my face. "There. That's quite secure." His expression changed. "Are you all right, Casey? You look a little flushed and your eyes are . . . I don't know. Glowing, I suppose. You're not feeling feverish?"

I managed to smile and shake my head, and I took his arm in the casual way we affected as husband and wife. "No, I'm quite all right. Truly. I . . . I expect I just felt a little emotional because of thinking about Daniel."

"Well, that's understandable."

I made some sort of conversation as we went down into the drawing room where one of the footmen had brought in our tray of tea, but my poor brain was reeling under the impact of what I had just discovered about myself, and I could feel the beginnings of pain. Chad had married me for convenience. Fortunately we were good friends, but I was well aware that he was not in love with me. When the reason for our marriage ended he would want to be free again, as agreed.

I told myself that I must take every care never to let him see what I felt for him. Sam had almost driven me to run away because of a similar situation, and I would have despised myself forever if I brought embarrassment to our home. With an effort I made myself concentrate on pouring tea and paying attention to Chad.

"... so I think you should know the truth, Casey," he was saying.

"The truth?" I frantically cast my mind back in an effort to recapture words barely heard. "Oh, you mean about ... about ..."

"The coin." He regarded me with puzzled amusement. "The coin on your bracelet. Are you with me, Casey?"

"Oh, I'm sorry, I seem to be in a dream this evening. Yes, I'm with you now. Daniel was in two minds about telling me where the four coins had come from."

"Yes, because he felt it might be dangerous knowledge, but that no longer applies. I see no reason for not telling you, if you would like to clear up the mystery."

I was thankful for any subject that would save me having to make conversation for the next few minutes, and said, "Yes, I think I would like to know."

"Well, of those four coins, yours has been defaced to make a charm, two have been melted down, and mine is therefore the only one of its kind on earth. But that doesn't include the waters that cover the earth. You see, the coins came from a forty-gun Spanish frigate which was believed to have been sunk off Cuba during a hurricane in seventeen ninety-four. It was called *Almiranta*, and it was carrying one hundred thousand of those very special coins in six chests."

He reached forward to take the cup of tea I had poured him, and lifted an eyebrow in amusement. "You don't seem particularly excited, Casey."

"Oh, I'm sorry." I tried not to seem flustered. "It's very interesting indeed, Chad, but when you live in Jamaica you hear lots of stories about sunken galleons and chests of treasure."

"I'm sure you do, but this is a rather special story because it's about rather special coins. Can you bear a short history lesson?" I nodded. "Well now, Charles the Fourth of Spain came to the throne in seventeen eighty-eight, and he was a weak man who was very much dominated by his wife, Maria Luisa. It seems she was a hot-blooded lady who had a favorite named Manuel de Godoy, and from seventeen ninety-two onwards it was young Manuel who virtually ruled Spain. I say young because he was made prime minister when only twenty-five."

Chad sipped his tea and gazed into the fire. I wanted to look at him all the time, but made myself sit decorously looking down at my cup. I did not feel decorous. I felt more like Maria Luisa, and was shocked at myself. Chad slipped a finger and thumb into his waistcoat pocket, then leaned forward to hand me a gold coin. One side bore the same coat of arms as the coin on my bracelet, but on the obverse was a female head and some Spanish words, among them "Maria Luisa."

"That's the coin Daniel gave me," said Chad, "and on it you can see the lady herself. As a means of currying favor with his mistress, Manuel de Godoy had one hundred thousand gold pieces of eight escudos struck in the mint at Mexico City, then a Spanish possession, of course. They were called Maria Luisa doubloons, and they were sent off to Spain on the *Almiranta*. Spain was at war with France, and the French were active in the Caribbean, so it was considered safer to send the doubloons by frigate rather than in a galleon. But the *Almiranta* went down in a hurricane, and the Maria Luisa doubloons went down with her."

I had pulled myself together sufficiently to concentrate on Chad's tale, and now I said as I returned the coin to him, "How did Daniel come to find those four specimens?"

Chad shook his head. "He didn't just find those four. He found the sunken ship, and it was quite a long way from where it was supposed to have gone down according to old records in the Kingston library."

I sat up straight. "Then it must have been somewhere off Jamaica. Do you mean he found the whole treasure, Chad?"

"So he told me, that day when he gave me the coin as proof of his discovery. He said one chest had broken open but the other five were still intact."

I was thankful that Chad's story had become truly intriguing, for it helped me to keep my mind on it. I said, "If Daniel found the sunken ship and was able to reach it, then it must be in fairly shallow water. I mean not much more than about fifteen fathoms. I don't think he would dive deeper than a hundred feet."

Chad's eyebrows lifted. "As deep as that?"

"Oh, yes. It's quite comfortable at ten fathoms as long as you've adjusted the pressure in your ears, and I don't think it would be any different at twice that depth—except that it's a long way to come up, and it gets too dark to see much. I've never been deeper than ten fathoms myself."

Chad looked at me wonderingly. "Sixty feet or more? It's incredible, Casey."

"Not really. Not even for a girl. Daniel told me that in the seas off Japan it's always the women who dive for pearls, they're better at it than the men. There's nothing very clever about it, Chad, truly. It's just something very few people have ever learned to do. I only came to it myself by a string of peculiar circumstances."

He smiled. "Yes. I doubt if many English girls would be happy to swim around for two or three minutes sixty feet under water. I've tried my hand at going down in a diving suit, and I must say I found it a rather menacing experience."

"Oh, it would terrify me. I would feel so trapped. I remember now, Liza once told me that you and Sam had been through a course of training as divers. Was that because you hoped to bring up the Maria Luisa coins from the *Almiranta*?"

Chad nodded and stretched out his legs. "Yes. When I talked with Daniel that day he not only gave me his confession, already prepared, but he also wanted to make what amends he could. He told me of the treasure, and said it would need a deep-sea diver to bring it up, but if I could arrange that, it was mine for the taking."

A memory came back to me. I said, "Was that the business you wanted to discuss with Oliver when we met at the races in Kingston?"

"Yes. I thought he might finance the project for a quarter share after costs had been paid, and I showed him the Maria Luisa coin, but I didn't tell him anything about Daniel. The longer we talked, the more I distrusted Oliver Foy. He was very keen." Chad glanced at me with a lifted eyebrow. "Is it possible he could have been in financial trouble, Casey?"

I stared in surprise. "No, I don't think so. He was the richest man on the island."

"So I understood. But Sam had some business friends of his in America look into Foy's affairs at the time, and they concluded that Oliver's father had transferred a large number of assets to charity before he died, leaving Oliver with a much reduced income."

"I couldn't speak to that, Chad. He always seemed to have plenty of money."

"Well, it's of no importance now. The fact is that I backed

away from having any dealings with Foy, and left the whole thing deliberately vague. I came home to England, and together Sam and I decided to train as divers, return to Jamaica, charter a suitable ship, and do the job ourselves. The following spring I wrote to Daniel in guarded terms to say I was ready to proceed with the matter we had discussed, and would be arriving in June with a colleague. Apparently the postman took the letter to a sister-in-law of Daniel's who was unable to read, and she took it to the minister of the church she attended. He opened it to find the address of the sender, and returned it to me with a short letter explaining the circumstances and informing me with regret that Daniel Choong had died in a storm at sea the previous September."

Chad passed his empty cup to me and made a wry grimace. "With Daniel Choong dead, as I thought, that was the end of the matter. Without him there was no way ever to find the sunken *Almiranta*." He nodded toward my wrist as I poured fresh tea. "That's why, when I first saw the charm on your bracelet and recognized it as a Maria Luisa coin, I asked if Daniel had ever told you where it came from. But as he hadn't, there's no hope of ever discovering where the *Almiranta* lies."

I sat thinking for a few moments. Sheba would have taken the letter to Mr. Royston, the Methodist minister, to ask him about it. I said, "When Mr. Royston returned the letter and told you Daniel had died in the storm, did he say anything about his running away or being sought by the police?"

"Ah, Royston. Yes, that was the name. No, he wrote no more than I've told you, Casey. I suppose he didn't want to launch into a long story."

"Well . . . thank you for telling me all about the Maria Luisa coins, Chad. I'm sorry I don't know where the *Almiranta* lies, but I can understand why Daniel felt such knowledge might be dangerous."

At that moment Dimmock, our butler on Tuesdays and Thursdays, entered the room to announce that it was a quarter to six and our guests would shortly begin to arrive. I performed my duties automatically that evening, but inwardly I felt as if in a dream, a feeling I had to struggle against in the days that followed. There was irony in the fact that I was now in the same situation as Liza, in love with a man who felt only friendship for me. The difference was that Chad and I were married, and I found it hard to conceal from Liza and Sam that I was in love with my husband. If I managed to do so successfully it was because we were all invariably busy and there were few occasions when the four of us were together.

At any other time I would have thought much more about Chad's tale of the Maria Luisa treasure, for it was a fascinating story and I might well have speculated on how Daniel had stumbled upon the sunken wreck, and off which coast it might lie. But my head was filled with the mingled joy and despair of finding myself in love with Chad Lockhart, who was certainly not in love with me, and I gave only occasional and hazy thought to the story he had told.

I could not know that this had planted a seed in my mind, a seed which in a matter of days would grow vigorously enough to break through the barrier that hid a particular memory from me, so that when the recurring nightmare came again it would be yet more terrible, and bring the threat of an early end to my marriage.

17

A WEEK LATER COLONEL BROWN CAME TO OUR ST. JAMES'S house for the first time. I had not seen him since the day of my wedding, and was surprised to find myself feeling genuine pleasure when Dimmock announced him. It was almost eight o'clock, and Chad was already at one of the whist tables, so I received Colonel Brown alone.

"Good evening and welcome, Colonel. How nice to see you here."

"You're very kind, Mrs. Lockhart." He bowed over my hand. "Forgive my late arrival but I was detained in the City."

"Please don't apologize. I'm afraid there are no whist players waiting to make up a table at this hour, but perhaps you were intending to make use of the poker room?"

"It's not really my game, Mrs. Lockhart. I lack your husband's genius, unfortunately."

"Then perhaps you would care to sit and take a glass of sherry with me until a rubber ends and Chad can arrange for a rotation?"

"Nothing would delight me more, Mrs. Lockhart. I am all the more grateful to your husband for inviting me this evening."

I felt a curious annoyance with myself for being pleased to

see this man again, for it was something I could not explain, and especially odd since I did not entirely trust him. This, too, I could not explain to myself. He had always been polite and courteous. Certainly his behavior had been eccentric, but I could take no exception to those eccentricities and in fact had rather enjoyed them. If he had reminded me of Daniel I could have understood my liking for him, but they were in no way alike. If he had reminded me of an older Chad, if he had been Chad's father perhaps, I would not have been puzzled by my feelings, but again there was no similarity. I did not know why I liked him, and did not know why at the same time I had doubts about him, except that some instinct seemed to warn me that he was not all he seemed. Perhaps this was because the way he studied me, never offensively but always with profound absorption, brought me a sense of embarrassment.

It was the same on this April evening as he sat in the drawing room with me, having accepted my offer of a whiskey and soda in preference to the sherry. His eyes were on me every moment, not watchfully, but as a man might study a painting to take in every detail.

"We haven't seen you about Greenwich lately, Colonel," I said as Dimmock put another log on the fire. "Have you been away?"

"Yes, I have, Mrs. Lockhart." Humor shone in his eyes. "I felt I had exhausted the possibilities of my two previous careers, as a would-be butler and an uninvited wedding guest, so I went abroad in the middle of January to attend to some small business matters, and I returned only a few days ago."

"I hope you had an enjoyable trip. I notice the Channel has been very rough for the last two weeks, according to *The Times*."

"You study reports of the weather at sea, ma'am? That's rare in a lady, I imagine."

"I suppose so, but the weather has long been a particular interest of mine. Do tell me about your trip. Were you on the continent?"

"No, Mrs. Lockhart, and not in the Channel either. I have just returned across the Atlantic to Liverpool."

"Ah, from America? That must surely be a fascinating country to visit."

"True enough, ma'am, but I wasn't there on this occasion. I was in the West Indies attending to matters of a shipping line in which I'm a partner. We carry cargo to a number of the Caribbean islands."

I smiled and said, "So you do not really need a position as a butler to keep you from idleness, Colonel?" I hoped my smile did not seem false. The last thing I wanted was to pursue a conversation about the Caribbean islands, and I was thankful when Chad came into the room at that moment.

"Good evening, Colonel." He came forward to shake hands. Then, to me: "May I steal our guest from you, my dear? Sir Graham has decided to dine now, which leaves me without a partner, and I thought perhaps the Colonel might care to take his place."

Colonel Brown stood up. "My dear Lockhart, since I must not trespass upon your wife's kindness by taking up more of her time, I shall be delighted to partner you. Will you excuse me, Mrs. Lockhart?"

"Yes indeed, Colonel, for I have some duties to attend to, but it has been a pleasure to see you again, and I wish you the best of good fortune this evening."

"Thank you, ma'am. I rather think your husband and I make a formidable partnership."

When they had left the drawing room I stood gazing down into the fire with a troubled mind. It was only when Colonel Brown, sitting there with his gray-flecked red beard, had spoken of his visit to the Caribbean that I suddenly remembered the moment off St. Kitts when Daniel had returned from the trading store to say that a man with a red beard was seeking the *Casey*. I had been alarmed at the time, and I felt an echo of that alarm now.

It seemed absurd to think that the man who sought us might have been Colonel Brown. If that were so, and if he had followed me to England, then what was his purpose? Was he friend or enemy? Apart from a few harmless eccentricities of behavior he had done nothing to interfere with my life in any way. After a few moments I gave a mental shrug and told myself not to imagine mysteries where none existed. To have heard about one red-bearded man and to have met another was not a particularly startling coincidence, and I had more immediate matters to occupy my thoughts.

I straightened a cushion, glanced quickly at myself in the looking glass, then went out to make my rounds of the card rooms before visiting Mrs. Fielding to see that all was well in the kitchen.

* * *

Drifting easily at eight fathoms I looked up and saw him gliding slowly toward me . . . Daniel, but with the body and limbs of a skeleton.

Horror struck into me like the blade of a spear. I wanted to cry out, to beg him to turn away, but I could make no sound underwater.

He kept coming, and the face became mercifully blurred, but the skeleton hand was very close, held out toward me, with a gold coin shining on the bony palm.

The waters boiled and foamed, hiding him. Impossibly, there was the sound of wind howling and roaring all about me. I was swept up, and I lay once more on the broken deck of the Casey, *staring down into the maelstrom beneath Alligator Gap.*

Something swung into view below me like a pendulum. Daniel, no longer skeletal, but sitting in a bosun's chair and in no apparent distress, calling up to me, his words no more than a whisper above the noise of the storm. "Eight-mile reef . . . tell Mr. Lockhart . . . tell him eight mile reef . . ."

The words were repeated again and again, yet I scarcely took them in, for from the darkness below Daniel I could see enormous open jaws rising slowly up to seize him. The monster's body was hidden from me. I saw only the gaping mouth, the vast red tongue, the immense teeth . . . and I fought like one possessed in my effort to cry out. But my jaws were locked, my tongue immovable, and I thought my throat would burst with the struggle to scream a warning.

Then another voice was speaking, and the nightmare dwindled as I woke . . .

I was sprawled half sitting across the bed, somebody's arms holding me, sobs bursting painfully from my throat, panting, shaking, swept with relief to have woken from the nightmare, yet still shivering with the horror of it.

The bedroom door was open. A lighted candle stood on the cabinet by my bed. Chad's voice, close to my ear, said gently, "Casey dear, you're quite safe. Wake up now, you've been having a nightmare. Don't be afraid, you're quite safe, quite safe."

I gave one tremendous sob of relief and collapsed against him. He wore a dressing gown over his pajamas, and I could feel the soft wool of it against my cheek. He moved a hand to stroke my brow, his voice a low murmur. "There now, that's better. You're quite safe, Casey. Just rest quietly for a moment.

You've had such a dreadful nightmare. I heard you in my room across the passage. Here, let me wipe your cheeks. You've been crying, poor dear. There . . . that's better. Now I'll light the gas, and you lie down again while I rouse Birchall and get him to send his wife down to take care of you."

"No, Chad, no," I quavered, my voice muffled against him. "Don't leave me. I'm sorry. Sorry to wake you. Just . . . just stay like that for a moment. There's no need . . . no need for Mrs. Birchall."

He said doubtfully, "Are you sure? I'm sorry to have rushed into your room as I did, but I had to wake you quickly."

My voice was a little steadier as I said, "Thank God you did. And please stay a little while. After all, it doesn't matter, does it? I mean . . . we are married."

"Why, so we are." His voice was cool and neutral. It was as if my mention of our being married had made him withdraw into himself, and I felt an ache in my heart. It was so good to be held in his arms like this.

With an effort I forced myself to sit up. "I'm all right now," I said briskly. "Do forgive me for making such a fool of myself, Chad. Would you pass my dressing gown from the chair there? Thank you." I slipped out of bed as he held the dressing gown for me to put on, then I tied the belt at my waist and pushed the hair back from my brow.

As he put a match to the gas Chad said quietly, "You weren't making a fool of yourself, you were having a nightmare."

"Yes . . . it's one I've had several times, but tonight there was more to it than before." I sat down on the edge of the bed, breathing deeply as if I had just emerged from a long dive. Chad adjusted the gas so it was not too bright, and blew out the candle. I said, "I don't want to keep you, but there's something important I have to tell you, something the nightmare made me remember."

The eyebrow above his drooping lid arched upward. "What do you mean, Casey?"

I wiped sweat and the dampness of tears from my face with the handkerchief he had given me, and tried to smile. It was not easy, for my heart was full of pain. I loved being married to Chad Lockhart, even though he wanted me in name only and as a matter of business. If I could have no more, if I could not belong to him fully, then I was content to be his friend and companion for the years that he needed me. But I knew that when I told what the nightmare had revealed to me it would set a very early term to his need.

As he sat down in the easy chair by the curtained window I was tempted to keep silent, tempted to pretend that I had spoken out of confusion, still half dreaming, but I could not do it. I held the key to release Chad Lockhart from the endless burden of a deathbed promise, and I loved him too much to withhold that key from him.

I said, "I know where the *Almiranta* lies, Chad. The nightmare made it come back to me. When I was . . . oh, fourteen, I suppose, Aunt Maude and Uncle Henry went for a sea voyage the doctor recommended after my aunt had a bout of fever. My nannie, May, who was Daniel's wife, was left in charge of me. I loved her as if she had been my mother. One day when the sea was very calm Daniel took us out for a full day's sailing on his fishing boat. We took a picnic, he rigged an awning, and that was the first time I swam in really deep water, because we went out northeast from Ocho Rios for eight miles. That was when Daniel told me about what he called Eight-Mile Reef."

Chad wore a small frown of puzzlement. "Sam and I studied the Admiralty charts for that area pretty thoroughly. The sea off that coast becomes very deep very quickly, and there was no mention of a reef."

"No, there wouldn't be, because it's not a true reef. It's a ridge no more than a hundred yards long and the same in breadth, more of a plateau I suppose, the top of a very steep underwater mountain, a long-dead volcano, perhaps. It's not a shipping hazard because it lies fifteen to seventeen fathoms below the surface, far deeper than the keel of even the biggest liners. So it wouldn't be charted, and I'm probably the only person in the world now who knows it exists."

Chad stared. "Are you serious?"

"Yes, completely. People who don't use the sea have no idea how immense it is. A hundred-yard plateau of rock a hundred feet below the surface would never be found except by people using one of those instruments to sound the ocean depth, and this doesn't lie anywhere near the line of the submarine telegraph cable."

"Daniel found it, though."

"By one chance in millions. He was testing a boat he'd built, and happened to be hove to directly above the ridge when he decided to test the free running of the little anchor winch to the full length of the cable. But when he ran it out, the anchor found bottom, so he went over the side and followed the cable down. That's how he discovered the ridge. I don't know whether he found the wreck of the *Almiranta* then or during a later exploration, but I'm certain he found her there, lying on top of Eight-Mile Reef."

"Wouldn't the reef and the wreck be visible from the surface?"

I shook my head. "Depth makes the water dark, and so does a field of dark weed growing on submerged rock. I could see nothing that day, even with the sea completely calm. Daniel didn't tell me about the wreck, of course, he only told me of his discovery of Eight-Mile Reef, and said we would keep it as a secret between us."

Chad pressed fingers and thumb to his eyes as if trying to focus his thoughts. "How did the nightmare tell you that the *Almiranta* lies there?" he said slowly.

"It made me remember, Chad." I tried to keep my voice light, so he would not sense the empty sadness I felt. "When the *Casey* was wrecked, Daniel was hanging by his lifeline from the broken stern, and I was pinned by the line, looking down at him. When he knew I couldn't move to help him, and the only way to free me was to cut himself loose, he called something up to me very deliberately. I was in such horror at what he was about to do that I didn't register the words properly, but they must have gone into my mind and lain hidden there. I heard them again in the nightmare tonight. He kept repeating, 'Eight-Mile Reef . . . tell Mr. Lockhart . . . Eight-Mile Reef . . .' "

Chad opened his eyes to stare at me. "He actually spoke my name just before he died?"

"Yes, Chad. You knew of the *Almiranta* and the gold coins, I knew where Eight-Mile Reef lay. He must have hoped that I would tell you, and that you would help me."

"But how could you tell me? And surely he would never have thought of such a thing in the moment before he died?"

I could not stop my voice shaking as I said, "It's exactly the kind of thing Daniel *would* think of in the moment before he gave his life for me. He believed I would survive, because I had only to scramble up the slope of rock to be safe. He knew I would be penniless and homeless. He loved me, Chad, and the words he spoke were all he had left to give me—a distant hope that I might somehow find you and give you his secret, and that in return you might help me."

There was a long silence. I went to my dressing table, brushed my hair back, and found a piece of ribbon to tie it behind my neck. In the looking glass I could see Chad frowning down at the floor. I had expected him to show delight, and was puzzled by his response. At last he said, "Casey, as you say, the sea is huge. Isn't it true that if anyone knew Eight-Mile Reef lay roughly eight miles northeast of a given point on the coast of Jamaica, they would still have to search many square miles of sea, and it could take years to find the spot?"

I turned from the glass and nodded. "Yes. That's true."

"Then how could Daniel find it at will?"

"Oh, he explained that to me on the day of the sailing picnic, and I've never forgotten. From eight miles out you can see Mount Diabolo and the heights above Ocho Rios, providing visibility is good. With a telescope you can make out Daniel's house, the church on Lucky Hill, another at Claremont, all sorts of landmarks on high ground. Well, Daniel took two bearings. With the church on Lucky Hill lying two points west of south, and with his house on a bearing of two hundred and twenty-two degrees, you know you're lying in a circle of a half mile diameter that contains the reef. Even then you can spend an hour or two of tacking back and forth with a trailing anchor to find the ridge. The bearings are easy to remember because they're all twos."

"And you could find it, Casey?"

"Yes." I turned to the glass again and pressed a hand over my heart to ease the ache in it. "Yes, I can find your treasure ship, Chad."

There was another long silence as he sat gazing pensively into space. At last he roused himself from thought, stood up, and came to where I sat. "We'll have to think about the whole matter," he said, and rested his hands gently on my shoulders. "Are you all right now?"

"Oh yes, I'm quite myself again, thank you. Perhaps I won't have any more nightmares, now that I've remembered what Daniel said."

"That would be a great relief. Keep your gas on, turned low, and we'll leave both our doors ajar. I hope you'll sleep well for the rest of the night, but don't hesitate to call me if you need me."

"Thank you, Chad. And thank you for being so kind."

He paused in the doorway and looked back at me. I saw

that quizzically amused look I had first seen long ago in Fern Gully. "I wonder what the lady is up to this time," he said.

A moment later he was gone, but several seconds passed before my tired mind realized that the lady he referred to was his old friend Lady Fate, of whose malice or whims he claimed to be a special victim.

I told Liza my tale the next afternoon, when I joined her at the agency. Much to my surprise we found when we returned home after the day's work that Chad had not mentioned it to Sam. I wondered if I had done wrong to speak, and went at once to Chad's room, where he was preparing for an evening at his club.

When I tapped and called out he came and opened the door, fastening the cuffs of a newly laundered shirt. "Hallo, Casey." His smile was pleasant, and he held out a wrist. "Here, it's your turn again now."

I stood with him just inside the open door, fastening his cuff links, trying to stop my hands from shaking for love of him, and said, "Did you not want me to speak about the *Almiranta*? I told Liza this afternoon, but then when we spoke of it to Sam, he said you hadn't mentioned it, so now Liza's telling him all about it. I'm sorry if you meant to keep it a secret, Chad, but you didn't say, and I didn't dream of not telling Liza or Sam. There, that one's done, now let me have the other cuff."

He held out his wrist and said lightly, "For goodness' sake stop worrying, Casey dear. Of course I intended to tell Liza and Sam. I happened not to speak of it to Sam this afternoon because... oh, perhaps because I felt it was your story to tell."

"But it's your treasure, Chad. Daniel gave it to you, and if it can be brought up you'll be free of all those ancient debts. I'm so glad for you." I kept my head bent, for my eyes felt moist with tears. "There, you're all done up now, and I must go and put the dinner on."

Sam was full of excitement and enthusiasm at my discovery. Liza was also excited, but rather wary with it. "If you and Chad," she said to Sam that evening, "are going to take Casey out to the West Indies so that she can show you where to go down in those awful diving suits, then I shall come with you. If I stay here alone I shall be worrying every minute of the day and night."

Sam said, "That's a great idea, Liza honey. A sea voyage

would do you good, you work too hard these days, and besides, I need someone to squabble with. Chad and Casey are real hard to provoke, but you rise to bait like a fish to a fly. You always have."

Liza looked at him sideways from narrowed eyes. "When I was six years old I bit you, Sam Redwing," she said. "Watch out that I don't do it again one of these days."

The following Sunday when all four of us were together Sam raised the subject of the *Almiranta* during our afternoon walk, as if an early attempt to raise the gold was to be taken for granted and the main question was how to go about it. Since it would be out of the question for me to visit Jamaica, he suggested that we should go to Haiti and charter a small island steamer with three or four passenger cabins in Port-au-Prince. It would be necessary to find a reliable captain and crew, no more than six in all, and these would have to be handsomely paid. It would be unwise even to breathe the word treasure in Port-au-Prince, said Sam, so he would set up a Seabed Survey Company, and he and Chad could purport to be surveying a route for a new submarine telegraph cable. To explain my presence and Liza's, it would probably be best if we were supposed to be the wives of the two surveyors, allowed by the company to join their husbands for this project.

"How about that, Liza?" Sam demanded, grinning as we strolled along the crest of Observatory Hill. "Casey and Chad are legal anyway, but could you bear to be Mrs. Sam Redwing for a spell?"

Liza looked out toward the skyline of London town under April sunshine. "I'll think about it," she said, smiling.

It was then that Chad began to speak, amiably and casually, but making it quite clear that he had no enthusiasm for rushing into this project of raising the gold from the *Almiranta*. "I don't want to be a wet blanket," he said, "but we'd be foolish to do this during the hurricane season, so for safety's sake it would have to be no later than the end of June. That allows very little time. Not enough, in my view, considering all the arrangements to be made."

"Ah, what's wrong with you, Small Fry?" said Sam plaintively. "There's plenty of time."

"What about Liza's agency?"

Liza said, "I shall ask Mr. Basset to provide staff to run it for me. He owns the Woolwich Domestic Agency, he has twice asked if he might buy the Blackheath agency from me, and I think he's rather sweet on me, so there won't be any problem. He'll be delighted to oblige."

"Sweet on you?" said Sam. "He's old enough to be your father."

"It's still very flattering," Liza said serenely.

"He's had time to develop good taste," I said. "His assistant, Mr. Craigie, is sweet on you too, Liza, and he's not even as old as Sam."

"What do you mean, not *even* as old?" Sam said indignantly.

Beside me, his arm linked with mine as we walked, Chad laughed and said, "May we come back to the subject, please? I accept that Liza can hand over the agency temporarily, but I can't do the same with my high-stakes gambling house. It's going very well, and I'm doing better than I hoped, but if I suddenly stop inviting people and close the place down for several weeks I'll never get my hand-picked band of customers back. They're not the kind of people to be played about with."

"But you won't *need* them back once we lift that gold," Sam said with a touch of exasperation.

"There's no guarantee that we can lift it," said Chad. "When we spent two months training at the Siebe and Gorman school we found that a diver can meet all kinds of problems on the seabed. There's a good chance we can raise the gold, but it's by no means certain, and I'm not going to risk substance for shadow."

Liza looked at her brother curiously. Sam was shaking his head, plainly baffled. "I figured you'd jump at the chance, Small Fry," he said. "But if you feel that way, I'll go out with Casey and do the job myself."

Liza said, "Don't be an idiot, Sam. Casey's married."

He made a dismissive gesture. "Ah, sure, but not seriously. And anyway, I was reckoning on you being along with us."

Chad said idly, "I can't spare Casey. It's out of the question, Sam. The *Almiranta* has lain there for a hundred years and more, and she's not going to run away if we wait till next year, so let's think about it again then." He pressed my arm. "I just hope Casey doesn't feel she's offered this splendid gift and I've brushed it aside without gratitude."

Sam gave a dour look. "She could well do."

"No," I said quickly, "no, I don't feel that way at all, Chad dear. I'm content for you to do whatever you think best."

I had been surprised by his caution and lack of enthusiasm, but I was truly thankful for it, and my heart felt light with joy, for now it would be at least another year before Chad could wipe out all debts and would no longer need me. I could never show my love, for I felt he would have nothing but contempt for me if I broke our bargain by trying to make our marriage real, but at least for another whole year I could be his wife in the way that I was now. This might fall short of all I would have wished, but I had known much of pain and fear and sorrow, too much to value good fortune lightly, and for me this was happiness enough.

On the Thursday of that week, at seven o'clock in the evening, I was with Chad in the drawing room of the St. James's house, making conversation with three gentlemen who were about to make up a four at whist with Chad. One of them was Colonel Brown.

Dimmock entered and announced Sir Graham Dean, one of our regular guests. Sir Graham looked unusually flustered, and after greeting me politely he turned to Chad and said, "Evening, Lockhart. Look, I'm somewhat embarrassed. There's a chap outside in my cab who wants to play poker here tonight. I scarcely know the fellow, but he was introduced to me at my club the other day, somebody's guest, and he buttonholed me there tonight, said he'd heard about your soirées and would like to come along."

Sir Graham dabbed his brow with a handkerchief, seeming uneasily aware of disapproving glances from the other gentlemen. "I've told the man this isn't a club," he went on protestingly, "simply a gathering of—ah—friends of yours, but he was frightfully pressing. Said that in fact he's an old acquaintance of both yourself and your wife, over from Jamaica I believe, so I thought I'd better bring him along and have a word with you before fetching him in. If he's been hoodwinking me, I'll go and send him about his business, double quick. Name of Foy, he says."

My heart seemed to turn over within me, and I held fast to the back of a chair as I felt the blood drain from my face. Foy? Who could be using Oliver's name? Who could have recognized me or traced me, or stumbled upon the truth of my identity? All eyes were on Chad, and I had a moment or two to recover from the shock as he said pleasantly, "I believe I once met a gentleman of that name, Sir Graham, so I'll send Dimmock to fetch him in. Meanwhile, perhaps you would go through with these gentlemen and make up a four? I don't wish my guests to be embarrassed if the fellow turns out to be an impostor. You gentlemen all know each other, I believe? I shall hope to join you shortly, and perhaps cut in for a rubber later."

Somehow I managed to smile and say the right words as the gentlemen excused themselves and withdrew. Dimmock went out with instructions to bring the newcomer in, and Chad turned to me. His face was impassive, but it seemed to me that the gray eyes were darker than I had ever seen them. He came and enfolded my clasped hands in his own. "Is it possible?" he said in a low voice.

"Oliver? No, no, I saw him die, Chad. It must be someone from over there who is using Oliver's name to . . . to let us know he has recognized me."

He nodded. "We'll see. Leave everything to me, Casey. We don't know what this fellow wants, but he's clearly up to no good, so brace yourself for a shock. Above all, don't be afraid. I will allow no harm to come to you." His voice was cool and without emotion, but the words were kind and I was fervently thankful for them. As he moved away to stand by the fireplace, Dimmock entered and announced, "Mr. Oliver Foy."

A moment later my husband walked into the room.

I STOOD AS IF IN A DARK LIMBO, ABOUT TO TOPPLE INTO A PIT where sanity had become madness, the true had become false, and logic had become unreason. For one hideous moment I felt this creature must be a corpse given the semblance of life by the voodoo magic of the obeah man. A zombie. One of the undead.

Then Chad's voice, still calm and unshaken, brought me back from the edge of the pit as he said, "That will be all, Dimmock. No more guests are expected. See that we're not disturbed, if you please."

I breathed deeply to steady myself, moved to stand beside Chad, and made myself look at Oliver Foy. He had aged much more than the three and a half years which had passed since the night I had fought him and fled from him, and the imprint of dissipation showed clearly on his face, but there could be no doubt that this was Oliver Foy, the man I had married in innocent hope, and lived with in secret pain and degradation. In his eyes as they rested upon me now was a look of such jeering triumph and anticipation that I almost cried out with terror.

"Good evening, Emma, my dear," said Oliver Foy. "Good

evening, Mr. Lockhart." He put down hat and gloves on a chair, then moved forward as if to greet me, but Chad's voice stopped him.

"Do not approach this lady, Foy. Do not attempt to touch her." The words were casually spoken, and when I half turned my head I saw that Chad stood relaxed, one hand on the mantelpiece, looking down absently at Oliver's feet.

Oliver said, "It is hardly for a bigamous husband to forbid me to approach my wife, Lockhart."

Chad said in the same casual voice, "I won't warn you twice," and as he spoke he lifted his head. I could see only his half-closed eye, but Oliver must have received the full impact of a look that made him start back a pace.

He recovered his composure, gave an unconvincing laugh, and said, "Clearly there are matters for discussion. May I sit down?"

Chad said, "We will remain standing while you explain your presence here, Foy."

"My presence?" Oliver had been thrown off balance now, and began to bluster. "What the devil have I got to explain, sir? There stands my wife, Emma Foy, and I have come to take her home to Jamaica!"

"This lady has been suffering from loss of memory for more than three years," said Chad. "You assert that she is your wife?"

"Eh? Loss of memory?" Oliver's eyes narrowed. "Ah, so that's the story? Well, it saves a scandal, which is all to the good. But you can't deny that *you* know Emma is my wife, Lockhart. You met her twice in Jamaica, yet you still went through a form of marriage with her."

"I have a poor memory for faces," said Chad, "and failed to note the resemblance. Perhaps you will explain how you came to lose your wife, Foy."

Oliver drew in a breath between his teeth, then nodded grimly. "Very well, I'll play your game for the moment, Lockhart. Three years ago last September the edge of a hurricane touched Jamaica. Lightning set fire to our stables. I was..." he glanced at me with eyes that threatened dreadful things, "indisposed with a fever at the time, but Emma ran out to help save the horses. Such was her concern for me that she locked me in our bedroom to make sure I could not risk my health by going out into the storm. I learned from the servants later that the situation was quite chaotic, with a high wind, teeming rain, and frightened horses running loose everywhere. There was constant lightning to add to the danger, and in fact my valet, Ramírez, was killed by a thunderbolt, struck full in the chest by a lump of fiery metal as big as a coconut."

Ramírez! The rain-drenched figure in the white shirt Daniel had pierced with his thrown fishing spear had been Ramírez, not Oliver. Lightning had melted the spear into a shapeless lump, and this had been taken for a thunderbolt. It was a natural assumption. Perhaps close examination might have proved it wrong, but the death of a servant would not have warranted that. The candlestick ... how had Ramírez come to be carrying the heavy silver candlestick with which I had struck down the monster who was my husband?

Oliver was saying, "... and so next day, when Emma was nowhere to be found, our doctor suggested that she may have witnessed this horrible event, and been so shocked by it that she temporarily lost her wits. She may even have been close enough to be physically affected by the thunderbolt. Her horse was found, saddled and bridled, near Rio Hoe, so it seemed she had ridden away in a daze and perhaps been thrown. When after a week we had not found her body, it was assumed she must have fallen down one of the sinkholes in the area."

This was the assumption Daniel and I had hoped for. We had never dreamed that the faceless figure advancing upon me through the storm could be anyone other than Oliver.

My husband went on, "In due course I announced publicly that I must accept some blame for both deaths. For my wife's, in that I did not prevent her rushing bravely out into the storm to save the horses. Then there was poor Ramírez. I managed to open the window and shutters of my dressing room, and saw the fellow hurrying across the courtyard to go to the blazing stables. When I shouted, he did not hear me above the storm. I hurled a tall candlestick down in front of him to attract his attention—the first thing to hand. When he came beneath the window I bawled orders that his first task was to find my wife and bring her back into the house at once. I suppose he carried the candlestick rather than leave it there, but it was in fact silver plate on copper, and perhaps this in some way attracted the thunderbolt which struck him."

Oliver had recovered his poise in the telling of his story, and as he concluded it he gave Chad the contemptuous look of a man who is certain he must win in the end. "Well, now you know how I lost my dear wife, sir," he said with heavy sarcasm. "I might never have found her again had it not been that Mr.

Carradine, the surgeon who has been teaching in hospitals on a number of islands in the Caribbean of recent months, came to Jamaica early this year. I met him at my club, and he was a guest once or twice at Diabolo Hall. One evening he told the the strange story of a little ship called the *Casey*, with a crew consisting of a half-caste Chinaman and a coolie girl. It seems they had been wandering the length and breadth of the Caribbean for several years, and one day they brought a desperately sick man to La Faucille in the teeth of a hurricane."

Oliver broke off and gave a shrug. "But you know this story better than I. The sick man was called Sam Redwing. The ship and the Chinaman were lost. The girl, known as Casey, brought the sick man to the hospital, where Mr. Carradine operated on him for appendicitis. The girl spoke only in crude pidgin or creole, but she carried a bracelet among her few belongings, a gold bracelet with a gold coin which had been made into a charm. Carradine was shown this by one of the sisters while the girl was sleeping off the effects of her ordeal. When he told me that the reverse of the coin bore a coat of arms and the date seventeen ninety-four, I knew I had seen it like years before, when *you* showed me a similar coin, Lockhart."

Oliver half turned away, looking back over his shoulder at Chad with hatred in his eyes. "You showed me the Maria Luisa coin and spoke of the *Almiranta*. You were interested in having me finance a search for the ship, and then you withdrew, damn you, with no explanation."

"Be so good as to refrain from swearing in the presence of this lady, Foy," Chad said without heat.

Oliver laughed and looked at me. "You mean this coolie girl? Oh yes, my dear. I learned the truth about you when I went to La Faucille. It was easy to piece things together from what they told me. Daniel Choong and that boat of his vanished from Ocho Rios on the night of the storm, and were believed lost. But you went with him that night, didn't you? The farewell letter he sent you deceived me, as it was no doubt intended to. You survived, and you both changed your names and the name of the boat."

He looked at Chad again. "The nuns told me how this man Redwing had sent her to England with a member of their order, Sister Clare. I've been here two weeks now, and after I'd spoken with Sister Clare at her Ealing convent it wasn't difficult to have inquiries made, and to discover that the coolie girl had become a young lady again, living with her new friends on

Crooms Hill by Greenwich Park." Oliver flashed a searing glance at me, and ran his tongue round his lips. "The inquiry agent I employed took only a few days to find out all about the Blackheath Domestic Agency, about Miss Liza Lockhart and her brother, and their friend Sam Redwing, about Miss Casey Brown who became Mrs. Chad Lockhart, and about these high-stake gambling evenings you organize here. In the face of all this are you still going to deny that this woman who called herself Casey Brown is in fact my wife?"

"I haven't denied it," Chad said musingly. "I've simply said that Casey was unaware of it because she lost her memory, and that I was unaware of it because I failed to recognize her as the young girl I met some years ago. I should now like to know exactly why you have come here, Foy."

"Why?" Oliver glared, and I saw a pulse of anger swell in his temple. "I've come for my wife, of course!"

"She will not return to you under any circumstances. You know why."

Oliver's mouth twisted. "The law will compel her. You may both be exonerated from a charge of deliberate bigamy, but the law will make her return to me . . . and will restore my marital rights."

A cold sickness rose within me, and I clung frantically to the memory of Chad's words: *I will allow no harm to come to you.*

Chad said, "Would you not prefer approximately one hundred thousand Maria Luisa pieces of eight, Foy?"

"What?" A mingling of disbelief and avarice shone in Oliver's eyes.

"You must surely have realized that Daniel Choong, a skilled diver, was the man who found the sunken *Almiranta*. That is how Casey came to have the coin, in the form of a bracelet charm he made for her, and it was from him that she learned the precise location of the wreck. For reasons which don't concern you, Foy, that treasure was offered to me by Daniel Choong. I now offer it to you, providing you agree to release Casey."

Oliver exhaled as if he had been holding his breath. After a long moment he said, "You'll fetch it up for me? Within the next few months?"

"Yes. Once you have signed a legal document acknowledging that our bigamous marriage was made unknowingly,

but adding that under all the circumstances, and without ac-
rimony, you wish to have your marriage annulled."

There was a brooding silence in the room, and it seemed
to me that the air was charged as if by a storm. Oliver stood
with a hand to his chin, tapping a fingernail against his teeth,
looking at me with glittering eyes. "A hundred thousand of
those coins?" he said at last.

"Approximately. One of six chests was broken open, apparently."

Oliver kept looking at me, and grinned slowly. "Suppose I
refuse your offer?" he said. "Suppose I insist on taking Emma?"

"Then I'll hang for you, Foy." There was an eerie softness
to Chad's voice, but it did not belie the words. Rather it gave
them added force. "I'll hang for you if need be," he said again.
"Doubt me at your peril."

Oliver took a step back, and his face was gray with fear. I
was startled myself, and turned my head to look at Chad. Again
I could see only the eye with the drooping lid, but I caught my
breath, for in his gaze there was no doubting the threat of
death, and the thin scar on the temple above that eye was starkly
white against the surrounding skin.

Oliver waved his hands as if dismissing some needless
digression. "Don't talk like a fool," he said roughly. "All right,
I accept, but there are details to be decided before the document
can be drawn up. When shall we meet for that?"

"On Saturday, the day after tomorrow, at ten o'clock in the
morning, at the offices of my solicitors, Foley and Pargiter of
Blackheath. My sister and Mr. Redwing will also be present.
You may bring your own legal representative." Chad pulled
the bell cord beside the fireplace.

"Very well." Oliver did not look at me again, but turned
and picked up his hat and gloves. "At ten o'clock on Saturday,
then."

Dimmock entered and said, "You rang, sir?"

"Show Mr. Foy out, please."

The door closed behind them. I fought to prevent my teeth
from chattering and to hold back a moaning sob. Chad said
reflectively, "I'm sure Sam's friends were right. That man
needs a lot of money, and needs it badly. Just as well for us."

"For *us*?" I pressed my hands to my cheeks, still dazed with
shock. "For me, Chad, yes. But...but you've given your
fortune away! Oh, dear heaven, you shouldn't. You mustn't.
I can run away somewhere, hide so he can never find me—"

"Hush now, hush," said Chad, and took my wrists gently to draw my hands down. "That must have been a worse ordeal for you than the hurricane, Casey, but you were quite splendid, and at least we know the whole truth now. The man who died was Foy's valet, and there was never any suspicion attaching to Daniel, or to you either as an accessory." He glanced at the clock on the mantelpiece. "I must attend to our guests. I wish to God we had Liza here to look after you, but perhaps if you go and lie down you'll feel better soon. I'll take charge here tonight."

I would have liked Liza to look after me, but what I longed for much more was to have Chad hold me in his arms and comfort me, as he had done that night when rousing me from the nightmare. With an effort I managed a small smile and said, "No, I won't lie down, I shall only keep reliving that moment when Oliver came into the room. I'd much rather carry on as usual."

He studied me with that odd look of his, one I could never fathom, then said, "Are you sure? You're very pale."

"I'll drink my sherry for once, and pinch my cheeks. I won't let you down, I promise."

He gave me a funny lopsided smile. "All right. We'll talk about everything tomorrow."

I said, "Just one thing now, Chad. Thank you with all my heart for what you did in these past few minutes, for not letting Oliver come near me, and standing up for me, and for all the things you said. But you . . . you threatened him, and that frightened me. You must never put yourself in jeopardy for me. Will you promise?"

He looked down sideways at me with a frown, and shook his head. "That's impossible, Casey dear. You're an investment of mine, and I have to protect my investments."

I held back tears and said as briskly as I could, "Yes. Of course. That's different."

Strangely enough I found no difficulty in doing what had to be done that evening. It was not only a relief to be carrying out my usual duties, but I also found that the performance of them seemed to be steadily abating the shock I had sustained. Some time later, in one of the whist rooms, Colonel Brown rose to his feet and came toward me as I approached the table at the finish of the hand being played. "Is that man Foy in the poker room?" he murmured.

I said, "No, Colonel, my husband did not invite him to stay."

"I'm very glad. I was in Jamaica recently, as you know, and Foy is up to his eyes in debt. He has also completely lost the respect his family once had, since he's now known to be a thoroughgoing rake."

"Thank you, I shall pass that on to my husband." I hesitated for a moment, then went on. "May I ask your opinion on a particular matter?"

"But of course, Mrs. Lockhart."

"It may be necessary for us to cease holding these soirées for a few weeks. If so, do you think our little circle of guests will take offense and be reluctant to visit us again when we return?"

His eyebrows lifted. "Good heavens, no. The whole point about your home is that it is not a club. You and your husband would naturally be expected to take a holiday for a few weeks in the summer, like any other family. Besides, I can assure you that an invitation to this house has become much sought after, Mrs. Lockhart, and those fortunate enough to be received here prize that privilege far too jealously to give it up on the grounds you suggest."

I said, "Thank you, Colonel. Now I must ask if you or any of your companions at table wish to dine shortly. If so, perhaps they would like to make their choice from Mrs. Fielding's menu."

Colonel Brown's words had been a huge relief to me, but I found it baffling that Chad could have been so wrong in thinking we would lose our guests. When I told him later what the colonel had said he only nodded absently and remarked that he had probably been overanxious about the situation.

I slept fitfully that night, but with no bad dreams. Next day, when I told Liza of Oliver's return from the dead, she was stricken with grief. We were in the agency office, where I had joined her after luncheon, and I put my arms about her and comforted her as she wept for me. Then I told her how Chad had dealt with Oliver, and she sighed with relief.

"Lost memory . . ." she said a little shakily, "and then buying that monster off with Daniel's treasure. Oh, that's very clever." She dabbed her eyes. "Chad's a very clever man, though I wouldn't dream of telling him so."

"Do you really not mind if he gives it all away, Liza?"

"Oh, pish and tush. You're much more important than a few chests of gold."

I reflected, loving her for her great heart, that perhaps I was indeed more important to her than gold. But to Chad, kindly though he was, I represented an investment, and it puzzled me that he seemed willing to give up a fortune to keep that comparatively tiny investment.

I did not see Sam Redwing's immediate response to the startling news of Oliver's appearance, for it was Chad who told him about it, but when Liza and I returned home that evening Sam said little and was very quiet when Chad called us together to discuss a draft of the agreement he had drawn up for his solicitors to put into legal form. He had already been in touch with Mr. Foley, the senior partner, and the draft was delivered by hand to Mr. Foley that same evening, so that the document would be ready for the meeting next day.

At ten o'clock the following morning we were sitting at a long table in a boardroom at the offices of Messrs. Foley and Pargiter. Mr. Foley, a thin man with gray hair, sat at one end of the table. Chad and I were on his right, Sam and Liza on his left. At the far end sat Oliver's solicitor, a Mr. Thompson, with Oliver on his right. Apart from a polite formal greeting by Mr. Foley, no words had been exchanged between Oliver and ourselves when he arrived.

Mr. Foley cleared his throat, picked up a foolscap sheet of heavy linen paper in front of him, closely written in copperplate handwriting, and said, "You hold a duplicate of this agreement in your hands, Mr. Thompson. It is to be a secret agreement, but will of course carry the full force of law in the event that either part attempts to default. In essence it states that Mr. Chad Lockhart and Mrs. Emma Foy entered into a bigamous marriage unwittingly, by virtue of the fact that Mrs. Foy suffered loss of memory lasting several years and had acquired a new identity. Mr. Oliver Foy believed his wife to be dead. He acknowledges that she is now essentially a different person from the woman he married, that she has no recollection of him, and that in these circumstances it would conduce to her happiness if the marriage were annulled on grounds which are obvious, thereby permitting her legal marriage to Mr. Lockhart."

The solicitor looked up from the document and said, "In passing let me say there is little doubt that the bigamous marriage will attract no legal penalties since there was no intention to break the law, and that the dissolution of the first marriage should suffer no legal hindrance. It is also my opinion that the Church of England will accept the dissolution under these circumstances."

He bent to the document again. "In consideration of Mr. Oliver Foy's natural distress at losing his wife by this unselfish act, Mr. Chad Lockhart will undertake to recover certain monies from a sunken ship, the *Almiranta*, within the course of the next three months, monies of a nature here specified in some detail, and to deliver such monies into Oliver Foy's hands. In the event of failure to recover the said monies, this agreement will become null and void, but the parties may negotiate a fresh consideration if both so desire."

Mr. Foley looked up again. "That is the nub of the matter," he said. "May I have your view, Mr. Thompson?"

The other solicitor and Oliver muttered together, then Mr. Thompson said, "Clause Four states that Mr. Lockhart shall be responsible for providing the ship and crew needed for the diving operation. My client agrees that Mr. Lockhart shall provide all diving equipment, but wishes himself to provide ship, crew, and diving attendants. The ship will be ready to sail from Port-au-Prince from June first onward."

Mr. Foley glanced at Chad, who looked down at the table for a few moments before saying, "Agreed." Mr. Foley nodded. "I shall have the clause amended. Are there any other matters you wish to raise, Mr. Thompson?"

Another muttered consultation, and the other solicitor shook his head. "Nothing further."

Sam Redwing struck the table softly with the palm of his hand. "I'm an interested party, and I've got something to say," he announced grimly.

I was startled by his manner, but this was nothing to the shock I felt at his next words. Pointing a finger at me he looked coldly at Chad and said, "Casey's the one who told us how to find that ship, and even now we probably couldn't locate the wreck without her guidance. But you seem to forget just who brought Casey here." He touched his chest with a thumb. "I did. Sam Redwing. She was a coolie girl who lost the boat that was her home and the man who was her protector. She was penniless, and I had her sent to England. I had her clothed and fed and taken into *my* house at *my* expense. I'm entitled to half that gold, Chad. Any way you look at it, I'm entitled to half."

Across the table from me Liza was sitting with a hand to her lips, white with distress, and I could feel the color draining from my own cheeks. This was a side of Sam I had never seen, and I would never have believed it if anyone had told me. His face was set like stone, his eyes bitter. There was a brief, dreadful silence when he finished speaking, then Chad said in a voice of ice, "It's a pity you didn't say this before."

"I never believed you'd have the gall to cut me out. But I'm saying it now."

Liza put a hand on his arm and said in a choking voice, "Sam dear . . . please."

He did not look at her, but said dourly, "If your brother can't see the justice of it himself, I'd have thought you might enlighten him."

At the far end of the table Mr. Thompson said, "This dispute between your clients is a serious matter, Mr. Foley."

Oliver spoke in a taut voice, "I'm not taking only half of what was promised."

Mr. Foley looked from Sam to Chad and said worriedly, "Perhaps we should suspend this meeting while—"

"No," said Chad, and though his voice was quiet there was iron in it as he looked across the table at Sam. "The issue is simple. Daniel Choong discovered the *Almiranta*. There's no question of treasure trove in those waters, so the gold belongs to whoever can recover it. Daniel Choong gave it to me, and I propose to fetch it up and use it as I please. You have no rights in it whatsoever, Sam."

I looked dazedly from one face to the other, sick with dismay and wanting to stop my ears. They were lifetime friends, yet now they were quarreling, and I was the cause. I wished I had run away the night before, so that this moment could never have come, but it was too late now. Liza's grief was as great as my own. She sat with eyes closed, two tears running slowly and unheeded down her cheeks.

Sam said brusquely, "Is that your last word?"

The hooded gray eye surveyed him coldly. "It is."

"So be it." Sam stood up, picking up his hat and gloves from the empty chair beside him. "If it was anyone else, I'd fight you on this. But for the sake of old friendship I'll let it go. You do what the hell you like, Mr. Lockhart, but you'll have to do it without me. Excuse me, ladies." With a brief nod to me and to Liza he moved to the door, where he paused to look back. "I'll pack a suitcase and I'll be away by the time you reach home. Next week I'll be going to Spain again for a month or so. Your lease of the house expires at the end of July. I'll have my solicitor write to you about it." He went out and closed the door behind him.

Liza stifled a sob. I clasped my hands in front of me in a vain attempt to stop them trembling. Chad sat staring down at the table. After a moment or two he lifted his head and said, "Nothing further then, gentlemen?"

Sam Redwing was gone from Heathside, and I still could not quite believe it. During the day there was little time to think, for we were feverishly busy making preparations to leave in just over two weeks, but at night I found sleep came slowly, for my head would begin to buzz with troubled thoughts.

I felt guilty, for it seemed to me that I was the cause of what had occurred. Without wishing it, simply by existing and by the ironies of Fate, I had destroyed the seemingly unbreakable friendship of the two men who, together with Liza, meant more to me than anyone else in the world. I said as much, both to Chad and to Liza, but in their different ways neither would hear of it. Chad declined to discuss Sam's departure, and would only say vaguely that being an American, Sam was inclined to act on impulse, but that given time he would forget his grievance and all would be well again. Certainly I was not to blame for what had happened.

Liza was equally quick to exonerate me, but I could see she did not agree with Chad's view that the quarrel was no more than a temporary flare-up. We only discussed the incident on one occasion, for I think we found it too painful for fruitless speculation, but Liza was as baffled as I was by Sam's behavior.

"It's so strange," she said one evening as we sat mending after dinner, with Chad busy in his study. "Sam is the most generous man in the world, and thinks so highly of you, Casey. Yet the way he acted that morning was as if he cared little for you and was possessed by greed. They say that gold can twist a man's nature, but I never dreamed it could happen to Sam. And Chad was strange, too, so cold and harsh and unbending. I've never known him to act in such a way toward Sam before. Well, there you are, it did happen and Sam's gone now." Her hands were still, resting in her lap, holding a woolen sock on a darning egg. It was one of Sam's socks, I noticed. Her eyes were weary, her face wan as she murmured, more to herself than to me, "Perhaps it's for the best."

My heart went out to her, but I could say nothing, for I knew what was in her mind; that perhaps it was best she should no longer go on living with the hope that one day Sam might return the love she held for him; that hope forever unrealized could be more painful than acceptance without hope.

There was no laughter in our home during those two weeks before we sailed. Our days were quiet and grim and purposeful. In the beginning Chad tried to persuade Liza to remain at home when we left for the Caribbean, but she was more fierce and peremptory with him than I had ever known her.

"I will *not* argue the matter, Chad. If you take Casey, I go too."

"But I need Casey as a guide. Oh, I know I have the bearings for Eight-Mile Reef, but there could still be problems finding it. Casey's a skilled sailor and knows the area. I might even need her for some shallow diving to locate the wreck. You can see a great deal more from a few feet below the surface than from above, and she can work ten times faster at that level than a man in a diving suit trudging about the bottom."

"Very well. You need Casey and you don't need me. But I shall go just the same, because Casey needs me. Do you think I can bear the thought of her being alone on deck with that monster Foy and his hired crew while you're grubbing about below in the wreck? And what about the journey out there? You can't expect Casey to share a cabin with you, but if I go along we can say that your wife is sharing with your sister because I'm too nervous to be on my own. Don't waste my time arguing, Chad, I have too much to do. Just book passages for the three of us in two cabins."

And so it was done. We could not get a passage direct from an English port to Haiti, but there were ships plying from Le Havre to this island, which had once been a French colony, and so we made arrangements to cross the Channel and spend one night in Le Havre before sailing for Port-au-Prince.

A curt note from Oliver, five days after our meeting at the solicitors' office, announced that he was sailing next day and had sent a telegram to a colleague in Haiti who would be making arrangements to charter the small steamship and crew required for the search, together with two men experienced in the work of diver's attendants, to man the air pump, winch, and lifeline.

Early in the following week, the firm of Siebe and Gorman, on Westminster Bridge Road, supplied one of their latest diving suits, together with all necessary air pipes, lifelines, and two air pumps. This equipment was tested and proved by Chad in the deep tank used by the firm for preliminary training of divers, then it was crated and sent on ahead to Le Havre so that it could be taken as cargo aboard the *Valence*, the ship on which we would travel to the Caribbean.

Meanwhile Liza and I were busy handing over the reins of her agency to Mr. Craigie and a clerk from the Woolwich Domestic Agency, who were to keep the business going during our absence. I was also engaged in writing letters for Chad to all the gentlemen who came regularly to play cards at our St. James's house, saying that we were going abroad for a few weeks' holiday, but would return later in the summer and would then look forward to welcoming them once more to our little soirées.

"It's strange," I said to Chad one evening when all the letters had been written and were ready to post. "They really do seem to enjoy themselves, even the ones who are the biggest losers."

Chad nodded. "You don't know gamblers, Casey. They almost all lose in the end, and the biggest losers are always the ones most anxious to try again. I only invite those who can afford to pay for their pleasure, so everybody is content. It's very convenient for someone like me, or for one or two rare people. Colonel Brown, for instance."

"Yes, but why, Chad? I mean, what's the difference between you and the others?"

He smiled absently. "We're not gamblers, Casey, we're not victims of the fever. That's the difference."

I cannot say that our voyage across the Atlantic was a happy one. The weather was good, our cabins were comfortable, and after one day of feeling a little queasy Liza found her sea legs and was troubled no more. But there were shadows hanging over us. Sam was not with us, Sam Redwing with his easy smile, his teasing, and his enthusiasm for whatever might be afoot. He had left no forwarding address and sent no word. I longed to write to him and say that we all loved him and longed for his return, but the best I had been able to do was to place a letter in his room on the day we left, hoping that he might come back and find it there.

Liza was as affectionate toward me as ever, but there was none of the warm bubbling chatter that made me laugh and at the same time endeared her to me. The sparkle of mischief was gone from those cornflower blue eyes, and one night I woke to hear her weeping softly in her sleep in the bed across the cabin from me. I went to her and stroked her brow, whispering little words of comfort, but made no attempt to wake her, and soon she was quiet again.

I did not know where the dividing line between the Atlantic and the Caribbean ran, but when I came on deck one morning to find we were passing through the long string of the Bahama Islands I knew we had entered the sea that not long ago had been my home. It was a hot day with a fair breeze, and I wore a light cotton dress with a wide-brimmed hat tied in place by a chiffon scarf knotted under my chin. Standing by the rail I looked down at the dark blue water, then away to a small island on our port beam, where sand and shallows turned the water to turquoise, and I thought how lovely it would be to strip off my clothes, pull on the faded shirt and short trousers of my years as a coolie girl, and dive down into that cool water just off the island. There, as a gull glides on air, I could swim and turn, circle and hover, weightless as a feather, renewing old acquaintance with that other world below the surface of the sea.

I had kept those well-worn garments, together with my goggles and my knife in its leg-sheath. Apart from Daniel's bracelet and the leather purse, these were the only things I possessed after the *Casey* was lost. I had kept them because I could not bring myself to throw them away, and now they lay in the tiny wardrobe in my cabin.

I heard a step, and Chad was beside me. He nodded toward the yellow and green of the little island, the sand and the palms. "Homesick, Casey?"

I shook my head. "No. I hope I have the chance to dive, and I suppose that's partly because I'd like to show off my one small ability, but I'm not homesick for the past. I was happy aboard the *Casey*, but in a way it was . . . a retreat from life, because I was hiding. I've never been happier than in these past months, with you and Liza and Sam. Well, until Sam left in anger."

"Yes. I'm sure it will come right, but I'm sorry to have put you and Liza to this distress."

I looked at him, puzzled. "It wasn't your fault, Chad. Or Sam's. It just happened."

He gazed out to sea and smiled wryly. "Well, perhaps."

On the third day of June we docked in Port-au-Prince. This was the capital and chief port of Haiti, the country where a century ago a black army of ex-slaves had risen against their

French masters and defeated them. It was now a very poor country with a few very rich men, and in the last sixty years had known a succession of seventeen rulers, of whom almost all had either been assassinated or overthrown by revolution. I had visited Port-au-Prince briefly at the end of my dreadful honeymoon on the west coast of the island. It was a sprawling, dusty city with poorly kept roads, but of recent years there had been some renovation of the docks, mainly financed by America, according to the captain of the *Valence*.

Oliver Foy was on the quayside to meet us when we disembarked, and I had to struggle against a sense of panic as I came down the gangway, for the sight of Oliver brought a kaleidoscope of pictures to my mind—memories of my wedding night, and of all that he had done to me, then and later, in the privacy of our bedroom. I set my teeth, took Liza's arm, and crushed those memories into darkness as we came onto the quay.

With Oliver was a pale-brown man of about fifty, a mulatto with a gaunt face and frightened eyes. He wore a rather grubby white uniform and a blue peaked cap. Liza and I stopped a few paces away as Chad approached the two men. There were no greetings. Oliver said, "This is Caragole, captain of the steamer *Liguria*. Since he normally carries passengers for short journeys on the coastal route there are only four passenger cabins, but that will suffice. He says he will need a crew of no more than three for this trip, one of whom can cook after a fashion. There will also be two experienced diving attendants he has hired. They work regularly with an American firm here whose divers are preparing the base for a new breakwater."

Chad said, "Do they speak English? And does Captain Caragole speak English?"

The captain answered. He had the accent common throughout many of the islands, but was easy to understand. "Yes, sir. I speak not bad. My crew, little bit, but mostly French creole. The two diving attendants, they speak English for all things about diving, except they speak like American men."

"Very well." Chad glanced up at a loading net being lowered into the after hold of the *Valence*, then addressed Oliver. "The equipment will be coming off shortly. Will you see that it's transferred to the *Liguria*?"

"Yes." Oliver glanced at the man beside him. "Go and do whatever's necessary for that, Caragole, and have the trunks of these passengers transferred at the same time. They will only require enough luggage here for an overnight stay, and they're prepared for that."

The captain inclined his head, gave a nervous smile, and moved away. Oliver turned back to Chad and said, "I've put out that you're a submarine surveyor, as you suggested, and that I'm a director of your company. The two ladies are your wife and sister. I've booked rooms here for you tonight at the best hotel, such as it is, and I recommend that you go straight there. I'll name no names, but one of the two ladies should remain out of sight as much as possible until we embark unobtrusively in the early hours tomorrow. I have a carriage waiting to take you as soon as your overnight cases have been brought off." Oliver said all this very quickly, in a monotone, as if he had rehearsed the words, and as he spoke I saw from beneath the wide brim of my hat that his eyes, puffy now with long years of dissipation, kept flickering toward me.

Chad said, "Does Captain Caragole know what we intend?"

"Not yet. He and his crew and the diving attendants will be told when we're at sea. It won't be possible to hide what we're about once we begin."

"Are they to be trusted? The commodity we seek is renowned for its temptation."

Oliver gave a short laugh. "Afraid they might be inclined to drop us over the side and take it for themselves? Don't worry. The name of Foy guarantees our safety. It's too widely known for them to risk any stupidity of that kind. They will also be told that a lawyer here and another in Kingston will have a statement of our intention and a list giving the name of each man in the crew, in case we fail to return." Oliver smiled, and there was something in his smile that made me shudder. "It happens not to be true, but that won't diminish its effect."

There was a short silence, then Chad nodded. "Very well," he said. "Let us proceed."

Five minutes later we were in a hot and dilapidated carriage rattling along a broad dusty road to a hotel called Le Coq D'Or, each of us with a small overnight case. At three o'clock next morning, after a short night's sleep, we left the hotel and retraced our journey. Twenty minutes later we were aboard the *Liguria*, installed in three of the small passenger cabins below the deck saloon. By four o'clock we had begun our two-day journey to Eight-Mile Reef, to seek the sunken *Almiranta*.

19

UNDER A MID-AFTERNOON SUN ON THE SIXTH DAY OF JUNE I
stood with Liza on the deck of the *Liguria* in the shade cast
by the empty passenger saloon, and watched Chad prepare to
make his second dive of the day.

Oliver and Captain Caragole watched from the bridge. The
two diving attendants were getting Chad into his diving suit.
Beyond them on the foredeck, the three men of the crew sprawled
under a makeshift canvas awning as they watched. All five of
these men were black, which was to be expected since not more
than one in a hundred on Haiti was white, and not more than
five in a hundred were mulatto. The diving attendants were
two brothers, Jacques and Louis, with a surname that sounded
like Borra. They were neither friendly nor unfriendly in manner, to us or to the crew, and they never smiled, but Chad said
they were good at their work and he was well satisfied with
them.

The three men of the crew were amiable enough, to the
extent that they had anything to do with us. I felt sorry for one
of them. He was a shambling giant of a man with the intelligence of a child, and always seemed to be the butt of the other
two, who called him Jonjon. He wore a rabbit's foot on a string

around his neck, and carried a machete in a sheath at the back of his belt, which reminded me of the many days Daniel and I had spent with machetes gathering coconuts.

It was quite clear that all the crew, and to a lesser extent the two brothers, were in fear of Oliver. So was Captain Caragole. Since Haiti was a place where influence and wealth were stronger than the law, Oliver probably had the power to ruin any of these men, if not to have them imprisoned on some flimsy and trumped up charge.

I was quick to note that the crew were also very nervous in Chad's presence, especially Jonjon. This was no doubt the effect of that drooping eyelid, which I remembered to have inspired great fear in Joseph on the day Chad and I had mended his cart in Fern Gully. We had laughed about the incident since, and Chad had questioned me with interest about the power of voodoo and the obeah man in the islands.

Now, as the Borra brothers were about to lower the helmet onto his head, Chad smiled toward us and said, "You ladies should envy me. It's beautifully cool down there." Liza blew him a kiss. After a moment of hesitation I followed suit. The helmet came down and was locked in place. At once Jacques began to work the air pump, and Chad plodded slowly toward the break in the rail where the ladder had been set, his monstrous boots thumping ponderously on the deck.

We had found Eight-Mile Reef late the previous afternoon. Since we had not revealed the bearings to anyone, or the objects on which the bearings were to be taken, it was I who had stood over the compass beside the helmsman, telescope in my hands, gradually conning the *Liguria* into the position where we could begin trailing a grapnel at thirty fathoms in search of the underwater ridge. Because the steamer was an unwieldy craft I had taken several hours to maneuver her to what I felt was the most exact point of the cross bearing; but then, to my pleased surprise, we had found the underwater mountaintop within two hours of commencing our snail's-pace trailing of the grapnel.

This meant that there was no need for me to dive, and I would therefore be unable to show off before Chad and Liza, but any disappointment I felt was more than balanced by relief that I would not have to display myself, half bare in boy's clothes, before the crew of the steamer, and above all before Oliver. When we found the ridge it had been too late to begin the long preparation for deep-sea diving. Captain Caragole put down a bow anchor, and next morning we watched Chad make ready to descend.

I had felt a measure of shadowy fear ever since we came aboard, and guessed that this was the result of being so close to Oliver. It did not help that his cabin was just across the passage from my own. Because of my nervousness I was thankful for anything to distract me, and kept asking many questions of Chad as he prepared for the first dive.

The cumbersome suit was made of solid rubber with a covering of tanned twill. The inner collar was drawn up around the neck, and an outer one came down over the breastplate to make a watertight joint. The helmet weighed thirty-five pounds and was of tinned copper. Its base screwed onto the breastplate by a segment bayonet fitting requiring only one eighth of a turn. There was a circular glass panel in the front of it, protected by a guard, and an oval panel at each side, for the diver's head would have to turn within the helmet. The great leaden-soled boots weighed thirty-two pounds.

Over light cotton underwear Chad had put on two woolen vests, long woolen pants, thick stockings, a woolen cap, and a shoulder pad before coming on deck. It was quite a struggle for his attendants to get him into the suit, but this apparently was as it should be. Then came the boots, and at last the helmet. As soon as this was in place the attendants began to work the pump, and I could hear the air hissing from a valve in the helmet as Chad exhaled. He clumped to the stout wooden ladder that had been lowered over the starboard bow, climbed slowly down it, and vanished beneath the rippling surface.

For a little while, as we leaned over the rail, Liza and I could see the light of the twenty-five-candlepower electric lamp in his helmet as he sank steadily down at the end of the lifeline, then it dwindled to a pinpoint and was gone. One of the attendants, Louis, spoke into a telephone, connected by cable to an earpiece and mouthpiece set in Chad's helmet.

After listening for some seconds, Louis looked up and spoke to Oliver, who stood clutching the rail, chewing his lower lip. "He reach bottom, mister. Not easy surface. Up and down. Rock and sand." The man listened again, then said, "He don't see ship. Now he will go east for sixty steps and make circle from there." Louis swung his arm in a curve from starboard to port. "If he don't find, we lift him clear, move boat east one hundred steps, try again."

More lifeline and more air pipe were paid out. Liza and I

stood with parasols against the morning sun, not speaking, thinking of Chad in those menacing depths, afraid for him. Twenty minutes went by. Louis squatted with the telephone to his ear. Chad had moved north and west. I was telling myself that if I quartered the area at a depth of a few fathoms, wearing my goggles, I would surely see some hint of the wreck below, and this would save Chad much slow searching. Then Louis suddenly spoke again, grinning. "He find!"

Liza clutched my hand. Oliver let out a wordless sound and struck the rail with a clenched fist. Soon a small cork marker on a length of twine floated to the surface, released by Chad, and five minutes later the process of bringing him up began. I knew from Daniel that if a diver had been below for a long time he had to be brought up very slowly, because the breathing of air under pressure had the effect of causing most dreadful cramps and even death if the diver were brought up too quickly.

Louis spoke into the phone, listened, then nodded to his brother, Jacques. "He say not too long. He rest five minute at eight fathom. No need for more."

That afternoon Chad went down again, and this time I felt a little less frightened. The *Liguria* had been moved to beside the cork marker, and the wreck lay almost immediately below us now. There had been a brush between Chad and Oliver an hour before this descent. Oliver was in a fever to see some gold, and began to give orders for a loading net to be made ready for lowering on the afterdeck derrick. Chad stopped him with a brusque, "We won't need that today, Foy. Perhaps not tomorrow, either. I'll tell you when."

Oliver glared, opening and closing his hands. "What d'you mean? The gold's there, so why not fetch it up?"

"That's why I'm here, to fetch it up, but this isn't a job to be rushed. Ask Jacques and Louis. I've found the wreck, but now I have to explore it to find the gold. That must be done very carefully, because it's easy to get a tangled lifeline. I'm not going down for a handful of coins, I have to get five chests up, which means I may have to break through some of the hull timbers with a crowbar to clear the way, and I won't be working on level ground. I may have to set up a winch on the seabed, to drag the chests out sideways onto a loading net for a vertical haul. If the chests are rotten, I may have to maneuver each one into a canvas sack. All I shall do this afternoon is try to find the chests and then study how best to raise them. I shall also be taking down the spare air pipe to test it under pressure, because Jacques was concerned about one of the joints when he examined it this morning. But don't expect to see any gold lifted today."

Oliver was angrily sullen, but there could be no argument, and without a word he turned away to join Captain Caragole on the bridge.

Chad remained below for over three hours that afternoon. Liza and I sat in the saloon, where a big fan set in the deckhead and driven by an electric motor stirred the air. From time to time we heard one or the other of the diving attendants in brief conversation with Chad on the telephone, but could deduce little from what was said. After one hour a crowbar was lowered to the seabed; after another hour and a half Chad gave orders that he was to be brought up. This took three quarters of an hour, with Chad resting suspended on his lifeline for three periods of fifteen minutes on the way.

Oliver was on deck with us as Chad stood with water streaming from his suit while Jacques unscrewed his helmet. It was barely off before Oliver was almost shouting, "Well, man? Why the devil can't you report progress as you go? D'you think I enjoy being kept in the dark?"

Chad said, "Too much talking mists the glass, and you can't wipe it clear down there, Foy."

"All right, all right. Well?"

"Good news. I've found the six chests, one split open. I've broken a path for fetching them out. Tomorrow morning I'll fix a winch in position to haul them clear. If all goes well, I should send up two chests tomorrow afternoon, and three the following morning. I shall have to spend the afternoon of that day shoveling up as much as possible of the scattered gold from the sixth chest and getting it into canvas sacks."

"Ahhh!" Oliver let out a long breath of triumph, and I saw his eyes glitter. It was a look I recognized, the avid look I had once dreaded as a sign that I would suffer cruel and demeaning abuses for his enjoyment.

Chad was as good as his word. By dusk next day two green and weed-covered chests had been drawn up from the depths and lowered to the afterdeck. They were of oak, bound with iron, not particularly large, but heavy, for each contained more than fifteen thousand Maria Luisa pieces of eight. When the first had been lifted from the loading net, Oliver sent all the crew forward and called for me to come from the saloon. I did not answer, I had yet to speak a word to Oliver, but I went out with Liza and stood a pace or two away as he broke open the two big rusting hasps with a hammer and cold chisel. Sweat poured from his brow as he worked, but I felt this was as much from greed as from effort.

The hinges groaned. He lifted the lid and forced it back. We looked down upon a mass of sodden oakum. Oliver made a dreadful sound in his throat, and I saw white foam at the corners of his mouth. He lunged at the oakum with clawed hands, and as it came away in a mass we saw that it was no more than a three-inch layer covering the dull gold coins beneath, coins of pure gold, untouched by a hundred years of lying beneath the sea.

Oliver was panting as if he had run a thousand yards, lips drawn back in a hungry grin. I could sense that he wanted to look at me, but could not take his eyes from the gold. "There it is, my dear Emma," he whispered at last, the words rough in his throat. "Just a part of your bride-price."

I touched Liza's arm, and together we turned and walked back into the saloon. I had to admit to myself that I was shaken by the sight of that gold and by Oliver's words, for together they brought home to me as never before the immensity of what I was costing the man I loved, who was no more than my friend and who owed me nothing.

We ate our dinner on the afterdeck in the cool of the evening as usual, a simple repast of cold roast chicken, bread and butter, some cheese, and a variety of fruit. A coop with a few chickens stood against the port rail, brought along to provide a change from fish, and Chad had arranged for a canvas screen to be set up across part of the afterdeck to give us some privacy. Oliver always dined in his cabin, then spent the evening playing dice with Captain Caragole in the latter's cabin, much to Caragole's reluctance, we suspected. By unspoken agreement we remained apart from Oliver except when some practical matter had to be discussed, and then Chad dealt with him. We had the saloon to ourselves whenever we wished, for the crew and the diving attendants spent their spare time either on the foredeck or in the forecastle, but in the main we preferred to sit in the open of an evening, behind the afterdeck screen.

I was deeply interested to know as much as possible about the wreck that my beloved Daniel had long ago set eyes on, and after dinner I persuaded Chad to move into the saloon, where there was a good bright lamp, and draw simple sketches to show us how the wreck lay, where he had found the chests, and how he was contriving to get them out.

He seemed amused by my many questions, but humored me by sketching on the writing pad I had brought from my cabin. "The ship's turned turtle," he said. "She's lying at sixteen fathoms with her keel up, and her back broken. Most of the timbers are still surprisingly sound. She's resting on a slight hill, like this." His pencil moved over the pad, and though the drawing was only diagrammatic I began to see the *Almiranta* in my mind's eye.

"Of course, there are great holes in the hull, pierced by rocks, or perhaps by cannons crashing through," said Chad, "and when you get inside you're in a topsy-turvy world. Instead of standing on the deck of a cabin you're standing on the deckhead." He smiled at Liza. "On what we landlubbers would call the ceiling. Everywhere is heavily encrusted with weed. I've seen several cannons, and a pile of cannonballs. I'll bring a cannonball up for you tomorrow, Casey, a souvenir of Daniel's wreck."

"Oh Chad, that's so kind of you. I'd love to have it."

He sat looking at the pad, tapping the pencil gently on it, eyes very thoughtful as if trying to make a decision. "There's one very remarkable thing," he said after a little silence. "I wasn't sure whether to speak of it because it's somewhat gruesome, but I don't think it will keep you awake nights." He put his pencil point on the drawing. "The chests are here, in what I imagine was probably the captain's cabin. Now, next to this there's another cabin."

He tore off the sheet and began a new sketch. "It lies aslant and upside down, like this. You remember I took the spare air pipe down to test it yesterday? The attendants pumped air down it for an hour while I got on with my work. Well, the current must have moved the air pipe a little, and when I went to find it I came through a gap here, into the other cabin . . . and as I walked up a slope I suddenly found my head above water." He drew a horizontal line across the sketch of the cabin, and a round ball to represent his helmet emerging from the level of the water. "Like this."

Liza stared. "But that's impossible!"

"No," I said quickly, for I had guessed the truth. "No dear, it's not impossible." I looked at Chad. "It's an air lock? The air from the spare air pipe was trapped in the cabin and couldn't get out, so you have a huge square bubble of air down there. Is that right?"

Chad laughed and put down his pencil. "Well guessed. But what surprises me is that the air was pumped down yesterday, and it hadn't leaked away by today."

I said, "There must be something sealing the planks of the deckhead from above. Or rather, the planks of the deck. Something in the cargo. Oakum, perhaps. Or even the weeds and barnacles could have made the place almost airtight. But why did you say it was gruesome, Chad?"

"Well . . . when I looked up, I was looking at what had been the deck of the cabin, and I saw a big desk there. It must have been bolted to the deck, together with the chair set in front of it. There are weeds hanging down, probably very puzzled to find themselves surrounded by air, but the extraordinary thing is that there's a man seated at the desk. Well, not a man, a skeleton, still wearing rags that were once clothes. He must have been trapped there in some way, between the chair and the desk, and he didn't fall even when the water was forced out and replaced by air yesterday."

Liza shivered. "Oh, how horrible for you."

Chad looked at me. "Strangely enough, I didn't find it so. You have to expect the seabed to hold sad and grim secrets."

I nodded. Daniel and I had once undertaken a diving job that involved working among drowned men trapped in a small ketch which had sunk off Puerto Rico. It was gruesome, yet I had not been as distressed as I might have been on land, perhaps because it would have seemed some kind of sacrilege for me to question or deplore what the sea had done.

Next day Chad descended again and sent up three chests in two hours. He then took forty minutes to come to the surface, resting at set depths to avoid suffering the agonizing cramps. In the afternoon he went down for what we thought would be the last time, with two very strong canvas sacks, to gather up the gold scattered from the broken chest. The loading net had been used for drawing up the other chests, to make sure they did not break open, but this was a cumbersome process. The sacks had metal handles and could easily be hoisted by a whip on the foredeck.

Oliver was in a state of huge excitement, pacing the deck, glancing at his watch every few minutes, and ordering Chad's attendants to ask how much longer he would be in finishing the work. After this had happened four times, Louis reported to Oliver with some unease that Chad had said he was too busy to waste breath answering stupid questions. Oliver swore viciously.

An hour and a half passed before Chad gave orders that he was to be brought up. Oliver was pale with fury, for he had expected Chad to call for the hook to be lowered so that the last of the gold could be hoisted. He had to contain his anger for more than half an hour while Chad was brought slowly to the surface, but as soon as the helmet was off he began a tirade. "What in God's name are you playing at, Lockhart? I wanted the job finished today! Are you hoping to filch some of the gold for yourself? Is that it? I warn you, don't try to break your bargain with me, or you'll rue the day!"

Chad ignored him as the brothers began to unfasten the great boots, and did not speak until Oliver's ranting ceased, then he said brusquely, "I'm pledged to bring the gold up for you, Foy, but not to work under your orders or to explain my actions. In fact, both bags are ready and only need hauling up."

"*What?* Then why the devil didn't you call for the hook and line?"

Chad said patiently, "Because as I dragged the last bag out, a large piece of debris shifted amidships, something heavy, a gun perhaps, and it slid down into a patch of sand not far from me. There was no danger, but it stirred up the sand so that I couldn't see my hand before my face. I wasn't inclined to wait an hour or more for the sea to clear. I'll go down and fetch the bags up tomorrow morning." The smoky gray eyes surveyed Oliver coldly. "It shouldn't take more than ten minutes, but don't pester me with questions while I'm down there, because you'll get no answers. Is that clear?"

Oliver stood mopping sweat from his face with a handkerchief, his hand shaking. After a moment or two he turned and walked away. Liza and I came forward, and Chad smiled at us as he stepped out of the heavy diving suit. He was not an elegant figure in his thick padding of woolen underclothes, but I felt so proud of him, for I could never have found the courage to go down in that monstrous prison of metal and rubber, and I yearned to throw my arms around him and kiss him.

He nodded toward something lying on the deck in a piece of netting, something he had brought out of the sea with him, and said, "A present for you, Casey. Be careful, it's heavy."

Jacques picked up the net and brought it to me, taking out the object it held, something round, coated with a mosslike weed, with black patches showing through. He held it out in cupped hands for me to look at, but I took it from him, wary of the weight, careless of the green slime, and felt a glow of delight as I said, "Oh, Chad dear, you remembered!"

In my hands I held a ten-pound cannonball from the *Almiranta*.

I slept poorly that night, troubled by nameless anxieties. At two in the morning I was standing by the open port of my cabin, looking out toward the invisible landfall of Jamaica on the horizon, wondering who might now be living in Daniel's house on the heights above Ocho Rios. I had just been able to pick it out with the telescope while conning the *Liguria* into position, and the sight had brought back many memories. As I stared now, I saw a small light appear in the blackness, a pinpoint but very bright. It blinked on and off for a while, then vanished. I wondered vaguely what it might be, but decided at last that it was a trick my eyes had played after looking at the stars to note if we had swung at anchor.

I longed to put on my dressing gown and go on deck for a while. It was unlikely that anyone would be about, but even the slightest risk of meeting Oliver was too much for me. To be wearing nightdress and dressing gown and to find myself facing Oliver would have opened too many old scars. After a while I went back to my bunk and fell into a fitful sleep.

At a little after half past nine o'clock next morning I stood by the rail with Liza and watched the light from Chad's helmet dwindle and vanish in the depths. I had woken early, and been up since dawn. Restless and wanting something to do, I had washed some of our underclothes and hung them to dry on a line behind the canvas screen on the afterdeck, including a shirt and cotton trousers Chad wore when not diving.

Oliver was a different man this morning, cool and formal, with no hint of the feverish rage that had possessed him the day before. Although it seemed foolish to be afraid, I was glad to have Liza with me, for I recalled how this calm and polite manner in Oliver had always preceded my worst moments with him.

Two minutes passed. The winch stopped turning. Louis spoke into the telephone, listened, then looked at Oliver and said, "He reach bottom."

Oliver nodded. "Very well." Two of the crew sprawled under their scrap of canvas awning, as usual. The giant Jonjon stood a pace behind Oliver and seemed to be keeping close to him as if ordered to do so. Captain Caragole was on the bridge above the saloon. I was looking down at the sea again when I heard Oliver say calmly, "Jacques, Louis, pay attention please. When the two sacks have been brought up, Jonjon will cut the air pipe with his machete."

I froze with disbelief, and slowly turned my head. Beside me Liza caught her breath in a sound like a sob. The Borra brothers, crouched over the air pump and their other equipment, were staring at Oliver, eyes wide and showing much white against their black faces. The two men under the awning sat up. After a silence Jacques said, "If air pipe is cut, he will die."

"Exactly so," said Oliver. "But that need not concern you. I shall be reporting to the authorities that Mr. Lockhart took the two ladies for a trip in the dinghy, and that an unfortunate accident occurred. Captain Caragole will support me in this."

On the bridge, Caragole stood gripping the rail. His pale brown face was twisted as if in torment, and he seemed shrunken with fear. Then he bowed his head, and his face was hidden by the grubby blue cap he wore. Dazedly I looked at the brothers again. Jacques was steadily working the pump. Oliver said, "I think you would be foolish to argue with Jonjon." Jacques twisted his head to glance at his brother, and some understanding passed between them. Louis looked at Oliver and lifted both hands, palms out, in a gesture that was very clear to me. The brothers were not prepared to interfere in a quarrel between two white men, and whatever happened would be none of their business.

Oliver looked at me from eyes that were heavy with mingled hatred, menace, and triumph. He said, "I shall respect Mr. Lockhart's wishes to be asked no questions while he is below, but I shall have the pleasure of making a few statements to him over the telephone before Jonjon cuts off his air supply."

If I could have seized the machete and killed Oliver at that moment I would have done it. I would have flung myself at him bare-handed if by nails and teeth I could in any way have prevented his purpose. I was in terror and in fury at the same time, yet underlying this there remained a cold thread of awareness and calculation, a sailor's understanding, hard won by experience both above and below the waves, of what the sea could threaten and how the sea might be foiled.

Beside me Liza said in a high shaking voice, "You are

insane, sir! You have declared your intention to murder my
brother! If you carry out this dreadful act I will never rest until
you hang for it!"

Oliver smiled politely. "My dear Miss Lockhart, I have a
house on a small island off Haiti, a place of retreat from the
world, known to few, where I can enjoy myself as I please. I
look forward to conducting both you and my dear wife there
very shortly, to help me pass a few idle weeks, perhaps."

I knew then that Oliver's mind had truly passed beyond the
edge of reason. Even the gold was not enough. He wanted his
revenge upon me as well, and was ready to kill for the accom-
plishment of his dreadful purpose. I caught Liza's arm. It felt
tense as a cable under stress, and I dug my fingers in painfully
hard, signaling her to heed me and follow my lead. Then, for
the first time since I had struck him down almost four years
ago, I addressed my husband. It was an effort to speak, and
my voice came hoarsely as I said, "We cannot prevent you,
but we will not stand here and watch you commit murder. We
shall go to our cabins."

"As you please." He snapped his fingers at the two men of
the crew. "Take the women down. Lock each one in her cabin.
Jonjon will go with you. Hit them if they make trouble."

Still holding Liza's arm I moved with her toward the companionway. The two men followed uneasily behind, not touching us. At a word from Oliver, the huge Jonjon joined them.
I could feel my poor Liza shivering as if with a fever, and as
we reached the passage where our cabins lay side by side I
breathed, "There's a chance I can save him. A tiny chance.
Pray for us . . . and don't give up hope."

She did not answer, but caught her breath suddenly, and I
knew she had heard my words. Ten seconds later my cabin
door was locked behind me. I wedged a chair under the handle
and began to drag off my clothes. Naked but for my cotton
drawers with the legs cut short, I opened the narrow cupboard
which served as a wardrobe. On one of the shelves lay my
trousers and shirt, my goggles and my diving knife.

I counted seconds in my head, breathing very deeply, making myself move steadily and without fumbling as I pulled on
the familiar coolie-girl clothes and strapped the sheathed knife
to my right calf. Through the open port I could hear Jacques
calling an instruction to the crew, and knew that the hook was
being lowered from a whip on the foredeck. Once it was down,
Chad would need only a minute to hook the bags in place, but

I would still have a little grace, for Oliver planned to speak on the telephone, no doubt taunting him and gloating before at last giving Jonjon the order to cut the air pipe.

I picked up the cannonball Chad had given me and slid it into one of my discarded stockings, then put on my goggles, pushed a small table into place beneath the port so I could climb on it to wriggle out feet first, and laid a towel on the lower edge for padding. Twenty seconds later I was hanging by one hand from the port, my feet less than a yard above the water, the cannonball dangling in the stocking from my free hand. I exhaled as fully as possible, then drew air into my lungs in the way Daniel had taught me, with a series of inhalations, forcing it down into the base of the lungs as if packing a trunk. In the instant that I let go I glimpsed Liza's face above me at the port next to mine, and knew thankfully that she would at least realize I was acting upon my whispered words.

Now I was sinking down through the cool green water I had once known so well, and it was as if I had left it only yesterday. I did not need to hold my nose when blowing air up through my ears to equalize the pressure on the eardrums, for in time I had found the knack of the Japanese women who dived for pearls, the knack of closing my nostrils from within. This was something Daniel himself had never quite managed to achieve.

If I had not been diving to save Chad I might have been a little afraid of the depth, for I had never been so far down before. But Daniel had, and the women pearl divers were said to go even deeper, so I had the underlying knowledge that the depth alone held small danger for me. Head down, feet trailing, I knotted the stocking to my belt, blew till my ears clicked yet again, and knew by the growing darkness that I must be well past ten fathoms. I barely saw the seabed until I was almost upon it, then I shifted the dangling weight and came into a horizontal position as the cannonball touched rock.

I could not see the wreck, but ahead of me was a yellow glow that could only be the lamp of Chad's helmet. Quickly I swam toward it, and as I drew close I saw in its light two sacks on a stout cable passing up in front of Chad as they began their journey to the surface. My eyes had adjusted to the darkness now, and as Chad turned I saw the wreck beyond him, lying in just the way he had described and sketched, with a patch of blackness marking the hole he had broken in the hull in order to winch out the chests.

I swam in front of him and hovered with head close to his

faceplate. Heaven alone knew what he thought at that moment. The light was full upon me, and it would have been impossible for me to see his expression even if I had not closed my eyes now to preserve my vision in the darkness. I held his shoulder with one hand, floated back a little, and pointed toward the wreck with an urgent stabbing movement.

After a few seconds his hand came up and gently tapped my cheek. I turned, opened my eyes, and began to swim for the gap in the hull. I had been underwater for some ninety seconds now, and subjected to greater pressure than I had known before, but I was not yet distressed. Chad was following me, I could see his lamp shining from behind me. He could not match my speed in his clumsy boots, but when I reached the gap and glanced back I saw that he was leaning forward a little in an effort to move faster. I was sure he had guessed my purpose now, and I suspected that Oliver had begun to speak on the telephone, gloating before he put the man I loved to a dreadful death.

Chad's sketches were in my mind as I turned right, groping through almost complete darkness. I was inside the ship, in the cabin where Chad had found the chests of Maria Luisa doubloons. If I continued straight on, through to the adjoining cabin, and if my hope was not in vain, then we might yet live.

Barnacled planking scraped my chest. It sloped up . . . gently up . . . and my head broke the surface of the water. I was in utter darkness, resting on hands and knees, letting out the air in my lungs and drawing in strange dank air, heavy with moisture, but full of life-giving oxygen. The huge air bubble trapped in the cabin had not leaked away. A faint glow touched the darkness about me. I turned and saw Chad's lamp shining through the water. His helmet broke the surface, further back than I had emerged, for he was walking upright. As he came toward me I could hear the regular hiss of the air valve, but while he was still thigh deep it stopped abruptly. Then I knew that sixteen fathoms above us, Jonjon's machete had sliced through the air pipe.

Chad came forward three lumbering steps and sank to his knees, hands lifted to his helmet, struggling to twist and unlock it from the breastplate. I lunged forward to help him. One of his hands touched my face, and I felt a finger pressed firmly against my lips. I patted the hand to show I understood. I was not to speak when the helmet came off, for my voice would be heard by Oliver on the telephone. I gripped the metal sphere as I had seen Jacques do, and twisted with all my strength. It turned, and together we lifted it from Chad's head, but he did not allow himself to suck in fresh air until he had lowered the helmet beneath the surface so that no sound could pass over the telephone. Then he said in a ragged, gasping voice that sounded strangely hollow in this underwater cavern, "No need to tell me what's happened, Casey. He's been telling me for the last minute or more. But he thinks you're locked in your cabin."

I said, "I was, but I climbed through the port. Come out of the water, Chad." I took his hand, and he plodded forward on the sloping deckhead of the inverted cabin. The light from the submerged helmet pushed back the darkness, and I glimpsed something suspended from above in the far corner, the huddle of bones seated at a weed-covered desk, just as Chad had described.

He said in a steadier voice, "Dear God, I thought I was having hallucinations when you appeared in front of me. But then Foy came on the telephone and began talking . . . "

"Yes. Sit down, Chad. We have to get you out of this suit, and there's no point in making a long job of it. I have my knife, and I'm going to cut the suit off you."

"Wait." He lifted the slack of his lifeline and hitched it over a broken beam that jutted from the bulkhead. "Just in case they try to haul my body up. Now Casey dear, is it really possible that you can get us both to the surface alive?"

"Yes." I was kneeling, my goggles hanging round my neck, peering to cut the straps of his boots. "We have to wait seven or eight minutes so they'll be sure you're dead. I expect they'll try to haul you up, but when they find the line's fouled, they'll just cut it, and we'll lose the light, but it won't matter by then. Chad, will you be in danger from cramps? We can't go up slowly." I dragged one boot off and started on the other.

Chad said, "No. If we surface from this depth within the next twenty minutes I shall be all right. But I'm no great swimmer. You must tell me what to do."

"Yes, I will. When I've got you out of the suit you must start breathing slowly and deeply, forcing all the air out, then inhaling fully, and so on. Daniel says it gives the blood a reserve of oxygen. When we're ready to go, you must fill your lungs for the last time, then hold on to my belt when we submerge. I shall follow your lifeline out of the wreck, then continue west for a little way so that we lie almost directly below the ship's stern. All that will only take about twenty seconds. I'll drop my weight and we'll go up together, facing each other, holding hands so that I can guide us both clear if we're right under the hull. When we start to go up you must begin to exhale slowly, and continue until we reach the surface. I shall slow down the ascent for the last two fathoms."

I had his other boot off now, and was carefully working the blade under the thick rubber of the legs. "The loading net is hanging down from the rail of the afterdeck," I went on, "and we ought to be able to climb it unseen. If we do, we'll be hidden by the canvas screen and the saloon. But after that . . ." I paused and looked up at him. "I just don't know, Chad."

The drooping eyelid twitched. "After that," he said softly, "you'll have done more than your share, Casey. Does Oliver have a pistol?"

"No, he didn't need one. He's using Jonjon with his machete as a threat, but all the men are afraid of him anyway."

"I see. This is more or less what I suspected, but it didn't occur to me that Foy might strike before I surfaced. I was a fool."

"You *suspected*?"

"I'll explain later, Casey, I hope. Give me the knife now." Two minutes later he was out of the suit completely, and stripping off his thick undergarments to leave only the short cotton drawers he wore beneath. Then he crouched beside me in the dim glow of the submerged lamp, and said, "In case we fail, there's something I have to tell you now."

"Chad dear, don't waste time, you must do three minutes deep breathing before we go up."

"Another minute won't make any difference, and this is very important." He began to speak quickly. "I have to tell you that I've deceived you, Casey. I couldn't offer a proper marriage with the debts I carried, so I persuaded you into a marriage of convenience, but that was a lie. I just wanted to keep you. I was afraid you would fall in love with some other man, and I'd lose you. I loved you so deeply I was able to hide all my longing, and simply content myself with having you as my dear companion. It was the best I could hope for. When you first said Daniel's gold could be raised I didn't want it, because if I paid my debts there would be no need for the gambling soirées, and our bargain would end. There, it's said now. I had to tell you I love you before we . . . before we gamble against the sea together."

I knelt and peered into his eyes, marveling at the words he had spoken, a glow spreading through my body to wipe away all the chill of the depths surrounding us. Abruptly the light from the submerged helmet went out. I smoothed my fingers over his eyebrows, then slid my arms round his waist and put my head in the crook of his shoulder. "Oh Chad, my dearest Chad," I whispered, "I've been deceiving you in the same way, ever since that evening when you put my bracelet on for me."

"Casey?" he said wonderingly. "You mean it?"

I nodded against him. "Yes, Chad. Don't say any more now." I turned my head, and as his arms held me I found his lips. It was a cold, wet, salty kiss, deep under the sea, with death very close, and with the grim denizen of the century-old wreck hanging above us; but it was the first kiss of love I had ever known, and one that I would remember till the end of my days.

With an effort I drew back my head and slid from Chad's embrace. "Start your deep breathing now, my darling," I said. "We'll go up in three minutes."

It was so simple, the ascent. I groped my way out of the wreck by following Chad's lifeline, then swam west for a short distance. He kept a hand on my belt and kicked his feet up and down in the way I had instructed him before leaving. Then we were gliding up, holding hands. To Chad I would be only a blur, for he had no goggles, but I could see him clearly as the light grew stronger, could see the thin stream of bubbles from his tight lips and nostrils as he kept up a slow exhalation.

The green brightness increased steadily. I was looking up, and saw the loom of the hull to my right. A movement of my legs inclined us that way a little, another movement slowed our ascent. Then we broke surface quietly, no more than ten feet from the stern. The loading net still hung down from the rail. We gripped the thick ropes, resting for a full minute so that Chad could quiet his breathing. It was as I hung there that I saw between the wide meshes a sight that made my heart jump with shock.

Only a quarter of a mile away, and coming steadily toward us under steam, was the *Casey*. I knew she lay broken at the bottom of the sea off La Faucille, a thousand miles away, but the lines of the little ship Daniel had built were unmistakable. She was sailing under bare poles, laying a feathery trail of gray smoke from her smokestack, and the only difference from the

Casey as I had known her was the blue line painted along her white sides.

I turned my head to Chad, and my eyes must have been round with incredulity as I whispered, "It's . . . the *Casey!*"

He put his lips to my ear and breathed, "It's Sam, just the way we planned."

I had suffered almost every emotion from terror to joy in the past fifteen minutes, and suddenly my mind would respond no more. Sam must be on the little steamer because Chad said so, but I was beyond astonishment now, and could not wonder at it. I could only feel a sense of dazed relief. There was shouting going on above us on the deck of the *Liguria*. The smaller boat turned a little, heading toward our bows. I saw on her side the painted name, *Miss Emma*, and again it seemed I must be dreaming. I would gladly have given myself up to the dream but for the anxiety I felt for Liza.

A man in shirt and trousers was sitting on the cabin housing, legs spread, a shrouded object in front of him. Now the boat was only a hundred yards away, and I could recognize the man as Sam. Another figure was at the deck wheel, a tall man in a suit of khaki drill, wearing a brown top hat. A man with a beard.

Colonel Brown. I registered the fact almost without surprise. Beside me Chad muttered, "Good God, look who Sam has with him!" I nodded. So this was something even Chad had not expected. The *Miss Emma* swung round so that she was lying with her bows toward the starboard bow of the *Liguria* and fifty yards away. I heard the engine reverse to stop her way, then it faded to an idling sound as she lay hove to.

Sam spoke through a megaphone. "*Liguria* ahoy! Let's see your passengers! Mr. Lockhart and the two ladies!"

Almost at once we heard Oliver's voice, also magnified by a megaphone. "Get out of my way, Redwing!" It was a raving bellow, almost a scream. "We're weighing anchor! Clear off or I'll ram you!"

Through the mesh of the net I saw Sam pull the blanket off the object in front of him, something metallic, on a tripod. Next moment there was a truly shattering noise, and splinters of wood came fluttering down from the wing of the bridge. Smoke hung in the air above Sam as he picked up the megaphone again.

"This is a Maxim machine gun I've got here, Foy. Now let's start again. Where are your passengers? The gold is yours and you can keep it, but we're here to take your passengers aboard."

There was a long pause, then Oliver's voice came again, strained and taut. "All right! Wait!"

Chad whispered, "He'll use Liza as a hostage. Up now, Casey, quick!"

It was easy enough to climb up the thick rope mesh of the landing net and over the rail. Nobody aboard the *Liguria* could see us, for we were doubly hidden by the canvas screen and the saloon. But from their position off the starboard bow, Sam and Colonel Brown could not fail to see us. The instant Chad was over the rail he stood up straight and held his forearms crossed above his head. It was a signal Sam evidently understood, for he had begun to raise the megaphone, but now he lowered it again and turned his head as if saying something to Colonel Brown.

Chad turned to me, and in his eyes was that absent look I had learned to recognize when he was concentrating on the play of cards. "You said Foy's using that poor half-idiot Negro as a threat?" he whispered.

I nodded, a new fear growing within me, a terrible fear for Liza. Chad said, "The obi sign. The curse of the obeah man. You told me they used blood and feathers and a witches' brew of muck. Is that right?"

"Yes." I could not imagine what was in his mind.

"Make up a bunch of feathers, Casey. Plenty by the chicken coop there. Tie them with a strip of cloth, and fix a small weight on somehow." He was unpegging the shirt and cotton trousers of his that I had washed and hung out to dry. I picked up half a dozen feathers, arranged them in a fan, and fastened the quills with a strip from one of my petticoats hanging there. For a weight I began to tie on a metal ring cut from one end of the washing line.

Abruptly I froze as Oliver's voice sounded again in a bawl of triumph. *"Now then, Redwing! Look at this, and listen! Lockhart is dead and my wife has barricaded herself in her cabin! But here's the other woman, his sister! You dismount that gun and throw it overboard, or I'll have this buck nigger here start cutting Liza Lockhart to pieces! You hear? To pieces!"*

20

CHAD LOOKED TOWARD THE *MISS EMMA*, LIFTED A HAND, AND opened and closed thumb to fingers several times, to mime a talking mouth.

Sam called, "Hold on there, Foy! Let's talk."

"No! Fling that gun overboard!"

"All right, all right! I have to unbolt it from the cabin housing! Give me two minutes!"

Chad had his shirt and trousers on now. He took the weighted bunch of feathers from me, gestured for my knife, pulled up a trouser leg to make a cut in his calf, and smeared the feathers liberally with blood. "We'll go through the saloon now, Casey," he whispered. "Keep out of sight when I go on deck. If I can just freeze Jonjon for long enough to get his machete, we've won."

I had barely grasped his intention when he took my hand and moved toward the stern door of the saloon. A moment later we were inside. The blinds at the windows had been lowered to keep out the sun, and it was dark within, except at the forward end, where the door stood propped half open to allow a draft. Chad halted two paces from the door, still in the gloom. Beyond him, framed as if in a brightly lit picture, I could see Oliver and Liza. He held her by the back of the neck with one hand, bent forward a little, her dress torn, his other hand holding her arm twisted up behind her back in a painful grip, one I well remembered. To one side of her stood Jonjon, machete gripped in both hands, eyes rolled up so that they seemed all white, sweating with what I judged to be the dread of doing what he would have to do if his white master so ordered. Oliver's face was alight with ugly joy. He was mad, but I could not pity him for he had always fed his madness. I could feel only dread and loathing.

Chad crouched a little, and his arm moved as he tossed the imitation obi curse high through the half-open door. To those on deck the thing that dropped fluttering to the timbers must have appeared to fall from the sky. I had heard that voodoo was even stronger in Haiti than in Jamaica, and kept my eyes on Jonjon. Sweat sprang from his brow like water from a squeezed sponge, his mouth fell open, a dreadful groan broke from his throat, and the great white eyes with their small irises rolled down to look obliquely at the bloodied feathers.

Then Chad stepped out of the saloon. I could not see his face, but to everyone on deck this was the man who had been at the bottom of the sea for the last fifteen minutes, imprisoned without air in a diving suit. I heard cries from men I could not see, but the shriek from Jonjon rose above them all. Chad moved steadily toward him, hair wet, clothes dry, a creature of fearful magic.

It was Oliver who broke the spell. Face bone-white, lips drawn back like a snarling dog's, he threw Liza aside so that she fell heavily in the scuppers, then pointed at Chad. "*Kill him!*" he croaked in a dreadful whispering scream. "*Strike, Jonjon, strike!*"

The giant black man wailed and backed away, his face gray. Oliver lunged toward him, screaming, "*Give me the machete!*"

I did not at first realize what happened next. I think Jonjon had no intent to harm his master, but he was in mortal fear of the risen dead that he saw in Chad, and he simply lifted his hands to ward Oliver off. But the machete was in those hands, and Oliver was upon it before he could save himself.

I heard a gasping cry, and Oliver stopped as if he had run into a wall. Then he half turned, eyes and mouth wide. I saw that he was impaled, the hilt and half the blade of the machete jutting from his chest. He tottered three steps back. The port rail caught him across the base of the spine. A fearful sound came from his throat as he arched back over the rail under the impetus of his movement, arms flung wide. His legs came up, and next moment he was gone.

Jonjon sank to his knees and clutched his head in his hands, keening and moaning. I ran out of the saloon. Chad looked at the men of the crew and the diving attendants. He jerked his head toward the forward companionway. "Get below," he said curtly, "and take Jonjon with you." Liza lay sprawled on the deck, unmoving. As I dropped to my knees beside her, Chad lifted his voice in a shout. "All right, Sam! Come alongside!"

There was blood above her ear and a swelling bruise along the side of her head. She had hit a rail or ringbolt in her fall. I looked up at Caragole on the bridge and shrieked at him. "Fetch a towel and water! *Move*, damn you!" I had never sworn before in all my life.

Liza's eyes flickered open and stared muzzily up at me as I pillowed her head. "Casey . . . ?"

"It's all right, darling. We're safe now. Just rest."

"Chad? You . . . saved him?"

"Yes, he's fine. Don't worry, dear."

"I knew you would. And . . . that was Sam, on the other boat? That was really Sam?"

"Yes. He's coming now. I think they planned it between them all along, he and Chad. They only pretended that awful quarrel."

She smiled faintly and whispered, "Men . . ." Then her eyes closed and her head became heavy on my thigh. Caragole crouched beside me with a towel and a bowl of water, his face shining with the sweat of fear. "It was not my wish, *madame*. I swear it. But a few words from M'sieu Foy can take my ship from me and put me in prison—"

Bathing the blood from Liza's head I snapped, "Get away from me. Go and drop fenders for that boat coming alongside."

"At once, *madame*." He scuttled away. A shadow fell across me, and I looked up at Chad. He said, "Is she badly hurt?"

I shook my head. "I don't think so. It's a mixture of shock and a bad bump on the head, but she spoke to me just now."

He let out a long breath of relief. "Thank God for that."

"Why didn't you *tell* us, Chad? I mean, about Sam. It was all pretense, wasn't it?"

He crouched and held the bowl for me. "Yes. We thought Foy might turn nasty after he'd got the gold, so I wanted Sam hidden away in reserve, out of Foy's reach, ready to appear at the right moment. But Foy had to believe that Sam was completely out of it. He had to be utterly convinced, right up to the end, and I'm afraid we relied on you for that. When we started the quarrel, your face and Liza's would have convinced anyone. There could be no shadow of doubt that it was genuine. But I had to keep the same sadness in you both, right up to the last moment. Foy was mad, and madmen are very suspicious."

I wrung out the towel and pressed it to Liza's head again. "Has Sam been waiting somewhere above Ocho Rios?"

"Yes, watching the *Liguria* with a telescope. That story I told about being unable to bring up the last of the gold yesterday was rubbish. I had to delay finishing the job until after I'd signaled Sam. I did that last night, from the bridge."

I remembered the distant pinpoint of light I had seen during the night. That must have been Sam answering the signal. Chad said, "I told him to come in at ten this morning. That was a mistake, I should have made sure he came in before I went down for the last dive, but I didn't dream Foy would strike so quickly or so murderously."

I could hear the engine of the *Miss Emma* close by now as she edged alongside. Sam was calling, and Caragole answered him. I said, "What has Colonel Brown to do with it all, Chad?"

"God knows, my darling. I expected Sam to have a friend or two with him, but I've no idea what Colonel Brown is doing here." He put down the bowl and moved away as the two men came scrambling aboard from the smaller boat, now grappled alongside. "Hallo, Sam. Good morning, Colonel. This is an unexpected pleasure."

Sam grunted, "What the hell's happened, Small Fry? We couldn't see properly." He hurried on without waiting for an answer and crouched beside Liza. "Oh, dear God," he whispered, and took her limp hand. "Liza? Liza girl? Liza honey?" He looked at me with stricken eyes. "Will she . . . will she be all right?"

"Yes, I'm sure of it. Hold her for me, Sam. No, with her head resting on your shoulder. That's right." I sponged with the towel. "The bleeding has almost stopped now, and I think she's more asleep than stunned. Once she knew we were all safe, she just let go."

Sam crouched with his arms about her. His face was like carved mahogany, his eyes sloe-black as he twisted his head to look about him, and I remembered the Cheyenne blood in him. "Where's Foy?" he said in a voice like flint.

"He's dead. Dead and under the sea now."

Sam bit his lip. "God damn," he said softly. "I reckoned to kill that one myself. Was it Chad?"

"No, the big Negro. I'll tell you later. Will you carry Liza into the saloon, please? I'll bring fresh water and a clean towel."

He lifted her easily, and carried her through into the cool twilight of the saloon. When I followed two minutes later he had laid her on one of the long cushioned seats there and was crouched beside her. I put down the bowl and gave him the towel. "Can you tell me what's to happen now, Sam?"

"Main idea is we all go aboard the *Miss Emma* and head for Nassau. There's going to be a ship waiting for us there. Cargo ship with passenger cabins, to take us back to England. The colonel owns more than half a steamship company, and it's one of his ships."

"Well . . . that's very nice. Sam, who *is* Colonel Brown?"

"That's for him to tell you, honey." Sam's eyes were on Liza as he knelt holding the cold damp towel to her brow.

I said, "All right. You stay and look after her, please. If we're transferring to the *Miss Emma* I can be more help on deck."

Out in the sunlight the shrunken figure of Captain Caragole faced Chad and Colonel Brown. The colonel was saying crisply, "Is that clear, Caragole? Mr. Lockhart will now go with you to your cabin and write out a brief account of how Oliver Foy attempted murder and you and your crew permitted it. When he has done this, you will sign the statement, certifying that it is accurate. Your crew will also sign it, or make their marks. When we have transferred the gold and your passengers, you may return to Haiti. There you may report the truth, if you're a fool, or you may report that Oliver Foy fell overboard one night when drunk. His reputation will invite belief. You will be quite sure to say that this occurred *after* your other passengers had disembarked at Nassau, and you will not speak of the gold at all. There are to be no inquiries pursuing any of my friends, you understand? If this should happen, your signed statement will be produced. Now is that quite clear, or shall I repeat it once more?"

Caragole shook his head and smiled a sickly smile of gratitude. "Is quite clear, sir. You will have no cause to show the statement. Not ever."

"Good." The colonel turned and gave Chad a friendly pat on the shoulder. "Would you care to go and start writing, my boy? I'll roust out a couple of the crew and start shifting your treasure chests." He looked toward me, and raised his brown top hat. "But I would be grateful for your wife's advice in the operation. I'm no sailor."

Chad said, "Casey isn't strictly my wife at the moment, Colonel. I imagine Sam has told you all about that?"

"He has indeed, but I'm not impressed by technicalities." Colonel Brown smiled and came toward me. "Good morning to you, Mrs. Lockhart. I'm more than delighted to find you safe and sound."

"Good morning, Colonel." I gave him my hand. "It's always a pleasure to see you, though I never thought to do so here."

"There are no doubt matters to be explained, Mrs. Lockhart, but perhaps they should await a more leisurely moment." He still held my hand.

"I'm sure you're right." I looked down at myself, "Oh, I hope you will forgive my attire."

"My dear . . ." His voice shook and he swallowed. "My dear, please don't say that. I have long wished to see you in the way you were described to me when I pursued that will-o'-the-wisp called the *Casey* through the islands."

Two hours had gone by, a time in which there had been so much to do that the shock of seeing Oliver stabbed through the heart with a machete had passed without making any deep impact on me. If anything I felt relief at his death, wicked though such a feeling might be. I suspected that everybody felt the same, including Caragole. Certainly nobody had suggested searching for the body.

The statement written out by Chad had been signed and witnessed. The chests and our luggage had been put aboard the *Miss Emma*. Now, under my instructions, Colonel Brown and Chad were ensuring that the weight in the forward hold was evenly distributed. We planned to make the journey under steam, for the trade winds were against us and I was the only experienced sailor.

Liza, awake again now and with bandaged head, lay just aft of the cabin on a bed made with cushions taken from the saloon of the *Liguria*. Sam was rigging an awning above her. Apart from a headache she seemed little the worse for her ordeal. In the five minutes we had been able to spend alone together she had wept with relief in my arms as she thanked me a dozen times for saving Chad. This made me feel very humble and embarrassed, for Liza Lockhart was worth three of me and I knew it. In the end I had stopped her thanks by teasing her, constantly saying, "Oh, pish and tush!" in the way she so often did herself.

Chad climbed out of the hold and the colonel followed, mopping his brow. Chad said, "What now, my darling?" Each time he spoke to me, each time he looked at me, I felt myself melting inside. I was so happy that as I went padding about my work with bare feet like the coolie girl I had once been, I found myself constantly smiling with joy. I said, "We can cast off soon. I've had some coal put in the fuel store from the *Liguria*, so we'll have plenty of steam for comparatively little fuel. I'd better go and stoke the boiler now."

Chad shook his head. "You've done enough for today, Casey dear. I'm sure the colonel and I can cope with the boiler if you'll just give your orders."

Ten minutes later, as I came out on deck after making up the two beds in the cabin, Sam emerged from the wheelhouse with a troubled frown. "Look, honey, we've taken it for granted," he said, "but can you *get* us to Nassau? It's a good six hundred miles, and none of us can navigate."

I laughed. As Oliver's wife I had come to dread all physical contact, but now I was so full of love that I wanted to touch my friends, to tell more than words could say, and the lightness that was in me made me bold to do so without fear of mis-understanding. I reached up and clasped my hands behind Sam's neck, looking up at him. "Sam dear, we have charts and a compass and a sextant, so I can take you anywhere you like in the West Indies."

He smoothed his hands back over my head and down my hair. Because it was long now, I had tied it back. "You're a great girl, Casey," he said.

"No, don't think too highly of me."

"Why not? First you bring me through a hurricane, then you bring Chad from under sixteen fathoms of sea. Who else could have done it?"

"Any freak of a girl who happened to become a sea gypsy and learned to sail and dive."

"More to it than that, honey."

"Oh, don't argue. You realize you men are in for a cramped voyage? Liza and I are sharing the cabin."

"Fine. We can sleep on deck forward, or in the hold if it rains. It's only for three or four days."

Chad's voice said, "When you've finished with my wife, Big Chief." He emerged from the after hold. Sam laughed and I let him go. Chad said, "We've got up steam, darling. The needle on the dial is where you wanted it to be."

I moved toward the wheelhouse. "Then we'll cast off and head northeast. That's roughly the direction. And while I'm calculating the exact course, you can be at the wheel beside me and practice steering. We'll all be standing watch for this trip, except Liza."

That evening I busied myself in the galley and contrived a reasonable meal. There were some provisions aboard, but we had also commandeered three chickens, a sack of flour, and some vegetables and fruit from Captain Caragole. As dusk turned to darkness, Liza declared that she would enjoy doing some little task, and insisted on Chad helping her attend to the washing up. Sam was at the wheel, the night air was warm, and Liza suggested that the colonel and I might like to enjoy the tiny breeze on the foredeck for a while before going to bed.

I was well aware that this arrangement was on Colonel Brown's behalf, but I did not mind. When we were sitting on cushions in the bows I said, "Are you an official person of some kind, Colonel? I can't think why else you should be involved in all this. Also, I gather from what you said a little while ago that you are the gentleman with the red beard who was inquiring on St. Kitts last September about the *Casey*, and about the Chinaman and the coolie girl who sailed her. Are you a policeman? Or perhaps a detective?"

"Neither, my dear." Colonel Brown was silent for a few moments, then went on, "Yes, I was trying to find the *Casey* for many weeks last year, until I came to Grenada shortly after you had been taken to England. It was there I learned what had happened, and how the *Casey* had been wrecked on La Faucille."

I said, "Why were you looking for us?"

There was a longer silence, and by his expression in the light of the moon it seemed to me that he was nerving himself to speak. "My name is not Brown," he said at last. "I adopted that name only because I found you had done so. My name is Delaney. Richard Delaney."

I stared. "But that was my father's name."

"Yes."

"I don't understand. Are you a relative—" I broke off, frowning. "Oh, you can't be my father! He was killed at Omdurman years ago, when I was a small child."

The man with the graying red beard said, "Your Aunt Maude and Uncle Henry felt it was best for you to believe so, and I had little choice but to agree." He ran a hand through his thick auburn hair; hair so very much like my own in color, I realized for the first time. "They disliked me intensely," he said somberly, "and disapproved of your mother marrying me. I was a junior officer without private income, which is a situation close to penury. But I loved your mother deeply, and she loved me in return, so we married. You were born a year later, and when you were four I was sent overseas. I was in Egypt when your mother died."

I knew I was hearing the truth, knew that this man must indeed be my father. Now I understood the strange intensity of interest he had shown in me, and also the instinctive liking I had felt for him. At any other time I would have been startled beyond words, excited, astonished, perhaps shy, but I had known so much of emotion in the past few hours that for the moment I could feel only a mild, pleased wonderment and curiosity.

He went on, "There was nobody to care for you, apart from your aunt and uncle, and even if I had left the army I was not competent to care for you myself. I appealed to Maude and Henry. They agreed to give you a home and bring you up, but they felt it essential that I should vanish from the scene. This was not out of malice, I believe. They genuinely felt that if you had a soldier father on the other side of the world, perhaps appearing every two or three years when on leave, it would undermine their authority and be continually unsettling for you." My father gave a small shrug. "Perhaps they were right. In any event, this was a condition I had to accept if I wished them to take you into their home. And so, as you became old enough to understand, you were led to believe that your father had died during the fighting at Omdurman."

The *Miss Emma* lifted beneath us to a gentle swell. A part of my mind told me that the wind had moved a point to the north, and the same part told me that this did not matter since we were under steam. I whispered, "And all these years . . . ?"

"Yes. I honored the agreement I had made. I did not write to your aunt and uncle, nor they to me. It was as if I had been truly dead—except, I beg you to believe, that I never forgot my daughter, Emma, never failed to think of her on special days. I rose to field rank, and later to command of a battalion. I had opportunities to marry again, but never wished to. Your mother, my dear wife Catherine, was the only woman I have ever loved."

My father stretched out long legs before him and crossed his feet. I knelt up, kissed his cheek, and said awkwardly, "Please understand . . . I can't quite think of you as my father yet. It will take a little time. But I do like you very much, I assure you."

He took my hand and touched it to his lips. "After so many years, I can afford a little time," he said quietly. "My fear was that you would feel I had abandoned you."

"No. I think you made a dreadful sacrifice for me. But why did you come seeking me at last?"

"Oh, my dear, I thought you were dead. Don't you see? When you were believed to have fallen down a sinkhole on the night of the bad storm, your uncle Henry wrote a letter to me, care of the War Office. He felt it his duty to inform me that my daughter had died."

"Oh, dear." I rubbed my eyes. "I'm so sorry. But I still don't understand why you came to look for me."

"The letter took months to reach me because I had left the Army by then. I had saved some money, and I bought an almost bankrupt steamship company in Liverpool. In two years I managed to transform it into a very profitable business, and was a rich man. That was when your uncle's letter, long delayed in the red tape of the War Office, finally reached me. I went out to Jamaica, saw Maude and Henry, and heard the story. I also went to see the minister at your church there, and he mentioned one or two things which led me to Sheba."

"Oh! She was the sister of May, my dear nannie, who was Daniel's wife."

"Yes, I know of all that. She was a little suspicious of me, I think, but she told me about you and May and Daniel. She also produced something very interesting, the detailed plans Daniel had made when designing his boat."

My father, Colonel Richard Delaney, patted the deck timbers beside him. "I was greatly intrigued," he said. "This was an ideal craft, combining steam and sail, for fishing and light cargo work, either off the coast or in trading between the islands. When I left Jamaica two months later I had financed a small yard and taken on sufficient men to start building these boats for sale, with an appropriate sum being paid to Sheba on each boat for having provided the plans."

"To Sheba? Oh Father, I'm so glad."

I saw him smile in the darkness, and again he touched the deck timbers. "This was the first of them, launched a year ago. I called her the *Miss Emma*, as Daniel did, and she was never sold."

I said, "That would please Sheba so much. Does she know you are my father?"

"Yes, I told her from the beginning, but it wasn't until I came out for the launching that she finally made up her mind to believe me and trust me. It was then she confided to me her secret belief that you and Daniel had run away together in the first *Miss Emma*. She said that Foy was what she called a beast-man, and told me how cruelly he had treated you. She believed you had asked Daniel to take you away, and that the night of the storm offered the ideal opportunity. She also believed that Daniel's boat would have survived the storm, and that is why I began to search the islands for a man and a girl, and a boat of this design. It wasn't long before I learned that there was just such a boat trading through the islands, a boat called the *Casey*."

I held his hand and said, "We changed the name. Daniel said it was a variation of my second name, Catherine, and it was useful as a boy's name, too. Dressed like this, but with my hair short, and keeping in the background, I was often taken for a boy."

My father said, "So I discovered, and this was quite confusing, but in the end I learned about the coolie girl called Casey Brown from the mother superior of the convent where you stayed for a night or two on Grenada. She told me how Sister Clare had taken you to England. I followed on the next boat, traced you to Blackheath, and took up residence there myself."

I looked at the stars, noting that Sam had allowed the *Miss Emma* to edge a little off course but was now bringing her back again. Laughter touched me as I said, "Why on earth did you pretend to want work as a butler?"

"Simply to speak to you. I was delighted to find how wonderfully the Lockharts had taken care of you, but I couldn't make myself go away. I wanted to be near you, to watch over you a little, in case you needed me."

I pressed his hand, and said, "You could have told me who you were."

"My dear, I had no right to intrude upon you after so long. Also, I was afraid. Afraid you would regard me as having turned my back on you for all those years, and that you would despise me for it."

"No. That isn't the way I think, Father, it isn't the way I learned from May and Daniel." I sat up straight. "Oh, I've just thought of something! You were there when I married Chad, and you must have known that Oliver, my husband, was still alive, because you spent many weeks in Jamaica, and Sheba spoke of him. Yet you kept silent." Another thought came to me and I put a hand to my head. "Oh dear, *you* didn't know I believed Oliver to be dead, so you must have thought I was deliberately entering into a bigamous marriage."

"No." He shook his head. "When I first heard the banns read, I concluded that you had lost your memory, or partially lost it, when the *Casey* was wrecked. But I kept silent because I didn't propose to destroy your happiness by speaking. I felt that Oliver Foy's wife was long dead, and in a way that was true, because it was as Casey, of the *Casey*, that you had become the woman I saw married that day."

"Not really married, Father."

"I count your happiness far more important than such considerations. Any guilt is mine, for clearly you were innocent. I held my tongue because it seemed impossible that anyone but myself would ever know the truth. When Foy himself appeared at your St. James's house I was stunned." My father touched my hand. "You were wonderful that night, my dear. I was so proud of you."

"It was Chad who carried me through, but I expect Sam has told you all that happened."

"Yes. There was plenty of time while we were living in Daniel's old house, keeping watch from there. He's a good man, Sam. And so is young Lockhart. You're in safe hands there, my dear."

I sensed that Sam had said nothing about my marriage to Chad being one of convenience only, and I was glad. I said, "How was it that you and Sam came together?"

My father looked up at the sky and smiled. "When Foy appeared I sent two inquiry agents to keep watch on the situation. On the morning that Sam stormed out of the meeting at the solicitors' office in Blackheath, he went home, packed a case, and left at once. He was followed, and when this was reported to me I went to the hotel in London where Sam had registered. I took the bull by the horns, and told him my true identity. Once he was convinced, he explained the plot he and Chad had hatched to counter any treachery on Foy's part. Sam planned to enlist the help of a friend or two for the task, but my advent made that unnecessary, especially as I controlled a steamship line, had a fleet of *Casey*-type boats here, and with Sheba's help could provide the perfect lookout position above Ocho Rios."

I saw my father's mouth tighten. "Even so, we weren't quite clever enough," he said bleakly. "That madman Foy would have slaughtered you all if you hadn't brought young Lockhart up from the wreck."

His voice broke on the last word. I slipped my arm through his, and leaned my head against his shoulder, as I had sometimes done with Daniel when we sat together under the stars. "As soon as possible," I said, "I shall marry Chad again, but properly this time. And I shall be very cross with my father if he sits in a pew at the back of the church. This time I want him beside me, to give me away."

At midnight I fed the boiler and relieved Sam at the wheel for the middle watch, leaving Liza sound asleep in the cabin. Chad and my father were sleeping on the foredeck. The air had lost its heat now, but I still needed no more than my coolie-girl shirt and trousers.

Sam said, "Did you get some sleep, honey?"

"A good three hours, and I feel wonderful. You seem to have got on very well with my father, Sam dear. He thinks the world of you."

"It's mutual. We all reckon he's a great character."

"Has Chad told you that we're in love and want to be properly married?"

"Oh, sure. I'm real happy for you both, Casey." He hesitated, then said with a diffidence I had never seen in him before. "Look . . . would you speak to Liza for me?"

I said, "What about?"

He sighed and shook his head. I glanced at the compass, and registered that the little breeze had moved another point or two north but was still carrying the smoke from our smokestack away aft. "Well," Sam said slowly, "it's difficult. See now . . . we've grown up like brother and sister, but after what happened yesterday, it's not like that for me any more. When Foy was holding her, threatening to have that Negro kill her with the machete..." He broke off and wiped a hand across his mouth. "I thought I was going to lose her, Casey. Suddenly I knew what she meant to me, knew how I'd always taken her for granted, and . . . and I really seemed to see her for the first time in my life."

I felt warm joy within me as I said, "What do you mean, Sam?"

"I mean . . . it came to me that I love her, Casey." His voice was low and troubled. "Maybe I've always loved her. One thing's sure, I can never think of her as a sister again. But if I tell Liza all this, she'll . . . well, she'll laugh, I guess. I'm just old Sam Redwing, who's always been around, a sort of adopted big brother she's cooked for, washed for, generally looked after. She'll think I've gone soft in the head if I try to explain, but I figured maybe if *you* talked to her, and . . . and tried to get her to think of me sort of afresh, and explained tactfully that I . . . well, you know."

His voice trailed rather despairingly away. After a moment I said, "Sam, do you trust me?"

He looked startled. "Only with my life, honey. Why?"

"Then do as I say. I'll make sure you're left alone with Liza some time tomorrow. Then you hold her hands, and simply tell her you love her. Then take her in your arms, and tell her again. Then kiss her, and tell her again. Don't try to explain anything. Just tell her."

He stared, and in the moonlight I saw mingled hope and doubt in his eyes. "But how do you think—"

"No, don't ask questions, Sam. Just trust me. Will you do that?"

He gazed at me, baffled, then nodded slowly. "All right, honey. If you say so."

"That's lovely. You're going to be a very happy man, Sam. Now you come give dis coolie girl good night kiss befo' you go close-eye along dem bockra frien' belong you."

He laughed softly and came to brush my cheek with his lips. "You're the captain. Good night . . . and God bless you, Casey girl."

It was half an hour later when a figure emerged from the shadows, coming from the foredeck beyond the cabin. I said, "Chad, my dearest. It's not nearly time yet. You have the morning watch, at four."

He came to stand beside me and slid his arm round my waist. "I was lonely for you," he said.

"But you must get some sleep if you're to stand watch."

"I know, my darling. I've brought a blanket, and I'll sleep on the deck here, beside you. But first I want to tell you how happy I am." He kissed my neck, just above the shoulder. "It was so hard, pretending to be cool and . . . no more than friendly. I had to remind myself all the time that I'd promised you a marriage of convenience, and that I mustn't touch you."

I looked at the moon. "If only you knew how I ached for you to touch me. We're so lucky, Chad. You can clear those wretched debts now, and even after sharing with Sam you'll have enough to do whatever you wish to."

"Yes, I suppose so, but that's not important. Our having each other is all that matters to me."

"I feel the same way. I know everything won't always be perfect, because life isn't like that. But we've both been tested in ways hard enough to make us appreciate being loved, and . . . oh Chad, we have the priceless gift of being good friends as well."

"Casey, can this boat steer itself for a few moments while I hold you and kiss you?"

"Yes, easily. You don't mind me looking like a boy?"

The smoky gray eyes were full of gentleness, and smiling. "You don't look like a boy, my sweetheart, and you don't feel like one."

A little later I sighed a long sigh and took the wheel again. "You'd better sleep now, Chad," I said rather breathlessly.

"Yes . . . but please, just five minutes of steering practice first." Standing behind me, he reached forward and rested his hands on mine, which were grasping the spokes. We had veered a little to port, and our hands moved together as I turned the wheel.

Chad said, "Like this?"

I whispered, "Yes. Just like this."

The *Miss Emma* came back on course. Our hands moved again to steady her there, and we sailed on under the stars.